HUBBERT & LIL

Partners in Crime

Gallagher Gray

IVY BOOKS • NEW YORK

Ivy Books
Published by Ballantine Books
Copyright © 1991 by Gallagher Gray

Library of Congress Catalog Card Number: 91-55181

ISBN 0-8041-0948-6

This edition published by arrangement with Donald I. Fine, Inc.

Printed in Canada

First Ballantine Books Edition: May 1993

CHAPTER ONE

1 When the phone rang, he was in the middle of a bizarre dream involving giant marshmallows, burning sun and a motorboat endlessly circling. He raised his head from the pillow and squinted, but Brenda's huge backside obscured the clock. He shoved her out of the way and her loud purring abruptly stopped. As he reached for the receiver, she turned her head and regarded him with yellow eyes, tail switching back and forth in annoyance. Eddie raised his massive head from his favorite spot on the heat coil of the electric blanket to stare at both of them sleepily.

"Yes?" T.S. peered at the illuminated dial of his clock and saw that it was nearly 8:00 A.M. He sat suddenly, pulling the phone onto the rug with a crash. Both cats stared at him in disgust.

"Yes?" he asked again. He would be late for work—the first time in thirty years. Where was the alarm?

"Mr. Hubbert?" The voice was female, but so breathless he could barely make out his own name.

"This is T.S. Hubbert," he said firmly into the phone. "To whom am I speaking?" Did he have any early appointments?

The voice grew stronger. "This is Sheila."

"Sheila?" He swung a leg onto the floor. "I'm on my way now."

"How did you know?" she asked.

"Know what?"

"That they'd stabbed him?"

1

He stared at the receiver. "Is this Sheila O'Reilly from Sterling & Sterling?"

"Of course it is!" Her breathlessness gave way to indignation. "Who else would it be? Mr. Hubbert, what is the matter with you? I called to tell you. They've stabbed Mr. Cheswick."

"What?"

"Yes. They've stabbed him. Right here at Sterling & Sterling. In the Partners' Room." Her voice unraveled and wavered. "My mother was the one who found him."

He stood up and stared at the controls of his electric blanket. No wonder he was covered in sweat. Brenda or Eddie had nosed the heat setting up again and it was nearly to nine on the dial.

"I'm sorry to disturb you on your first day of retirement," Sheila added politely.

Of course. He sat down again on the edge of his bed. It was Friday, March 1. He was a retired man. It was to have been his first day to sleep late in three decades.

"Someone stabbed Robert Cheswick?"

"Yes." Sheila was efficient once again, accustomed to supplying him with information. "I rode in with my mother as usual—you know how she likes to be here no later than 7:30 and today she was a couple of minutes late and really in a tizzy about it. I left to take the elevator up to the third floor, but I hadn't even gotten down the hall when I heard her screaming. Of course, I went flying back and it was awful. Just awful. He was lying back in his chair."

"You saw him?" He was fully awake now, one eye on his closet. What did one wear when one was retired?

He heard voices in the background and frantic whispers from Sheila.

"Sheila? I'm still here." Perhaps his tan slacks and a sweater.

"Hubbert?" An overconfident male voice blasted through the receiver. Brenda and Eddie heard the echo and stirred.

T.S. sighed. Edgar Hale.

"Hubbert? Are you there, man? Say something."

A steady drizzle dribbled down his windows. It was the perfect day to sleep late.

"Yes, I'm here. Of course, I'm here. Where else would I be at 8:00 A.M?"

"You'd be here," the voice boomed back. Edgar Hale was nearing sixty, but his voice would make a drill sergeant proud.

"I'm retired now, Edgar. Remember?" Someone had stabbed Robert Cheswick? It was certainly unexpected.

"Not any more," the voice ordered. "This is serious. The girl is right. They've stabbed Robert."

"Who is 'they'? Why do you keep saying 'they'?"

"How the hell should I know? That's the job of the police."

"Then why are you calling me?" He was retired now. He could talk back.

"Stop talking back and get down here. The ninny that took your place will make a mess of it. Start handing out employee anxiety surveys or some other nonsense. I need someone who can take charge. I can see the headlines now. There has never been tabloid mention of Sterling & Sterling in two centuries. You've got to help us out."

"I can't stop the press, Edgar. You know that."

"Never mind. You know what I mean. We need you here."

Whether they really needed him or not, it was gratifying to hear the Managing Partner beg. Besides, in all his years as Personnel Manager at Sterling & Sterling, no one had ever been murdered before. At least not in the Partners' Room.

"Be right down," T.S. promised. A murder. Well, it was certainly more interesting than interviewing the slack-jawed sons of clients. He whistled as he pulled on his slacks and a sweater. No tie. He was his own man now, master of his destiny, no longer enslaved by the confines of Sterling & Sterling's fashion code. Besides, it would drive Edgar Hale crazy.

2 He trudged down the dripping steps into the blackness of the subway entrance, joining the affluent throng stamping toward the downtown train. The light bulb was broken and he pressed into the damp and stamping crowd blindly. Water dripped off of rain hats and umbrellas, spattering his face. He took perverse pleasure in possibly being the only man within miles not wearing a tie. It was really quite absurd—millions of men wearing strips of cloth around their necks each morning. Why had he never realized it before?

He tuned out the sounds of an ongoing battle in his subway car. Just the usual morning squabble. An impeccably dressed executive had inadvertently snagged an extremely loud old woman's stockings with his umbrella.

T.S. had automatically bought the *New York Times* but, after seeing no mention of the murder, occupied himself instead with wondering who in the world might have stabbed Robert Cheswick.

It could have been anyone, really. Even him. He had not particularly liked the man. In fact, he had loathed him for over twenty-five years. And he suspected nearly everyone else did, too, with the exception of the bank's German and Japanese clients, who seemed to find him secretly amusing.

In truth, Cheswick had been born and bred a horse's ass and was as pompous as they came. By the time T.S. had joined the firm thirty years before, Cheswick had already settled down to a steady life of intimidating secretaries and junior clerks. There had never been any question, what with his esteemed ancestors, that Cheswick would rise to the very top. T.S.'s own ascent had been far rockier and less assured.

But it wasn't the silver-spoon background T.S. held against Cheswick. It was really his teeth. They were large and protruding and when Cheswick laughed, he'd throw back his head and bray, lips peeling back like a donkey's.

It was ironic that Cheswick had given the big retirement speech honoring T.S. at his reception the night before. Suppose Cheswick had been killed by a burglar simply because he'd had the bad luck to be there late at night? On the other hand, dead or not, T.S. wasn't sure he was ready to forgive Cheswick yet for the dreadful speech he had made. His words would have been more appropriate for a retiring mechanic, and the speech was so tedious that the murderer could conceivably use it as grounds for self-defense and claim that Cheswick was trying to bore him to death.

Such thoughts were getting T.S. nowhere. Thinking of the retirement party only reminded him of the golf clubs. Why in the world had they given him golf clubs? He'd never played in his life.

Golf clubs. It was depressing to think that you could work somewhere for thirty years and your co-workers know so little about who you really were.

It was this thought that would not leave his mind as the subway screeched to a halt at the Wall Street stop. He joined the crowd silently shuffling up the stairs and wondered: how well had anyone really known Robert Cheswick?

3   Albert, the elevator man, had heard all about the murder by the time T.S. arrived on the stonecut doorstep of Sterling & Sterling, Private Bankers. A facade of genteelness was being maintained at the discreet Wall Street entrance, but T.S. spotted scores of official vehicles clogging the side street and extra guards were posted there.

"Morning, Albert," T.S. said to the short, trim man in a smart burgundy and silver uniform. The elevators were automatic, but Sterling & Sterling maintained an air of toadying service for older clients by posting Albert in the lobby during working hours anyway. He'd been with the firm for more than forty-five years and now earned $50,000 a year, for pushing the occasional button and tipping his hat. Good heavens, when was the old bugger going to retire?

"Morning, Mr. Hubbert, sir." Albert lowered his basset-like eyes respectfully. "Terrible thing, sir, isn't it?"

T.S. nodded. "Certainly is terrible, Albert. Right here in the Sterling offices." He found himself whistling a tune as he watched the floor indicator crawl downward.

Albert eyed him suspiciously. "Surprised to see you here, sir."

"What's that?" T.S. asked as an elevator door opened and a throng of people thrust him into the car.

Albert stood on tiptoe and shouted, "I thought you were retiring, sir."

"Yes, well." T.S. could think of no other reply as the crowd turned to stare at him. He detected a pitying air in several of them and was suddenly conscious of his tieless collar peering out from under his raincoat. He imagined they were probably staring at the inevitable neck wrinkles he had recently discovered, creeping across his skin like a warning: there's an old man lurking inside, biding his time, and there's nothing you can do to stop him.

Well, let them stare. He was retired, but not dead yet. He surveyed the smartly dressed employees and determined that his best defense would be a strong offense.

"Morning, McIntyre. Johnson. Felstein. Jeffers. Miss Block." He nodded his head at each person as he took inventory. Most were too engrossed in the folded papers open on their arms to do more than mumble back. Cheswick could have been stabbed in an elevator with twenty-five of this crowd and there would have been no witnesses.

"Morning, Mr. Hubbert," an incredibly young fellow echoed dutifully. His hair was slicked straight down on his head with some kind of gel and brushed back in a style that made him look like a pompous middle-aged gigolo with a sixteen-year-old face.

T.S. recognized him vaguely. Someone's nephew. A recent hire. He remembered now—a name like a candy bar.

"Good morning, Clarkson," he replied with as much savvy as he could muster. After what seemed an interminable silence, the elevator doors opened and he escaped into his kingdom—the third floor of Sterling & Sterling, Personnel Department.

The receptionist had evidently been weeping over the tragedy and was startled to see him. "Mr. Hubbert," she said, dabbing at her eyes. "What are *you* doing here?"

He ignored her unintentioned insult; it was a pity to be so young and uninformed. "Terrible thing, Margaret. Terrible thing." He found himself shaking his head, a reflexive action developed at countless employee funerals. He passed a series of stunned employees, apparently so shocked over the murder that no one was getting any work done. He sighed.

He had often observed this mass emotional response during his many years on the job. An unexpected death would trigger it for sure. Especially heart attacks. Never mind that few had known or liked the dead one. Something about a sudden death opened up their emotional faucets. It was a wonderful way to spice up a dull routine.

He wandered into the center of his own office before he realized that Miss Fullbright had already moved in. Hanging plants dangled from the ceiling and brushed his head. Well, he thought, she can certainly move quickly when she wants to. In all other respects, Miss Fullbright took inordinately long to reach a decision, weighing countless psychological pros and cons. She had been chosen as T.S.'s successor by a number of partners, who, tired of being outmaneuvered by the actions of a more experienced Personnel Manager, hell bent on spending *their* money, had decided that a friendly puppet government was in order. They had certainly found their man in Miss Fullbright. She had been raised to obey and was in her element at Sterling & Sterling.

"T.S.!" Miss Fullbright was clearly startled by his appearance. She sat on his custom radiator cover, looking out over Wall Street. Rapidly moving clusters of people slogged forward in the morning drizzle. An ideal view for venting sorrow.

"Felicia." He was uncharacteristically confused for a moment, his coat folded in his arms. What did one do in such a situation?

"Oh, go ahead and hang it up," she grumbled ungraciously, turning back to her appropriately depressing view.

Felicia Fullbright was a tiny, slender woman, naturally graceful but so uncaring of this grace that she appeared, instead, to slink about and frequently made other people nervous. Her shapely legs were spoiled by the clunky, uncompromising conservatism of her shoes, a style that male executives had snidely dubbed "power pumps." Her pretty heart-shaped face and delicate, almost feline, features were likewise marred by her very visible suspicions that others were out to undermine her. He sometimes wondered where she had acquired this stubborn defensiveness and why she had sacrificed her sleek feminity to its power.

He hung his coat on his usual hook in the rack, squeezing it in next to her bulky fur. No worry about animal rights in Miss Fullbright's mind. She had earned her fur coat and she was going to wear it well.

He sat on the edge of the sofa and waited. He had no idea what to do next.

"You're looking very relaxed today," she said, staring at his sweater and slacks.

"Well, I am retired." He straightened the cuffs of his sweater and cleaned a small smudge off of his right shoe. She was the last person he was going to apologize to.

"Glad *you* remember that." She was most unattractive when she pouted. Miss Fullbright had never been very good at hiding her feelings from T.S. It was as if she expected him to ferret them out anyway, so what was the use? It was true that he was abnormally gifted at reading other people's motives, but that had been bred of his long years in Personnel. She took his skill, however, as a personal assault on her dignity and frequently resorted to being blunt with him and little more.

"Edgar insisted I come in and field the press," he said. "I'm not sure why. I am sure that in every other respect of the Personnel Manager job, he will want you to carry on as planned."

"I'm sure." She slouched sullenly toward his huge oak desk and sat down in the swivel chair. Her small frame was dwarfed by it and when she tilted back, her feet lifted off the floor. If she thought it made her seem imposing, she was mistaken. She looked instead like a little girl who was playing in her daddy's office.

"Felicia, I don't want this job anymore. It's yours. I assure you I have no intention of hanging on." She was startled into momentary speechlessness and he continued. "But I can tell from Edgar's voice that it will do you absolutely no good to protest this move. Particularly as your first act in office. It would be unseemly for the Personnel Manager of Sterling & Sterling to protest in such a manner. Especially a woman. The lady doth protest too much, remember?''

"Yes, I see your point." The whining was gone from her voice and her one saving grace, competency, had crept back in.

He sighed. "Where shall I make camp?"

Her lovely brow furrowed and she pushed impatiently at her impeccably razored short hair. "I hadn't thought about that."

"How about in Sheila's area?" he suggested. "There's an empty office there."

Sterling & Sterling had advertised recently for an employee benefits assistant. In the meantime, there was a perfectly good office in the back going begging, where there was less of a chance that people would know he'd returned. Besides, if anyone knew what was going on, it would be Sheila.

"How about by Sheila?" Miss Fullbright echoed. She smiled as she looked up. "Now that's a good idea. You'll be in the back." She considered her words and colored slightly. Her dignity was most important to her. "What I meant to say was, it's a discreet location. Let me call her now."

When it came to intercoms, computers and all the gadgets of a modern office, Miss Fullbright was a well-oiled cobra. She used them perfunctorily and ruthlessly. Punch, punch and she was ready to move on to the next task.

"She's on her way. Poor child. Her mother discovered the body, you know."

"Yes, I heard."

"Awful, isn't it?" Her tone belied her words. "I can't imagine the impact on employees. It might be a real trauma." She leaned forward and gazed at him in expectation. "What do you think, T.S.? Should I call in a psychologist and offer special grief counseling? Perhaps I should take an Employee Pulse." This was the name she had given to the endless series of surveys she delighted in passing out to all employees.

Usually on important subjects, like whether the cafeteria should continue to include raisins in the rice pudding.

T.S. rose as Sheila entered the office. "Actually, Felicia, I think the best thing would be to let this matter ride its course unchecked." He headed gratefully for the door and stopped for a parting shot. "Besides, if you ask me, the employees seem to be enjoying this." He winked and left his baffled successor staring after him.

"So," he said, comfortably seated in Sheila's office. "The torch has passed."

"Oh, please." She rolled her eyes and reached for a fresh tissue, blew her nose lustily and tossed it into the trash can across the room with the accuracy of a Boston Celtic. "Working for that woman is going to be a real pain in the ass."

"Now, now Sheila. She's very well trained and experienced in the field." He had never sat in Sheila's visitor chair before. It was a huge wood and leather contraption, as oversized as she was, and ostensibly designed to put distraught employees at ease as they poured out their troubles to the "medical benefits lady." T.S. sank deep into the leather, suspecting that it was more likely designed to prevent anyone from escaping.

"She's a whiner," Sheila replied as if that ended the discussion. The phone rang and she ignored it. "I can't take any more calls," she explained. "Margaret will have to cover." She sighed and rubbed at her temples. "How are Brenda and Eddie?" Because she had cats of her own, Sheila never failed to ask after his own.

"They're fine. Slim as ever." In truth, they were nearly as big as seals. "Tell me about this morning," T.S. asked when she remained silent. He wanted to know what he was walking into before he delivered himself upon the sacrificial altar of Edgar Hale and the NYPD. He could count on Sheila for an accurate picture of events.

Impeccably raised in a New York middle-class Irish home, Sheila had entered the department as a receptionist at the front desk five years ago, attracting a steady stream of male employees on obvious reconnaissance. She looked like an otherwise fierce Amazon cursed with unruly, perpetually childish blonde hair. She towered above the other women in the department—and many of the men. But her imposing physical presence was at odds with her sympathetic and often shy demeanor, a contradiction that made her spectacular smile that much more effective. In fact, she unconsciously disarmed nearly everyone she met. This, combined with her unfailing politeness to applicant after applicant, no matter how scruffy, had done wonders for the Sterling & Sterling image.

If Sheila had a fault, it was excessive empathy for her fellow men and women and an overactive imagination when it came to their suffering. Probably her Catholic school upbringing. As a result, she was terrible at turning people down for jobs, but this trait had made her the ideal choice for a vacant employee benefits job. She had quickly established herself as the perfect person to approach when your wife was ailing or your child had succumbed to drugs or you had to get a second opinion on a hemorrhoid operation. She would never take your troubles lightly—your sorrows were her sorrows.

Sheila began dabbing at her eyes, as if the memory of the discovery might trigger a new round of tears. "It's very upsetting," she almost whimpered. "Mr. Cheswick got me my first job here, you know." Sheila's mother had been Robert Cheswick's secretary for nearly thirty-five years and the partner had referred Sheila to Personnel as a favor.

"Oh, hogwash, Sheila!" T.S. could not help replying. "Your first job paid nothing. How grateful can you be?"

She sniffed and mumbled. "The benefits were good."

"Not for Cheswick they weren't. Now get a hold of yourself. Tell me what happened."

She blew her nose dramatically, paused as if to collect herself, and launched into narration. "Mom found him early this morning. Very, very dead. It was not like the movies at all." She gazed at him blankly. "It was really rather ugly." She sighed and fiddled with her letter opener, flipping it from hand to hand and stabbing idly at her desk pad. She stopped suddenly, stared at the opener and, appalled, threw it down with an involuntary shudder.

"We rode in together on the subway as usual. Mom likes us to spend that time together. It gives her a chance to keep nosing into my life." She waited until he nodded his head sympathetically, then continued. "Anyway, because we were late, she was in no mood to talk. Acted like it had been my fault or something. She makes such a big fuss if we're even two minutes behind schedule. He really has her trained." She shook her head. "*Had* her trained. I don't know what will become of Mom now."

"Another partner will snap her right up. She's really an excellent secretary."

"Yes. She would be." Sheila reached for a tissue as if she expected her self-control to fail her momentarily. "I walked her to her desk because the bank is deserted that early. Sometimes it can get creepy down there. That marble really echoes."

T.S. knew what she meant. He was convinced it was deliberately planned so that even the most confident senior executives would find their resolve reduced to mush from the conspicuousness of their every footstep as they walked the long marble hall to the Partners' Room.

"I was in a really good mood, you know. I'd had such a good time at your retirement party and then I'd gone out to a bar later and . . . well, I had a good time." She colored slightly and continued. "I was sort of whistling as I walked down the hall. No one else was there, of course. I was thinking about maybe cutting my hair like . . ."

"About Mr. Cheswick?" he interrupted tactfully before she could get started.

"Well, I was halfway down the hall when I heard Mom scream. And I mean *scream*. She let fly with this shriek that grew and grew and just hung there. I was so scared I dropped my shopping bag and these oranges I'd brought to work with me rolled everywhere. I'm on another diet, you know. This time I mean it."

He nodded. She was given to gaining weight quickly. Just the same, he did want her to get to the point.

"I went running back as fast as I could." She held out one nicely shaped leg for him to see. "Of course, these stupid heels make it impossible, but just the same I went flying through the swinging doors into the Partners' Room and there he was. Dead as can be. Slumped backwards in his chair. And that stupid old-fashioned chair had tilted back on its swivel and my mother had a hand on the arm of it while she screamed, so it was jostling up and down. He was jerking like some kind of puppet. I just can't tell you." She was too absorbed in the morbid details to consider crying, he noticed. "His face had this wide grin just frozen on it. Ugh. And Mom would not quit screaming. I had to grab her by the shoulders and shake her until her glasses fell off. I practically had to slap my own mother."

She paused and looked at T.S. to see the impact of this terrible statement.

"Perhaps you should have."

"Well, I didn't." She picked up the letter opener and stared at it speculatively. "I thought it was a heart attack. I mean, you know those old guys. You expect them to die of heart attacks. All they think of is making money all day long. They deserve to die of heart attacks. But it wasn't a heart attack, I can tell you that." She stared T.S. right in the eye and paused for effect. "It was a knife. A long, thin knife with a weird ivory handle. Sticking right out of his rib cage just above the heart. *I know.*" She emphasized these last words and leaned forward. "I'm CPR trained. It was right above the heart and angling down. Someone knew just where to stick it."

He had no idea what one replied to such a statement and merely nodded.

"So I checked his pulse. Definitely dead." She shivered again. "His hand was very cold and very heavy. Well, Mom, of course, was just standing there aghast that I would touch a dead person. She opened her mouth like she was going to scream again, but no sound came out. Then she started whispering something like, 'Go get help, get help, get help.' Over and over again. Which was almost as creepy as Mr. Cheswick being dead. So I made her shut up and sit down and catch her breath, then I went out the swinging doors to look for a guard. But I couldn't find anyone that early and I was afraid Mom might faint if I left her in the same room as a dead man, so I went back in. She was just sitting there clutching her pocketbook, mumbling to herself. I led her out of the room and called the police. At first the operator wouldn't believe me. She kept asking me to repeat the address. It was really quite irritating. She wanted me to stand in the drizzle to direct the ambulance. I told her an ambulance wasn't going to do much good and that my catching pneumonia wouldn't help things, either. Just then I saw Frank coming down the hall.''

"Frank?" T.S. asked.

"You know, the security guard who still wears a crewcut. I sent him to the side entrance to flag down the cops and warned Mom not to let anyone else in the Partners' Room, not that she would have been any help, since she was still practically in a trance. Then I got her some hot tea from that little closet they have hidden away off the Partners' Room.'' Sheila leaned forward and dropped her voice slightly. "Did you know there's three bottles of scotch stashed in there behind the styrofoam cups?'' She lifted her eyebrows.

"Yes, I did.'' They'd been there for years. But they belonged to an old partner without any real duties and T.S. didn't begrudge him his snorts.

"Anyway, I brought Mom her tea. She had turned into a zombie at this point so I tried to call my father to tell him he better come get her. She can be Miss Efficiency, you know, but if anything upsets her routine, she turns into a three-year-old.'' She delivered these observations with the knowing air of a pop psychologist on a talk show. "Dad wasn't home and by this time it was about ten minutes to eight and I heard the elevator start moving. I knew people would be arriving soon and I didn't want them asking Mom a lot of questions and upsetting her more, so I made her sit in that little reception area right by the Partners' Room. Fortunately, Mr. Hale was one of the first people to arrive and since he's the Managing Partner, well, no one is going to argue with him or ask him stupid questions. I let him take a look and explained to him that the police were on their way and it was crucial no one disturb a thing. I know that because of Brian, of course.'' Sheila's husband and father were both NYC policemen and she loved to contribute gruesome details about their run-ins with occasional murders and soured drug deals as part of her coffee cart conversation.

''Mr. Hale was a mess himself, of course. Kept staring at Mr. Cheswick. Seeing his own face on the corpse, I suppose.'' She shook her head. ''You know, for partners, they can really be a bunch of little kids sometimes.'' He knew exactly what she meant. ''I happened to make a remark about what you might say to all this and Mr. Hale jumped right on it. Said we had to call you right away. Insisted I phone. I reminded him you were retired but he didn't want to hear it. As soon as he grabbed the phone from me—I hate people that do that—the other partners started arriving. You know how they are about trying to get in earlier than each other. One by one, they walked in through the swinging doors and stopped dead in their tracks.'' She was nonplussed by her choice of words. ''I finally told Mr. Hale that he had to stand outside the swinging doors and keep everyone out. They were all quite angry that they couldn't get at their desks.''

She fiddled with her empty ashtray and tapped it against the desk. ''I always thought it was silly how they all had to work in the same room anyway. How can they get anything done there? It looks like Ebenezer Scrooge time. All those rolltop desks.''

''I expect they do most of their work at lunch and visiting clients and on the banking floor anyway,'' T.S. explained. It *was* like Ebenezer Scrooge time. She had an excellent mind for capsulizing the truth.

''The cops were here within ten minutes. I'm surprised it took them that long. To hear Brian talk, you'd think they always got there when the body was still warm.'' She rolled her eyes again. T.S. had discerned over the past few months that her marriage was going steadily downhill and that she was not particularly disturbed about the trend. "This big fat lieutenant or something took over. He was really very pushy. Didn't even say thank you or anything that I'd preserved the scene of the crime. Just grilled me like I was a suspect or something. Wanted to know why I wasn't more upset. Practically accused me of disturbing evidence. I told him I was married to a cop and knew better and that if not for me, he'd have found a room full of fourteen alive partners and one dead one, with all the evidence trampled and them working as if nothing out of the ordinary had happened."

"Good thing it was Cheswick," T.S. interrupted. "With some of the others, it might have been days before anyone noticed they were dead."

"I beg your pardon?" She stared at T.S. with wide eyes.

"I'm making a joke, Sheila."

"Oh." She plunged back in. "Anyway, the fat lieutenant started right in on Mom, didn't care a bit that she was so upset. But she snapped right out of her trance, sat straight up and informed him that she was married to Tommy Shaunessy, who outranked him by a mile, and that he better treat her with a little more respect. That stopped him dead. He backed right off, apologized to Mom and told a guy to take her into one of the conference rooms to wait until they could find Dad. I tried the same thing—telling him I was married to a cop—but I guess Brian didn't impress him as much as Dad because I had to give my statement to this policewoman who acted totally bored and obviously thought I was some kind of an airheaded secretary. I don't know who she thought she was." She shook her head angrily. "They do have nice uniforms, though. Gray slacks and blue blazers. She had a gold shield, too. Looked very smart. I noticed that her hair was curled into this braided bun."

He could think of nothing to say to this and simply sighed.

"But they finally said I could go if I promised to stay on the premises in case they had more questions. Let me tell you it was quite a relief to walk through those swinging doors. And you know what?" She waited patiently for T.S. to ask.

"What?"

"It was disgusting." Her eyes glittered with excitement.

"What was disgusting?"

"The Main Floor was swarming with employees kind of loitering by the entrance to the Partners' Room. Pretending they had to run an errand past the place."

T.S. nodded. He knew the syndrome well. It also happened when someone was fired and word got around. Coworkers seemed overcome by lemminglike urges to visit the scene of the incident and rubberneck.

"All these partners' secretaries were trying to get a peek and pump me for information—especially Mrs. Quincy. The executives were trying to act real cool, but you could tell they were trying to look in between the doors. Desperate to know what was going on." She shook her head. "I was practically mobbed and my phone's been ringing off the hook. But to tell you the truth, I didn't feel like talking to anyone."

If these words betrayed her enthusiastic narration, T.S. wasn't going to let on.

"I holed up in here and waited for you to arrive. It really hit me hard. It was ugly seeing a dead man. With a knife sticking out of him and all."

"Yes, I can imagine." The knife intrigued him. It nudged at his memory, but he couldn't quite pinpoint it.

"Perhaps you should go home early?" he suggested.

"Yes. That might be nice. If the lieutenant will let me." She made no move to go. "Someone has to get Mom home after she gives her statement. She is very upset. I doubt she could find her own way to the bathroom right now."

"She worked for him for many years," T.S. reminded her. "She probably saw as much of Mr. Cheswick as your father."

"More, I expect." She shook her head again. "Anyway, she ought to be in bed right now with a mug of hot lemonade and rum. That would take care of her."

"Sounds pretty good to me," T.S. remarked. "Perhaps you should consider it yourself. Is Brian on duty?"

She stared at the wall. "I can take care of myself." Suddenly she grinned wickedly. "Do you suppose anyone would notice if we went and looted one of those bottles of scotch?"

He could think of one partner who would. "Probably not," he said.

"You know what the worst part of the whole thing was?" Sheila asked.

"What?" He had the feeling that he was about to hear something very important. He often got this feeling during an interview, when he had let several moments of silence pass before asking a question. Silence made people nervous, made them spill their guts, and he'd developed antennae for when something big was about to pop out.

"His fly was open," she nearly whispered.

"Whose fly?" he whispered back, before catching himself and switching to his normal tone of voice. "Whose fly was open?"

"Mr. Cheswick's." She leaned back and explained. "Not that I'm in the habit of inspecting these things, of course." T.S. shook his head and murmured something nonsensical in agreement. "But there it was. I couldn't help but notice. I could even see that he had on white boxer shorts with these little green bows printed on it. Pretty silly for a partner. I couldn't see any flesh, but something about his fly being open really gave me the creeps."

T.S. nodded in agreement. He knew what she meant.

"It just seemed so nasty," she said.

CHAPTER TWO

1 It was time to see for himself. He heard the murmur of employees' voices as he strode down the Main Floor, a cavernous marbled cathedrallike space divided by a large center aisle that led to a smaller, oak-paneled foyer manned by alert valets who hovered about an enormous pair of swinging doors. Behind these doors lay the inner sanctum—the Partners' Room itself.

He wondered briefly if he would even get past the swinging doors, but he need not have worried. Jimmy Ruffino, loyal valet to the partners for more than two decades, stood guard beside a uniformed cop and grabbed T.S. by the elbow at once.

"Thank goodness you're here, Mr. Hubbert," he cried, as if expecting T.S. to somehow raise Cheswick from the dead.

"Yes, well. Thanks, Jimmy." He could think of no other suitable reply. The cop stared at them curiously.

"It's Mr. Hubbert, Personnel Manager," Jimmy explained.

"Former Personnel Manager," T.S. corrected with a weak smile.

"The one that Mr. Hale has been insisting be present," Jimmy added.

"Oh yeah? Boy, can that old guy howl." The cop seemed infinitely bored with his role. "If you being here means the old codger will leave us alone, you're welcome to *entre vous*. Anyone would be an improvement over that guy." The uniform jerked his thumb in the air and gave a sign that T.S.

could enter the inner sanctum. He was so fat, T.S. had trouble squeezing past. What had happened to fitness requirements?

On the other hand, though the cop was overweight and spoke bad French, he was absolutely right about Edgar Hale. Just about anyone was an improvement over the Managing Partner.

T.S. pushed through the swinging doors. The body was screened from general view by an expensive Moroccan leather screen usually reserved for decoration. Forensic technicians moved about the screen quickly and dispassionately in an efficient choreography of detached involvement. Mesmerized by the clinical dance unfolding before him, T.S. stood in the doorway and stared until a familiar, booming voice interrupted his reverie.

"It's about time, Hubbert," Edgar Hale barked by way of greeting. "What took you so long?"

Edgar Hale, Managing Partner of Sterling & Sterling, stood stiffly at attention under the portrait of Samuel T. Sterling and his four sons that was displayed over a never-used fireplace at one end of the Partners' Room. Hale bore an uncanny resemblance to the founder himself, down to his tubby pugnaciousness, scowling face and hair that remained stubbornly dark despite his age. Yet he was related to Samuel Sterling by temperament and station alone. Perhaps it was the constant diet of power that had shaped their images in such a like fashion.

If so, Edgar Hale was hungry. Obviously relegated to his spot, he stood with his arms folded, glaring at each and every man and woman who dared move around him as if he wasn't there. His grim expression made it clear that he suspected they were purposefully tramping mud and sludge onto Sterling & Sterling's impeccable rose carpet. He glared at the crowd with curious, smoky green eyes that smouldered with barely suppressed anger and frustration. "What a day for Boswell to be out," he finally shouted to no one, cracking under the unexpected strain of being ignored. John Boswell was in charge of the firm's Management Committee and second in importance only to Edgar Hale himself in the partner pecking order.

"I understood he was taking a small vacation this weekend," T.S. dared to say.

"So what the hell is your excuse?" Edgar Hale demanded. He had found a target. "Where have you been? I called you over two hours ago."

"I hung up my coat first," T.S. barked back. "Okay by you?" There was no answer to this relatively daring retort, an unusual response given the Managing Partner's customary surliness. Ever since Edgar Hale's wife had died, he'd been a world class grouch. It was one reason why T.S. had retired as soon as he could.

T.S. counted to three beneath his breath and resolved to remember that he was retired now, above and beyond the reach of partnership politics. Fate had thoroughly tainted the genteel veneer of Sterling & Sterling, throwing them into a panic where appropriate reactions were not pre-ordained. They needed *him* now, to hold their hands. Edgar Hale would just have to realize that, sooner or later.

"What did you think you were attending here? A golf game?" The old man glared at T.S.'s sweater and slacks. So—it was going to be later, *much* later.

"Look, Edgar," T.S. replied, knowing the old man hated to be called by his Christian name. "I'm retired now and here as a personal favor. I'll wear what I want."

The old man tried to stare him down but soon gave up with a grunt of extreme dissatisfaction, and switched gears. "Who cares what you're wearing?" he said gruffly. "Just get to work and untangle this mess."

"I'm hardly qualified to solve a murder," T.S. pointed out.

"I didn't ask if you were qualified," Edgar Hale thundered. "I just said to do it." He stomped out the door, leaving T.S. standing in a sea of assorted official uniforms and activities, ebbing and flowing about him as if he were invisible.

"Who the hell are you?" A nasal voice heavily rimmed

with a New York City accent startled him out of his confusion. T.S. found himself staring at the forehead of a roly-poly, swarthy man whose thinning black hair was combed over his scalp in a last ditch effort to hide impending baldness. T.S. noted the suit—straight off the rack and badly fitting—at the same time he noticed the man's massive torso. It strained his shirt, a huge chest barreling down to a waist gone soft. The man was short and slightly plump, but unmistakably powerful. T.S. took a reflexive step backwards, sending the fireplace rack and tools tumbling over with a tremendous clanging. He was instantly pinned in the silent scrutiny of dozens of pairs of trained eyes until, as if on mass cue, the steady hum of activity began again and a multitude of tasks resumed.

T.S. retrieved the tools with disgust, savagely clanging them back into place. He was *really* getting tired of people screaming in his face. "My name is T.S. Hubbert. I'm the retired Personnel Manager of Sterling & Sterling. I am here at the request of Edgar Hale, Managing Partner, and I don't like it any more than you. And while we're at it, who the hell, may I ask, are *you*?"

The man had observed T.S. during this speech with an expression vacillating between contempt and amusement. He stared at T.S. passively, then casually dug wax out of one ear and shrugged. "I'm Lieutenant Abromowitz. I'm in charge of the scene. You can remain since the old man made such a stink. But stay where you are. I don't want anyone interfering with the physical evidence. It already looks like a tribe of Ubangis tramped through here."

"I understood the young lady who called the police did an excellent job of preserving the scene," T.S. replied stiffly. If this guy was any indication of the brilliant minds at work, they could go ahead and file this one under "unsolved."

"That what she says?" Lieutenant Abromowitz allowed, before adding cryptically, "That's what they all say."

Before T.S. could think of a suitable reply, they were interrupted by a scrawny young cop wearing a uniform shirt T.S. estimated was at least three sizes too big and pants that were too small. The kid's skinny legs poked out from the bottom of the trousers, leaving an inch thick strip of pale white skin before meeting black rubber boots. His hair stuck out like dried wisps of straw, though it was brushed flat in front as if he had at least tried to tame it. He looked like he'd escaped from a prison farm for minors in Ohio and taken a wrong turn somewhere, landing in the big city by mistake.

"Um, lieutenant," the little cop stammered nervously. "No one can find Tommy Shaunessy." He gulped as if expecting the lieutenant to smack him with a riding crop at any moment.

"Who the hell is Tommy Shaunessy?" Lieutenant Abromowitz demanded.

"You know. The secretary's husband."

"Oh, him." The lieutenant scowled. "Not home yet?"

"No sir. And his precinct says he didn't have the night shift like he told his wife. In fact, he's due in any minute to start his real shift."

Abromowitz sighed. "You'd think these guys could come up with more original stories." He rolled his eyes and turned to T.S. "Every cop who plays around thinks he can get away with it by claiming night shift."

The younger officer waited nervously, gulping as if his throat were dry. T.S. wondered how anyone could be intimidated by the lieutenant.

"Keep trying," Abromowitz ordered his man. "But don't tell the wife. You never know when we'll need cover ourselves." His laugh veered between lascivious and familiar, which equaled repugnant in T.S.'s estimation. "If he's not in within the next ten minutes or so, I'll question her myself without him. Wouldn't hurt to have the best on the job, anyway, since she was the first on the scene and knows the victim so well. Might have noticed something useful. In fact, tell everyone to lay off her. I'll handle this myself. Make sure no mistakes are made."

As the skinny cop hurried away with his instructions, T.S. was appalled to realize that the lieutenant had actually turned to him and winked. "You married?" he asked T.S. in a repellingly confidential tone.

T.S. was not opposed to winking on principle. He had even been known to wink himself, specifically in the event of specks of dust, eye infections and, occasionally, small children. But he was vehemently opposed to winking at tawdry indiscretions and pretended not to have noticed. "No, I'm not," he replied stiffly.

The lieutenant stared at him as if he found this peculiar. "Hmmmm," he said, eyeing T.S. even more closely.

"Well, are you married?" T.S. asked back defensively.

"I was," the lieutenant countered, as if daring T.S. to make something of it. "Until a couple of months ago. What's it to you?"

T.S. made a mental note to remember to congratulate the newly divorced Mrs. Abromowitz on her recent good fortune, should they ever be introduced.

The lieutenant gave T.S. one more suspicious glare, then tucked his clipboard under a sweat-stained armpit and took a couple of steps toward the screened-in area before pausing and turning back to T.S.

"You're the Personnel Manager here, you say?" he growled at T.S.

"Was. I retired yesterday."

"You don't look much like a Personnel Manager to me." Abromowitz eyed T.S.'s sweater and slacks.

T.S. drew himself up to his full height. "Maybe I'm on my way to a golf game. Why is everyone so preoccupied with my dress?"

"In this weather?" The lieutenant jerked a thumb toward one heavily draped window. "Don't get so defensive. Geeze. I was gonna say I liked your sweater."

"Thanks." He spit the word out with a lack of graciousness quite unlike him, then attempted to regain his dignity. "I assure you I will not be in the way. I have no doubt that you are quite capable of performing your duties without my interference. But if my presence here comforts the partners, I see no harm in it."

"Okay by me." The man tapped his pen against his two front teeth and stared absently at T.S. "Not that anyone here seems to need too much comforting. If you know what I mean."

"This is a very reserved firm," T.S. explained out of the side of his mouth. "Tradition."

"Yeah. Tradition." Abromowitz folded his arms and dangled the pen between two fingers. "I'm interested in the traditions around here. Been here long?"

"For thirty years." T.S. noticed the bright glare of lights behind the leather screen. A still photographer emerged and signaled a video cameraman, who shouldered his equipment and stepped behind the intricately tooled barrier. Robert Cheswick had been a rich man. They were taking no chances and pulling out all the stops on this one.

"Thirty years? That's long enough. You probably know a lot about this place. Being in Personnel and all." The lieutenant was scrutinizing T.S.'s face openly, as if searching for bloodstains on its surface. T.S. fought an undeniable urge to scratch one of his cheeks and casually reached up to do so. The lieutenant followed his move.

"You're the guy who had the retirement party last night, aren't you?" the lieutenant pointed out.

"Well, yes," T.S. admitted. "It was given for me. I didn't pick out the date."

Abromowitz nodded and stared at him without comment.

T.S. stared back at the lieutenant and noticed for the first time how tired he looked. There was a small spot of crusted egg still clinging to the lieutenant's chin. He, too, had probably been called out of bed. T.S. resolved not to hold it against Abromowitz personally for being a buffoon. He'd hold it against the NYPD.

"I probably know more than anyone else about Sterling & Sterling," T.S. reluctantly admitted. "It was my job."

"Including the financial aspects of it?"

"What do you mean?" T.S. wondered if anyone would notice if he just craned his neck a bit to try to see over the top of the screen.

"How profits are divided. Which partner gets what. That kind of thing."

"I know the procedures they follow to allocate profits among partners," he answered. "But the actual shares—no one knows that but the partners themselves. And, I assume, the IRS."

The lieutenant considered this. "I can do without actual amounts for now. Just the procedures will do. Feel free to throw in your impressions of the parties involved."

It was T.S.'s turn to stare at the lieutenant with a cross between contempt and amusement. "On the record?" he asked incredulously.

"Some on. Some off. I can be discreet."

T.S. was appalled to realize he'd been winked at yet again. "It's a complicated situation," he began.

"I've unraveled some pretty complicated situations in my time," the lieutenant interrupted with a tight smile. "Try me."

"They hold a meeting once a year to hash out which partner gets what percentage of overall profits. It's tied pretty closely to the performance of each partner's area of business."

The lieutenant seemed genuinely interested. "That sounds pretty simple to me."

T.S. shrugged. "Maybe. But if you're suggesting that money had anything to do with this, I can assure you that you are very much mistaken."

"Why is that?" The lieutenant took a step forward and breathed into his face. The smell of a garlic and onion bagel, tinged with coffee, wafted past. But not far enough.

T.S. could not retreat further back without crashing into the fireplace screen, so he stood his ground as firmly as was possible under the circumstances. This resulted in his bending over backwards while the lieutenant leaned over him like a sergeant preparing to chew out a boot camp inductee.

"Money would be the last thing a Sterling & Sterling partner would get murdered for," T.S. tried to explain.

"Oh, I think you'd be surprised. It's nearly always money.

Or love. Or love of money.'' The lieutenant laughed at his own joke. T.S. merely waited. ''But this guy looks a little old for love, if you ask me.'' Abromowitz gazed at T.S. with a scrutiny that seemed better suited to a suspect. Perhaps it's the only expression in his repertoire that approached thought-fulness, T.S. decided charitably.

''Maybe,'' T.S. conceded. ''I'd certainly be surprised at either motive.''

''Why's that?'' he demanded, blasting T.S. with another burst of bagel breath.

''Sterling partners all have more money than they could possibly ever need and would consider it the height of gaucheness to bring up the subject of their earnings in a conversation, much less question the decision of the other partners once a consensus had been reached. Nor, in my opinion, would any of them murder on its behalf.''

''Hmph'' was all he got in reply to his eloquent theory, a frequent reaction among strangers unused to T.S.'s some-times formal way of speaking. It was a trait T.S. was uncom-fortably aware of, but powerless to change. His articulate stiffness was the legacy of a most demanding schoolteacher mother.

A voice from behind the screen interrupted their chat. ''Hey, Manny!'' a female voice called out. ''Want one more look before we wrap things up here?'' Another unseen voice laughed mirthlessly at this unintended pun and a look of irritation crossed the lieutenant's face.

''Yeah. Hold up. I'll be right there.'' He stared into T.S.'s face for a moment, then wagged his pen at him for emphasis. ''I want to talk to you some more. Don't go anywhere.'' He eyed T.S. as if he were about to bolt the room.

''Maybe.''

''Maybe? What's maybe? Wait here until I get back.''

T.S. had made up his mind. ''I'd like to see the body.''

''Oh you would, would you? Not quite the well-bred gen-tleman you seem?'' A distinct note of scorn crept into the lieutenant's voice.

''I talked to the young woman whose mother discovered

the body,'' T.S. replied calmly. "Something she said stuck in my mind and I can't figure out what. I thought taking a look would stimulate my memory.''

"Oh, well, in that case," the lieutenant made an exaggerated bow and swept his hand forward. "Be my guest. In fact, let me carry you there on my back. We're desperate for assistance. We have only fourteen officers professionally trained in solving murders to assist us here today.''

T.S. gritted his teeth. He hated sarcasm in others. "It was about the knife, I believe.''

"You know about the knife?'' The lieutenant was gazing just above T.S.'s head now, nodding as he spoke.

"The young woman who discovered the body told me. I think I know where it came from.''

The lieutenant's acerbic demeanor crumpled as he wearied of his game. He tucked his clipboard back under one arm, shrugged, and gestured for T.S. to follow.

"What do I care?'' he said with a sigh. "Be my guest.''

It was just as Sheila had described it. Robert Cheswick lay splayed back in his chair, jostling slightly as forensic specialists brushed past. One knelt at the base of the desk, scraping carpet fragments into a plastic bag. Another carefully printed labels and affixed them to a pile of plastic bags containing various objects piled on another desk nearby. A woman dressed in gray slacks and a navy blazer lifted a wilted boutonniere off the desk with small tongs and dropped it into a small plastic bag. A cameraman was noisily breaking down lights.

"Look familiar?'' Abromowitz asked.

"I beg your pardon?'' T.S. stared at the body. Cheswick's head was thrown back, the neck exposed. T.S. noticed with a start how old the dead man looked. His crepe-paper skin stretched tightly over brittle bones and small wattles hung from his chin. The grin Sheila had described looked more like a grimace, the fleshy lips pulled back over his trademark prominent teeth.

"The corsage,'' Abromowitz said impatiently. "Why's the

guy wearing dead flowers to your retirement party? Was that his idea of some kind of a joke?"

T.S. stared at the brown and shriveled flowers closely. "That's a boutonniere," he corrected the lieutenant. "I don't remember his wearing flowers at all to my party."

The lieutenant rubbed his chin and looked away.

Cheswick's eyes were open as he gazed up at the huge chandelier inset into the room's dome. His pupils were gray and lifeless and tiny pinpoints of light were reflected in his flat irises. His jacket was neatly folded in the visitor's chair by the side of his desk.

"That's the same suit he had on last night," T.S. remarked. The lieutenant nodded as if he already knew this.

Just above the center of his chest, angling up with an incongruous delicacy, was the intricately carved ivory handle of a knife. It was yellowed with age and glowed in the chandelier's glare. A dark stain spread across the front of Cheswick's impeccably tailored shirt, the color curiously echoed in the delicate burgundy stripes that continued through the fabric. The victim's hands dangled at his side and T.S. noticed the age spots studding the clawlike flesh. How had death been able to make him instantly so much older?

Sheila was right. The partner's fly was unzipped and the whimsically patterned boxer shorts peeked out, drawing attention to his crotch area. T.S. sighed. He had not liked Robert Cheswick but no one deserved to die like this. It was undignified and an affront to the pride with which he had occupied his desk while living.

"So? Look familiar?" The lieutenant asked again, standing to his right and drinking in the scene as if seeing it for the first time. "The weapon, I mean."

"Yes." T.S. leaned forward and studied the handle carefully. His first suspicion was correct. "There's only one like it in the world to my knowledge. It was given to the firm in 1823 by a grateful African king. We had made it possible to bring trade to his Ivory Coast kingdom. He was an unusual man by all accounts. Ahead of his time."

"You're a wealth of historical info, aren't you?" The lieu-

tenant spoke without much enthusiasm. He seemed preoccupied, lost in the scene at hand, as if looking at it long
enough would bring the solution. "Where was it usually
kept?"

"In the first conference room down that small hallway."
T.S. indicated a smaller set of double doors opening out from
the side rear of the Partners' Room. "The one with the ivory
and blue drapes. It's usually kept in a case. There were some
gold coins and other antiques with it. On velvet. It made a
nice display for visitors."

"Where?" the lieutenant barked, startled. Before waiting
for a reply, he screamed for the skinny cop who had broken
the news about Anne Marie's husband. The kid skidded immediately to a hasty arrival at the lieutenant's elbow.

"Where's the secretary who found the body?" Abromowitz demanded.

"I think she's in a conference room somewhere," the cop
whispered back, gulping for air and darting his eyes nervously to the side. A number of bystanders had slowed their
work to keep an eye on the evolving scene. The lieutenant's
eyes narrowed dangerously. He looked like a bad-tempered
wart hog about to charge. Even T.S. felt the urge to step
back.

"Not the first one down that hallway?" the lieutenant
asked in a dangerously sarcastic and calm voice. "Get her
the hell out of there *now*," he suddenly bellowed, startling
the room into its second immediate halt of the hour. "Charlie! Dennis! Jack!" Abromowitz screamed each name like
an accusation and a trio of detectives leapt to attention from
their impertinent perches on the partners' desks lining the
far row. They stared at him nervously.

"Charlie," the lieutenant attempted to say calmly, but
immediately abandoned the cool approach in favor of rage.
"Someone has invited a witness to sit her fat ass down right
in the middle of a room crucial to evidence. This guy says
the knife came from a showcase in there. Get her the hell out
of there now. Find out who showed her in there in the first
place and why no one noticed the joint was ransacked. I want

to know whose responsibility it was. Jack, you go with Charlie. See what you can lift off the case and take her prints
while you're at it. Dennis, you stand by.''

The lieutenant turned his back on the men and clumsily
changed the subject, hoping, in vain, that T.S. had not noticed that a monumental gaffe had just been made. He took
in the Partners' Room again slowly, moving his eyes carefully down the double row of rolltop desks. ''What I can't
figure out is why all the partners sit in here. You'd think a firm
like this could afford to give everyone his own office.''

T.S. wasn't fooled by his changing of the subject or his
apparent ignorance. It was a technique many executives tried
at meetings when they were setting a rival up for a fall. ''Most
of them do have their own offices elsewhere in the bank. This
arrangement is just tradition. It goes back two hundred
years.''

''Where's his office?'' Abromowitz nodded toward Robert
Cheswick.

''On the second floor. In Private Investments. He has a
small office where he keeps some files and a desk. He liked
it down here on the Main Floor, though. Kept his secretary
down here with him, too.''

''He doesn't look like he likes it too much now.'' Abromowitz motioned over Dennis, who had lapsed into his familiar
pose of boredom. ''Dennis—hit the victim's office on the
second floor. Ask that guy in the monkey suit to show you
the way. Make sure Jack gets the prints from there when he's
through down here.''

The detective left silently and T.S. stared at the body. As
he took in the open fly and the spreading dark stain, he felt
the lieutenant's arm across his shoulders.

''I want to talk to you some more, Mr. Hubbert,''
Abromowitz said, giving T.S. a squeeze. ''Some more about
tradition, eh? Give me half an hour to question the broad,
then I'll meet you in your office. Don't worry. I'll find it.''

The broad? Anne Marie was many things. A broad was
not one of them. T.S. left the Partners' Room, shaking his

head. He doubted the lieutenant would be able to find his office, much less the murderer.

2   Their talk lasted more than an hour. It consisted of the lieutenant barking perfunctory questions at T.S. about his retirement party as well as exhaustive inquiries concerning financial arrangements at Sterling & Sterling. T.S. sat calmly at his desk while Abromowitz paced the floor, fiddled with the blinds, chomped on gum and scribbled an occasional note.

T.S. had long ago regretted having answered the phone that morning when Abromowitz started to go around again.

"You say that new partners are picked each November?"

"That's correct," T.S. replied. "If any new partners are selected."

"Who chooses new partners?"

"The existing partners do. I do not know the process. I doubt they vote. It's probably obvious and something that emerges over the year."

The lieutenant considered this information thoughtfully. "So there may be some disappointed honchos here? Someone who wanted to make partner and didn't?"

T.S. allowed himself a brief smile. "There may be. Probably about a dozen or two people a year think they should have been made partner. Maybe two or three of them seriously had a chance and didn't make it. The number grows each year."

"Why's that?"

"The partners at Sterling & Sterling tend to be much older than the partners you might find elsewhere on Wall Street. They tend to stay partners longer, take much longer to retire and, if I may say so, are extremely reluctant to relinquish the power they have spent a lifetime building."

"Yeah," the lieutenant agreed. "I saw a couple of them pass by. They looked old enough to me."

"Old enough to murder?" T.S. asked. The thought of another partner at Sterling & Sterling waiting for Cheswick behind the drapes struck him as slightly absurd.

Abromowitz had stopped pacing and stared thoughtfully at his clipboard. "Could be. Or maybe a younger honcho. Someone passed over for partner." He looked up.

"Then how do you explain the open fly?"

"Stranger things have happened." The lieutenant shrugged. "Maybe some young hotshot was trying to show the old guy it would be worth his while to back him but something went wrong." He ignored T.S.'s incredulous stare and changed the subject. "Tell me about Robert Cheswick."

"Truthfully?" T.S. began. "I'd say that not too many people liked him. Although I wouldn't really call any of the partners likable, with one or two notable exceptions. These are men who are almost solely concerned with making money, lieutenant. That's why they're partners and we're not. And it has been my experience that a sole preoccupation with making money doesn't leave much time for such mundane pursuits as making friends or maintaining warm employee relations."

"And Robert Cheswick in particular?"

"I suspect that most people thought he was a horse's ass."

The detective stared at T.S. "Is that on the record?"

T.S. sighed. "You seem to think I believe this is some kind of a joke. I assure you, I do not. He may not have been the warmest man in the world, but he didn't deserve to die like that."

"I'm glad to see such a sense of public spirit in a public relations flak."

"I'm the Personnel Manager," T.S. said yet again, wearily. "Retired."

The lieutenant turned back to staring at the heavy green drapes. "Go on. I'm interested in your perceptions of him. Not many people liked him, huh?"

"No. Not even the other partners, I don't think."

"Why is that?"

"Why didn't they like him? Same reason the rest of us didn't. He was pompous, overbearing and incompetent."

"How'd he get to be a partner?"

T.S. gave a short laugh. "The old-fashioned way. Family.

His father was a partner here before he left to go into politics. His great-great-grandfather was the founder's right hand man.''

''Silver spoon, huh?''

''Sterling,'' T.S. said. The lieutenant did not smile.

''What about his private life?''

''It was private, so far as I know.'' T.S. shrugged. ''I'm not being facetious. He didn't have any close friends among the other partners. Most of them tend to bunch together in groups of two or three. I believe he belonged to the same Connecticut country club as several of the other partners, but I never heard of his taking part in the usual activities. He didn't play golf. He didn't play tennis.''

''What about playing around?''

''Pardon?'' For a fleeting second T.S. thought he'd been propositioned.

''Did Cheswick play around?''

T.S. stared at him for a moment before answering. ''You'd have to ask his wife. As far as I know, sex was pretty far from his mind.''

''What about that secretary of his? For an old dame, she isn't bad looking.''

First she was a broad. Now she was an old dame. He'd better set the lieutenant straight before he started calling her ''Toots.''

''Anne Marie Shaunessy has been his secretary for nearly thirty-five years,'' T.S. told him with as much dignity as he could muster. ''She is a devout Irish Catholic and would be absolutely the last person at Sterling & Sterling to have an extramarital affair.''

''That's just your opinion,'' the lieutenant pointed out. ''Her old man's playing around. Maybe she wanted a little revenge. Tit for tat.'' He guffawed offensively.

''And that's just *your* opinion. You have no proof her husband is playing around and it isn't relevant anyway. Besides, if Anne Marie and Robert Cheswick were having an affair, I assure you I would have gotten wind of it. I hear just about everything that goes around,'' T.S. admitted.

"Really. Then what exactly did get around about Robert Cheswick?"

T.S. sighed and gave up. It was now nearly 2:00 in the afternoon and he wanted a chance to talk to some employees before he left. "The word on Robert Cheswick was that he wasn't very smart, that he was exceptionally stingy with employee bonuses, that he intensely disliked younger executives who were in any way threats to his power, and that he was something of a wimp, I guess. He had no outside interest that established his masculinity. He didn't own racehorses. He didn't play golf or tennis. He wasn't into sailing. That sort of thing. Most of the other partners had one hobby they could brag about. These are competitive men."

"Not even when he was younger?"

T.S. thought for a moment, back to his early years at Sterling & Sterling when he and Robert Cheswick had been moved along parallel paths, with different destinations clearly apparent. "A long time ago, I believe he was . . . well, more like the other partners. They were all younger then. Sowed some wild oats."

"You sure it was a long time ago?" The lieutenant looked up at the clock, then checked his own wristwatch.

"Yes, I'd call thirty years a long time ago. When I first got here, Cheswick was still known as a playboy, I guess. Like every other kid who joins the firm and knows he doesn't have to worry about making partner. That it's in the bag. Girls probably fell all over him. He would have been quite a catch. It might have hurt him if he kept it up. Rumor had it that his father flew in from Colorado to make sure he got the message. I don't know the details. Shortly after that, I know he married a lovely woman and settled down. But I really don't think it's relevant to what happened today."

"Well, if you don't think it was for money or love," the lieutenant asked, letting sarcasm creep back into his voice, "what do you think it was for?"

"I really don't know," T.S. replied. "But I intend to find out." He hesitated before asking the dreaded question. "Do you think he was killed by an employee?"

"Let's just say it's possible he knew his murderer." The lieutenant nodded. "How reliable are your night guards?"

"Extremely reliable. This is Sterling & Sterling."

"So if they say that no one entered or left the building last night without their knowledge, you'd believe them?"

"Absolutely," T.S. said. "I would certainly consider the check-out list accurate. They're mostly retired policemen. They'd understand the importance of the truth."

The lieutenant shrugged. "Unless the truth would make them look bad." He drummed his fingers impatiently against the desk. "It's my experience that such lists are useless. For now I want your personnel files and financial records on the dead man, all other partners and top executives. We're going to be taking a close look at securities trading patterns. There's a lot of big money in insider trading these days. I need them by tomorrow."

"Tomorrow's Saturday," T.S. protested, although he had no other plans.

"You think murderers take the weekend off?" the lieutenant asked in a careful voice as if he were talking to a particularly slow-witted child. "Detectives don't."

"I'm telling you, you're wasting your time if you think it's money."

"Don't tell me my job." The lieutenant moved toward the door and stopped for a final glare. "I only have so many people and right now something tells me we'll find the answer in those files." He stomped out, leaving T.S. staring at the door.

CHAPTER THREE

1 As soon as Lieutenant Abromowitz released him, T.S. fled to the privacy of the rest room. Perhaps cold water could revive his dignity and relieve the mysterious fright he felt. Robert Cheswick had looked so old, so very old—all hanging skin and sharp, protruding bones. Yet, they were not so many years apart in age.

T.S. felt better after splashing cold water on his face. For one thing, he did not look any different today than he had the day before. Retirement was not the instantaneous sentence of age that others had implied. His German heritage assured T.S. of wonderful bone structure. His face was still unarguably firm. Relentlessly rosy skin stretched over wide, flat cheeks and a determined chin. Why, he was wrinkled only a little bit around the mouth and eyes and, he would admit it, the jowls. But only a little. After all, he had retired early, he was barely fifty-five. Besides which, he was determined not to be vain and his body had yet to betray him.

It was true that a sturdy disposition and reliable constitution had bred in him years of carelessness about his body. He ate and drank what he wished without thought, at least he had until a few years ago. When he was sick, it never lasted more than a few days. His was definitely a low-maintenance body. An extra ten pounds or so around his hips appeared to be the only price he'd have to pay for his neglect. And that was not so bad as others that he knew. After all, his back was still straight, his shoulders erect and his walk still firm and confident. He brushed a lock of graying hair from his broad forehead, uncovering a new nest of wrinkles.

But at least he was not balding. On the contrary, he had a full head of robust, though graying, hair. Altogether, he felt, he could still lay claim to the mantle of middle-age.

The door swung open and young Clarkson entered, his unlined face flushed with the enthusiasm of youth for life. He looked up with startled, sparkling eyes and jumped to attention when he saw T.S. It was time for T.S. to move on with his duties before the child called him "sir" and crumbled his illusions. T.S. mumbled a greeting and escaped.

His next task was one that required experience, bearing and great tact. A younger man or woman would surely flub it. It was time to jump-start the bureaucratic public relations machine that Sterling & Sterling reserved for major deaths. It had last been used when Hobart Cummings finally succumbed to pneumonia at the age of 106, a fact that seemed to garner more public interest than the illustrious career he built ushering Sterling & Sterling into the modern Wall Street era.

Robert Cheswick's death was certainly no threat to the Dow Jones industrial average either, but, nonetheless, T.S. dutifully pulled the ever-ready obituary from the files. He had updated them all during his last vacation, using a battery-operated typewriter that packed neatly in his beach bag. Some may have thought it macabre that he would sit sipping rum funnies along the shores of St. Thomas, tapping away at the obituaries of the partners. But it had given him great satisfaction at the time—the perfect combination of work and pleasure.

Cheswick's obituary was, in the final analysis, rather sad. It concerned itself mostly with where he had come from and not where he had gone. A full paragraph was devoted to his ancestors, particularly his late father and grandfather. T.S. reflected on how hard it was to get a break, even in death. But he had to leave the paragraph in. For it was, after all, Cheswick's greatest accomplishment—to have carried forth the genes of a financial dynasty. Unfortunately for the family name, he had fumbled the ball a bit here as well, failing to produce sons and fathering instead two horsey-looking young ladies who had the misfortune to resemble their father instead of their lovely mother. Which reminded T.S. that he needed to visit Lilah

Cheswick and express his condolences. Her remembered image flooded him with warmth and triggered the emotions of a younger time. Surprisingly, it calmed him—his confusion was the assurance of youth he'd been seeking all morning. But he would not think about Lilah yet, not with work to do.

He met Lieutenant Abromowitz again outside of what was now Miss Fullbright's office. The detective stood thoughtfully in the doorway, gazing blankly at his shoes. He hardly noticed T.S. when he squeezed past and lumbered off in search of the elevator in a kind of trance. What possible illumination could Miss Fullbright have cast on anything? She was perched back on the window ledge, staring out at the drizzle with great concentration. T.S. coughed discreetly and she jumped, her automatic smile fading once she saw it was T.S.

"Oh, it's you," she said, not bothering to mask her disappointment.

"I've been pulling the file obituary together. I thought you'd like to see it."

This news agitated her greatly and she hopped to her feet. "But I wrote one," she said. "It took me all morning." She handed him five pages of single-spaced typing, with a great many words underscored and bold-faced.

T.S. scanned it quickly and resisted even a gentlemanly groan.

"Miss Fullbright," he said, holding the offending document daintily between two fingers. "This is surprisingly . . . poetic, I would say. Perhaps you missed your calling."

She simply stared at him, as suspicious as always. "I feel something like a fool," she finally said. "I didn't know an obituary had already been written."

"Yes," T.S. said brightly, sweeping an arm over a discreet oak file cabinet. "Copies of them are all right here. Every one." He did not like his competency questioned, even in a roundabout way, and thus could not help adding, "I believe I noted it in the procedures book that I prepared for you."

She looked at T.S. as if she did not believe him. "I must have missed it," she said.

"Section Two, pages fifteen and sixteen, if I'm not mistaken."

"Oh, I'm sure you're not," she answered archly.

He forged onward. "You only need to update them when a partner performs some extraordinary deed that should be noted in the event of his death."

"As extraordinary as getting stabbed in the chest?" she asked sweetly.

T.S. gazed at her silently. He had not realized she had any sort of sense of humor at all. The thought was encouraging. The humor was not.

"Thank you for reminding me," he said. "We'll have to deal with that in the official obituary. But I do suggest that we save your version for use as a special supplement to the *Sterling Times*, with proper credit, of course. And work together on revising the official version here before sending it out."

But having circled and sniffed the territory before making a stake to her claim, Miss Fullbright had clearly made the decision to deal with the living, leaving the dead to T.S. Hubbert. She tapped her initialed gold Cross pen on her impeccably polished teeth and stared at T.S. blankly, as if her mind were far away. T.S. knew this to be a gambit. It was her favorite way of attempting to gain control—making others wait while she collected her thoughts.

But T.S. also knew that collecting even all of Miss Fullbright's thoughts couldn't possibly take very long and so he was content to wait her out. He settled in and mulled over possible ways to phrase the violence displayed in the Partners' Room below in palatable terms for the public. Perhaps, "To their great regret, the Partners of Sterling & Sterling announce the untimely death of their esteemed colleague Robert Cheswick." Yes, that was the way. Make no mention of the stabbing at all. "Untimely" would have to suffice. Certainly the phrasing fit. Dying on T.S.'s first day of retirement was nothing but untimely, although the general public was unlikely to appreciate the nuance.

"So what do you think, T.S.?" Miss Fullbright was staring at him brightly.

"An excellent idea," he answered promptly, wondering what in the world he had just sanctioned.

"I knew you would agree. I think a team of three psychologists should do it. We'll install them in the department and anyone who feels the need to vent his or her feelings can visit on company time."

Oh, dear. Edgar Hale would pop a cork. "Perhaps you should suggest employees visit during their lunch hours, or have the, um, team available before and after working hours as well," he ventured to say.

"Then no one will go." She became visibly grumpy when anyone disagreed with her, and at such times had a tendency to pout. It was not a becoming habit.

"I'm sure an employee in distress will welcome the opportunity for . . . ah, relief at any cost. And reach out for help even after working hours." It was a good thing he was retiring—the jargon of modern human resource management made him feel plain silly. Relief. Reaching out for help. Honest to god. Employees would leap at this chance to goof off, even if they had to pretend to miss Robert Cheswick to do it.

She grunted in a very noncommittal, though ladylike, fashion and T.S. decided to escape. He rose and handed her back her obituary. "This will make a lovely testimonial."

"What?" She stared blankly at her papers. "Oh, that." She looked up at T.S. "What do you think of Manny?"

"Who?"

"The lieutenant." Her pen clicked against her teeth at a more rapid pace.

"Abromowitz? He seems, well . . . confident." It was the very best he could do. He could hardly tell her he'd found the loutish lieutenant as dumb as a deaf St. Bernard.

"Yes, isn't he? So confident and . . . so in control." She smiled at T.S. brightly and briskly patted her papers into a neat pile. "It's good to know we're in such competent hands." She stared back out the window and sighed.

2 It took him an hour to revise the official obituary and send it out by messenger to the dailies, along with eight-by-ten-inch glossies of a younger Robert Cheswick, his horsey teeth hidden behind tightly pressed liver lips in a true Wall Street mogul smile. He had barely finished notifying the financial periodicals by phone when a discreet rapping sounded at his office door.

"Come in," he called out and Albert the elevator man stepped timidly through the door, his small burgundy cap twisting in his shaking hands. He was followed by a stocky man in his early fifties, resplendent in a gray and burgundy security guard uniform complemented by his closely cut gray hair.

"Good afternoon, Albert. Mr. O'Hare." T.S. nodded to both men.

"We've come about the list, Mr. Hubbert, sir," Albert began in a quavering voice. The man was so nervous that T.S. found himself tapping his foot in time to Albert's fearful trembling. Or was it anger?

"The list?" T.S. asked. "Come in. Come in." They inched further in the door until Timothy O'Hare, a security guard, finally moved quietly to stand by the window.

"The list of people who checked out late last night," O'Hare explained. He unfolded a piece of paper and set it gingerly on T.S.'s desk. "I made you a copy of it, sir. So that you can see for yourself that we're thorough. The lieutenant doesn't believe us." O'Hare's normally soft voice swelled in anger. "He thinks we left to go to the bathroom or let people pass through the lobby without signing in."

"Or maybe even fell asleep," Albert piped up indignantly.

The guard tapped the list with his finger angrily. "He reminds me of my old lieutenant. And why I retired as soon as I could." Like many Sterling & Sterling security guards, O'Hare was a retired police officer.

"We would never do that, Mr. Hubbert," Albert interrupted, his voice squeaking in anger. "Why, Sterling & Sterling is entrusted to us. We'd never let someone through the lobby without stopping them. If someone killed Mr. Cheswick last night, sir, his name is on that list." He eyed the paper fearfully.

"Even when we know people, we make them sign in," O'Hare pointed out.

"Not just their names, but their employee numbers, too."

"Even Edgar Hale himself, sir. I've stood up to him many times and insisted he check in and out."

T.S. swiveled his head back and forth as each man spoke, following the exchange with interest. He wasn't interested in the words so much as who would come out on top of this seemingly endless battle for most uncompromising lobby watchdog.

"Why, Timothy even stopped Mrs. Cheswick last night," Albert protested, throwing the contest in favor of his opponent. "Didn't you?"

Timothy looked embarrassed. "Not really. She didn't actually say she wanted to go in. She just wanted me to call and see if her husband was there."

"Lilah Cheswick? What time was that?" T.S. asked with interest.

"About 9:00, sir. She had her limousine waiting outside. Thought Mr. Cheswick might want a ride home."

"And no one answered at his extension?"

"No, sir. And Mrs. Cheswick, she just got in the car and left."

"Did you tell the lieutenant that?"

"Of course." O'Hare rolled his eyes. "He shrugged like it was no big deal and started grilling me again on whether I had left the lobby unattended."

"We keep telling him we would never do that," Albert squeaked.

"He'll get us fired, sir. You know how Mr. Hale is. And the more I told the lieutenant I would never leave my post, the more he acted like I was lying."

"I told the lieutenant you were both most reliable," T.S. assured them.

"He doesn't believe you either, sir," Albert said. "I know because he questioned me again on his way out. I was there until 7:00 P.M., just like I said I was." He wagged his hat angrily.

"I'm sure you were, Albert," T.S. soothed.

"And I took over then," the security guard added. "I didn't even leave my post to go to the bathroom until my coffee break at 10:00 and another guard took over for me while I was gone. We're under orders not to leave the lobby unmanned, not even for a minute. Ever since that . . . well, you know. Ever since that unfortunate surprise in the Partner's Elevator. And we follow orders, sir."

He remembered the unfortunate surprise all too well. They had concocted some story about a visiting pet dog to mollify the more refined employees. But the real message had been inescapably clear: at least one employee felt the partners were worth no more than a pile of . . . well, he would think of it no more. Such a prank was nothing in the face of murder.

T.S. looked at the clock. It was getting late. "I'm sure you both followed orders exactly," he assured the men. "Believe me, I'll back you up."

"He's barking up the wrong tree, sir," Albert added, his brown eyes even sadder and more basset-like than before. "We think this list is important."

"There's only one way in and one way out at night," Timothy declared. "What does he think? That we leave the windows open for people to creep through?"

T.S. took both men by the elbows and ushered them out the door. "I appreciate your coming by, gentlemen. I will personally emphasize to Edgar Hale that neither of you was remiss in your duties." Albert started to reply and T.S. was forced to tighten his grip, marching them firmly out the office door to the main elevators.

They were still shaking their heads angrily as they entered the down car, inventing improbable scenarios for each other.

"The cops must think we smuggle burglars in with the laundry," Albert muttered under his breath.

"Or pull up easy chairs and snooze the night away," O'Hare answered bitterly as the doors closed upon them.

"Perhaps he thinks my grandmother did it," Albert offered as a last retort, his squeaky voice fading down the elevator shaft.

Despite their excess indignation, T.S. watched them go with sadness—sadness because he believed them. And, if they were right, the killer's name was on that list. A list that contained the names of some of Sterling & Sterling's finest employees.

3 T.S. checked his watch and pocketed his copy of the late check-out list. He was due to meet Auntie Lil for dinner at 6:00. He would have just enough time to sneak an early drink. He hoped Frederick would be on duty at the bar.

It was just his luck. Faced with a crippling workers' strike, the *Daily News* was publishing a temporary afternoon edition in a bid to regain readers—and making the most of Cheswick's gruesome death. The minute he hit the sidewalk, T.S. heard the cry: "Blue Blood Runs Red on Wall Street! Blue Blood Runs Red on Wall Street!"

It was shouted from every corner, including the one not thirty feet from where they had carried the body away. A cluster of curious people, all holding newspapers, stood staring at the imposing entrance to Sterling & Sterling and, for a brief instant, T.S. thought that the crowd had taken up the cry. But, of course, it was the newspaper hustlers and they were doing a brisk business indeed. T.S. resisted for perhaps three seconds before digging for change and tucking the screaming headline quickly beneath his arm. He looked around but no one he recognized had spotted him.

Well, it was no crime to purchase a tabloid on an occasion such as this. Besides, he may have been quoted for all he knew.

4 And there he was, in a paragraph attributing possible motives: "According to an unidentified knowledgeable source, the subject had no known enemies or personal problems which may have contributed to his death."

"Damn thee with faint praise," he muttered beneath his breath.

"What's that, Mr. Hubbert? Like another?" Frederick stood over his bar like a lord of old, his handlebar mustache

carefully waxed, his arms stretched wide along the length of
the bar's polished oak surface. He was the perfect man to
preside over the bar of Harvey's Chelsea Restaurant, an es-
tablishment that still managed to preserve a veneer of gentility and hushed elegance—if you ignored the occasional
construction worker, with tastes a cut above his usual crowd,
such as the one who sat at the end of the bar nursing a beer.

"Oh, why not?" T.S. said amicably to Frederick. After
all, he was an unidentified and knowledgeable source. And
certainly knowledgeable enough to know when another drink
was in order.

"Meeting Auntie Lil tonight?" Frederick placed a healthy
Dewar's and soda in front of T.S. Olympic-sized, in fact.
The man could read his mind.

"Who else?" He raised his glass in cheers and sipped.

"You could do a lot worse," the bartender allowed. "Believe me, I've seen them all. Give me Auntie Lil any day."

As if on cue, Auntie Lil entered the restaurant, seemingly
borne in on a gust of cold wind that followed her. She wasted
no time in getting right to the point, hissing to T.S. loudly
across the entrance floor even as the maitre d' struggled to
relieve her of her coat. She never gave it up willingly.

"It was a woman," she whispered ominously. "I know."

T.S. looked around, but Harvey's hummed on, blissfully
unaware that Robert Cheswick had been stabbed.

"Now, Auntie Lil." He took her elbow and steered her to
the dining area entrance, hoping to slip her past the bar without stopping. "How can you be sure?" She wore a black silk
pants suit—Auntie Lil loved pants—and the fabric rustled
agreeably beneath his touch. Her perfume smelled of apples
and her white hair was upswept with a smart lacquered comb.
Her thick hair framed a strong, almost masculine face that
had been referred to as handsome in her heyday, primarily
because of the stubborn and confident spirit that emanated
from it. Her skin was remarkably unwrinkled for her age.
She swore she used nothing but soap, but T.S. tended not to
believe her because she also swore her eyes were perfect and

he had one afternoon discovered a pair of reading glasses hidden beneath the cushions of her couch.

Her German heritage was evident in the strong, rounded chin and her prominent apple cheeks—much like his own face. She used a light brush of powder and a sprinkling of rouge because it suited her elegant clothes, not because she needed it. As sturdy as they come, Auntie Lil was the type of woman who had settled whole states in pioneer days.

They never bothered to wait to be seated at Harvey's. Auntie Lil preferred to charge forth unfettered, taking the dining area by storm. Because their favorite table was seldom occupied this early, the maitre d' had long since given up reining in Auntie Lil. She strode through the dining room, her firm step belying her eighty-four years of age. Auntie Lil liked to sit in the rear, looking out over the other tables so she could remark on fellow diners while they ate. She also liked the extensive dessert cart to be parked to her right, so she could take her time and gauge which concoction was proving most popular before making her own selection.

She gave the double chocolate mousse pie a long hard look before answering her nephew. "It was a stabbing. Am I correct? Right above the heart?"

"I see you've been reading the *News*." He made no mention of his own copy, which he had given to Frederick once he was through.

"How else am I supposed to keep current?" She looked about the dining area and waved the waiter over with a broad sweep of her sturdy arm.

"What does one have to do to get a drink around here?" Auntie Lil muttered.

"Well, how does the fact that he was stabbed prove it was a woman?" T.S. mulled over whether or not to order another drink while she was at it. However, Auntie Lil was staring at his full glass rather fixedly and he gave the notion up.

"Because I saw it happen once before." She announced this with great conviction, leaning forward and staring him intently in the face, using her most forceful whisper. She had a most intimidating habit of voicing her opinions in a conspiratorial and confident manner, moving her body closer so that it was virtually impossible to disagree.

"Ms. Hubbert." The waiter nodded his head and beamed. She was a notorious overtipper. "The usual?"

"Yes, please. Heavy on the Tabasco." She drank Bloody Marys and Bloody Marys only, regardless of the time of day. She could easily drink T.S. under the table.

"You saw it happen before?" he asked. Auntie Lil was an endless fount of information and stories on human nature, having spent six decades in the fashion industry as an assistant designer. It was an occupation that suited her practical nature well. She took the illusions and dreams of some of the biggest names in haute couture and forged them into reality with her sharp eye, skillful hands and uncompromising perfection. Even today, at her advanced age, she was in demand during peak seasons.

"Yes. In 1938. My best cutter, a Sicilian woman whose husband had run off with a dancer. Her name was Maria, I believe. If not, it should have been. She'd taken a lover. An Albanian, I recall. Someone she knew from the neighborhood. She obtained a job for him at the warehouse unloading dresses. Soon after being hired, he had the bad taste to leave her for a fat housewife of his own nationality. At least Maria said she was fat. 'A filthy pig of a woman' were her exact words. For all I know, she looked like Sophia Loren. She's Albanian, isn't she?"

"No, she certainly isn't," he said firmly. Auntie Lil had to be corrected forcefully and at once or else she was capable of carrying a misconception to the grave. "And she stabbed the housewife?"

"Sophia Loren?"

"No, Aunt Lil. Maria. Your employee." All this talk of stabbings was starting to get to him. He waved anxiously at their waiter. Perhaps a fresh drink after all.

"No. She did not." Auntie Lil plucked a bread stick from the basket and examined it closely before biting into it with gusto. "She stabbed the Albanian." Crumbs flew as she talked. Auntie Lil waved what was left of the bread stick as if it were a baton, using it to emphasize her points. "She stabbed him right through the heart. I saw it all. Out in the hallway near the water cooler during a break. Absolutely no warning. She used her finest scissors, a German pair. Impeccably crafted, of course."

"He died?"

"Certainly. She was the best I've ever seen with the scissor. An unerring sense of where and when to cut. He died without a sound. Crumpled at her feet. She stood over him staring down as if a tramp or street bum had dared to block her regal passage. It was majestic and terrifying. Black eyes flashing. Dark hair flowing over a white smock."

Auntie Lil would no doubt have trod the boards on the Great White Way had it been more respectable for a young girl in her day.

"What happened then?" he asked.

"I disarmed her. Walked right up to her and demanded she hand over the scissors. She did, too. Meek as a lamb. Then I let her sit in the office until the police arrived. It was too late for the Albanian, of course."

Of course. Auntie Lil figured prominently in all of her stories. He had no doubt that most of them were true.

"And you surmise from this that Robert Cheswick was stabbed by a woman?"

"Yes, I do."

Their drinks arrived and they sipped for a moment in silence, Auntie Lil making a great show of testing the degree of spiciness before dismissing their waiter.

"I believe I'll have the shepherd's pie tonight," she announced to T.S. out of nowhere. It had never been her habit to follow the conventional confines of a conversation. "All this excitement has me feeling very much the pheasant."

"You mean peasant, don't you?"

"No. I had it once and it was far too dry." Auntie Lil refused to admit that she was slightly deaf in her left ear. "You have the liver and onions," she ordered. "Tell them not to overcook it."

"I was thinking more along the lines of the prime rib," T.S. protested.

She snorted at this. "You need the liver. Look at you. Your color is terrible."

"Yours would be, too, if you'd spent all day with disagreeable detectives."

"Yes, aren't they? Think they know everything. What did they withhold from the press?" she asked, her eyes glittering.

T.S. paused to let her squirm a bit, not above getting his petty revenge when he could.

"Well, come on. What is it?" She spoke almost like a man when she had to wait, her already husky voice deepening and taking on a certain kind of power from impatience.

Abromowitz had said nothing about keeping quiet. Probably thought him too unimportant to matter.

"They found him with his fly unzipped."

"I knew it," she crowed. "They always withhold some important detail. They always do. And now I know it, too. How exciting."

"There was also a dead boutonniere placed on his desk."

"A dead one, you said?" She leaned forward, eyes glittering.

"Yes. Wilted and brown."

"How curious. Symbolic, no doubt." She leaned back to consider the information. "He could have been on the way to the bathroom," she finally said. "That's why his fly was down."

"It's half a flight up."

"Perhaps he was, um, playing with himself," she ventured.

"Auntie Lil!"

She waved the waiter over to take their orders. "I'm teasing you, Theodore. I'm sure it's a significant development."

She ordered for them both, then suddenly scrutinized him closely. "Where is your tie tonight, Theodore? You look like you're on the way to a golf game."

"I'm retired now," he virtually moaned.

"Yes. I quite forgot." She eyed him again closely. "I

think it's quite suitable in that case. You pull it off well. What a lovely sweater. I gave it to you, didn't I?''

"No, you did not." She was forever taking credit for his best clothing. "I bought it in Ireland last year."

"Hmm. Didn't bring me back one."

"I brought you that lovely shawl," he protested.

This mollifed her. "So you did," she said, settling the subject.

She began again. "I am positive it was a woman."

He had known even before she arrived that the murder would be the sole topic of conversation at dinner. If truth be told, he had looked forward to the opportunity to discuss it all with her. Auntie Lil's observations tended to be remarkably perceptive and correct, although collectively they presented a bleak view of human nature.

He started at the beginning and told her the entire story, from Sheila's recounting of the event to his own observations to his conversations with lieutenant Abromowitz and the lobby guards.

"The lieutenant sounds like a pompous ass," she noted briskly, having listened carefully to his entire account. Even her chewing, normally lusty and quite an event, had been hushed and unobtrusive.

"He seems positive that money is behind the killing, or some sort of insider trading scandal. He's equally convinced that the killer could easily have slipped by the guards."

"He may be right," she conceded generously. "But I doubt it. Pompous people don't have hunches, you know. They're too full of themselves to see things clearly."

"Unfortunately, his hunch, correct or not, means that I must go in tomorrow to pull together all the records he's requested. It's quite a lot. Personnel files on all partners and top executives. The financial records will have to come from the treasurer."

"Tomorrow is Saturday," she pointed out.

"All the better. No one will be there but the security and cleaning staff."

He could tell immediately he was being set up by the careful way she raised her Bloody Mary, staring into it as if an image might materialize in its murky depths. For a moment, he thought she might even have fluttered her eyelashes, but then, she was far too forthright for that. Bluntness was her only approach.

"I want to come," she announced.

"Whatever for?"

"To see the crime scene."

"The body has been removed."

"Of course it has." She was insulted by his assumption that she knew nothing of such techniques. "There may be something the police have overlooked."

"I don't know if they'll let us back in." He wondered if the police guard would still be posted.

"I'll take the chance." She stared at him sternly, almost daring him to refuse.

She would be a monumental pain in the ass at the office. Her normally inquisitive nature would no doubt go wild faced with rows of personnel files containing the most minute information on well over fifteen hundred lives.

"Aren't you busy tomorrow?" he asked.

She snorted and speared her last forkful of shepherd's pie with gusto. "Doing what? Who'd want to bother with an old woman like me?"

This he knew not to be true and merely another symptom of her rather dramatic approach to life, but he also knew when he was beaten. "Fine, then. I think I can manage it." He would surrender with grace.

The change in her was astounding. She briskly wiped her mouth with the linen napkin, folded it neatly at the side of her plate, pushed away her Bloody Mary and reached for the ice water. She threw it back like whiskey, slammed the glass back down, then reached into her cavernous black cloth bag for her notebook and gold fountain pen. "This is what we're going to do," she began.

T.S. stared, a half-chewed chunk of cold liver dangling from his open mouth.

"For god's sake, Theodore. Close your mouth. You're go-

ing about it all wrong. And so is that Lieutenant Abromowitz, bless his arrogant heart.''

"You planned this," he accused her.

"Of course. When will we ever have the chance again?''
She leaned forward and whispered urgently to him. "When
will we ever have the chance again, Theodore? You have the
time. I have the time. We both have the brains.''

"Thank you for the benefit of the doubt," he interrupted.

She snorted again. "Of course you have the brains. You
inherited them from me.''

He did not attempt to explain that it was impossible for
him to inherit anything from his father's sister. Besides, his
own mother made the same accusation: "You're just like that
Hubbert woman," she would spit out in scathing tones.
"Bullheaded.''

Auntie Lil had thought it all through. "They're on the
wrong track. But they're also not going to listen to us.''

"Who are we?" she asked just as the waiter approached.
He paused, startled, as Auntie Lil threw out her hands and
proclaimed, "We're a couple of crazy people to them if we
try to intervene in their investigation! You are maybe useful
to some extent, but me, I'm an unknown.''

She again leaned forward, this time shaking her fist and
whispering, "We have the power. Compared to the police,
we're invisible. We can find out things they can't.'' She sat
up straight again, fixed the waiter with a piercing gaze and
nearly growled, "No dessert tonight. Get us the check.''

He stared at her in surprise and walked away muttering,
his tip in danger.

"People talk to you. I know they do. You're always telling
me of someone's marital problems. Or someone preparing
to run off with someone in accounting.''

He nodded and pushed his plate away. "Yes, employees
do talk to me.''

"They know," she said wisely, nodding her head in full
expectation of his agreement.

"What do you mean, they know?''

"There is a reason why Robert Cheswick was stabbed and that reason is at Sterling & Sterling. I can feel it."

"How?" he asked her, genuinely puzzled. "What do you mean?"

"They left him there on purpose, Theodore. Out of sheer contempt. Left him cold and lifeless and totally without power, stripped of all life and dignity in front of his colleagues." She shook her head angrily. "And they exposed him, too."

"His skin wasn't showing," he corrected her.

"Oh, who cares if his dingus was hanging out or not? That's not the point. The point is passion. Ugly passion. It's not financial." She snorted again. "What poppycock. Those men are cowards. Do you think Ebenezer Scrooge would have had the courage to murder? I think not. All they care about is money and earning more of it. It's a game to them. They're not going to risk the pleasure they get from the game to obtain a little bit more." She nearly rolled her eyes at the very notion.

"So what is the reason?" he asked her, wishing he could share in her conviction. It was true the older partners would never murder for money. But what about the younger ones? Did he really understand the new generation of Wall Street whiz kids? T.S. was no longer so sure that he did. He was old and getting older every day.

"The absence of an apparent reason makes it all the more important and difficult to discover," Auntie Lil insisted. "It will be something small to us. But very large to the murderer."

"Where do we begin?" He was intrigued by this notion. As usual, he found himself beginning to be swept along by her enthusiasm for life, one trait he had regrettably not "inherited" from her.

"Tomorrow, we go in. You gather up your files. I want to look them over before we give them to that detective. Then we take a look at the scene of the crime."

When he nodded, she made a small check on her notebook and flipped to a new page. "Now, we also must get Anne Marie Shaunessy over to my house for brunch on Sunday. She was his secretary and may know more than anyone those things that no one is supposed to know." While T.S. was translating this convoluted statement in his head, she moved briskly onward. "Can you call up Sheila?" she asked. "And get her over for brunch as well?" Auntie Lil was familiar with T.S.'s fondness for Sheila and knew all about her family.

"Certainly," he said, happy to be able to offer something to the cause. The thought of having brunch with Sheila on an otherwise dull Sunday was appealing.

"But just the women," Auntie Lil made clear.

"Not me?"

"Certainly you. I meant tell them both to leave their husbands at home. We don't need a bunch of overgrown boys masquerading as policemen butting in with suggestions and acting superior."

He quite agreed with her assessment of Shaunessy and O'Reilly. "Fine," he said.

"We also need to talk to Cheswick's widow," she decided. "I remember her well. I last saw her at that benefit luncheon in 1986. Lilah is her name, correct? She has quite a sensible mind."

"Correct." He thought of Lilah again. A tall, athletic woman with strong features and a frank demeanor who had grown old with grace, refusing to dye her hair and standing out as the only gray-haired wife at the infrequent partner social functions. An island of honesty in a sea of silver and tinted coiffed ladies.

"You had a thing for her once, as I recall," she reminded him needlessly.

T.S. sighed. Auntie Lil never forgot a single fragment of his nearly nonexistent personal life. His "thing" had consisted of a minor crush nearly thirty years ago, shortly after he joined the firm, when he had met Lilah at a party for the young turks at Sterling & Sterling. Not yet married to Robert Cheswick, she had arrived on one of her first dates with the partner-to-be. T.S. had spent the evening talking opera with her, delighted at her intelligence and daring.

Appalled she was going to marry a horse's ass like Cheswick, T.S. had made the mistake of mentioning their encounter to Auntie Lil, who, even then, was a terrible busybody when it came to his life. She'd championed the banner of Lilah Cheswick until months after the wedding, only dropping it reluctantly when he fabricated a pert young secretary in the Foreign Investment area simply to gain some relief from being constantly reminded of what he did not have.

"It's never too late," she announced to T.S., interrupting his thoughts.

He stared at her. "What are you suggesting? That I call her up and say, 'Sorry your husband was stabbed and by the way, would you like to get married?' "

"Of course not." She sniffed, offended at such implied bad manners. "That would be inexcusably rude. I meant that it's still not too late to get married to someone."

"You never got married to anyone," he pointed out.

She shot him a steely glance and her eyes snapped with brilliance. "That, my dear Theodore, does not mean I was never asked."

Having put him in his place, she switched subjects again. "Finally, I want you to tell me in great detail what happened at your retirement party, and we'll need to go over the list of employees who left late last night."

"That's going to take a while."

"I know. That's why we're going to your house for a nightcap." She snatched the bill from the waiter's hands and rummaged through her purse for a credit card.

"You think that the list is important?" T.S. asked.

"For our purpose, it has to be." She stacked two embroidered handkerchiefs, a dog-eared address book, a large Swiss army knife, several pens and a box of colored pencils, three packs of mints and what looked to be a broken charm bracelet on the tablecloth before she produced a credit card from the depths of her bag. She flashed T.S. a triumphant smile. "Found it."

"Anyway, we have to start somewhere," she continued matter-of-factly. "Unlike the lieutenant, we haven't an army of investigators to pore over security trading tracks. And we certainly can't investigate everyone at Sterling & Sterling. I think it's unlikely the killer would have tried to stay hidden in the building all night. There was no guarantee the body would not be discovered before morning. And I think there was a body well before morning.''

''But if he was killed during the evening, that would mean there could be a connection between my party and his death,'' T.S. said.

She batted at the air absently. ''The papers said he was killed between 10:00 P.M. and 3:00 A.M. He doesn't get in that early, does he?''

''Not to my knowledge,'' T.S. answered reluctantly.

''Then we must assume he was stabbed after attending your retirement party.'' She stared at him impassively.

''You sound as if this makes me guilty of something,'' he protested.

''You are guilty of drinking too much at your party at a time, it turns out, when your memory could have proved crucial. But we'll see what we can do about that.''

''What? What are we looking for?'' He was catching her zest for the hunt, but lagging behind in ingenuity. The effect was annoying, as though he were in a parlor game and the only one who did not know the rules, thus doomed to fail from the start.

''We're looking for *clues*, Theodore. For god's sake. Haven't you ever read a detective novel?''

''One or two.'' In truth, he'd read hundreds. ''Have you?''

''Maybe,'' she said vaguely. T.S. was relieved to see she was her same overtipping self as she signed her credit slip and scribbled in the gratuity quickly, her mind having automatically computed the amount as she spoke. She opened her bag and scraped the pile of assorted junk back in, snagging a napkin in her haste. T.S. watched it disappear, without comment.

''What are we waiting for?'' she asked as she rose and walked majestically through the now crowded dining area, nodding to several patrons and waving at the staff.

T.S. followed obediently, wondering where in the world he was being led.

CHAPTER FOUR

1   They sat at the dining room table in front of the sliding glass doors that led to his thirty-fourth floor terrace. York Avenue snaked before them, winding uptown through the shadows of nearby highrises before disappearing into the fog. T.S. had to be content with the view through glass, for Auntie Lil refused to set foot on the actual terrace, convinced that she might fall, be propelled off by a gust of wind or be seized by a sudden impulse to jump. She was a great believer in the theory that the human race functioned largely according to impulse and was constantly waiting for one to overcome her, unaware that no impulse in the world had a chance next to her steely self-control.

T.S. knew this well. He had yet to see her take any action without a great deal of calculating forethought, but he was not about to tell her that. Besides, the truth was that the great height and endless lights stretching under his feet made him a little bit dizzy himself. He was far more content to stay within the cozy confines of his apartment.

His personal life was, of course, as meticulously organized as his professional existence. Each room in his apartment had a purpose and was carefully furnished to fulfill that purpose in as expeditious a manner as possible. The living room was spare and uncluttered—a large blue rug covered the floor as his sole concession to fashion. He preferred the simplicity of bare wood because it was easier to clean. There was a low-slung, sleek couch stretched along one wall with two matching armchairs arranged on each side. He'd chosen a special gray upholstery fabric that was guaranteed to repel dirt, dust, cat hairs and other foreign objects for either his lifetime or the lifetime of the couch, he never could remember which. He liked to keep his copies of *Personnel Manager Monthly* neatly arranged on the coffee table in vertical rows that were offset by corresponding rows of *The New Yorker* and *Cat Fancy*. The ashtrays were banished to a special drawer lined with cedar chips. T.S. usually found smoking messy and intrusive, depending on the smoker, and made guests ask before they were allowed to taint his carefully humidified air.

Since he was a man of simple tastes and rarely had company, the kitchen was tiny. His one indulgence was bottled water and an entire shelf of black olives stuffed with anchovies, a brand available only in Spain. The local grocer brought T.S. a carton each time he returned from visiting his family there. T.S. had invested some of his relative wealth in a coffee machine that looked as if it required a license to operate, plain bone china, and heavy sterling silverware of a geometric pattern that annoyed Auntie Lil for no clearly discernible reason. The attached dining room held a heavy oak table and four matching chairs that, while a bit large for the area, had been the only heirlooms he had chosen from his parents' house. The set had belonged to his mother and he was not above judicious sentimentality. A low sideboard along the wall held a dozen each of water and wine glasses. He'd had both sets for over a decade now and had yet to break a single glass, an achievement Auntie Lil found amusing.

The rest of his apartment was equally utilitarian. His bedroom held a bed and dresser set of fine quality but too modern in design for Auntie Lil's bohemian tastes. Several Broadway show posters on the wall provided a rare peek into his private passions, as did a stack of programs on the bedside table that had been carefully saved through fifteen seasons of the Metropolitan Opera (center orchestra, ten rows back, just to the right of the oboes).

There was a spare bedroom in the unlikely event T.S. should have overnight visitors. Sometimes Auntie Lil would

sleep over if they found themselves out late, but most of the
time he used it as a home office. It had all the charm of a
Pentagon briefing room and was lined with tall bookshelves
filled with tomes on theater, opera, psychology, and the latest
non-fiction. He arranged his books by subject and height,
with alphabetical preference awarded by author should the
heights of any two books match. Every volume was hardback
and retained its original, immaculate paper cover, mainly
because he gave his best seller detective and mystery paper-
backs to a neighbor down the hall before Auntie Lil could
tease him about them. They were his passion. He loved to
read about murder and mayhem before falling off to sleep
each night. It made him feel even safer, not to mention more
satisfied, to be so cozily surrounded by his own peaceful,
well-ordered kingdom.

But T.S. was most proud of his bathroom, kept scrupu-
lously clean by a cleaning lady so bored at the lack of dirt
that she had nearly scrubbed the enamel surfaces away. He
was proud because he'd had a special closet constructed at
one end to hold Brenda and Eddie's litter box. A discreet,
small swinging door was inset into the larger closet door and
afforded unlimited entrance to his pets. All T.S. had to do
was open the larger door slightly and shut it again to automatically send a shower of deodorant spray over the contents
when the cats were done. It had been an ingenious, germ-
free solution to the housekeeping problems Brenda and Eddie
presented, well worth the ribbing from Auntie Lil.

Of course, the extreme cleanliness of his home meant that
every time Auntie Lil entered, he had to endure the same old
joke: "Anyone home?" she would call out, then move from
room to room, shouting back at him, "Nope. No one lives
in here either, it's obvious." She'd finish by holding up a
white-gloved finger and saying, "I'm sorry to have to tell
you this, Theodore, but once again I've found a speck of
dust."

He'd been spared Auntie Lil's comedy routine that night.
She was too interested in getting down to business. They
sipped hot tea, per her orders, while T.S. told her, as well

as he could remember, the sequence of events at his retirement party. It was easier the second time around and his earlier rehearsal with Lieutenant Abromowitz helped encourage new memories. Auntie Lil interrupted often with questions that seemed to lead nowhere. But he was not fooled—Auntie Lil was always leading somewhere.

"Where was it held?" she asked him.

"In a lounge on the thirteenth floor."

"Oh, dear."

"It was quite a nice lounge," he protested. "We have client seminars there. Heavy red brocade curtains along the walls. Lovely furniture."

"There was food?"

"Of course." He was slightly offended that Auntie Lil was failing to grasp that his retirement had been a big deal. "They pulled out all the stops, you know. The staff from the Partners' Dining Room put on quite a spread: shrimp, roast beef, caviar. Usually they just set out cheese dips and chips."

She leaned over and patted his hand. "I understand, dear. It was much nicer than when, say, a custodian or messenger retires."

He wasn't sure if he should be mollified or not.

"Who decided who was invited?" she asked.

"I did. That is, anyone with over twenty-five years at the bank was automatically invited and I submitted a list of additional employees I wanted as guests."

"Why wasn't I invited?" she asked archly.

"Employees only. Just in case you had any doubts about the partners being cheap. Even when they're being generous."

"Have you got the guest list?"

"Of course." He was slightly offended. He knew exactly where it was—in the third file back in the middle drawer of his large home desk. Everything in its place and a place for everything. He retrieved it within seconds.

Auntie Lil scanned it carefully. "Who decided that Robert Cheswick would be the one to speak?"

"He did." T.S. allowed himself a rueful smile. "Technically, I reported to him. I would have preferred no speech at all. But it wasn't worth making a fuss.''

"What time did he get to the party?" Her interrogation style was distressingly like that of Lieutenant Abromowitz.

T.S. thought for a moment. "About an hour and a half after it started. Maybe about 6:00. After the jumbo shrimp ran out. I remember Mrs. Quincy—she's Edgar Hale's secretary—complaining long and loud about how cheap the partners were to only put out five pounds of shrimp, which would have been plenty if she hadn't been there, when in walked Cheswick, stopping her in mid-gripe *and* mid-bite.''

"Was he usually late for those kinds of things?"

T.S. thought again. "No. He usually arrived right at the start and left early. I always suspected he wanted to get a head start on the bar.''

"Did he drink more than usual last night?"

"There was no usual for him," T.S. admitted. "He sometimes hit the bar hard and fast. Probably trying to down it all before the other partners arrived.''

"Did he drink a lot last night after he arrived?"

"He started right in, as I recall," T.S. said. "Jimmy was acting as bartender and had stashed a bottle of Dewar's for me behind the bar. Cheswick spotted it immediately. I made a joke out of sharing it with him. He took full advantage of my generosity.''

"In front of the other partners?"

"There were only five or so there, but, yes. He did continue drinking quite heavily in front of them. I think John Boswell may have said something to him.''

"John Boswell?" she asked. "The handsome partner?"

"Yes. I saw him pull Cheswick aside and behind the heavy curtains. They had quite a discussion.''

"That may be important, dear.''

"Probably not. It may have been a business matter that needed to be settled that evening or he may have been telling Cheswick to lay off the booze.''

"How was the speech?"

"Cheswick's? Dreadful. It sounded like he was talking

about his butler retiring or something. Or else someone I'd
never met.''

"Those kinds of speeches always do,'' Auntie Lil soothed.
"Was there anyone at the party you didn't recognize?''

"No, of course not. It was my party.''

"No one? What about guards? Catering staff? Maids?''

"It was the same handful of people. Regular staff whom
I can recall,'' T.S. insisted.

"What time did people leave?''

"Well, the party had started at 4:30 P.M. I guess the partners can't bear to give up more than half an hour of official
time for these things. Some people actually left the party at
5:00. You know the type. Work ends at 5:00, even if it isn't
work. Most people left about 6:30 or 7:00 when the food
and drink started to run out. The hardcore stayed until 8:00
or so. A handful beyond then, most to help clean up.''

"When do you have to start signing out in the lobby?''

"At 6:00. And Albert and the rest of the guys run a very
tight ship. I tend to believe them when they say no one got
past without signing in or out.''

Auntie Lil was nodding wisely, as though he had confirmed some great hunch.

"What?'' T.S. demanded. "Why are you nodding?'' It
was really quite annoying, this feeling of always being one
step behind her.

"Nothing, really dear. Don't get excited.'' She patted his
knee. "But I do think it's time to compare your party list
with the late check-out list.''

They moved to the dining room table. Brenda lay sprawled
on the smooth glass surface. Auntie Lil pulled out the napkin
purloined from Harvey's and waved it at the cat in a futile
attempt to shoo her away. When Brenda only lifted her head
and glared, Auntie Lil resorted to smacking the beast's bottom with her handbag. This time, Brenda gave a light growl
and sullenly leapt from the table with a heavy thump.

"Honestly, Theodore. Can't you train them?''

"No,'' he said, pulling out a chair. "I can't.'' He sat at
the table and watched her remove her pen and notebook from

her bag. "By the way, Auntie Lil," he pointed out, "you stole that napkin from Harvey's."

"Did I?" She held it in her hand and stared at it vaguely. "Oh, dear. Not again. I thought it was my handkerchief." Sighing, she blew her nose on it daintily and stowed it carefully away in her bag. "Now, where are those lists?"

He smoothed the two lists on the table between them and they peered at the names together for several silent moments. Finally, T.S. turned his head and asked: "What are we looking for anyway?"

Auntie Lil pulled a blank pad toward her. "That list is the list of employees who checked out late, right?"

"Correct. Anyone who leaves past 6:00 P.M. must check out." He ran his eye down the photocopied list.

"Starting at the top, I want you to tell me if that person had been invited to your party. If not, there was another reason they left late and we need to verify that. If they were at the party, you'll just have to search your gin-soaked brain to try and remember if they signed out at the correct time."

"Scotch," he said.

"I beg your pardon?"

"Scotch-soaked brain."

"Of course. How careless of me." She numbered the pad evenly down one side. "Then we simply look for something that doesn't fit."

"Like what?"

"Like someone who came to your party and stayed late but never signed out. Or someone not invited to your party who stayed late to work for the first time ever. Or a name we don't recognize. Remember, the party ended by 8:00, so pay special attention to anyone staying later than 8:00 without a good excuse."

"It will still take us forever," T.S. protested.

"Not really," Auntie Lil pointed out. "When's the last time you saw Robert Cheswick alive?"

He thought for a moment. "Around 7:30. I remember because we finished the bottle of Dewar's at 7:15 and Jimmy said it was the fastest time ever. Thanks to Cheswick, of course. He left soon after, saying he had to catch up with some work at his desk. Not that I believed he was capable of work at that point, of course.''

"Then, for our purposes, we can eliminate anyone leaving before 7:30." Auntie Lil drew a heavy line through over half of the list.

"What about the people I know personally?" T.S. asked. "I think we could safely eliminate some of them."

Auntie Lil peered at him over the top of her glasses and shook her head sadly, as if disappointed with her favorite pupil. "My dear Theodore. Trust no one. I'm willing to trust you, but even that is a stretch, you know."

He started to protest but noticed the twinkle in her eye and calmed down.

"Now let's get started. Everyone after 7:30." She drew several columns in across the empty page. "This is just a preliminary list, of course. Once the time of death has been officially fixed, we may be able to narrow it further."

"If the guards are telling the truth about everyone checking out," T.S. added.

"If the guards are telling the truth. Which reminds me—" Auntie Lil made several notations on the pad. "Who were the guards on duty that night?"

He told her and she wrote down their names, then looked up and smiled thinly, her expression suspiciously like Brenda's. "They're our first two suspects."

I wouldn't want to cross *her*, he thought—and not for the first time.

It took nearly an hour to cross-check the two lists and compare the comings and goings of employees with what memory T.S. could muster. By the time they were through, they had a list of over a dozen names with comments and notations beside each. T.S. stifled a yawn and Eddie, lying at his feet, stirred and stretched in sympathy.

"Hang in there, Theodore. We're on the home stretch. I want you to tell me what you know about each of these people and I'll note it on their sheets."

It took another twenty minutes for this step, but T.S. had

to admit that it was most satisfying to have a neat pile of suspects when they were through.

Auntie Lil tapped a finger on the pile. "The murderer may well be among this crowd."

He glanced over their names and sighed. A handful of partners, the firm's biggest client and some of its most loyal employees. Including several of his favorites. T.S. sighed again and stared at the notebook.

"What is it, dear?" Auntie Lil asked, patting his hand tenderly.

"It just occurred to me that if the killer is on this list, chances are good that I helped to hire whoever murdered Robert Cheswick."

"It certainly can't be construed as your fault."

"No, but I can't help feeling responsible."

"Well, then, Theodore," Auntie Lil said quietly, "make up for it." She sat up straight and looked him right in the eye. "Get me in there tomorrow and help me find whoever murdered Robert Cheswick."

"Or die trying?"

"Knock on wood when you say that," she ordered, reaching out to rap him smartly on the head.

2   T.S. was relieved to see that only a Sterling & Sterling security guard was posted in front of the Partners' Room on Saturday morning.

"Good morning, Frank," T.S. greeted him heartily. "This is my Auntie Lil."

"Pleased to meet you, ma'am." The guard touched his hat in salute.

"Are you the Frank who was on duty the night Mr. Cheswick was killed?" Auntie Lil inquired with a breathless manner as if it were all too exciting for her.

"I'm afraid so, ma'am, though I didn't see a thing. We don't come through here at night on our regular rounds if the Main Floor doors check out." He shrugged ruefully. "The most excitement I got was spelling Timothy out in the lobby and being questioned by the lieutenant about it."

"Working weekends?" T.S. asked him.

"Yes, sir," the guard replied. "Need the overtime. Putting two through college, you know."

T.S. nodded in sympathy. "Yes, of course. Frank, Jr. and Tiffany, if I recall."

"That's right, sir. Frank, Jr. is going to be a lawyer."

T.S. resisted the temptation to express his condolences. "I'm surprised there's no police guard posted," he said instead.

"They felt it unnecessary, sir. This being the weekend and me willing to do duty." Frank's stance had relaxed and he appeared unaware of Auntie Lil's not very subtle attempts to peer around him into the room.

"I hear the lieutenant's a bit gruff," T.S. remarked.

"Yep. He's a real piece of work," Frank agreed. "Seemed damned and determined we'd let someone slip past." He nodded toward Auntie Lil. "Excuse my language, ma'am."

"Well, you aren't the only one who got a hard time." T.S. stepped closer to the man and spoke quietly, as if he didn't want to upset Auntie Lil with the gory details. "It was something to see how he operated. I was there, of course, during the investigation. Mr. Hale insisted. I saw the scene, the body and everything. Had to spend all afternoon answering questions for the police."

Frank nodded, impressed. "I always found police work quite interesting, sir," he said. "Lots of the other guards have experience on the force and I like to hear them talk."

Auntie Lil looked ready to stage an end run around Frank. T.S. made his move while there was still time. "You don't mind if my Auntie Lil takes a peek at the room, do you?" He gave the guard a wink. "It's the most exciting thing that's happened to her in a couple of years."

The guard gazed at Auntie Lil fondly. "Of course not, Mr. Hubbert, sir. Just don't touch anything, ma'am." He spoke to Auntie Lil carefully and slowly as if she were a child. Fortunately, he turned back to T.S. as Auntie Lil slipped in the room, thus missing her expression at being treated in such a manner. T.S. was also grateful the guard had not wagged a finger at her—Auntie Lil had looked like she wanted to bite him.

"What were they doing yesterday, sir?" Frank asked, his security lapse already forgotten.

T.S. obliged him in great detail, unsure of how long Auntie Lil wanted to have the room to herself. He elaborated on the number of lab personnel and how they had both a videotape and still camera photographer. He spoke of the scraping and sampling that went on, the positioning of the body. He even added a few details such as the way the body had jumped and swayed when someone touched the chair. Frank seemed particularly gratified at that. But T.S. was careful to omit mention of the dead man's unzipped trousers and the dead flowers left behind.

"You were in the lobby that night?" T.S. said after running out of juicy details.

"Just for about half an hour or so," Frank admitted. "Timothy takes a break about 10:00 and I come in from my rounds on the night floors to spell him. He's dedicated, that man. Won't even go to the bathroom unless I happen by to sit in for him. So I like to give him plenty of time."

"See anything unusual?"

"No, sir. Couple of people working late. Nothing unusual there. The night shift nipping out to dinner, maybe. Some of them smelled like they were on liquid diets, if you know what I mean. I made everyone sign in and out."

"So, no one you failed to recognize?"

Frank shook his head. "Afraid not. They were all familiar faces. I may not know their names, but I sure know their faces."

"What about on your rounds? Anything unusual?"

He shook his head. "Nothing. Of course, there's a lot of floors for me to cover alone," he added almost apologetically.

"I quite understand," T.S. assured him. "I remember when we cut back the night security staff several years ago."

T.S. had just finished explaining his role in unofficially aiding the investigation as a personal favor to Edgar Hale when Auntie Lil strolled casually out of the Partners' Room. She laid a gloved hand on Frank's arm.

"Thank you, Frank," she said and gave a near-girlish squeal. "That was very exciting."

"You're most welcome, ma'am." This time the guard nearly bowed as he touched his hat.

"Theodore," she turned her wide eyes on him. "All this excitement is getting to me. Do you think I could rest in your office awhile?"

"Of course." He took her arm helpfully and waved good-bye to the guard. "I'll fill you in later, Frank. Thanks for your time."

Frank nodded and stared after them as they strolled to the main elevator.

She was hissing mad. *"The most exciting thing in years?* Really, Theodore. How patronizing."

"You wanted to see the scene, didn't you?" he hissed back. "Besides, you interrupted me just as I was getting to the good part." Their footsteps echoed loudly through the cavernous Main Floor.

"It was most informative," she admitted grumpily once they were alone on the elevator.

"What did you find?"

"It was what I didn't find. His desk was bare," she said.

"Perhaps the police cleared everything away. Put it all in bags," T.S. suggested.

"No." Auntie Lil shook her head. "I don't mean literally. He had the usual. A brass pen holder, a small calendar. A stapler. Some paper clips in a silver dish. But he hadn't a single family photo or memento."

T.S. thought carefully. "You're probably right. He wasn't a sentimental man. Despite his lovely wife."

"It's even more than that," she insisted. "The other partners all have personal effects on their desks. A brass replica of a sailboat. Gold trains. Miniature golf clubs. Graduation photos of their children. And nearly all of them have the same unusual paperweight, a heavy oversized sterling silver spoon on a round base with their initials carved on the handle. But

Cheswick didn't have one. In fact, he had nothing. Not one single personal item. Do you know what that proves?''

''No, I don't,'' T.S. admitted, annoyed that he had to. ''What does that prove?''

''He was a man who had totally shut off his emotions. On purpose. As if he were trying to block something out.''

T.S. was dubious. ''Perhaps.''

''Not perhaps. Definitely. There was a conscious effort not to see the world around him, other than the bank. He didn't want to admit his private life existed. Nothing must show. I find that peculiar, don't you?''

He considered the question. ''I suppose I find it sad,'' he finally answered.

''And another thing.'' Auntie Lil placed one white-gloved hand on her chin and mused. ''I could not find a single file in his drawer marked 'Correspondence' or 'Personal Correspondence' or 'Personal' or anything like that.''

''You went in his drawers?'' T.S. asked faintly.

''Oh, don't worry, Theodore—I wore my gloves.''

''That wasn't my concern.''

''Well, I didn't disturb a thing.'' The doors opened and she stepped briskly through, then waited for T.S. to lead the way. ''I must ask Anne Marie tomorrow about that paperweight and those files.''

He stepped out into the hushed darkness of the deserted Personnel Department. Auntie Lil pushed up right behind him, practically propelling him into the shadows. He bumped his head on a door jamb. She was anxious to get started with the files.

T.S. felt along the wall for the light switch. ''You're sure you didn't disturb anything?'' The department slowly flickered to life under the greenish tint of fluorescent lights.

''Of course not. I wasn't there to rummage. I merely wanted to observe.'' She followed T.S. briskly down the hall. It had been several months since he'd been there on a weekend and the normally busy work areas suddenly seemed ominous in their emptiness. He hesitated before he turned each corner, until Auntie Lil poked him rudely in the bottom with her umbrella.

"Really, Theodore. What are you afraid of? The boogey-man?"

"There was a murder in the building," he replied stiffly, tentatively turning another corner. What was the matter with him? He was certainly spooked.

"Well, the murderer is the last person who'd be hanging around," she declared, poking him again. Patience was not one of her virtues.

"Let's go in here," he said quickly, leading the way into his old office. Miss Fullbright had moved in even more plants before she had left for the weekend, and entering the room resembled hacking one's way into the jungle.

"Good heavens." Auntie Lil poked at a hanging fern with her umbrella. "Who took your place? The Jolly Green Giant?"

"Felicia Fullbright. And they're only green because she just bought them." T.S. cleared away room on the sofa. "They'll die soon enough. I've seen a cactus kick off in her presence. But she just keeps trying."

"Oh dear, you mean that silly woman with the short brown hair is the one who took your place?" Auntie Lil had ex-humed Miss Fullbright's memory from her large store of faces met at T.S.'s annual holiday party.

"Yes, well—I wouldn't put my money on her as the mur-derer. She's more the type to psychologically test someone to death than stab them." T.S. quickly found the partners' personnel folders in the bottom drawer of the wooden file near the antique globe. "Here you are." He dumped a hand-ful onto the cushions next to Auntie Lil. "These are the partners' files. Abromowitz wants them first."

"Why?"

"He says that if a thief is killed, you look among thieves for the murderer. If a prostitute is shot, you check out the pimps. And if a financial whiz is stabbed, chances are good there's finance at the bottom of it." T.S. was rummaging through the drawer for the remainder of the files.

''How very narrow-minded of him.'' She held a slim volume up to the light. ''They aren't very thick, are they?''

He retrieved the rest from the drawer and sat next to her, the folders piled between them. ''Give me a Personnel Manager who maintains an eternal vigil on his bosses and I'll show you the unemployed.''

''So these folders essentially end once the gentleman is made a partner?'' she asked. Edgar Hale's folder was spread open on her lap.

''That's right. Other than the addition of their official obituary. There are also press clipping files kept by an outside service, although making the papers is generally frowned on here at Sterling & Sterling.''

Auntie Lil scanned the left side of the folder. It contained a contents sheet which listed numerous and various documents with a space next to each for initials and a date. Many of Edgar Hale's documents had been signed for in a spidery handwriting using old-fashioned fountain pen ink.

''This is quite an old folder, if I may say so myself,'' Auntie Lil said without looking up. ''Who is R.I.P.?''

''That's Ralph Peabody. Mr. Ralph Peabody. He was the Personnel Manager of Sterling & Sterling before I took over. He'd been here for years. I thought he'd never leave and give me a chance at the job. He'd already waited out one Assistant Personnel Manager. But he finally threw in the towel in 1973 and I took over.''

''I remember. You were quite anxious to push the poor man out.''

''For heaven's sakes—he was ancient!''

''Hmmph. What does the *I*. stand for?''

''I haven't a clue,'' T.S. admitted. ''We all called him Mr. Peabody, even the Partners. He was an old-fashioned sort of fellow. The kind of employee who was so subservient you called him 'Mr.' to try to lessen the embarrassment to yourself.''

''Rather ghoulish initials, wouldn't you say?'' Auntie Lil remarked cheerfully.

"Yes, rather. Is that Edgar Hale's folder? Aiming high on your list of suspects?"

She nodded, absorbed in her task of thumbing through the yellowed documents contained within. "I just picked him at random," she mumbled, annoyed at being interrupted.

"Anything interesting?"

"He took off for several months in 1957 for a trip to South America with his parents, but only took a week off for his honeymoon a few years later."

"That sounds like the Edgar Hale I know." T.S. held up a deteriorating file. The spine was peeling off and the documents inside were so neatly written they might have been penned in calligraphy. "Remember old Hobart Cummings? Look at this first entry—1892."

"Well, he's out as a suspect," Auntie Lil said in a businesslike fashion. "Give me one more partner and then I'm ready for Robert Cheswick."

T.S. had never flipped through the partners' files before, having considered it beneath his dignity to give in to his curiosity. But now he happily paged through the many legal, medical and other official documents. Nearly every file contained some evidence of a school certificate or diploma, a medical check-up clearing them for proper health before hire, the background investigation report required before they were allowed to handle securities, letters of recommendation from clergymen and headmasters and perfunctory reports on their performance while employed at Sterling & Sterling. Every file ended with the brisk notation, "Made Partner," with a date scrawled next to it. These two terse words literally closed the book on their employment at Sterling & Sterling and signified their lofty ascension into the ranks of the ruling class.

Auntie Lil finally snapped the last partner's folder shut and stared out of the window at length. T.S. waited, watching her.

"What did you find?" he finally asked when she made no sound.

"It's curious," she said simply, reopening the last folder on her lap.

She held up the folder. It was Robert Cheswick's and it looked exactly like every other partner's folder. "Did you find something?" he asked.

"It was what I didn't find more than anything else," she said. She tapped an elegant finger on the back cover, above the glued pocket. Several documents were stuck in the back of the pocket, the remainder being clipped in the middle by metal fasteners. "Look at that," she commanded and handed it over.

He peered at the inside back cover. The folder was constructed of heavy brown cardboard, now faded and yellowed in spots. "Look at what?"

"See the outline of a larger piece of paper there?"

He peered closely and the outline of a large brown square emerged. A document had been stuck closely to the back cover, preventing part of it from yellowing.

"It's been removed," Auntie Lil said. "And look at this." She leaned over and flipped back to the inside front cover where the contents list was clipped and pointed at a neatly blacked-out listing under the category "Other." Someone had meticulously inked out an earlier entry, and marked out the date as well. The initials "R.I.P." appeared next to the obliterated entry.

"Your Mr. Peabody removed a document," she pointed out unnecessarily.

T.S. scanned the bottom entry and nodded. "It was removed right before Cheswick was made a partner. Nothing unusual in that."

"It isn't unusual to remove confidential documents from official files?" Auntie Lil asked increduously.

"Not really, I'm afraid. It was probably a simple reprimand memo from an earlier supervisor. Peabody felt it would be embarrassing to keep it in the file of a partner and removed it. I'm afraid it's been done before and since." Auntie Lil looked so disheartened, he sought to cheer her up. "But still, it was very observant of you to notice."

She sulked for a moment, but then perked up. "What about the fact that Cheswick, Hale and that John Boswell fellow all took a few months off during the summer of 1957? I suppose that's not unusual either?"

He shook his head and shrugged. "Sorry. It's been a tradition for some time, it seems, for young men sure to inherit the Sterling mantle to take off for a few months after they've been here for several years. To give them a chance to prove their manhood before they settle into their boring careers."

"How very silly," Auntie Lil observed. "Prep school boys running around on safaris, expeditions and sailing trips around the world. I don't imagine they fooled a soul. Probably took their servants with them."

"Perhaps it's an affectation. I don't know. But it seems to be expected."

"Theodore," Auntie Lil began in a tone of voice that made him pause. "I just don't know."

"Know what?" He began to gather up the partners' files and put them in a box.

"Whether Robert Cheswick's file is as innocent as you say. I still think there's something here. That missing memo, perhaps."

"Maybe so, but it goes to the lieutenant today." T.S. looked at his watch. "He doesn't think they'll be much use but I promised to drop them by so his men can go through them. Will you wait here while I pull out a few more files from the main drawers? He wants the top execs and employees who worked with Cheswick, too."

She nodded and continued staring at Cheswick's folder. "So long as I can take a peek at the rest of files."

"All of them?" He stopped and stared at her. "You said you'd control yourself."

"Just a quick peek," she assured him brightly. "You never know."

T.S. quickly located the other files Abromowitz had requested. They were fatter and more complete than the earlier files as Sterling & Sterling had responded to the challenges of modern life by stepping up employee surveillance. When he returned to his old office, Auntie Lil was again flipping through the partners' files.

"Find anything else?" he asked her. Although she could not have heard him approaching over the plush carpet, she didn't flinch when he spoke. She was a hard woman to spook.

"I don't really know, Theodore," she admitted. "I've never actively investigated before. Let's take a look at those."

He handed over his armful of new files. She scanned each file with the precision of a machine, devouring every document at a single glance and flipping pages with a skeptical snort, as if not believing any of the information contained within. "What a dull lot," she finally said, and this remark, somehow, irritated T.S. greatly.

She continued flipping through them and paused only when she reached the file of Anne Marie Shaunessy, Cheswick's secretary. "Heavens," she said. "She earns plenty for a secretary. My mother was right—I should have learned how to type."

T.S. shrugged. "Very senior employees sometimes get way out of whack with salary scales. We can't very well stop giving them raises. They'd complain to other employees and it wouldn't be worth the bad publicity. Of course, Anne Marie does make more than most secretaries. It's a real bone of contention between her and the others. Cheswick is cheap with the staff, but has always been consistently generous with her."

Auntie Lil stared at him with a raised eyebrow.

"No," he replied firmly. "Definitely not. Believe me, I'd have heard. Neither one of them was having an affair, with each other or anyone else."

Auntie Lil tossed the file back on her pile. "Not bad for a young girl in the 1950's from Brooklyn coming straight out of Our Lady of Perpetual Help Secretarial High School."

"Yes," T.S. nodded. "I always loved hiring young secretarial trainees from there. The name was so apt. And they were lovely girls. The school's closed now. Anne Marie was one of the very first secretaries we ever recruited right from high school. It was the perfect training ground for Sterling &

Sterling. There's nothing like a Catholic school education to teach you how to conform.''

Auntie Lil seemed lost in thought and said little as they drove to the First Precinct, ignoring T.S. and sometimes scribbling short memos in her pocket notebook. She even volunteered to wait patiently in the car while he dropped the folders off.

Abromowitz was nowhere to be found and a busy sergeant took the box from T.S. gruffly, shoving it to the side of the counter without much enthusiasm.

''Have a nice day,'' T.S. said sarcastically, receiving a suspicious grunt in reply.

Auntie Lil remained silent during the ride to her apartment in Queens, finally perking up when he turned onto her street. It was a quiet, tree-lined block with large brick apartment buildings no more than six stories high. Children played on the sidewalks under the close supervision of their mothers, and the noise and bustle of Manhattan seemed very far away.

''Did you invite Anne Marie and Sheila to brunch tomorrow?'' she asked as he escorted her to the elevator.

''Yes. They'd be pleased to come. I bribed Sheila with promises of your famous Bloody Marys.''

''Good work. We'll have to get a few in her mother. Loosen her up. As his secretary, she may know something without realizing it.'' Sometimes Auntie Lil displayed a disturbing familiarity with the less orthodox ways of achieving her means.

''I'll be glad to be bartender if you'll do the mixing,'' he offered.

''In that case, I'll be glad to do the cooking if you'll do the dishes.'' The elevator doors closed on her merry laugh and he was left to salute an empty lobby, already conscious of the lack of Auntie Lil's lively and invigorating company.

CHAPTER FIVE

1 The brunch had been scheduled for 10:00 A.M., despite the severe protests of Auntie Lil, who considered any time before noon absolutely barbaric. However, Sheila had indicated she had important plans for later in the day and would prefer to come over following church. T.S. knew it was her usual practice to attend early mass at Our Lady of the Sorrows with her mother each Sunday and he didn't want to interfere. She could probably use the religion this week in particular, he reasoned, after coming face to face, literally, with death.

Besides, while Sheila was on her knees praying, T.S. would be on his knees cleaning. For a woman with such an orderly mind, Auntie Lil had a remarkably chaotic home. It was a typical middle-class Queens apartment building on the outside—an anonymous, all brick design—but on the inside, Auntie Lil's apartment looked as if someone had tried to store six decades of outdated Smithsonian exhibits in four small rooms. Shelves and tables were crammed everywhere, and every surface overflowed with carved figurines, music boxes, antique cosmetic cases, bits of costumes and scraps of patterns, ashtrays from every hotel between New York and San Francisco, at least ten pairs of scissors, opened and un-opened boxes of crackers and cookies, and handfuls of notes first written as reminders and then promptly forgotten. He found one note, stuffed in a vase, dated over a year ago: "Pick up Santa suit from dry cleaners." He wondered if it had been retrieved yet, but wasted no further time trying to decipher what Auntie Lil was doing with a Santa suit. It made his brain hurt to even consider the possibilities.

To compound the confusion and, he suspected, eliminate any question of engaging a cleaning woman, Auntie Lil purposefully stored her most precious possessions side by side with flea market junk, declaring that she liked all equally and labeling him a snob when he protested. In the living room, a collection of exquisite vases had been shoved to the rear of a cupboard to make way for a large bowling trophy she had found on the street and decided she liked. In the bedroom, she'd filled a valuable pewter commode from the 1700's with thousands of poker pennies. This same democratic policy applied to her books: they were stored in haphazard piles along the hallway wall, hardback and paperback teetering together, first editions of Poe buried under *Reader's Digest* condensed book collections from the 1950's.

But Auntie Lil did not really collect objects. As was to be expected of someone so exquisitely nosy, she preferred to collect people instead, displaying her favorites in dozens of framed photographs that dangled precariously from her walls. Captured moments of Auntie Lil smiling with African kings, gripping the hand of a former prime minister of Japan, and posing with a group of somber German businessmen were interspersed among photos of more common faces snapped during one of the many trips she'd made over her lifetime. One of her favorites was from several decades before: she was posed atop a large pile of discarded tires, next to an entire family of broad-faced strangers who ran a junkyard outside of Vancouver. She could no longer even remember their names, as was the case with many of the photos, but she still cherished their faces and, T.S. presumed, the memories they represented.

Her furniture consisted of a jumbled mixture of various antiques and period styles given to her as gifts by grateful employers and a life's worth of admirers. She had a tendency to obscure the beauty of these pieces by draping bolts of fabric over her tables, chairs and couch, perhaps because it made her feel more at home after so many years in design showrooms. But working in haute couture had apparently had little effect on her sense of aesthetics. Heavy brocades were piled indiscriminately on top of cheery ginghams, creating a cacophony of pattern and color.

The only place in the entire apartment that displayed any semblance of discipline was Auntie Lil's clothes closet. It was meticulously organized. Coordinated outfits, mostly pants suits, hung in color groups subdivided by fabric. Her jewelry and shoes dangled from special racks inset into the door, a system T.S. had so admired he'd duplicated it in his own, far neater, apartment.

Unfortunately, Anne Marie and Sheila would not be spending their time in Auntie Lil's closet. Which meant that there was plenty for T.S. to do before they arrived. There was little he could accomplish in terms of fundamental organization, and he had long since learned that it was futile to try and change Auntie Lil's habits. But he could at least make a quick pass at surface sanitation. He spent the hour before the brunch folding up odds and ends of cloth, which, by long practice, he knew fit under her bed. As he worked, he could hear Auntie Lil clattering and singing in the kitchen, drowning out the sounds of his cleaning, he suspected, to avoid feeling guilty.

He dusted the surfaces of dozens of photographs, rearranged her shelves as best he could and essentially shoveled out the living room, banishing its treasured debris to the far side of her bed. When he was done, he vacuumed the cozy space he had created, noticing, to his surprise, that her sofa was white. He could have sworn it was flowered, but perhaps that had simply been a favored bolt of cloth. If Sheila or her mother asked for a tour, the game was up. But T.S. suspected they were both astute enough to know not to push their luck and probably too polite to pry.

They rang Auntie Lil's buzzer promptly at 10:00. T.S. welcomed them into the apartment with a bow. Anne Marie sailed past, regally dressed in a gray suit that almost shimmered as she walked—the finest of Sunday finery. Not that she was ever dowdy. She was still a striking woman, even in her fifties, small with the dark Irish coloring seldom seen unadulterated anymore. Her skin was a pale porcelain but her eyes and brows were nearly black. Her hair retained a glossy ebony shine, no doubt with a little help from Clairol at this point in her life.

Sheila, on the other hand, looked as if she had seen far better days. She was distinctly crowded in Auntie Lil's cluttered apartment and towered over her delicate mother with all the grace of a robot. Her short blonde hair had been unsuccessfully combed: small clumps sprouted from the back of her head like tiny haystacks beneath a tattered knit hat that looked as if it had been discarded by a lumberjack. Even Sheila's green eyes seemed murkier than usual. They gazed at T.S. in resigned agony, rimmed with red and a barely perceptible crust of old makeup she had failed to remove from the night before.

"Enter, ladies," T.S. said, completing his exaggerated bow.

"Hello, Mr. Hubbert," Sheila said woodenly, pulling off her knit hat and shaking her head vigorously. Drizzle flew about the apartment and Anne Marie rolled her eyes.

"Really, Sheila. You act like a Labrador retriever sometimes." Her mother pulled off her gloves in rapid, ladylike movements and draped them over T.S.'s outstretched arm as she sashayed by. She had certainly regained her composure since the murder and elected to sit right smack in the middle of Auntie Lil's white sofa, her gray silk suit a muted contrast to the snowy tones surrounding her. Sheila had managed to throw on the black-and-green print dress that she usually dragged out on Mondays when she was too tired to pick out anything else.

Purple circles beneath Sheila's eyes gave her away. "And how has your weekend been so far, Ms. O'Reilly?" T.S. asked innocently. Anne Marie appeared not to notice, instead carefully noting every detail of Auntie Lil's decor. She smoothed the skirt of her suit repeatedly, listening absently as T.S. teased her daughter.

"I feel awful," Sheila muttered back. "Too many drinks last night."

T.S. rubbed his hands in what he felt was a courtly manner. "Ah, yes. Drinks. Who would like one of Auntie Lil's famous Bloody Marys?" He directed the question to Anne Marie but did not miss the shudder that passed over Sheila's face.

"Perhaps it's a little early for you, Sheila," he suggested tactfully.

"Perhaps," she echoed faintly. "I believe I'll start with a ginger ale."

"A Bloody Mary sounds like just the thing," Anne Marie said cheerfully. "I've been through quite an ordeal." Although her coloring was even paler than usual, the excitement had caused her dark eyes to sparkle even more. They glittered in their depths and he was startled at the intensity. She looked almost as if she were enjoying the tragic break in her normal routine.

"Good morning, ladies!" This exuberant cry came from Auntie Lil, who popped in from the kitchen looking like a demented and overgrown Tinkerbell. She wore a pale pink jumpsuit covered with an enormous frilly white apron. A large bow tied it all together just above her butt and poked out on each side. She peered happily at Sheila and took in Anne Marie's suit in one professional glance, blinking slightly before turning her cheerful gaze back to Sheila. "How are you today, dear?" she asked.

Sheila stared at the apron, struck dumb by the sight, but Anne Marie rose to the occasion. "How lovely you look, Auntie Lil," she said, springing over to kiss her cheek. "It was very kind of you to invite us to tea. My husband pulled duty today, you know, and I would have been left all alone in that great big house."

Anne Marie had the disconcerting habit of talking in a rather breathless manner in social situations but reverting to the clipped, efficient tones of a drill sergeant when on duty as a secretary. Today, she elected to use her social voice and the girlish tone was at odds with her more mature appearance.

"I thought it was a bad time for you to be alone," Auntie Lil told Anne Marie, waving her spatula about as if it were a magic wand. "It's important to talk about these things, so they don't just prey on your mind."

Before anyone could reply to this, she disappeared back into the kitchen. T.S. wondered just who was preying on whom and fetched the pitcher of Bloody Marys.

Auntie Lil had been very specific about the order of events and had instructed T.S. to ply Anne Marie with at least three Bloody Marys before bringing up the topic of the murder. Brunch would be timed to occur near the end of her fourth Bloody Mary and T.S. was to leave the important questioning to Auntie Lil during the meal. It was a huge amount of liquor for a normal woman but, as Auntie Lil reminded her nephew, Anne Marie grew up in a fiercely Irish home and was no stranger to alcohol.

As Auntie Lil clanged about the kitchen, T.S. chatted with Anne Marie about all the fascinating topics he had long ago learned to explore with the automatic pilot portion of his brain. She sipped her drinks happily, even taking them with her on her frequent trips to the bathroom, and seemed unaware that she was rapidly consuming an unwise amount of alcohol. Each drink heightened the gleam in her eyes and encouraged her enthusiasm for conversation. Twin orbs of red spread over her porcelain cheeks, lending a girlish prettiness to her face.

Feeling something like a rat, T.S. refreshed her drink for the fourth time and asked her how she was recovering after the terrible events of Friday.

She needed little prompting and launched into a long and detailed description of her discovery of the body, a story familiar to T.S. by now. But in her version, Sheila had been the one who grew quite upset, while Anne Marie had been the one to calm her down and instruct her on what to do. At this part in her mother's story, Sheila rolled her eyes and requested a Bloody Mary after all. A few sips into the hair of the dog, she, too, relaxed and sat patiently through her mother's version.

The clanging and banging in the kitchen grew louder. T.S. was alarmed. Auntie Lil was not the world's best cook and there was no telling what would end up on the table. Finally, however, he caught on that the noise was a signal. Untangling himself from Auntie Lil's overstuffed armchair, he announced that brunch was served.

He led the way into a small narrow dining area that divided the living room from the kitchen. A sideboard against one wall held exquisite china from Hong Kong, brought back to Auntie Lil by a grateful designer in the 1930's. Auntie Lil had arranged the table beautifully with linen, silver and a huge bouquet of flowers, creating an air of elegance calculated to impress Anne Marie. T.S. made a show of insisting their guest sit in the place of honor. The three of them sipped their Bloody Marys and waited for Auntie Lil, T.S. with a trepidation learned from previous meals and the two women with benign innocence.

He should not have worried. Auntie Lil had spent the time in the kitchen well and now marched back and forth with great fanfare, producing platters of crispy waffles and strawberries, an obscene amount of bacon—his heart constricted at the very thought—eggs scrambled with peppers and onions, fruit salad, a pitcher of fresh orange juice and a pot of fresh coffee. Grateful his duties were largely over, T.S. dug in with a gusto matched only by Sheila's. Amazingly enough, the hangover appeared not to affect her appetite for food, and the two of them gobbled happily while Auntie Lil skillfully guided her guest's narration.

"It's really very puzzling that someone would kill Robert Cheswick," Auntie Lil said, spooning strawberries on top of Anne Marie's waffle. "Don't you agree?"

By now Anne Marie would have agreed to a wrestling match. She took another healthy sip of her Bloody Mary and nodded in agreement. "Who would want to kill him?" She picked daintily at her food and pushed it about her plate.

"Have you any idea at all?"

"The police think insider trading must be behind it," Anne Marie repeated with great confidence. Being married to a cop gave her great respect for the NYPD and she had repeated the lieutenant's explanation automatically. T.S. noticed that her speech had the very slightest slur to it, a defect that seemed to come and go.

"Oh dear, and I always thought the police were immune to fads," Auntie Lil said absently, searching about the table for the orange juice, as if that were the most important thing on her mind. "But what do you *really* think, dear?" she asked in an offhand manner. "After all, you were close to him. You have an intuition, shall we say, that they lack."

Anne Marie nodded in agreement, closed her eyes and appeared to think it over carefully. T.S. watched with a mouthful of eggs and for a moment was afraid she'd fallen asleep. "I don't really know," she said at last. "Mr. Cheswick was a very private man. I really couldn't say. It could be insider trading. Maybe he had tried to stop them. I suppose anyone would kill for enough money."

"Perhaps he was killed *for* his money?" Auntie Lil suggested.

Anne Marie crunched loudly on her celery while she thought this over. She seemed to like the idea. "That could be. Wouldn't that be something if it was his snooty wife after all?" She picked up her Bloody Mary again and twirled the liquid with her pinky, then sipped at it and smiled daintily at T.S.

T.S. concentrated on dissecting a waffle, his conscience nagging him badly. What had they sunk to? Getting respectable middle-aged women drunk and pumping them for information? This was not the glamorous detective life he had envisioned. It was, in fact, nearly tawdry.

Sheila was crunching away busily on her bacon, her eyes moving rapidly from one person to another as they spoke. Hangover or not, she wasn't going to let a single thing get by her.

"But if it wasn't money," Auntie Lil asked Anne Marie, "what else do you think it could be?" Auntie Lil had touched neither cocktails nor food and was skillfully pushing eggs about her plate. She preferred black coffee, only, until the afternoon.

A dreamy look crossed Anne Marie's face and she stared off at the wall. The words came slowly from her lips. "That's the funny part," she said softly.

"What?" T.S. interrupted, unable to help himself. Auntie Lil was miffed at his interference but kept silent.

"The mystery of it all," she replied. "He seemed such an ordinary man to be killed in such an extraordinary way. It's a joke on us all. Don't you think so?" Anne Marie looked around the table at their faces as she spoke. "We all thought we knew him so well. Robert Cheswick. Tweed jackets. Pipe. Connecticut manor. But somewhere, beneath it all, even he had a dirty little secret." She laughed thinly but it tapered quickly to a sigh. "I think he was killed for some reason that no one else knows but him."

"No one but him and the killer," Auntie Lil pointed out.

Anne Marie looked vaguely discomfited and sought refuge in her waffle.

"You must have known most of his secrets, my dear," Auntie Lil said gently. "After all, you were with him for many years."

"Since high school. He was so kind to me. We were both young then." The dreamy look returned, the Bloody Marys floating her back decades. "I started work there when I was only eighteen and didn't know a single soul. Not one person. They were all so young and handsome then—the partners today, I mean. Still human beings. Full of fun. Before money and power took over." She sighed. "Robert Cheswick was one of the most human of them all. He gave me time off when Sheila was born. He was very good about keeping my job open. He had another girl, but let her go so I could have my job back."

"I think that's the law, Mom," Sheila said between enormous gulps of scrambled eggs. She had demolished three pieces of toast and was starting on her fourth.

"It wasn't the law at the time," Anne Marie corrected her

daughter primly. "He gave me an entire year and a half off. He was really a very thoughtful man."

"He was?" Now it was T.S.'s turn to be skeptical. This unexpected canonization of Robert Cheswick wasn't sitting well with what he knew. "He didn't strike me as a particularly thoughtful man."

Anne Marie looked insulted. "He was very quiet about those kinds of things." She wiped primly at one corner of her mouth. "I expect he will roll over in his grave when he finds out that the investigators are poring over his personal papers. I suppose they're even going into his private finances?"

"You bet they are," T.S. told her. "I'm sure they'll ask you about it."

"I've nothing to hide." She looked at him sharply, then relaxed and sipped at her drink. "They'll only find out I'm right," she predicted. "Why, did you know he sent his wife flowers every week for nearly fifteen years? It's right there in his checkbook."

That did surprise T.S. It seemed to him that Robert Cheswick had failed utterly to appreciate his wife.

Auntie Lil perked up. "You, of course, know about his small thoughtful gestures. Why, I expect you knew even his failures. The faults he kept hidden from others."

"Of course," Anne Marie admitted. "I knew everything about him." She stared unexpectedly at T.S., who, surprised to find himself the sudden center of attention, swallowed a quarter of a waffle without chewing and managed to shake his head and nearly choke to death at the same time. Sheila pounded him vigorously on the back while Auntie Lil and Anne Marie chatted, oblivious of his distress.

"Had Mr. Cheswick been under a great deal of strain?" T.S. asked her in a strangled voice when he was able to speak again. "Had he been making more mistakes than usual?"

"Not that I could tell." Anne Marie shook her head. "Between you and me, of course, he's never been a real *friendly* man to most people. He seemed his usual starched self. Poor Jimmy's raise came up last week and Mr. Cheswick turned him down flat. No surprise there. You've got to know how to handle him.''

She certainly did, if her own healthy salary was any indication. ''Jimmy Ruffino?'' T.S. asked. ''The partners' valet?''

Anne Marie nodded. ''He's been there nearly twenty years and, believe me, I know how hard it can be with Mr. Cheswick in charge of your raises, rest his soul. But poor Jimmy's wife is ill and he really needs the extra money and Mr. Cheswick wouldn't even let him speak. Just told him things were tough, that the firm was losing money and that no one was getting a raise this year.'' She chewed her toast daintily.

''But that's not true,'' T.S. said indignantly. ''Sterling & Sterling made more money last month than they have in two hundred years of months.''

''Oh, I know that. But Mr. Cheswick always said things like that when you asked for a raise. Sometimes I wonder why I . . .'' Her voice trailed off and she hiccuped.

''Did you speak to his wife, dear?'' Auntie Lil asked. ''She must be terribly upset.''

''Oh, I doubt it.'' Anne Marie gave Auntie Lil a look that totally mystified T.S., although Sheila nodded wisely at its meaning. ''She'd be upset, of course, because being upset was appropriate and everyone would expect her to be upset.''

T.S. was piqued at any suggestion that Lilah Cheswick might not be entirely perfect, but stifled his anger and consciously ignored Auntie Lil's lifted eyebrows.

''They weren't really very close,'' Anne Marie explained. ''If you want to know how Lilah Cheswick is, you'd be better off asking another partner we know . . .'' She stopped suddenly as if she'd gone too far, thought better of continuing and sipped her drink quietly.

Auntie Lil cleared her throat gently and did not pursue the matter. She made a great show of filling up everyone's coffee cups. T.S. knew she was stalling for time.

''Do you pay all his personal bills?'' Auntie Lil asked in

an offhand manner. "It's amusing how men like Mr. Cheswick neglect their own financial housekeeping."

"Everything. From the barber to the dry cleaner to
Bloomingdale's at Christmas time. He'd have a buyer there
pick out some nice things for his wife and daughters. Money
was no object."

"Did you notice any unusual bills or checks recently?"
T.S. asked.

She thought for a moment. "No. The police asked me that
already. Just the usual."

"I suppose the police asked you for his personal files?"
Auntie Lil suggested.

Anne Marie shrugged and examined her toast. "No. They
acted like I was stupid, to tell you the truth. But they went
through his desk thoroughly. I'm sure they found them. It
wasn't my fault they seated me in a room needed for evidence," she continued indignantly. "How was I to know not
to touch anything?"

"You touched the case the knife came from?" T.S. asked
faintly.

"Of course I did. It had been left open. I thought I should
straighten up in case one of the partners needed the conference room. I didn't know the knife came from there."

T.S. thanked the fates that had steered him into his own
job and away from working for Abromowitz. Someone was
going to catch hell. Sheila stirred restlessly beside him, trying to sneak a look at Auntie Lil's antique cuckoo clock. Her
afternoon plans must be important.

"What about that unusual paperweight he had?" Auntie
Lil remarked, unconcerned about Sheila's growing desire to
bring the brunch to an end. "I noticed that quite a few of the
partners have them. What is their significance?"

Anne Marie stared at Auntie Lil. "You mean the silver
spoons? When did you notice them?"

"Well," Auntie Lil hedged, suddenly intent upon gathering up the dishes. "I was in there once and remember
them, for some reason. That's me. Latch on to some silly

detail." She was not, T.S. noticed, going to confess to Anne Marie that she had rooted around the scene of the crime.

Anne Marie put her chin in her hand as if, by this time, her head could use the extra support. "I don't think he ever had one, actually," she said. "But it's an honest mistake. Nearly all the older partners have one. They got them from Mr. Peabody, the old Personnel Manager, a long time ago. It used to be a real status symbol when Mr. Peabody presented you with one of those on the day of your first promotion. He didn't give them to everyone, just to the ones he thought would be partners one day. It was a game with him. The back has an inscription that says, 'You're on the way to the top' or something like that." Anne Marie was quiet for a moment. "I didn't think it was such a nice tradition for the people that didn't get one. It was like an acknowledgement they'd never make it. They made him stop doing it because of that, around the time you came, T.S."

"But in Cheswick's case, it should have been obvious from the start that he'd be a partner," T.S. protested. "Surely he would have received one."

Anne Marie nodded slowly and shrugged. "That's true. He would have had to embezzle funds in his underwear to screw that up."

"Mother." Sheila gave Anne Marie a horrified look and was rewarded with a defiant gaze from her mother.

"Perhaps I'm mistaken," Anne Marie admitted. "I just never noticed it, is all."

They still didn't know for sure if the paperweight was missing from Cheswick's desk. T.S. made a mental note to find out if the police had confiscated it. He could not recall having seen it the morning of the murder.

It was just past noon by the time Auntie Lil skillfully guided the brunch to an end. The drizzle had stopped and a brilliant sun streamed in through the apartment's tiny windows. Anne Marie had a bit of trouble manuvering into the living room and Sheila ended up firmly guiding her tipsy mother out the door with a grim smile.

"Runs in the family," Sheila said by way of farewell, as

she leaned her mother against the elevator door. "It's a good thing I'm driving her home."

"Mass," Anne Marie declared suddenly. "Drop me home and then I'm going to change clothes and catch the afternoon mass. Say a prayer for his soul."

Great, T.S. thought. She'd pass out the second she dropped to her knees.

"Perhaps we overdid it plying her with drinks," T.S. suggested as he sat on Auntie Lil's plump sofa and compared notes.

"Perhaps," Auntie Lil said, ready to dismiss the subject. "You would think she'd hold her liquor better. I do." She sniffed rather disdainfully. "Which reminds me, I believe I deserve a drink myself now. Did she leave us any?"

"That's not quite fair," T.S. protested, rising to pour her a drink. "You're the one who told me to force it down her."

She changed the subject instead of arguing the point. "Did you see that suit she was wearing?" Auntie Lil raised her eyebrows and made a genteel *tsk-tsk*ing before taking a healthy gulp of her drink.

"What about it? It looked good on her," T.S. admitted.

"Brilliant deduction." She glared at him in mock irritation. "It was pure Japanese raw silk," she announced. "Worth at least $700."

"Sorry I haven't your vast store of design world knowledge," he told her irritably. There was something about dresses and makeup and secret female looks that was so totally beyond his realm of existence that they made him feel instantly foolish.

"Never mind," Auntie Lil decided. "I can see you're getting grumpy. You think the personal files and paperweight are missing, too, don't you?"

She was right, but T.S. hated to give her that satisfaction. "It's highly likely the police took them before you got your chance to snoop around."

"Can you find out?"

"I'll try," he said. "But what would that prove?"

"What I've been saying all along. The clue to his death

lies in his personal life—a closely guarded personal life. What else did you pick up on?''

T.S. was ready. ''That business with Jimmy Ruffino.''

''Yes. What a stingy man Robert Cheswick must have been.'' Auntie Lil thought hard. ''You know, for someone supposedly reluctant to talk, Anne Marie certainly cast a lot of suspicion on people.''

''Bloody Marys have that effect, I believe.''

''Maybe.'' Auntie Lil searched her living room as if a hidden clue awaited her behind the familiar knickknacks. ''We're missing something. I wonder if Anne Marie's holding anything back.''

''Auntie Lil—we gave her six or seven Bloody Marys. I don't think she could have held something back if she wanted to.''

''Those Irish women. They can store their liquor like camels store water.''

T.S. reviewed the brunch conversation once again. ''We know he really liked Anne Marie. Holding her job open and all.''

''Yes. That is a bit unusual for that day and age. A year and a half is a long time to keep a job open. That would have been, when, T.S.?''

''Sheila is in her early thirties now. Let's make it easy and say that it would have been around 1960.''

''Did anything unusual happen in 1960?''

''That was the year Kennedy beat Nixon, wasn't it?'' T.S. said helpfully.

She looked at him. ''I hope you're not going to try to blame Richard Nixon for this, too,'' she said coolly. ''I meant at Sterling & Sterling.''

''How would I know? I wasn't even there yet. They were still struggling along without me.'' He was met by a chilly stare. ''I'm sorry,'' he protested. ''But what are we looking for anyway?''

''*Clues*. Did you catch what she said about his wife?''

''It sounds like vicious gossip to me,'' he replied stiffly.

''Oh, Theodore.'' Auntie Lil shook her head and patted

his hand. "You would have made such a romantic. It is possible that Lilah was playing around, I'm afraid."

He glanced at the ornate clock near the sideboard. It was
later than he had expected and he needed to get on the road.

"Am I running you off with my philosophizing?"

"Not at all. It's just that you've reminded me. I really must
be going." He rose to retrieve his raincoat from her hall closet.

"Where are you going?" She looked so small and expec-
tant sitting on the sofa, he was nearly tempted to bring her
along. Nearly.

"I told Lilah Cheswick I would stop by. Express my official and personal condolences." His hat had fallen from the
shelf and he rummaged around the crowded closet floor in
search of it.

"How interesting. See what you can find out. Ask her
if . . ."

"I know what to ask her," he interrupted, calling over his
shoulder as he groveled and pawed through boots. "And I'll
call you later to fill you in." He saw his hat in the back on
the floor and as he reached for it, a large stack of hidden
magazines tumbled to his feet. He stared at their titles: *True
Detective, Crime Watchers, Detective Story, Real Cases, Private Eye* and several other similar titles. He quickly flipped
through the stack. Auntie Lil had saved several years' worth
of issues.

He piled them carefully back together and concealed them
beneath some scarves. This was information he'd save for
future ammunition. You never knew when you needed an ace
card with Auntie Lil. A little something to keep her in line.

Smiling, he jammed his hat cheerfully on his head and
popped in for a good-bye kiss on the cheek.

"Please give her my regards," Auntie Lil murmured by
way of good-bye. "Such a lovely woman," she added
vaguely. "Always has been."

He left before she could get started.

2   The Cheswick house was an immense affair, wedged
between a sloping green lawn and a strip of private beach on

Long Island Sound. The door was opened by a wizened old woman, hunched over with age. Her white hair sprang out at odd angles and she cradled a pair of long shears in her hands. A shawl was draped about her shoulders and her feet were encased in dingy cotton stockings and thick black leather shoes. She looked for all the world like the witch in *Hansel and Gretel*. T.S. took a quick step back and was rewarded with wheezy laughter.

"What do you think? I'm going to stab you or something?" She wheezed some more, quite merrily, and T.S. thought it prudent to smile back. The old woman's voice was as high as a flute, reedy and cracking with age.

"No, of course not. I was expecting Lilah. Mrs. Cheswick," he said hastily.

"I just bet you were. Must have been a rude surprise." She cackled some more and shouldered past T.S. "She's out back. I'll tell her you're here. Keep your pants on." She inched her way around the bushes, snipping the shears ominously, and made for the edge of the enormous house. T.S. watched her disappear around the corner in astonishment. Not quite the well-groomed butler he had half-expected.

Lilah Cheswick arrived around front instantly to lead him breathlessly into the mansion. The house itself was full of curving stone hallways, drafty rooms and antique furniture that T.S. was sure had been passed down through both family lines.

Lilah was as lovely as always, her now-white hair smoothed off of a face flushed red with exertion. Perhaps she had been outside riding to take her mind off of her predicament. She was a tireless horseback rider and maintained a strong, athletic figure. T.S. enjoyed watching her movements, the rise of her arm, her confident stride, the well-coordinated twirl she executed once she had seated him in the library.

He also admired her honesty. She was grave, but hardly the grieving wife. She bore no signs of having been crying, her green eyes were steady. Sorrow was not keeping her indoors weeping.

She handed him a Dewar's and soda without having to be reminded what he drank. He thought of the evening so many years before when they had sat by themselves at the side of the party and she had fetched him drinks all night while they talked and laughed and made fun of the other guests.

"Did I remember correctly, Theodore?"

"You remembered." He smiled and raised his glass in toast. Other than Auntie Lil, she was the only person in his entire life who called him Theodore. He had forgotten what a pleasure it was to hear her say his name.

"Who answered the door?" His voice contained more bewilderment than he had intended to let escape.

Lilah laughed at his expression. "That was Dierdre. I'm sorry if she startled you. She's been with Robert's family for as long as I can remember. She even took care of him when he was young and she was nanny to our daughters."

"Good heavens. She must be ancient." He considered the tactless implications of his remark and had the grace to blush.

She laughed away his uneasiness. "I'm afraid you're exactly right."

"I'm terribly sorry, Lilah," he said simply, growing serious. "It was an awful way for it to happen."

"Yes, it was." She sat on a stool near his feet, staring into the fire that blazed in the enormous stone fireplace. "It was very unlike Robert to die that way." She looked up at T.S. "I know people didn't really like him and I can't say I blame them. He could be very cold. But I didn't think anyone hated him enough to kill him. To stab him. Did you?"

He could think of no suitably discreet reply and merely shook his head.

"To me, stabbing indicates passion and, believe me, there was no passion in Robert's life. I would have been less surprised if he had killed himself. He had so little love of life left in him."

"You seem to have accepted it well." It was all he could think of to say.

She stared into the fire. "I hardly knew him, Theodore. When he died it was almost as if a stranger had been stabbed." She stared up at him. "I suppose that's sad. To have so little feeling when your husband passes away. But it was his fault, really. He kept himself a stranger for so many years. It must have taken a real effort."

For the first time, a trace of bitterness entered her voice. T.S. watched highlights from the fire dance in her hair.

"Would you?" she was asking him.

"Would I what?"

"If you had married me, would you have stayed a stranger? Am I so terrible? I always thought I was kind of fun." She looked again into the fire and sighed.

"I always thought you were kind of fun, too," T.S. admitted. He could not bring himself to say more.

"Well, Robert must not have thought I was worth it. I know his parents pressured him to marry me. But I could have been a real dog. I always thought I was reasonably attractive."

"You are," he assured her.

"And intelligent."

"More than most," he hastened to agree.

"So what was it that Robert hated about me so much? Do you know that in over twenty-five years of marriage, he never once gave me a compliment. Never seemed to notice how I looked. Never expressed an opinion on his children. Never brought me chocolates. Never once sent flowers, not even on our wedding anniversaries. He used to give me such gauche presents for Christmas. Just whatever trendy fad was all the rage that year. I never understood him and I certainly don't understand why he was killed."

"Do you want to find out?" he found himself asking faintly, his mind on her remark about the flowers. What had Anne Marie said about flowers?

"Yes, I do," she said immediately. "I'd like to find out what it was I missed in him for so many years."

"I'm trying to find out," he said gallantly, responding to the plea in her voice.

She looked at him blankly. "Find out what?"

"Who killed him."

"I thought the police were investigating."

"They are. But I think they're quite wrong. They say it's money behind it."

She laughed bitterly and gulped the rest of her drink. "You're right about that. Robert would never stoop to dispute about money. Why should he? If you count my money, we have more than God. Big deal. The only real benefit is that you can afford the best. Speaking of which, would you like another drink?"

He nodded, primarily so that he could watch her walk across the room. She was an extraordinary woman and had been wasted on Robert Cheswick.

"Will you answer some questions for me?" he asked.

"Fire away." She settled in again at his feet. "But I warn you, you probably know more about him than I do. I thought you had all kinds of surveillance in Personnel."

She was one of the few people ever to tease T.S. and he quite enjoyed the sensation.

"No. We stop amassing intimate details once a person makes partner."

She laughed again. "Not to worry. If anything interesting ever happened to Robert, it was before he made partner. Believe me. He was already a fuddy-duddy by then, but he practically turned into his own grandfather once he made the big *P*."

T.S. asked about Cheswick's personal papers. He had none. They were all at the office. He had planned to stay at the Yale Club the night he was murdered and she had not been alarmed when he didn't come home. No, she was sure he had not been having an affair at any point in their marriage. He was far too prompt with his departures for work and arrivals home. She was quite adamant on this point.

"Besides," she added for good measure, "he knows that the one thing I absolutely would not tolerate would be that. I'd agree to a robot marriage, but not that. The only thing he cared about by the time he married me was appearances and he would have done anything to maintain them.''

He thought of Anne Marie's unfinished comment about Lilah's own fidelity but was at a loss as to how to approach the subject.

''Are you close to anyone?'' he asked and immediately felt like an ass.

''What do you mean?''

''I mean, any other . . . partners.'' He stumbled around for a way out. ''Partners, as in Sterling & Sterling partners. Or brothers or . . . fathers, maybe. Yes. Fathers. Someone to help you make the arrangements and deal with the lawyers.''

''I suppose so,'' she said, cutting off his babble. ''John Boswell took care of the funeral arrangements yesterday. I have no problem handling the lawyers myself.''

''John Boswell?'' he asked and his voice nearly squeaked. What in god's name was the matter with him?

''Yes. John Boswell.'' She looked at T.S. strangely. ''Are you all right, Theodore? Is the fire too hot?''

''No. Not at all,'' he said, straightening up and attempting to look cooler. ''I'm fine.'' Had his voice actually squeaked? ''Did your husband leave behind any clue as to whether something had been bothering him lately? A letter? A note? Did he make any unusual phone calls? Anything at all?''

The desperation in his voice caused her to consider his remark as carefully as possible. ''Well,'' she said slowly. ''I don't know. It's possible. We slept in separate bedrooms. He could have made a call late at night. I wouldn't have known about it. Or perhaps he left something in his bedroom. Would you like me to look?''

''Would you?'' Of course he would. It wasn't the fire that was blinding him. Heavens. Here he was fifty-five years old and being left tongue-tied by a woman. He needed a moment to regain his thoughts.

''Be right back.'' She left the room with the sure grace of an athlete and bounded upstairs. A quick scurrying in the main hallway alerted T.S. that their conversation had not been as private as he had thought. It was more shame at having his bumbling witnessed than anger that prompted him to investigate the sound.

He was not surprised to find Dierdre beside a vase of flowers, polishing it with a dirty cloth. She was hardly taller than the stand the vase stood on.

"Just cut them," she told T.S., but he was not fooled by her innocent demeanor.

"You were listening in, weren't you?" he asked her.

She shrugged, her round, sloping shoulders rolling up and down. "So what if I was? I have a right. I knew him better than anyone."

"You don't seem too upset," T.S. observed.

She defied him with a laugh. "That's because going and getting killed is the most surprising thing that boy has done in years." She suddenly stopped, as if realizing that a stranger would find her reaction peculiar.

"Of course I loved him," she nearly hissed. "I was probably the only one. I used to change his diapers. He was a bright boy. Full of fun. Full of life and laughter. Yes, laughter. You think I'm crazy, but it was true. Always wanting to try new things. But his father bled all the spirit out of him. Every drop. Finally broke him completely. I could tell you the day, but I won't." She shook her rag angrily at T.S.

"He hadn't been my Robert for a good thirty years," she said softly. "So you'll just have to forgive me if I temper my grief with some satisfaction at the surprising way he managed to get himself killed. It was a flash of the old Robert and I was glad to see it. He died a long, long time ago. Believe me. You don't know what it was like for him. Growing up an individual and being squeezed into the mold his father made for him."

T.S. had listened to the articulate words spilling rapidly from her mouth with a speechless astonishment. And he was further astonished when she suddenly turned her back on him and walked briskly away. He soon learned the reason why, when he heard Lilah descending the stairway.

"Making friends with Dierdre?" Lilah asked. She held a

small slip of paper in one hand. "She's really a lovely woman, you know. Quite well-read."

He was still too stupefied to frame a proper response. "She was . . . telling me how much she thought of Robert," he finally finished lamely.

"She loved him more than anyone. Including me. Here." Lilah held the piece of paper out to him. "He was using this as a bookmark. That's all I could find. The book was called *The Changing Face of Capitalism*. Do you want that, too?"

"Good heavens, no." He unfolded the paper and stared at it. The words made absolutely no sense. "Magritte," he read aloud. Lilah stared at him blankly.

"He's written 'Magritte' down twice and underlined one of them." He looked up at Lilah. "Know a Magritte?"

"I'm afraid not. It may simply have been a book he wanted to read, a painting he wanted to buy." She shrugged. "I would help you if I could, Theodore. Really I would." She smiled at him and he felt the old confusion flooding back.

"I have to be going," he managed to say without swallowing his tongue. From now on, Auntie Lil would handle the Lilah interviews. He'd made a mess of it.

Lilah took both of his hands in hers and smiled. "You were very sweet to come so far to see me, Theodore. And if I need any help, you'll be the first person I call."

He nodded, smiling dumbly back, promising himself that if he didn't trip on the way out, he would consider at least his exit a success. She fetched his coat herself and he wondered aloud where the rest of the servants and children were.

"What servants? I keep Dierdre because she belongs here but, of course, she's retired and spends most of her time in the garden. I have a maid come in three times a week and the kids are at college. They're coming home tomorrow for the funeral. He wasn't close to them, either. They hurt for him a long time ago."

"Why did you stay married to him?" he asked her suddenly.

"What? And leave show business?" She swept a strong arm around the great hallway and gave a mirthless laugh.

He kissed her on the cheek as he departed. Her skin was warm and soft beneath his lips and he was rewarded with a dazzling smile that followed him all the way to his car. He turned for a final wave good-bye to find her leaning against the door, watching his departure.

"Good night, Theodore," she called out, charming him with her little girl wave. "Don't let the bedbugs bite."

"John Boswell," he thought bitterly as he pulled out of the driveway and headed toward home. He shook his head. He should have guessed. He really should have known. How could she ever get mixed up with someone like John Boswell?

He'd failed utterly at distancing himself from the problem. And, he reminded himself, he'd forgotten to ask her why she'd stopped by Sterling & Sterling the night that her husband was killed.

CHAPTER SIX

1   The sunny weather of Sunday afternoon continued into Monday morning and T.S. arose filled with vigor, his troubling thoughts of murder, spiteful partners, age, unfaithful wives, strange servants and lost chances banished by a good night's sleep.

Hoping to avoid a repeat of Friday, he stood for several minutes in front of his tie rack looking for a compromise candidate. He would wear a tie, but one only he would like. That would show them he was now his own man. There were several possible choices and he considered them carefully. He rejected the string cowboy tie brought back to him from Sante Fe by his cleaning lady, and settled instead on a wide crimson silk, given to him last Christmas by Herbert Wong. Wong was a loyal Sterling & Sterling messenger, now retired, who for years had brought gifts back from his vacations as thanks to T.S. for having been granted a job nearly fifteen years before. The mementos ranged from plastic coasters painted with hula dancers to a Mexican sombrero. Last year, Wong had traveled home to Singapore and returned with a special tie for the esteemed Mr. Hubbert.

Mr. Wong was not of the American culture and thus actually grateful to have a job. These kinds of employees were, on the whole, the only ones T.S. found himself liking these days.

The tie was intricately embroidered with an enormous dragon, its bottle green scales giving way to a golden mane and black eyes. The widest part of the tie highlighted a gaping dragon mouth, featuring long white fangs and orange fire spitting forth. It was just the thing to keep him going. He selected a pair of matching red socks for good measure and completed the ensemble with an impeccably cut charcoal gray suit.

Once on the subway, he quickly found mention of the murder on page 1 of the *Times* Metropolitan Section, indicating the power of Sterling & Sterling's influence on the city's financial circles. The brief article tastefully recounted the incident, providing no new information on the crime. The murder was described in such a low key manner that the deed came off sounding practically routine. But with the murder in the *Times*, the story had surely spread across the nation. Clients, kooks and the press would inundate Sterling & Sterling with phone calls. This thought made him hurry and he waited impatiently in line for coffee at the mobile cart before charging into the Personnel Department.

He should have stayed in bed. It became immediately apparent that chaos reigned supreme in his former kingdom. Margaret, the receptionist, scurried from desk to desk, dropping off handfuls of messages and grabbing phones two at a time. She handed him a stack of memos before he could slip by, and shot him a grim glance.

"Mr. Hale has called three times," she squeaked and scurried off again. He stuffed the messages into his pocket, rounded the corner and smacked directly into Sheila. She had a pencil stuck behind one ear, a pile of medical files under one arm and two cups of coffee stacked one on the other balanced in her free hand.

"Going into hiding. They're driving me crazy," she shouted as she sped by. Her eyes shimmered with a desperate gleam. "The blue rinse crowd is at me. They haven't a thing to do and everyone is calling me for details!"

As head of employee benefits, Sheila oversaw the welfare of Sterling & Sterling retirees. With news of the murder spreading, they had called from Florida to Arizona, and every state in between and beyond. No doubt crazy Miss Turnbull would be next.

A former typist in the defunct steno pool, Miss Turnbull

took a morbid and unseemly interest in the deaths of Sterling & Sterling employees, especially fellow retirees. Not a demise went by without Miss Turnbull sending Sheila clipped obituaries and any personal details she could dig up. It was a ghoulish hobby for someone so advanced in age as she. Although T.S. had not actually seen her for years, in his mind Miss Turnbull always wore a black cloak with a white dress beneath and stood looking down on Sterling & Sterling survivors with the beady eyes of a vulture. No wonder Sheila was going into hiding.

He was looking forward to the calm of his makeshift office but this was not to be. Lieutenant Abromowitz sat in his seat, waiting patiently for his arrival. T.S. stopped in the doorway, coffee cup in hand, and stared. Abromowitz was happily inspecting the contents of T.S.'s desk drawer without any apparent attempt at discretion.

"There's hardly a thing in here," the lieutenant said in lieu of a greeting. He held up a box of paper clips and a pen, then stuffed them back in the drawer, slammed it shut and smiled at T.S. "Brought me coffee? Great, I'm only half-awake this morning." Abromowitz reached for the coffee and T.S. relinquished it automatically.

"Good morning, Lieutenant. Please have a seat." Sarcasm was wasted on Abromowitz but it didn't stop T.S. from trying. He stood by his own desk, looking around for somewhere to sit.

Abromowitz moved a stack of partners' files off of the extra chair and patted the seat. "Thanks, I did. Here, take a load off. Say, did you see your old office yet?"

"Yes. I noticed it this weekend when I came in at your request and spent my entire Saturday looking for files."

"Looks like a regular botanical garden in there." He pried the plastic top off of the coffee and sniffed appreciatively at the aroma. "That Miss Fullbright's a talented lady."

Talented? She was the Lizzie Borden of the plant world. Pruned her poor greenery to death. T.S. sat reluctantly in the visitor's chair, staring at his commandeered coffee. "Is there something I can help you with this morning?"

"Yeah, you can." The lieutenant dipped the tip of his tongue in the liquid. "Any sugar in this?"

"One pack," T.S. replied grimly.

"Perfect." He slurped loudly at the steaming coffee and T.S. watched the vapors longingly. Abromowitz took his time deciding what to do, then abruptly shoved the stack of personnel files over to T.S. "These are useless," he said in a tone of voice that clearly implied T.S. had planned it that way.

"It's all I've got," T.S. reminded him firmly. "I told you I thought they'd be of little help."

"These aren't of little help. They're useless. There's nothing in there but petty stuff that happened twenty, thirty years ago. I want the trading records of all partners and executives. What stocks they've bought. What bonds they've sold. You're required by law to keep them. We can subpoena them, you know."

"You're welcome to all the financial records you can lay your hands on. I don't know what else there is. I asked the treasurer to get them to you on Friday."

"Yeah, well. He didn't." The lieutenant arched an eyebrow and regarded T.S. thoughtfully. "You're not by any chance hiding anything in those financial files?"

"Don't be absurd. And give me my coffee back." T.S. reached over and reclaimed his cup. "I'll call Stanley Sinclair this instant if you'll kindly get out of my seat."

The lieutenant stood up silently and moved to the window. T.S. wiped off the rim of his cup and glared at Abromowitz as he dialed the treasurer's extension. He didn't know what was worse. Dealing with Abromowitz or dealing with Sinclair.

Stanley Sinclair, Treasurer of Sterling & Sterling, was an unabashed sycophant from way back. He lived to serve the partners, never disagreed with anything they said, and raced to point the finger of blame whenever anything went wrong. T.S. had long loathed the man's stalling, servile ways and he was angry that the financial files had not been sent to Abromowitz as requested.

Naturally, Sinclair did not answer his own phone. This was beneath his standing. Instead, a breathless voice answered, "Good morning. Office of the Treasurer. Sterling & Sterling, Private Bankers. Mr. Sinclair's line. How may I help you?"

By the time the introduction was over, he'd nearly forgotten why he was calling. "This is Mr. Hubbert in Personnel. Put Stanley on the line."

"I'm sorry, sir. Mr. Sinclair left explicit instructions not to be disturbed by anyone. May I take a message?" This was delivered in a confident tone, full of the expectation that such orders dare not be breached.

"Get that toad on the line now or I'll be sitting on his desk within three minutes with Edgar Hale on the line."

There was a sharp intake of breath and the voice asked, "Who did you say this was?"

"Mr. Hubbert. The Personnel Manager." Forget retired, let her sweat.

"Yes, sir."

T.S. could feel Abromowitz staring at him as he waited and he looked up and glared back. Abromowitz mouthed the words, "Very masterful," and T.S. turned his back on the oaf to sip his coffee before he lost his temper again. He stared out the window at the blue sky and white clouds with longing.

"This is Mr. Sinclair speaking. How can I help you?" The treasurer had refined being supercilious to an art, having practiced just the right voice inflection for years.

"Can it, Stanley. This is Hubbert. You were supposed to have the financial files to the police on Friday before you left. What happened?"

"There's been a problem. Mr. Hale agrees." Stanley Sinclair had a high, reedy voice that never failed to grate on T.S.'s nerves.

"No. You have a problem right now. Lieutenant Abromowitz will be in your office in precisely three minutes and I expect you to have those files ready." He hung up the phone and decided he didn't care if he had any authority anymore or not. He just wanted to get Abromowitz out of his office and into someone else's. Preferably Stanley Sinclair's. If ever two people deserved each other, they did.

"Efficient this morning, aren't we?" Abromowitz remarked sarcastically on his way out the door.

T.S. shrugged and took off his coat. "Sinclair is two flights up," he said. "I assume you can find your way." When the lieutenant glowered at him, T.S. lowered his big gun. "By the way, get any fingerprints from the conference room?"

The lieutenant's frown deepened. "That secretary's, of course. Everything else was wiped clean. Including the showcase that held the knife." He paused and looked T.S. over. "I don't see any need to mention what happened, do you? I mean, about the misunderstanding?"

"You mean the contamination of evidence by the carelessness of your men?" T.S. spread both palms up and shrugged. "You give a little. You get a little."

The lieutenant sighed. This was one game too dangerous to play any longer than was absolutely necessary. "What do you want to know?"

T.S. stared at Abromowitz thoughtfully. How could he phrase it without arousing suspicion? "Mr. Hale was anxious to know if you had removed anything from the premises," he finally said. "Anything from Cheswick's desk."

The lieutenant stared back at him. "Dead flowers. Blood scrapings. That's all. Like them back?"

The paperweight had been removed by the killer. But why? If Cheswick had even had one. Anne Marie hadn't thought so. How could he find out for sure?

"What about personal papers?" T.S. risked, pushing his luck.

"The guy had none. At least we haven't found them yet. I'm going to talk to the secretary again. And you've used up all your favors." The lieutenant turned to go, but paused just before he disappeared around the corner. "Just one more thing," he added, "your partner was loaded at the time of his death. Extremely drunk indeed."

T.S. threw his coat onto the windowsill and loosened the

dragon tie. He hated not having a few minutes of peace in the morning. And he had a feeling that the chaos was just beginning. Remembering the many phone messages, he took them from his coat pocket, thumbed through them quickly and tossed them in the trash.

2   Four more sips into his coffee, Mrs. Quincy charged in the door. As secretary to Edgar Hale, she was Sterling & Sterling's most senior administrative employee, the self-proclaimed queen of all partners' secretaries and head busybody of the entire firm. She had an unattractive habit of constantly scowling and bossing everyone, even other partners, around—with the sole exception of Edgar Hale. Rebukes or attempts to put her in her place sailed right past her without effect. He might have liked her had she merely been a character but, as it was, she was an unpleasant woman and stirred up far too much trouble for his taste.

"What is it, Mrs. Quincy?" He was attempting to restack the rejected files.

"Mr. Hale sent me up personally," she declared. "Since you refuse to return his calls." She seated herself in his visitor's chair with all the aplomb of Queen Elizabeth. "He says there's an emergency and he must meet with you at 11:00 A.M. in the conference room on the second floor." She waited impatiently for his reply.

"An emergency? Very well. I'll be there. What is this about?"

"I am not at liberty to divulge that, but if you ask me, it is something that you should have anticipated. As it is, Mr. Sinclair had to cover for you."

He turned his head slowly and stared at her. It seemed as if the dragon on his tie was sending him signals of strength, that if he opened his mouth and roared, flames of fire would lick over Mrs. Quincy and singe her hair into a frazzle. It was an appealing thought. "Mrs. Quincy, I am retired. I technically have no responsibilities here other than those that I choose to perform as a favor. I have nothing to oversee and, thus, nothing to overlook. Understand?"

She stood her ground firmly. "I'll tell him you'll be there. The Management Committee, as well as Mr. Sinclair, will also be present. Mr. Hale has asked me to get all new details on the investigation from you prior to the meeting."

He doubted that, but it was a good try on her part. "Two new developments, Mrs. Quincy," he said sweetly. She waited expectantly, ears on the verge of quivering. "Number one, Sterling & Sterling is about to get some very bad press indeed because Stanley Sinclair is too stupid to cooperate with the police and number two, we have concrete evidence that a partner's secretary murdered Robert Cheswick."

She stared at him with open eyes and he nodded wisely. "Yes, we found a piece of paper on the floor by his feet. He'd written part of a name on it in blood: 'QUIN' it began, before he ran out of life. You don't know who that might be, do you?"

He was greeted with an icy stare. He smiled back. Mrs. Quincy leapt up from the chair, looked as if she might slap him, whirled on her heels and stomped from the room, plowing down Herbert Wong in the process. The messenger was hovering about the door, angling to be invited in.

"Herbert," T.S. said loudly, hoping to shame Mrs. Quincy. "Are you okay? Let me help you brush off your jacket." Mrs. Quincy, however, had long disappeared and T.S. simply shrugged and waved him in the door.

"Mr. Hubbert, sir," the elderly man said with a bow. "A good morning to you this fine day." When he straightened up, dignity settled on him with a quiet authority. T.S. suspected that Herbert Wong, though meek, was, in his own quiet way, a most unusual man. He was tiny, meticulous in his appearance, and just beginning to round out with old age. Sienna age spots had seeped up through his burnished skin and this, combined with his thickening middle, made him look like a large, ripening pear. His thinning white hair had been carefully combed back over an extremely round and shining scalp in anticipation of his meeting with the hallowed Mr. Hubbert.

"Good morning to you, Herbert. You're looking fine. Retirement agrees with you. I wish it did with me." T.S. sat quickly in his chair, stifling the reflexive urge to bow back that always seized him when confronted with the custom. "Would you like to sit down?" He waved toward a chair and the retired messenger stealthily moved toward it, shuttling sideways with a curious gait. What in the world had gotten into the man?

"You are wearing my tie!" Mr. Wong cried suddenly.

T.S. jumped up from his chair, nearly spilling the rest of his coffee.

"You are wearing my gift," Mr. Wong cried again, his face breaking into a grin.

"What? Oh, yes. So I am." They stared down at his tie together and T.S. fingered the embroidered scarlet dragon.

"A fine tie," Mr. Wong finally said into the silence. "A fine tie."

"Yes," T.S. agreed. "One of my favorites. Absolutely." He sat back down and folded his hands on his desk, coughing discreetly. The retired messenger beamed at him. "So, Mr. Wong," T.S. finally said. "What can I do for you?"

"For me?" He leapt to his feet. "No. Not for me. I have come to see what I can do for you." He bowed again, then stood tall and proud. "I have heard you are investigating the untimely death of our partner and I wish to offer you my services."

"Your services?" T.S. asked. "The obituary has been delivered."

"No, no. Not as a messenger. As your investigative assistant." The old man bent low and thrust out a tightened fist, banging it back into his chest with a thump that made T.S. jump a second time. He definitely needed to cut back on the caffeine.

"I have training," Mr. Wong said, lifting up one leg and bending his other knee in a crane-like stance. "It is not a joke. As a young boy." He held up a fist and let T.S. inspect it. "It's very strong. Could be useful."

"Yes, well, Herbert. I don't know what to say." T.S. stared at the man for a moment. "It's very kind of you to offer. But I'm leaving that sort of thing to the police. I'm really just unofficially assisting in some of the paperwork. A few inquiries. Things like that.''

The elderly messenger seemed quite dejected at this news. He stared for a moment at T.S., then shook his head. ''It's not right,'' he said. ''They should put you in charge.'' He moved over and pounded T.S. on the back. ''You are a fine man and very, very smart. Much smarter than the partners, even, I always say. They should put you in charge.''

T.S. managed a smile. ''Thank you, Herbert. I appreciate the vote of confidence.''

''Well, then it looks like we all have confidence in the esteemed T.S Hubbert.'' Felicia Fullbright lounged against the doorjamb, watching the scene with amusement.

˜ Herbert Wong looked carefully from T.S. to Miss Fullbright and back to T.S. ''I must go,'' he said quickly, bowing again and backing toward the door.

''I'd lay off those Bruce Lee movies if I were you,'' Miss Fullbright advised the retreating messenger sweetly. Mr. Wong contented himself with a dignified bow in reply.

''President of your fan club?'' she asked T.S. as she straightened out an imaginary twist in the large bow she wore in lieu of a tie.

''Thank god for employees like Herbert Wong,'' T.S. replied fervently. Who was she to make fun of his hires? Especially ones that had been at Sterling & Sterling for fifteen years—almost twice as long as she had.

''An employee like Mr. Wong may well have stabbed Robert Cheswick,'' she pointed out, making a beeline for the visitor's chair. ''He's on the list of people checking out late that night.''

''Won't you come in, Miss Fullbright?'' he asked, a shade too politely, as she flopped into the chair's still-warm seat.

''Thank you, I will.'' Her face was flushed scarlet, but when he saw that her neck was equally red, he realized she'd been badly sunburned over the weekend.

''Looks like you had a wonderful weekend outdoors.'' He

looked with longing again at the blue sky outside. It was probably a great day for golf. If only he golfed.

"I've got some problems here and I need your advice," she said, ignoring his attempt at small talk.

"My advice? I'm sure you're perfectly capable of handling anything."

"Of course I am, but no matter what I decide, I'll be wrong so long as you're here. I'm not stupid, you know. Retired or not, if I don't get your okay, they'll hang me. This way they'll hang you." She shot him a glance. "I'm not the naive person you think I am. I know the office politics around here."

Yes, she had probably spent all weekend analyzing them while she lay out too long in the sun. Made a flow chart or two. "How is the trauma team?" he inquired pleasantly.

She looked at him suspiciously but his face remained impassive. "They're fine. I put them in the empty classroom down the hall."

"Line going out the door yet?"

"I haven't noticed. I expect it will take a day or two for word to get around, even with my memo."

"Well, if things continue as they've started today, I may be first in line to see them." He picked up his coffee and took a healthy gulp. Perhaps Sheila had a Valium he could cadge, though that was hardly discreet and might be taking his newfound freedom a bit too far. His mind fled Miss Fullbright momentarily and settled on Mrs. Quincy's message. He could not imagine what emergency Edgar Hale had discovered that could top the stabbing of a partner. And what could Stanley Sinclair have to do with it? T.S. smelled a dead rat and its features were suspiciously similar to those of the treasurer's.

"What's the problem?" he asked Miss Fullbright, hoping to extricate himself rapidly from this conference.

"Several things. For one, absenteeism skyrocketed today. It's absurd and we're terribly shorthanded. Some people will take any excuse to stay out of work."

Normally he would have shrugged it off and hoped that

the situation improved the next day. But he was no longer in any kind of mood to be charitable. "Have everyone called and tell them they must bring in a doctor's note tomorrow or they'll be fired. If they can't get a note, they had better be here by 2:00 this afternoon. Next problem."

Miss Fullbright stared at him. "Isn't that a bit severe?"

"They're slackers, all of them. Cheswick was stabbed. They weren't. Next problem." He ran his hand under his collar and loosened the dragon tie. My, but it felt good to be decisive and not worry about treading lightly for a change. Retirement was certainly exhilarating.

She leaned forward and smoothed her skirt nervously. "I was just curious. How is the investigation going? Found out anything the police have overlooked?"

T.S. shrugged. "Not really. Anything else I can help you with?"

"One more thing," she added quickly. "I thought a memorial service in-house for Mr. Cheswick would be appropriate. A candlelit gathering on the Main Floor, perhaps. With a small string quartet, flowers, some speeches and suitable refreshments."

"How about a mariachi band and flamenco dancers?" he suggested. Her mouth fell open. "Come, come, Miss Fullbright. Hold a memorial service twenty feet from where he was stabbed and on company time to boot? Besides, no one liked him anyway and he himself would loathe the idea of employees leaving their desks to mingle about sipping white wine in his memory. The official memorial service is scheduled for Wednesday evening. Let those in his department go an hour early so they can be sure to get there on time. That should do it."

Miss Fullbright made another quick notation on her list, rose in a businesslike fashion, pushed her glasses up on her nose and nodded good-bye to T.S.

"Let me know if I can assist you in any way," she offered curtly.

"I will. Good day." He hesitated a moment, revenge percolating irresistibly in the depths of his mind. "Miss Fullbright—I have a meeting to attend at 11:00. I think it might be a good idea if you accompanied me. Let you test the waters.'' It was the perfect way to get even with her for her shoddy treatment of him. Let her see what she would be up against for the rest of her life.

She shrugged as he followed her to the door. T.S. resisted the urge to bolt it behind her. Instead, he quickly shut it and leaned against it for a moment to catch his breath. She had said something important and he couldn't put his finger on it. Something to do with Mr. Wong.

So much for secluded office space. With all the interruptions, he had not been able to complete a single task he had planned. He and Auntie Lil had agreed that quietly interviewing certain employees might yield information they would otherwise be reluctant to reveal to the police, but a systematic approach to interviewing employees was rapidly proving impossible. Now the afternoon would have to be used for the interviews. He hoped the emergency conference would not take too long.

He sat down and made his interview list. First was Mr. Dorfen, the partner who sat directly behind Robert Cheswick. T.S. hoped that Mr. Dorfen was taking it easy on the hidden Scotch and would be in a condition to talk intelligently. Auntie Lil had also requested he talk to the biggest gossips at Sterling & Sterling. Without any doubt, she'd meant Effie Abacrombie, head switchboard operator, and Francine Crisp, head teller. The two women saw and talked to numerous employees each day and were key stops on the employee grapevine.

He was spared the task of calling Effie Abacrombie when she buzzed him just as he was about to leave for his meeting.

"Mr. Hubbert, thank god you're there."

Everyone seemed to be thanking god for T.S. Hubbert this morning, except, perhaps, T.S. Hubbert.

"The main line has been going crazy all morning with reporters and such," Effie said in her firm voice. "What am I supposed to do with them? They want to speak to Mr. Hale but Mrs. Quincy says she'll kill me if I put one more through.

She's got her hands full already. It seems Mr. Boswell took off on a business trip without warning anyone and she's having to help his secretary field calls from clients. She says she's sick and tired of taking messages.''

The thought that Mrs. Quincy might be having a bad day cheered him immensely. He then had a vision of Miss Fullbright popping in and out of his office all day with petty problems and clumsy attempts to pump him for information. He made a fast decision. ''Put all calls from the press through to Miss Fullbright here in Personnel,'' T.S. said. ''She's been designated official spokesperson and will know all details.''

That would keep her out of his hair.

''Thanks, Mr. Hubbert,'' the operator said. ''Roger. Will do.'' She was a war movie buff and used military jargon whenever possible.

''And, Effie—is Anne Marie in today?''

''Yes sir. Came in claiming she couldn't let Sterling & Sterling down no matter what she was going through. Overreacting a bit, if you ask me. You should see her dress. Black silk. Some people never seem to run out of . . .''

''I'm sure she looks stunning,'' T.S. interrupted. ''But could you ask her to help out Mrs. Quincy in any way she can? Maybe she could lend a hand with Mr. Boswell's calls or something.''

''That's a ten-four, Mr. Hubbert. What else?''

''That's all for right now, Effie. And thanks. But if you have a moment sometime today, could you come up and see me? I'd like to talk about some things with you.''

''Have I done anything wrong, Mr. Hubbert?'' As a long-time employee, Effie was well schooled in the art of being intimidated.

''No, no. Not at all,'' he soothed. ''I simply need to hear your point of view on some things.''

''On the murder?'' she said cheerfully. ''I heard you were investigating.''

''What? Where did you hear that?''

"Oh, I hear a lot of things. And I'm betting on you, Mr. Hubbert, sir. I'm betting you get him before the police do."

"Thanks, Effie. But don't bet too much." He hung up and sat for a moment, trying to decide if he was pleased about this vote of confidence or chagrined at being a topic of grapevine conversation.

3   At 11:00 A.M. precisely, T.S. found himself jammed in a small conference room designed for no more than four people. Unfortunately, seven now occupied the space, including T.S., Edgar Hale, plus three out of the four partners on the Management Committee, a smug Stanley Sinclair, and a baffled Miss Fullbright. Only John Boswell was missing. Edgar Hale gave his empty chair a dirty look and announced that the meeting would begin.

"We can't wait for Boswell any longer. Damned irresponsible of him to take off at a time like this." He glared at the assembled crowd as if they had abetted Boswell in his flight. "Look here, Hubbert," he continued. "Quincy is being driven mad by all these press calls and now she's hounding me. Get that damn Anne Marie to help out, won't you? No use paying her to sit around moping."

What a sentimental, understanding fellow Edgar Hale was. "Actually, Edgar," T.S. replied happily, "I've already assigned Anne Marie to help out your secretary and arranged to have all press calls switched over to Miss Fullbright here." T.S. loved telling him he'd already done what he wanted. It irritated the old grump immensely and he was forced to sniff around for a new victim.

Edgar Hale stared at Miss Fullbright as if he'd never seen her before, apparently forgetting he had once informed T.S. that he thought Miss Fullbright would look a hell of a lot better in a black negligee than those silly red suits she wore.

"For those of you who have not yet had the pleasure, I'd like to introduce Felicia Fullbright," T.S. said in response to Hale's blank stare. "Since she is taking over as Personnel Manager, I felt it appropriate she be involved. Particularly since this is an emergency. ˙ The men stared at Miss Fullbright and she shrank back in her seat.

Edgar Hale resumed his thunderous expression and reclaimed control of the table. Behind him, a gleaming silver coffee service was laid out on an oak sideboard. No one had dared moved to take advantage of the refreshments, with the exception of the youngest partner present, Preston Freeman.

Freeman was out of the Corporate Finance area, was described as a genius and never seemed to pay attention to a thing except his mergers and acquisitions. Even now, he sat with a full folder open in front of him and was busily making notes in the margins of legal documents. He took no notice of the events swirling around him. He had a cup of coffee at his elbow and absently sipped from it every now and then. He brought in millions to the company each year and could have publicly pissed on the Managing Partner without fear of censure. T.S. envied him his nonchalance.

Stanley Sinclair sat stiffly to the right of Hale, guarding a stack of files conspicuously stamped ''Confidential'' in bright red ink. Anyone looking for juicy details would know immediately that the files represented paydirt. The treasurer was an extremely thin man, given to exaggerated, almost foppish gestures. He wore his hair slicked back in a currently popular and pompous manner, a style that highlighted his receding hairline and caused his rodentlike face to appear even more pinched at the top. He was impeccably dressed in a suit nearly identical in cut and color to those of the four assembled partners, but there the similarity ended.

Stanley Sinclair would never be a Sterling & Sterling partner and it seemed that he was the only one who did not realize it. He had taken the route of extreme toadyism to reach his relatively powerful position but, while his subservient attitude may have gotten him raises in pay and rank, it had cost him the respect of most of the partners. As a result, he would never attain the loftiest of positions.

T.S. had seated himself as far away as possible from Sinclair and anchored the other end of the table. Miss Fullbright sat meekly beside him. The remaining partners filled in the sides. The chair to the left of Edgar Hale remained empty, in case John Boswell showed up late.

"Gentlemen, we have a problem," Stanley Sinclair said abruptly in a manner he thought masterful. T.S. noticed, however, that Sinclair's voice had squeaked on the word "we" and this gave him the courage to smile. Sinclair stared sternly back at T.S. "And I think the time to stem the flow of trouble is now," he ended pompously.

T.S. felt a yawn coming on and was powerless to stop it. He found himself the center of attention, hand clamped over his gaping yaw. "Excuse me," he murmured.

"I'll handle this, Sinclair," Edgar Hale thundered and slapped the table with a palm. He held a thoroughly chewed cigar in the other hand and waved it about as he spoke, sending little flecks of tobacco flying about the conference room. T.S. rooted for one to land on Sinclair's smirking face.

"T.S., Stanley here says that the lieutenant has asked for all of the firm's financial records."

"That's correct," T.S. said calmly. "The police feel strongly that financial considerations are a possible motive and they wish to cross-check recent personal transactions of all partners and senior executives with those of Robert Cheswick. They are also checking all significant money transfers and any recent or unusual transactions involving clients with whom Cheswick was familiar."

"But that's impossible!" Hale sputtered.

"Not at all." T.S. smiled. "I'm sure Mr. Sinclair here has kept impeccable records. He's an excellent administrator."

"That's the point, Hubbert," Sinclair whined. "I was able to stall that detective by giving him the firm's trading accounts first, but he'll want the private records next. If he hadn't been called away by his office this morning, he'd be paging through them at this very moment." He patted the stack of records. "No thanks to you."

Edgar Hale butted in before T.S. could reply. "Sinclair here says he believes this investigation is merely a cover for the IRS. That they're trying to double-check our financial transactions without giving us the benefit of knowing it. Trying to sneak in unofficial audits without warning, you might say. That's a serious allegation.''

T.S. fingered his dragon tie and considered his words carefully. Not that he was planning on being prudent. He was no longer concerned with such mundane niceties. He smiled in reply to Sinclair's glare and winked at Miss Fullbright, who nervously coughed behind her hands.

"This business about the IRS is horseshit,'' T.S. said. Preston Freeman put down his pen and looked up. "Sinclair sees IRS conspiracies everywhere. He ought to work for one of those cheesy television shows that investigate assassinations.''

"See here, Hubbert. I resent that! This is a serious matter.'' Sinclair clutched both sides of his stacked files. Edgar Hale stopped in mid-bite and his cigar dangled carelessly from between his lips as he watched the two men joust.

"It certainly is a serious matter,'' T.S. agreed. "Robert Cheswick has been stabbed. I think *that's* the real emergency. What exactly are you suggesting? That the CIA or FBI murdered Cheswick so that the NYPD could act as undercover agents for the IRS and get at financial transactions that are open to them anyway? That sounds nuts to me.''

Miss Fullbright blinked at this and Preston Freeman suppressed a smile. Sinclair looked momentarily stunned but quickly rose to the bait.

"I'm suggesting no such thing! You have no right to twist my words. Robert Cheswick was obviously murdered by some common intruder looking for cash. It's unlikely to happen again at Sterling & Sterling for another two hundred years. That danger is past. What I'm pointing out is a very real present danger. The IRS, on hearing about the murder, convinced the local police to cooperate in a little investigation of their own. It's the perfect cover for them. Believe me, the real danger in this situation lies far beyond the murder of Robert Cheswick.''

By the end of his speech, Sinclair's features had taken on a fiery glow and his collar appeared to have tightened considerably around his neck. His Adam's apple bulged desperately above the rim, as if trapped in place with nowhere to go.

"You see IRS conspiracies everywhere, Sinclair," T.S. pointed out. "You blew up this smoke screen when they wanted to film that movie in the Partners' Room. You thought the same thing when that magazine wanted to take a photo of the *outside* of the building, for god's sake." The room had grown even more silent and Edgar Hale was listening carefully to T.S. "Now I suggest that you are about to cause a great many more problems for Sterling & Sterling than you've ever dreamed of," T.S. concluded.

Edgar Hale looked carefully at both men. "Like what?" he barked.

"Like dragging this out in the press even further. Think of the publicity. We refuse to hand over records that may lead to the solving of the murder of our esteemed colleague. What are we hiding? What are we afraid of? The police are convinced it's insider trading. Rumors like that could kill our Corporate Finance business in a week. For what? Those records could be subpoenaed in an instant, believe me. Lieutenant Abromowitz is not easily amused. They have nothing else to go on. I'm told that no useful physical evidence was found at the scene. And that Cheswick was thoroughly potted when he was stabbed. Now that would look good in the press if it ever got out. 'Sterling Partner Dead Drunk. *Literally.*' And something tells me Abromowitz would be more than happy to hold that over our heads if we failed to cooperate in any way."

It was the longest speech he had ever made without interruptions from Edgar Hale. T.S. was, in fact, so startled at having everyone's attention that he simply trailed off his words at the end and clasped his hands in front of him.

"What do you suggest?" Preston Freeman asked quietly. He had abandoned his files and was now listening intently.

"Give them anything they want," T.S. said. "Let them follow us into the bathrooms and coat closets if they like. Cooperate fully. Give them an office to work out of. Offer phone lines and secretarial support. Feed them. Let them talk to everyone they wish. Give them access to each and every employee's and partner's trading account. For the sake of the bank's reputation, which is irreplaceable, we must resolve this and go on.''

"Can't we take a more active role in solving this?" someone asked.

"I'm trying," T.S. admitted. "I'm doing some looking around of my own. Maybe as an insider I'll be able to find some things out." He shrugged.

"You think someone here at the bank did it?" Preston Freeman asked slowly. He leaned forward, staring at T.S. intently.

T.S. shrugged again. "It's possible. The timing of the murder and the fact that the murderer kept his cool and carefully wiped the surfaces clean lead me to believe that the act was premeditated, with Robert Cheswick clearly the target.''

They all sat in silence, considering this information. Even Stanley Sinclair looked startled. Characteristically, it was Edgar Hale who broke the silence.

"Well, you better come up with something quick," he said to T.S., his usual gruffness tinged with a note of desperation. He glared at Sinclair. "I'm not keen on our private transactions going public and I want this to end. Sinclair, I want you to stay on top of Abromowitz, you hear me? Be so helpful he can't take in a thing. Stay on top of him, understand?''

"Yes, sir," Sinclair said crisply. He shot a glance at T.S., trying his best to eke out a small measure of victory from the meeting. "I'll take care of the situation. Don't you worry.''

"Keep him off Hubbert's back," Hale continued, chomping hungrily on his cigar. "He's right. The big problem here is our image. We epitomize discretion and gentility. If this drags on much longer, our clients are going to start questioning our integrity and our reputation. We can't afford to let that happen." He looked around the table slowly at everyone present as if each individual were in some way doing his best to impede progress. He stopped at the empty chair reserved for John Boswell.

"Where the devil is Boswell?" he asked. No one answered. "Never mind," he dismissed the matter with a wave. "Cooperation, then. It's cooperation all around and smother them with kindness." He stood up from the table and slammed his chair back into place. "Now let's get back to work and make some money."

His abrupt and carefully timed exit was upstaged by the whirlwind arrival of his secretary, Mrs. Quincy. She came flying in the door, her bun askew and glasses slipping sideways on her face. Her skin was flushed scarlet and she seemed unable to breathe.

"Mr. Hale! Mr. Hale!" she gasped, running headlong into her boss. Hale bounced off the sideboard and went toppling over the table, knocking his chair over, tripping over Preston Freeman and eventually landing in Miss Fullbright's lap. The two of them immediately tipped over backwards. There was a flurry of shrieks, a waving of legs, flashes of lingerie, muttered curses and numerous scrambling sounds.

Several confused seconds later, Edgar Hale huffed to his feet and left Miss Fullbright lying unceremoniously on the carpet. He gripped the edge of the conference table tightly with both hands, his knuckles showing white. Mrs. Quincy stood, her hand to her mouth, staring at her boss.

His voice was quiet and precisely controlled, the tone deadly in its exaggerated politeness. "What is it, Mrs. Quincy? What urgent news have you brought us now?"

The panic-stricken woman pushed her glasses back up on her nose, then turned the gesture into a sign of the cross. "It's Mr. Boswell, sir," she whispered. "He's washed ashore. He's washed ashore at Orient Point."

CHAPTER SEVEN

1 Reactions to the news varied. T.S. observed them all with great interest. He himself felt a great sadness, less for John Boswell than for Sterling & Sterling. This second death made it clear that the first had been no accident, that the motive had more to do with the bank and less to do with the individual—and that chances were good the killing would continue if the reasons were not uncovered. And it strengthened the lieutenant's theory that financial impropriety was the motive, a situation that could easily mean death to the firm itself. And however much he made fun of Sterling & Sterling, it had been his home for over half of his life and T.S. had come to respect the integrity it strove to preserve. Boswell's death would hurt it greatly and he searched his mind for ways to stem the damage.

Stanley Sinclair reacted to the news with sudden silence. He stared straight ahead at the wall, his face impassive. Only his eyes moved in his head and they shifted nervously from wall to wall. For once, his precious files were forgotten. A few seconds later, an almost imperceptible tremor passed through his body and his eyes reflected a puzzlement quickly replaced by the darkness of an even stronger emotion. Perhaps fear.

Miss Fullbright grasped his arm at the news and clung tightly to T.S. He looked down at her. Her lower lip had started to quiver and her eyes glittered nearly black. He resisted the impulse to draw away. She was not really of such stern stuff that two murders would not affect her greatly, but he had not expected it to, well, almost excite her.

Meanwhile, the Management Committee partners were

staring at Mrs. Quincy as if the messenger bearing bad news deserved immediate execution. She stared wildly back at them, her body pressed against the wall. Her tongue was hanging out in a near pant, as if she were facing the firing squad. Her worst fears had come true. She expected to be arbitrarily dismissed from her job at any moment.

Only Preston Freeman retained his composure. He stared down at the open file before him, his lower lip stuck out thoughtfully. He was certainly a cool one.

The biggest change occurred in Edgar Hale. As T.S. watched, it seemed as if the Managing Partner actually shrank in size. His shoulders sagged, his stomach became a paunch, his face drooped and he stubbed his cigar down absently in the ashtray. He ran a hand tiredly through his thinning hair and wrinkles appeared on his forehead. Putting a hand out to steady himself, he lowered himself into Boswell's empty chair and placed his head in his hands. He changed from a contentious and volatile leader to a weary and frightened old man before their eyes.

T.S. took it upon himself to break the ominous silence. "How did you hear this, Mrs. Quincy? Are you sure?"

Everyone's eyes shifted to T.S. and the secretary relaxed her posture, answering almost politely in her relief at being removed from the center of attention. "Yes, sir. I'm quite sure. Mr. Boswell's housekeeper called to notify us. The police just told his wife and she is too distraught to make the formal identification. They were hoping someone from the office could do it."

"Yes, of course," T.S. said automatically. "Send Jimmy, he'll be able to take it." As valet to the partners for decades, Jimmy Ruffino could be counted on to undertake the unpleasant task with bearing and aplomb.

"Did she give any details?" The assembled group let T.S. lead the way.

"Only that he was found this morning about 10:00 A.M. by two women who were painting seascapes from a bluff out on Orient Point, sir," Mrs. Quincy replied.

T.S. nodded. He knew the area. It was a small seaside town on the northern claw of Long Island.

"He'd drowned," she continued when no one responded. "They say there was no question of reviving him. They are checking the marina now. He had a sailboat, you know. It was his pride and joy."

Edgar Hale nodded at this statement and T.S. remembered that John Boswell had probably been Hale's closest friend at Sterling & Sterling. As the nearest to him in terms of power, Boswell was one of the few individuals Edgar Hale could relax around or confide in. T.S. looked at the grieving man, then addressed the group.

"We don't know if there's a connection. This may be a sad coincidence." He sighed. "However, the media will certainly connect the two incidents, whether rightly or wrongly. I suggest we keep this to ourselves for now. I will ask that all calls be forwarded to my department. There's very little more we can do except cooperate with the police."

He stood up to signal that the meeting was over and Miss Fullbright followed his lead. The members of the Management Committee hesitantly stood as well. Stanley Sinclair virtually sprang to his feet, tugging his files under his arm and walking stiffly to the door. Edgar Hale remained seated, staring quietly at the smooth polished surface of the table. T.S. patted the man's shoulder on his way out the door and stopped to speak to Mrs. Quincy. "Perhaps Mr. Hale would like a cup of tea. And then he may want you to call his driver. It has been a difficult day for him."

"Yes," Edgar Hale echoed, raising his head. His voice was uncharacteristically soft. "Please have my driver bring the car around. I must drive out to see Megan Boswell. I am sure she will need a steady hand and a friend to guide her through this."

Miss Fullbright followed T.S. from the room, nearly trampling his heels in her haste. He turned to glare but she had been transported in her excitement or fear and took no notice of him, instead gliding past and heading for the elevator in a near trance. He stared after her.

He was saddened and sickened by this latest news but, most of all, he was filled with resolve. There had to be more they could do to get to the bottom of the murders. He would not sit idly by while the police got bogged down in money transfers and stock transactions. His first talk would be with Sheila.

2 He entered her office without knocking. She was attempting to end a phone conversation with an anxious retiree.

"No, Mrs. Gladden. I'm sure no one is out to get Sterling & Sterling employees. Mr. Cheswick's death was probably an accident of some sort. Perhaps he was surprised by a burglar. I doubt the killer will be in Arizona any time soon."

There was a silence, and she looked up at T.S., rolling her eyes to the ceiling. "Yes, I'm sure. And please don't hesitate to call me if you need me. Good-bye." She hung up the phone and sighed, rubbing at her temples. "It's been like this all day," she said and waved for T.S. to sit down. "Some of them are really frightened. I can't imagine what they think. That some maniac is picking names at random from the Sterling & Sterling employee directory?"

T.S. tucked his feet beneath the chair. "Sheila, John Boswell has been found drowned in Long Island Sound."

She had been reaching for the phone again, but froze at his pronouncement. The blood drained from her face and her lips trembled against her suddenly pale skin. The lips moved but no sound came out. She moved them again and this time a very faint "What?" floated to T.S.'s ears.

"I'm sorry. John Boswell has been found drowned in Long Island Sound."

Sheila leaned back in her chair and stared intently at her feet, then pressed a hand over her eyes and sighed.

"I'm sorry. I didn't mean to upset you." He had not expected her to be so distressed at the news.

"I'm all right," she said weakly. "Just surprised. One was enough. But two . . ." Her words trailed off and she stared to the right of T.S.'s head.

"Yes. It's all the more tragic because I doubt it's a coincidence. They found the body this morning. We don't know any details yet. I'm afraid I need your help.''

"Of course. What can I do?'' She spoke quietly, still stunned.

"Are you and your husband on speaking terms?''

"Yes. I say good morning and Brian says good-bye. He's been working the night shift at his precinct. Probably on purpose.''

"Do you think he could get us the details on Boswell's drowning? I don't think Abromowitz is going to be much help. I think they've brought him in on the drowning and he's not going to have time for someone like me.''

"What makes you say that?''

"He was called out of here suddenly this morning by his office, according to Stanley Sinclair. It had to be because of Boswell. The police would connect the two immediately.''

"As they should,'' she said without emotion.

He nodded. "As they should. But I need to know details. Anything that might help us. I admit that my investigation started out as a scheme to humor Auntie Lil and relieve the pending boredom of retirement. But I don't like the looks of this at all. I saw Edgar Hale turn into an old man before my eyes. People may be in danger. People here at Sterling & Sterling. And I don't believe the police are on the right track. They're convinced that financial hanky-panky is behind Cheswick's murder, but I just don't see it. He was an honest man, if nothing more.''

"What do you want to know?'' She had pulled out a small pad and a pen and was ready to take down instructions.

"Everything you can find out about the circumstances of Boswell's death. Was anything found with him? Was there anything missing? What was he wearing? Were there any similarities between his condition and that of Cheswick?''

"Such as what?'' she asked.

"I don't know. Anything. His fly being down. A knife in his chest.''

"Okay,'' she said quietly. "What else?''

"I'm positive they'll do an autopsy. See if Brian can find

out the results. And they're looking for his sailboat now. Let me know when and where they find it.''

She nodded and finished her notes, pushing the paper over by the phone. ''I get the picture. When do you need it?''

''As soon as you can get it.'' He drummed his fingers on the desk. ''And there's one more thing, if you could keep it quiet.''

''Of course.''

''Find out if the police took Cheswick's private files from his desk. I tried to ask Abromowitz but could get nothing out of him.''

She stared at him and made a note on her pad. ''I'll see what I can do. But it may take a while. Brian will have to find someone he knows who's working on the case. Someone who'll talk to him.''

''I understand. But it's very important. We need your help.'' He stood to return to his office. He wouldn't be talking to John Boswell after all. But there were others.

3   Word of Boswell's death had not yet leaked to the press, as was obvious by the lack of calls being put through to Miss Fullbright. On the other hand, it was apparent that the news had quickly spread throughout the employee population. T.S. spotted clusters of people whispering on every floor he visited, most with genuine expressions of alarm. He even saw a few tears. John Boswell had been a well-liked man, one of the rare people in power at Sterling who had actually worked hard on his way to the top.

Auntie Lil was home and answered the telephone immediately. He came straight to the point. ''There's been another murder.''

There was a sharp intake of breath on the other end of the line. He could almost see her shaking her head wisely. ''I'm not surprised, Theodore. Not surprised at all.''

''They've found another partner. This one was drowned.''

''Are you sure it was murder?''

''I am. But it's not official.''

''Don't tell me who,'' Auntie Lil said. ''Let me guess.'' She got it right on the second try. T.S. was impressed.

"How did you know?"

"Something I saw," she said.

"Well, you've got to tell me. I'm the one over here in the middle of it. How do I know what to ask about if you don't tell me everything?"

She sighed. "It's nothing, really. Just that unimportant matter you pooh-poohed about memos possibly being removed from some of the partners' files. John Boswell was one of them."

"But that was maybe thirty years ago," he protested.

"Yes," she said firmly. "It was."

"I've got to go now. I'm going to go ahead and interview employees anyway. Boswell's death makes it twice as important. I'll let you know what happens."

"Shall we do dinner tonight?" she asked brightly.

"I don't know. I have a feeling it's going to be a very long day. I'll call you later."

She was disappointed but he could not help that. He didn't even know what he was searching for, so how could he know how long it would take?

4   Auntie Lil had suggested that an interview with Frederick Dorfen, the partner who sat behind Cheswick and Boswell, might prove useful. But T.S.'s fears were realized when it became apparent that the elderly partner was quite drunk.

"Hello there, T.S.," Mr. Dorfen said cheerfully, folding his long frame into the visitor's chair. He was very old but still exceedingly dapper, his pure white hair full and carefully combed. A white linen handkerchief peeked out of the pocket of his custom-made suit. He looked the perfect picture of a distinguished and competent Wall Street executive. Unfortunately, in the opinion of his fellow partners, his time had passed. It was not the highest endorsement of their compassion, as Frederick Dorfen had served the firm quite well for five years as Managing Partner. True, it had been three decades before—and he had been replaced quickly by younger men—but he was still acknowledged by many to be the last remnant of the old Sterling & Sterling tradition of gentility.

What a difference the years could make. T.S. could smell the scotch plainly on his breath, and the partner's eyes were slightly unfocused, almost dreamy.

"Mr. Dorfen. How good to see you again, sir." T.S. shook his hand warmly. He remembered Frederick Dorfen in his prime, cutting a swath through the crowded banking floor. Confident, handsome, the epitome of Sterling elegance, Wall Street's version of Errol Flynn.

"Call me Fred, T.S. You're old enough now." The old man slurred his words slightly and leaned a bit too far to the right.

T.S. sighed. Just once, he'd like his illusions to remain untarnished.

"What is it you want to see me about?" Mr. Dorfen asked. "It's not that Miss Butterworth is it?"

"I beg your pardon?" T.S. looked at the old man quizzically. "What would Miss Butterworth have to do with me?"

The old man flapped a hand and leaned back. "She's always threatening me with sex discrimination if I don't stop making remarks." He leaned toward T.S. "She likes it, though, you know. That tough old bird." He placed the tips of his fingers carefully together and crossed his legs. The maneuver took quite a long time. After all, they were extremely old legs and he was drunk. "She protests but I can tell she likes it. Who else is going to compliment her on her legs? I wouldn't do it if it didn't keep her young." He leaned forward in a conspiratorial manner. "The most I ever do is pinch her old bottom now and then. I'm surprised she can feel it at all through that steel girdle she wears." He leaned back and gave a dry laugh that turned into a coughing fit. Alarmed, T.S. waited until he recovered, then decided that he had better get right to the point before the old man passed out at his feet.

"You sit behind Robert Cheswick and John Boswell, Frederick," T.S. said.

"What?" The old man appeared confused at the change in subject but recovered after a moment. "So that's it. You're poking into their deaths. Most surprising, it is. Most surprising."

"It surprised you?"

"Of course it did. Who'd want to do away with those two?" Mr. Dorfen shook his head. "Cheswick was a regular prune, acted older than I am. And Boswell was just a fool who thought that if he chased skirts all day it would keep him young."

"Does that mean they deserved to be murdered?" T.S. asked.

Mr. Dorfen looked properly rebuked. "Of course not. I admire you for looking into it. What is it you want to know?" He held himself rigidly in the chair as if he might slide off onto the floor if he relaxed. As, indeed, he might.

"Did you notice anything unusual about either of them recently?"

"Unusual?" The old man considered the question, rubbing his chin with a hand as he thought. "I suppose so," he said at last.

T.S waited, "Well," he finally prompted when there was no response. "What? What was unusual?"

"Cheswick was even touchier than usual. Very grouchy, in fact. I am his senior, you know. It wouldn't have hurt him to show a little respect."

"What precisely did he do?"

"Practically accused me of snooping through his mail." Clearly the old man's pride had been hurt. "Came in each morning and snatched up his damn letters and looked at me like I was going to paw through them or something. I have plenty to do, you know, without going through other people's letters."

"I'm sure you do," T.S. soothed. "Anything else?"

"He was drinking heavily," the old man said darkly.

T.S. was tempted to ask if he'd been nipping at Dorfen's bottle, but resisted the urge. "How do you know?" he asked instead.

"How do I know?" The man gave a well-bred snort. "He'd come back from lunch stinking of the stuff." Mr. Dorfen tapped his nose slowly. "Don't think I'm so old that I don't have good refractory nerves."

"Olfactory," T.S. corrected.

"Those, too," the old man said firmly.

T.S. sighed. "Anything else unusual?"

Mr. Dorfen tapped his fingers together absently and bounced a foot lightly as he thought. "He was very bad about returning his phone calls," he finally said.

"How do you know?"

"That bossy secretary of his kept coming in and reminding him that so and so had called again and asking what was the matter with him that he wouldn't call back. Nagged him something fierce. She's a pushy one, even if she is a looker."

"In other words, he was preoccupied?"

"Yes, very preoccupied." The old man nodded his head, satisfied at the diagnosis. "That's all I can think of."

It hadn't been much, but at least T.S. had tried. He rose and extended a good-bye handshake. Instead, the old partner grabbed his hand and hoisted himself out of the chair, mumbling his thanks.

"Thank you for stopping by, Frederick. You've been most helpful."

The old man bent to smooth the creases in his pants. "Glad to be of use." He straightened up. "Glad to be of use." He strode to the doorway and turned back to T.S. "Believe me, Cheswick was being a real grouch. Just ask John Boswell."

"Frederick—John Boswell is dead, too. Remember?"

"That's so. That's so." The old man nodded his head and looked perplexed. "Keep forgetting. Butterworth told me." He sighed. "Too bad. He could have told you what they were arguing about."

"Who argued?" T.S. asked quickly.

"Argued, hell. Those two fought." The old man laughed in disbelief. "They fought, man. Two tremendous arguments. Right in the middle of the Partners' Room. Once on Tuesday and again on Thursday. Everyone was out to lunch but me. Jimmy Ruffino caught them arguing the second time and they shut up immediately. But as for me, they act like I'm not even there. No respect. You'd think I was wallpaper. I saw the whole thing. A regular shouting match." He *tsk-tsk*ed and shook his head. "Hardly a suitable way for partners of Sterling & Sterling to behave."

"What were they arguing about?"

"I haven't a clue." The old man shrugged. "I heard Boswell telling Cheswick that he had better get his mind back on work or the firm could lose millions. That he was imagining trouble. It would be easy to take care of, Boswell said. Then Cheswick told Boswell he was one to talk, that his extracurricular activities would get them all in trouble one day. That's all I remember. You think I eavesdrop or something?" He turned to go, then whirled back to T.S., raised one hand in the air and added jauntily, "Just meet me for a margarita at Magritte's."

"What's that?" T.S. asked. "What did you say?"

"Meet me for a margarita at Magritte's!" the old man repeated cheerfully.

"Who is Magritte?" T.S. asked.

Mr. Dorfen clung to the door frame with a shaky hand and leaned forward, his eyes narrowing as he attempted to focus them. "She was something else," he said. "Quite a liar, you know. A bunch of lies. Still and all, it's very sad. Very sad indeed."

T.S. stared at the old man. "Who was she?" he asked him. "Tell me more."

Mr. Dorfen peered at him intensely and an almost sly smile broke over his face. "It's just some old joke we used to say," he finally told T.S., shaking his head. "Can't remember how it started. I hadn't heard it in years until I overheard Cheswick whispering it to Boswell the other day."

He staggered cheerfully out the door and left a bemused T.S. behind, shaking his head in exasperation.

5 T.S. had decided it might save time and prove clever to interview the firm's biggest gossips together, but shortly into the proceedings he realized he had been out of his mind. Between Francine Crisp and Effie the operator, more misinformation and crazy theories flew about the room than you might find at a group therapy session out at Creedmoor, the city's most notorious mental hospital.

The two women sat, wide-eyed, in front of him. They were

a study in unfortunate contrasts. Effie was plump, to put it kindly, with upswept gray hair and a pair of ancient light blue cat's-eye glasses attached to her ears with silver cords. Rhinestones winked out at him from the frames, as the glasses balanced precariously on the tip of her large, wide nose. She wore a purple, two-piece polyester pants suit. Thank god she was seated behind the main desk all day.

On the other hand, Mrs. Crisp was very small and birdlike and wore her hair chopped off short in a style much too young for her pinched, wrinkled face. She was neatly decked out in a gray flannel pants suit, looking more like a doorman than a teller.

"We heard you were going to solve the murder, Mr. Hubbert," Mrs. Crisp said.

"Murders," Effie quickly interrupted. "We heard about Mr. Boswell today."

"Perhaps," T.S. said carefully. "I'm looking into it. So are the police, of course."

"The police!" Mrs. Crisp snorted. "Why, when my daughter's home was burglarized and they found out she had no insurance, they said there wasn't even any point in filling out a report. Imagine!"

"There's talk of embezzlement," Effie interrupted in her excitement. "Wouldn't it be something if old Mr. Cheswick had been embezzling money all these years?"

"Yes. We think maybe with an accomplice," Mrs. Crisp added. "We figure that Mr. Boswell found out and the accomplice first killed Mr. Cheswick and then Mr. Boswell to keep from being uncovered."

"Mr. Cheswick's nerves were in a terrible state last week," Effie said confidently. "He was probably afraid of being found out. We think he was going to confess the whole thing out of guilt. That's why he had to be silenced. See what we mean?"

They stared at T.S. expectantly.

"Well, it's a theory," he conceded.

"The question being . . ." Here, Mrs. Crisp paused

dramatically and pointed to the ceiling. "Who is the accomplice?"

"I know," Effie said importantly.

"You know?" Mrs. Crisp eyed her co-worker suspiciously. "Or you're guessing?"

"It's an educated guess," the other woman retorted angrily. "Let me just ask you—who keeps the financial records around here?" When no one replied, she continued. "And who's in charge of auditing key accounts? And who raises such a stink whenever *anyone* wants to look at them. Answer me that?" She stared at T.S. but he wasn't about to fall into her trap.

He sighed. "Who, Effie?" He'd give her that much.

"Mr. Stanley Sinclair, that's who." She announced this triumphantly and Mrs. Crisp looked at her in admiration.

"Well," Mrs. Crisp said. "Who would have thought it? It doesn't surprise me a bit, though. I've never liked the looks of him. Got a face like a rat and never says thank you when he cashes a check."

"Take my word for it, Mr. Hubbert. He's the one." Effie nodded her head wisely and crossed her plump arms over an abundant bosom. "I'm going to tell that Lieutenant Abromowitz the very same thing the next time he shows his face around here," she declared. "But I wanted to give you a head start. On account of I'm betting on you to figure it out before the police."

"I appreciate the tip," T.S. said graciously. "Can you tell me anything else unusual about Mr. Boswell or Mr. Cheswick these past few days? Anything you may have heard from other employees? About the dead men, I mean," he hastened to add.

"You mean like Mr. Boswell buying the diamond necklace?" Mrs. Crisp said very self-importantly.

"Oh, ho—you didn't tell me that," Effie accused her.

"Some things are private between a man and a woman." The teller crossed her arms primly and perched in a superior manner on the edge of her chair.

"Now, Mrs. Crisp," T.S. said soothingly. "What diamond necklace? Is this firsthand knowledge you have?"

"Of course it is. I saw it with my own eyes." She shot Effie a triumphant look.

"You mean," T.S. hazarded a guess, "Mr. Boswell showed you this necklace?"

"He certainly did. On Thursday. He came down to the teller's window and cashed a large check. I'm not at liberty to say how large, but it was for $5,000."

Effie was obviously impressed. "Imagine!" she said, eyes wide.

"I said to Mr. Boswell, 'What are you doing—running away from home?' And Mr. Boswell, who always stops to make a joke or two, not like some people I know who were recently murdered, said that he was on his way to buy a very special present for a very special lady. When he returned, he came right by the tellers' windows and showed it to me. He was very excited. Just like a little boy. He kept asking me if I thought the lady would like it. I told him I thought Mrs. Boswell would love it and he started laughing and clapped me on the back and told me what a good sense of humor I had." She sat back proudly after this speech, as if waiting for Effie and T.S. to agree that she did, indeed, have a good sense of humor.

"Hmmph. You might have told me that before." Effie crossed her arms and turned away from Mrs. Crisp. "Of course, what's that got to do with embezzling?" She was upset that she'd been bested at providing T.S. with juicy information and she thought hard to come up with something better. "It so happens," she said importantly, "that I know an interesting piece of news myself."

Mrs. Crisp was clearly skeptical and merely snorted.

"It may not pertain *directly* to the murders," Effie acknowledged, "but you should know about it anyway, Mr. Hubbert."

T.S. suppressed a sigh and asked, "What is it, Effie?"

"There's going to be big trouble between Anne Marie and Quincy, I'll tell you that right now. They were fighting like cats and dogs in the ladies' room. I was in one of the stalls and they didn't know I was there, so I just kept real quiet. No sense making things worse, I always say. Quincy tells

Anne Marie she's not working hard enough, Anne Marie tells Quincy to mind her own business. Then Quincy tells Anne Marie she's putting on airs and Anne Marie lets on as how she thinks Quincy dresses like a cow.''

"A cow?" Mrs. Crisp asked incredulously. "There's going to be trouble now."

"I just think Quincy is jealous because of all the attention Anne Marie was getting from certain partners, may they rest in peace."

"Now that's not true and you know it, Effie," Mrs. Crisp protested. "Anne Marie has never believed in going out of her station, even as a young girl, when so many of those other women let themselves be fooled by the young men, no names mentioned. I was always happy just to get a man like Mr. Crisp, of course. Anne Marie would never have a thing to do with a partner."

Effie sat back grumpily. "Maybe. But you have to admit that Anne Marie makes no secret about getting a bigger salary than Quincy. And that's what Quincy really hates. Mark my words, there's trouble ahead between those two."

Great. It was just what T.S. needed. A cat fight on the banking floor. "Well, thanks for the warning, Effie." He could see that he would get no other useful information from the two of them and stood up politely. "Thank you, ladies, for stopping by."

"Thank you!" they echoed in chorus.

"It's so exciting to be part of an investigation," Mrs. Crisp breathed.

"Let's keep this under our hats for now. Shall we?" T.S. suggested as he showed them to the door.

"But of course," Effie declared, as Mrs. Crisp murmured her agreement. They chatted quietly between themselves until they turned the corner.

T.S. stared after them and then could not resist poking his head into the department's main entrance room. Just as he suspected, Effie and Mrs. Crisp were racing toward the elevators, elbowing each other in matronly haste, both eager to be the first to spread the news.

* * *

6   Jimmy Ruffino, partners' valet, appeared promptly in the doorway less than five minutes after T.S. called down for him. He was extremely pale and looked frightened.

"Is there something wrong, Mr. Hubbert?" he asked anxiously, twisting his hands in worry. "Have I made some mistake?"

Good heavens, being a valet to the partners certainly bred subservience. "No, not at all, Jimmy. I just wanted to talk to you."

The man crept timidly into the room and sat on the very edge of the visitor's chair, as if he might get an electric shock if he were to actually sit back and relax. "Talk to me about what?"

"A couple of things. I'm looking into the murders for Mr. Hale, you know." T.S. looked him over. "Are you feeling well?"

"Certainly, sir, it's just that . . . well." He shifted uncomfortably in the chair. "I had to identify Mr. Boswell's body this afternoon. It was a bit upsetting."

"Of course. I'd forgotten. I'm surprised you came back to work."

"I thought Mr. Hale might need me. And I wanted to take what I'd seen off my mind, sir, if you know what I mean."

"I can understand that. It must have been awful."

"A terrible sight." Jimmy shook his head. "It looked like Mr. Boswell, but it didn't, if you know what I mean. Puffy and pale." He shuddered. "I'd rather not discuss it, if you don't mind, sir."

"Of course not. I didn't call you up here for that anyway. I thought you might be able to help me in my inquiries."

"If I can."

"Mr. Dorfen says that Cheswick and Boswell were arguing over the past few weeks. He overheard a few intriguing things and said you'd interrupted one fight."

Jimmy nodded. "Yes, I heard the yelling. It was around lunch time and they were the only ones in the Partners' Room. It was about a week ago, I guess. I went in on purpose." He shook his head. "I've never heard such behavior in there. It was most irregular."

"Did you hear what they were yelling about?" T.S. asked.

"I'm afraid not, Mr. Hubbert, sir. I got the impression it was, well . . ." He colored slightly and reached up to loosen his tie. "Well, actually it seemed to be about a lady."

"A lady."

"Maybe. I could be mistaken."

"Why do you think that it was about a lady?"

"Mr. Cheswick was yelling something like, 'It's her, I tell you. It's her.' Then I heard Mr. Boswell laugh and Mr. Cheswick got even angrier."

T.S. considered this information. Could a woman link the two of them in some way? He tapped his pen against the desk, then stopped abruptly. Had they been arguing about Lilah Cheswick? Had Cheswick heard the rumors and confronted Boswell about his wife? Had Boswell denied them? *Were* the rumors true?

"Have you told the police any of this?" T.S. asked.

"No one's inquired of me, sir. Should I volunteer?"

T.S. thought of Abromowitz and shook his head. "No. They say they know what they're doing." T.S. stared at Jimmy thoughtfully. He remembered his name on the late check-out list. "What time did you leave the night Mr. Cheswick died?"

"Right after your party . . ." he began to say, then stopped and was silent.

"Right after Mr. Cheswick left the party?" T.S. prompted.

"No, sir," Jimmy admitted. "I tried to talk to him about a matter first. It was a mistake. He'd had too much to drink. I should have waited. But it was the weekend and I was . . . very worried about it."

"About your raise?" T.S. asked kindly.

"Yes," Jimmy bowed his head and shuffled his feet. "He'd refused me earlier but I need the money badly and was hoping to change his mind. Mona is very ill, you know, and the bills are killing us. At first, I was going to ask Mr. Boswell to intercede with Mr. Cheswick on my behalf, but when I went to find him in the Partners' Room, Mr. Boswell was talking on the phone with someone. He was angry and I didn't dare interrupt. I saw Mr. Cheswick come out of the bathroom and start to enter the Partners' Room. But as soon as he saw Mr. Boswell, Mr. Cheswick stepped behind a door and started to listen in. He was hiding. Then I followed him to the hallway outside of the Partners' Room and tried to talk to him about my raise, but Mr. Cheswick just laughed at me and walked away.''

Poor Jimmy, T.S. thought. To serve a man so faithfully and then be so completely dismissed during a time of need. ''What happened then?''

''I sat in the dark anteroom for a few minutes and regained my composure,'' Jimmy said quietly. ''When I felt able to . . . face things again, I gathered my hat and coat and left. Mr. Boswell was gone by then and Mr. Cheswick was sitting alone at his desk.'' Jimmy sighed. ''I went home and told Mona. She wasn't surprised.''

T.S. shook his head sadly. ''Thank you, Jimmy. If you think of anything else, please let me know.'' The valet rose and nodded, walking quietly to the door.

''Jimmy,'' T.S. called out. The valet stopped and turned back to him. ''I'll see what I can do about the raise.''

Jimmy stared at him quietly. ''Thank you, Mr. Hubbert.''

It might have been his imagination, but T.S. thought Jimmy's shoulders rose slightly as he marched out the door.

7   T.S. waited at the office until past 6:00 P.M., hoping that Lieutenant Abromowitz might call looking for more information and give T.S. a chance to ask questions of his own.

When the phone rang in early evening, he had just finished jotting down his tenth preposterous theory about why anyone would kill both partners. It was Sheila, calling from home, her voice breathless.

''Can't talk long, Mr. Hubbert. I'm going out to dinner in half an hour.''

''Did you find anything out?'' he asked anxiously.

''Found everything out.'' Her voice was confident and happy. Things must be going well between her and her husband for a change. "Brian knew the guy who actually took the call from the Greenport cops."

"Greenport?"

"Yeah. Orient Point's too small to have a police department. Are you ready for the inside poop?"

T.S. grabbed a pen and a pad of paper. "Ready."

"Number one, you can bet the murders are connected."

"Why's that?"

"He was found floating face down in Long Island Sound. His trousers were unzipped. His fly was open. Catch my drift? No pun intended."

He did indeed. "What else?"

"He had a dead corsage pinned to his sailing jacket. They think he was probably drugged first, then thrown overboard. He was a good swimmer, you know."

"Keep going."

"They found his boat docked at Greenport this afternoon. It's a twenty-eight-footer. You usually need two people to sail it, but one person could do it if he knew what he was doing. No one remembers seeing it come in. There's not too many people around this time of year. They think it docked in the early, early morning. There's trains and buses that leave for New York City not even thirty yards away from the marina, so whoever brought it in could be there and gone on the early commuter run within minutes if they timed it right."

"What else?"

"A couple of funny things about the boat. For one thing, there weren't any signs of a struggle. There's two berths. One was neatly made. The other was stripped of linen and pulled down like he'd slept in it, then thrown the linen overboard."

"Or someone else did."

"Or someone else," she conceded. "But that's not the weirdest thing."

"What is?"

"They found a half-empty pitcher of margaritas on the little table in the galley. Two glasses. Both wiped clean. But they left the pitcher of margaritas just sitting there. Like on purpose. They wanted it found.''

Margaritas, again? Magritte wouldn't be far behind, he reasoned. ''That's curious. Boswell doesn't strike me as a margarita type. What else?''

''They had the wife look over a list of everything found on the boat. The pitcher and glasses she's never heard of before, says it's cheap stuff and doesn't match her crystal. And there's a gun missing.''

''A gun?'' T.S. asked.

''Yes. Apparently he kept one under the wheel for protection. It was in a drawer with his nautical maps. I guess because of the summer boat traffic. You know, the Hampton crowd. Drugs. Stuff like that. He thought you couldn't be too careful. The wife asked about the gun right away. And sure enough, it's missing.''

''What kind of gun?''

''Oh shoot, Mr. Hubbert, I don't know. I guess I should have asked.''

''Never mind.'' He made a note on his pad. ''You've done great. You'll be in tomorrow?''

''Certainly,'' she said. ''If I'm not too worn out from tonight!'' She gave a girlish giggle. ''Oh—and one more thing. Abromowitz was put in charge because this is such a visible case. He wanted it for his career and pulled a few strings. Word is he's a real department politician. But he hasn't got much investigative experience. He thinks the zippers and corsages and stuff are just false clues to make it look like a nut killer instead of someone who knows the victims and was involved in financial hanky-panky with them. But the detectives on the case aren't so sure. I guess they don't like Abromowitz any more than you. I gotta run.'' She hung up before he could agree.

He checked his watch. He'd call Auntie Lil after all. It was later than their usual dining time, but the thought of going home to an empty apartment was infinitely depressing.

CHAPTER EIGHT

1 He related the day's events to Auntie Lil in detail over dinner. She listened to him intently, for once interrupting only occasionally. Her thick lamb chops sat untouched and cooling on her plate, though she hunched over her meal as if guarding it from T.S.'s probable assault. Dinner could wait. She was mostly interested in the details of Boswell's death and Stanley Sinclair's reaction. Murder was one of the very few topics to take precedence over eating on Auntie Lil's list of priorities.

"You say he seemed frightened when he heard of Mr. Boswell's death?"

"Well, everyone did," T.S. admitted. "But Sinclair was different. He withdrew into himself as if he were thinking it over very carefully. As if he knew something everyone else didn't."

"You don't like this Stanley Sinclair at all, do you, Theodore?"

"No, he's a toad," T.S. admitted. "How can you tell?"

"You adopt a faintly condescending tone whenever you speak of him. Not to mention that you said his face was ratlike. Equine would probably have applied just as well. Your choice of adjectives is telling."

"It is a ratlike face," he protested stubbornly. "I'm only trying to be accurate."

"No doubt. But he's not the rat we're after. I still say it's a woman. There was so much passion behind Cheswick's death. Could men be so passionate about money?"

T.S. thought it over. "Well, if anybody could . . ." He let his voice trail off.

Auntie Lil ignored him. "Where is this diamond necklace Boswell bought? It wasn't for his wife, we both know that. The police don't know about it. That means it's gone."

"Gone where?"

"That's the $5,000 question." Sipping the last of her Bloody Mary, Auntie Lil set it down daintily. A waiter sailed past, bearing two frosty drinks on a tray. She stared with great interest. "What are those things, Theodore?"

"Frozen margaritas. The bartender loathes making them. Please don't order one. He'd never forgive me."

"I have no intention of ordering one." She cocked her head to one side and put one hand against her chin, a move T.S. recognized as one of intense concentration. "It's funny," she mused, "how margaritas keep popping up. Margaritas and someone named Magritte."

"What do you mean?"

"Well, first Mr. Dorfen comes out with that funny saying and then there's a pitcher of margaritas, of all things, found on the sailboat."

"There may be no relation. Mr. Dorfen is drunk most of the time, and who knows what he really remembers. And if Boswell was romancing some woman out there, what could be better on an unexpectedly sunny day than a pitcher of margaritas?"

"Still." She stared after the drinks. "I think we had better remember that, dear." She made a notation in her small notebook: "*Margaritas?*"

"What should we do now?" he asked her. "I mean, about Stanley Sinclair."

"You think he may be in on it?" she asked.

"He was adamant about trying to keep all eyes off the private files," T.S. pointed out.

"Yes, but that seems to be rather his habit, isn't it? It sounds more like an IRS fetish to me, Theodore."

"Fetish?" He smiled at her. "What do you know about fetishes?"

She smiled back, looking rather like the cat who had already swallowed three mice and had no need for more. "Theodore, my dear, we did everything you did back when I was young. And they're still doing it. Remember that. The years may change. The nature of people does not."

"Should I phone Abromowitz about the Stanley Sinclair theory?"

She surveyed her candied carrots carefully, selecting the thinnest for a tentative taste before demolishing the entire dish. "By all means, tell the lieutenant," she said with her mouth full. "I'm sure he'll be in the mood to entertain theories." She took notice of her potato for the first time. Within seconds, it was gone.

T.S. looked at her carefully. "In other words, he hasn't got time for us and he'll think we're nuts."

She wiped her mouth carefully with the napkin, then folded the linen into a square. "I think that he probably has already started investigating Mr. Sinclair if he made the ruckus you say about the files. I think that he's probably up to his ears in possible theories and motives and will probably be in no mood to take us seriously."

"Should *we* forget Sinclair?"

"Absolutely not. You felt he knew something. You've been hiring and firing and talking to employees for thirty years, Theodore. I trust your intuition implicitly."

He felt an inordinate amount of pride at this compliment. "So what do you think I should do?"

"I think," she said, placing the napkin carefully to the side of her plate, "that you should ask Mr. Sinclair about it first thing in the morning."

It was just like her to make the impossible really quite simple.

2   The dinner with Auntie Lil had revived his self-confidence. They had sorted out several trails and the smaller mysteries were starting to fall into place. He felt now that together they might be able to puzzle out the answer to the big question and prevent more murders from occurring.

It was this hope that occupied his mind as he returned from his dinner. "Evening, Maumoud," he said politely to the doorman, as was his custom.

But this time Maumoud, instead of tipping his hat, looked at T.S. in a positively secretive manner and came out quickly from behind his desk. "Mr. Hubbert," he whispered, although there was no one else in the lobby, "there is a woman who wishes to see you." He stared at T.S. breathlessly and T.S. was slightly offended that the idea should appear so radical to the doorman. Did the world think him a eunuch?

He looked around the lobby. "What lady?"

"The one in the limousine." He raised his eyebrows and twitched them in the direction of the street.

A limousine was parked directly in front of the fire hydrant near the apartment building entrance. "That limousine?" T.S. asked.

"The very same," Maumoud whispered back. He touched T.S.'s arm and leaned even closer. "What is this, Mr. Hubbert? You are breaking the hearts of ladies these days?" T.S. looked at him blankly. "She was crying," the man explained, sounding impressed. "The driver came in and asked for you, but I could see the lady through the front window and she had a handkerchief pressed against her face."

Alarmed, T.S. moved to the door. "Did she give a name?"

"No, the driver said to tell you only that the grieving widow wished to speak to you." Maumoud's eyes grew round and he eyed T.S. carefully. "What is it you are mixed up in now? Does your Auntie Lil know?"

"Know?" T.S. buttoned his coat back up to the collar. "This whole thing is entirely her fault."

He stepped back out into the cool March night and strode rapidly to the limousine. He had a very good idea of who it was, but it was still a shock to find a tearful Lilah Cheswick in the backseat.

The driver solemnly opened the door for T.S. and he slid in beside her. Her ladylike sobs filled the car and he was too surprised to ask why she was crying. She was too busy crying to offer a reason.

Oh dear, he thought to himself. And I prided myself on reading human nature. Please don't tell me Lilah Cheswick is involved with murder. He saw twenty-five years of his most secret fantasies swirling slowly down the drain.

"You're going to hate me, Theodore," she sobbed through her lace handkerchief.

T.S. moved closer to her and gently pulled her hankie into her lap. "I seriously doubt that, Lilah. What is it? How can I help you? Surely it can't be as bad as all this?"

She sniffled and gulped at the air. "It is." She wiped the corner of one eye with an exquisitely embroidered black glove. "Oh, it is."

She had not cried at hearing of her husband's death. What possible news could have brought her to this?

"Do you want to come in?" he asked her. "We could have a drink and you could tell me about it."

"No," she said in a tiny voice, evading his eyes. "You won't want me in your apartment when you hear what I have to tell you."

"That's nonsense, Lilah," he assured her. "Nothing could do that. Just tell me."

Her tears were almost too much for him. As accustomed as he was to dealing with corporate and human problems, he had never been able to steel himself to seeing a woman cry. And when the woman was Lilah, well, that was almost too much to bear.

"I know you like me, Theodore," she said slowly. T.S. glanced at the partition between the seats to see if the driver was listening. He was leaning against his door, apparently asleep, and T.S. fervently hoped that the seat divider was soundproof.

"Yes, of course I've always liked you," he encouraged her. "Go on."

"I wish that things could have been different," she said, examining her handkerchief. "Even though I haven't seen you very often over the years, I always think of you at the oddest times. And it's important to me what you think of me.'' She looked at him briefly and a flash of the confident and vibrant Lilah surfaced.

"I think very highly of you," he offered and immediately felt foolish. It was far too formal a thing to say.

"I want you to keep thinking highly of me. That's why I'm here. I wondered why you asked me what you did on Sunday. You know, about if I was being taken care of by . . . anyone else. By another *partner*, you even said.'' She looked at him in an accusing manner and he was ashamed. "Don't look that way, Theodore. It's me that should be ashamed. I'm the one who's been a fool. I should have known he wouldn't be discreet about it. Why should he? He's never been discreet about any of his affairs. I expect you know that.''

"I knew John Boswell was . . . a bit of a ladies' man.'' T.S. looked uncomfortably at the chauffeur again. How could the man sleep through this?

"A bit?'' She laughed bitterly. "He was always the worst. And I've known him since college. I couldn't understand why Megan would marry him.'' She was silent for a moment. "But then, Megan could never understand why I married Robert.'' She shrugged. "I allowed many humiliations, but I would never have allowed the kind of humiliations that John put Megan through.''

"But you were . . .''

"An affair is different. I chose that. And I took a damn long time to decide. He's been trying to get me into bed for twenty-five years, you know.'' She looked at him for agreement and it was all he could do to keep from blushing.

"But why now?'' he asked.

"For one thing, Megan doesn't—didn't—give a damn about him anymore. She's been, well, intimate, with her groom for ages now. Oh, don't look so shocked, Theodore. We're human, too. She needs comfort just as much as the next person.''

T.S. did not interrupt with the news that he had always managed to find his comfort in other ways.

She cleared her throat delicately. "Besides, I lied on Sunday when I said that I'd gotten used to the way Robert was. I never got used to it. It always hurt. My husband never even noticed my existence. For over twenty-five years, I rode my horses, went to my luncheons, raised our daughters, never had an affair and pretended that it didn't matter. Finally, I just couldn't do it anymore.''

"But why are you telling me this?'' he asked.

"Because I know you've heard rumors. And because I saw him the day he died.''

"Boswell? You saw John Boswell yesterday?''

"Yes.'' She folded her handkerchief efficiently and stowed it away, as if she were through with nonsense like tears. "He came to my house on Sunday morning. He had quite an agenda. He wanted to apologize for standing me up the night Robert was killed. He wanted to let me know he had made the funeral arrangements and I was not to worry. And he wanted to tell me that he didn't want to see me anymore.''

T.S. was appalled. Lilah stared at his face and shrugged.

"Don't be humiliated for me,'' she said. "I knew what I was getting into. It was certainly no great love affair. We'd slept together exactly three times total since New Year's Eve. That was when I weakened. At the partners' New Year's Eve party. All the wives were there. I guess he'd pretty much exhausted all the other possibilities by then and decided to start over with me. He was very flattering and it suddenly seemed to me the most natural of resolutions to do something, anything, to break out of the pattern I was in. So I agreed to start seeing him. But once I agreed, he lost much of his enthusiasm and I've seen him very little since. You want to know the funny part? He wasn't any better in bed than Robert. I would just as soon have been by myself, reading a good book, or out riding one of my horses.''

T.S. gulped and looked at his shoes for comfort.

"I don't want to tell the police, Theodore,'' she said to him. "And Megan Boswell is one of my closet friends. I couldn't face her if she knew.''

"Couldn't you just say he came over to express his condolences?''

"He was supposed to be at a business conference in Japan. At least that's what he told his wife. Megan would smell an immediate rat."

T.S. stared thoughtfully at the floor. "Where was he for the rest of the weekend then? Did he tell you anything that may be important?"

"Yes," she said simply. "That's why I'm here. I may be an adulteress, but I'm not a murderer. I'd like to see whoever killed them caught."

"Killed them? You're assuming Boswell was murdered by the same person?"

"Of course. There's hardly been a pickpocket in the two hundred years of Sterling & Sterling's history and suddenly two partners die in three days. John Boswell drown? He nearly made the Olympic team in swimming. He would never have drowned."

"What did he say that was so important?" Remembering Auntie Lil's methods, he pulled his notebook from his pocket and prepared to take notes. Lilah stared at him pointedly. "It's just for my own use," he assured her.

"Do you think this will make up in some small way for what I did to Robert?"

Robert Cheswick was dead. Lilah Cheswick was not. "I think it's more a question of what he did to you," T.S. reminded her gently. "You're only human, remember?"

"Yes. I am. That's what I hate. Being so predictable."

He managed a smile. "You're one of the least predictable people I know."

She began. "He arrived at my house about 10:00 A.M. He didn't even call first, just showed up. I suppose he knew I would be furious about Thursday night. The night Robert died. John was supposed to meet me at a little French restaurant in the Village while Robert was giving the speech at your retirement party. But John never showed up. I waited about an hour, then left. The maitre d' was very kind and kept apologizing on his behalf. I decided to stop by my husband's office around 9:00 or 9:30 P.M. to see if he was still there. He'd been staying quite late in the weeks before his death. I thought maybe he could join me for dinner. I'd assuage my conscience and pride all at the same time.''

''But the guard couldn't find him?''

''No. I thought he must have already left to spend the night at the Yale Club. So I returned home. I was quite upset. You see, John had mentioned our taking a long weekend together. He had said we could christen his boat for the season and take her on a three-day sail, maybe to Block Island. Megan was in Oregon visiting relatives and I told Robert I was going to a spa for the weekend. It was to be our first trip of any length together. But John stopped mentioning the trip about a week before we were to go and I had counted on making final plans at the restaurant. So there I was. Stood up. And no excuse to tell my husband as to why I wasn't going away. I felt like a fool.''

She spoke harshly, as if she deserved the punishment. ''In the end, I didn't need an excuse. When they called me on Friday morning and said Robert had been murdered, I tried to call John, but his housekeeper said he had gone for the day. He wasn't at work, either. I took a real chance by calling him there. I think Robert's secretary answered the phone. I tried to disguise my voice, but I doubt I fooled her. The picture became very clear to me—John had met someone he preferred more than me and wanted me to just go away. So I called his house again and left a message to call me. Then I began to telephone my own family with the bad news about Robert's death.''

''Did Boswell call you back?''

''No. He had his housekeeper call early Saturday to say that he was taking care of the arrangements. That I was not to worry. That he would call in a few hours. He didn't, of course.'' She pulled a pack of cigarettes from her evening purse and lit up, smoking with an angry vengeance. T.S. marveled she'd been able to hold off so long. ''I gave these up and now I'm giving up giving them up,'' she said.

''Perhaps I'll have one,'' T.S. agreed, surprising them both.

''Only if you don't tell Auntie Lil,'' she warned.

He smiled. "I won't if you won't."

The cigarettes were comforting. They puffed away like two kids sneaking smokes behind the barn.

"What did he say when he arrived on Sunday morning?"

"He made some terrible joke about the rainy weather and how it was good we hadn't gone out on the boat. The look I gave him made him stop in his tracks. He then said he was terribly sorry about Robert, that he knew it was an awful strain on me. All the things he was supposed to say."

"Where had he been on Friday and Saturday?"

"I don't know. With someone else, I'm sure. He didn't say that, but . . ."

"When did he last see your husband?"

"He said he'd had an argument with him about some business matter and last seen him around 8:00 Thursday night. He tried to make it sound like that was why he'd stood me up. I wasn't buying it."

"Was he upset about your husband's death?"

She ground out her cigarette in a silver ashtray attached to the front seat and shrugged. "To be perfectly frank, I don't think he gave a shit. Let's face it. Robert was a terrible drag on the bank. He'd exhausted his connections and usefulness some time ago. He had apparently bungled some big accounts lately and was growing mean as a defense against criticism. John's lack of sorrow wasn't the curious thing."

"What was curious?"

"He didn't seem surprised. I was still in shock about Robert. Not from grief. Just from surprise. Who would bother to stab him? But John didn't act surprised at all."

"What else did he say?"

"He tried to say that he had never thought I was serious about going away with him for the weekend and that's why he hadn't gone through with our plans. I heard better excuses than that thirty years ago in college."

"You're sure he didn't really believe that? Going away with him was an extraordinary chance for you to take."

"Of course I'm sure. I'm not a total fool. Just selectively foolish. He found someone better, that's all. No doubt someone younger. With Megan out of town, it was too good an opportunity to waste on me.''

"Do you have any idea who it might have been? Did she have a name? Was it Magritte?"

"No," she said, staring at T.S. curiously, but giving no sign that she remembered seeing the name on her husband's bookmark. "And I didn't feel like pressing him for details. He was anxious to go at that point and I was anxious for him to leave. He didn't even bother to hang up his jacket. He was all dressed up in his captain outfit and ready to go out on his boat." She spoke bitterly. "I don't even know if I told him good-bye or not." She stopped, considered this statement, and abruptly burst into tears again.

T.S. fumbled for his handkerchief and pressed it on her. He had never gotten used to giving emotional advice and was reduced to patting her on the shoulder repeatedly with an occasional "There, there."

"If I'd known he was going to be killed, I'd certainly have told him good-bye," she choked out through her sobs.

"Was he concerned about his personal safety?" T.S. asked her when her new tears subsided.

She sniffed. "I don't remember. I was too upset." She gave a long sigh, shook herself and sat up straight. "That's it. That's all. No more tears. Damn, I was a fool. I am far too old for things like this."

T.S. unclenched her left hand from a fist and patted it gently. "If we worried about making fools of ourselves, we'd never get a chance to live."

"That sounds like Auntie Lil." She considered the advice briefly, but spent little time weighing its merits. "What am I going to do?"

"I don't know," he admitted. "It's important that they know Boswell's whereabouts on Sunday. Especially if foul play was involved."

Lilah leaned foward suddenly and tapped on the partition. The chauffeur woke suspiciously quickly, hopping to attention.

"Where are you going?" T.S. asked her.

''To the police. I'll tell them he came by at 10:00 Sunday morning to express his condolences. They can figure out the rest on their own.''

He reached for the door handle. ''Thank you for trusting me,'' he said quietly.

Her smile was brief and lacked its usual brilliance. ''Thank you for not judging me,'' she said. ''I'm having a little trouble standing myself these days. My only consolation is that Robert never knew.''

He blessed the discretion that had kept him from telling her about the overheard argument between her husband and Boswell. Was she the woman they'd fought about? If she was, T.S. preferred to leave her with some peace, even if his own had been uncomfortably disturbed by the knowledge that the rumors had been true.

He watched the sleek black limousine pull away from the curb, then walked slowly through the lobby, ignoring Maumoud's admiring glance.

Women, women, women, he thought. But who was Magritte?

3 Auntie Lil's suggestion to confront Stanley Sinclair in the morning sounded simple, but the execution of it was proving impossible. T.S. arrived at the office early, stopping only to buy the *Post* and the *Times*. The *Times* had no mention of Boswell's murder, but the *Post* had gotten hold of someone who had talked and the headline screamed *Floating Love Nest Turns Deadly*, with a subhead proclaiming: *Killer Stalks Wall Street Elite*. The pitcher of margaritas figured prominently in the story as did a mysterious blonde he'd been spotted with at the marina. That was news to T.S. There went Megan Boswell's dignity. Anyone reading it would have gotten the impression that John Boswell had been found floating naked with the pitcher still clutched in one hand and the blonde in the other. Everyone connected the two murders, it seemed. If not already, they would once the media got through.

With this thought came the recognition of Stanley Sin-

clair's expression the day before. *He* had immediately connected the murders. Not out of fear. Not out of coincidence.
But because of knowledge. T.S. lowered the *Post* to his desk
and debated whether to get coffee first or call right away. He
called.

"Mr. Sinclair is not in yet," a secretarial voice informed
him.

T.S. left a message and wondered. He was still not in by
10:00 A.M. and T.S. left yet another message. By 10:30 it
was apparent that he was not the only one to have noticed
Sinclair's absence.

Edgar Hale stormed into his office just before 11:00 A.M.,
a copy of the *Post* under his arm. He seemed to have recovered from the death of Boswell, as he was sputtering and
roaring in his usual manner, anger fueling his storm.

"Did you read this?" he screamed at T.S., waving the
paper above his head. His face turned an alarming shade of
red. "This is a fine thing for the memory of my friend and
an equally fine thing for the reputation of Sterling & Sterling."

"Sit down, Edgar. Sit down." T.S. put his hands on the
old man's shoulders and, surprisingly enough, Edgar Hale
obeyed. He sat in the visitor's chair with a plop and flipped
angrily through the newspaper. "My god, they make him
sound like a Sybarite! Like he fell overboard during a drunken
bacchanal."

"They have to sell papers," T.S. explained.

"Yes, and I'm selling respectability. Respectability which
is rapidly going down the drain."

T.S. made soothing noises but Edgar Hale's cork was
popped too far to be worked back in.

"That's not the worst of it, Hubbert," he hissed. He was
a rather short man, but stocky, and now he hopped to his
feet and leaned across the desk, anger building to a fever
pitch. "Do you know who is missing today?" he said. "Do
you know?"

T.S. knew, but he wasn't about to bite.

"How curious," Edgar Hale said in a suddenly deadly

calm voice. "How curious that our Mr. Sinclair should not have come in today. His wife has no idea where he is. Says he left for work as usual."

T.S. did not reply.

"Don't you find that odd, Hubbert?" Edgar Hale breathed in his face and T.S. caught a whiff of peppermint mouthwash. "Don't you find it odd that he would try to stonewall those records and now conveniently not show up?"

"Yesterday you found his IRS theory quite convincing." Touché. T.S. suppressed a satisfied smile.

"If that snake," Hale began, ignoring the comment, "if that slippery snake has stolen one penny from this firm, one single penny, I will personally kill him. I will kill him myself with these bare hands." He threw the newspaper to the floor and held up his two hammy hands for T.S. to admire. "These are the hands of a former championship wrestler." T.S. remained wisely silent.

"Can't you see it?" Hale shouted at T.S. "He was embezzling money and Cheswick and Boswell found out. I never liked that man, Hubbert." He shook his head angrily. "Never trusted him. Too slippery. Too eager to please."

Sure. It was T.S.'s experience that people were only too eager to bend over when others offered to kiss ass. "What are you going to do about it?" T.S. asked.

"I have every single employee in the auditing department poring over his records. And I'm going to help them personally. I don't give a good goddamn about confidentiality. I don't care who knows what stocks I bought or when. I want to know what that weasel was stealing from me." He slammed a palm down on the desk and T.S. jumped. "I've told Abromowitz everything. They've got people in with us. This is going to ruin us. The scandal. No one has ever embezzled money from Sterling & Sterling."

"No one?" T.S. asked faintly.

"Not since 1887!" the Managing Partner roared back. "Okay? When $567 was taken by a bank clerk. Clean enough record for you?"

"Yes, yes of course. I wasn't being facetious." T.S. sought to calm the man but he was clearly in a frenzy.

"Stanley Sinclair will live to wish he'd never seen the doors of Sterling & Sterling opening before him. I'll tell you that much." Hale sat abruptly down again. "I'm going to nail that bastard," he finished quietly.

Long after he had left, T.S. sat at his desk remembering the fury in the old man's face and the strength that anger had lent him. Hale had been strong. He had been determined. He had, indeed, been convincingly murderous.

4   Shortly after Hale stormed out the door and slammed it—leaving a flying maelstrom of loose papers and curse words behind him—Auntie Lil called, lending a calm voice among the mayhem.

"Theodore, dear? It's Auntie Lil. Did you speak to Mr. Sinclair?"

"No, he seems to have disappeared." There was silence on the other end.

"Edgar Hale himself came to tell me. A most pleasant experience." He picked up loose sheets of newsprint with his free hand as he spoke.

"That's odd," she said in a small voice.

"I'll say it's odd. Kind of suspicious, too, wouldn't you say?"

"It's very bad news."

"Bad news for Sterling & Sterling. And us. It looks like Abromowitz was right about money being the motive."

"No, Theodore, that's not what I mean." There was a silence again while she thought things through. He waited impatiently.

"What? What? Come on, Auntie Lil, I've just had Edgar Hale throw a temper tantrum of mammoth proportions and the police are hot after Stanley Sinclair and, to top it off, Lilah Cheswick is somewhat less pristine than I've been dreaming of all these years. Are you saying the police are wrong? Is that what you're telling me?"

"This is a dangerous situation," Auntie Lil said. "Mr. Sinclair is in danger."

"I'll say. Edgar Hale is going to dismember him."

"No." Her voice was polite but firm. "I don't believe he stole any money. I do believe he's guessed who the killer is. Something fell into place for him. Something between your meeting yesterday and this morning."

T.S. was silent. He wanted to believe her. It would be better for Sterling & Sterling if she were right. Anything would be better than having your treasurer steal the coffers out from under your nose and then knock off two partners.

"Are you there, Theodore?" she asked crisply.

"I'm here."

"Before the news of Boswell's death came, how did Mr. Sinclair act?"

"Like his usual annoying paranoid self."

"Exactly. Like his usual self. The same way he acted on the previous occasions when he believed the IRS was trying to infiltrate Sterling & Sterling."

"So?" T.S. said doubtfully.

"It was Boswell's death that changed him. He didn't know about the death."

"He may just have been surprised the body was found so quickly."

"No," Auntie Lil said quickly. "The newspapers are trumpeting a floating love nest."

"That's just hype."

"No, Theodore. Why would John Boswell go out on a boat with Stanley Sinclair if he knew he was stealing? It would be the height of folly. Why would a bed be used and drinks laid out?"

T.S. was silent. She had a point.

"It was Boswell's death that shed new light onto the killings. Sinclair has connected the two deaths and he's frightened. Probably with good reason."

"So you think he's gone into hiding?" T.S. asked.

"Yes. Because he's in danger, too. Something connects

the three of them. If we can find out what, we'll have found out why. Where would he hide?''

"I have no idea," T.S. admitted. "He's not really that smart a man. Sneaky, but not smart."

"Is he brave?"

T.S. thought of Stanley Sinclair. "Good heavens, no. He's a coward."

"Then he must have told someone where he was going. Someone he could trust. His wife perhaps. Is he married?"

"Yes. Just recently. How she can stand him, I don't know."

"He probably thinks the same thing in his heart of hearts. 'How can she stand me?' He sounds like a man who hates himself."

"Of course he does. He always goes along with the crowd."

"Whatever. But that's why he'll trust her. Because he knows that, for some reason he can't understand, she loves him. If we can talk to her, she may help."

"I'm sure the police have thought of that."

"It's the police she's prepared for," Auntie Lil said confidently. "She won't be prepared for me."

5   They waited outside the Long Island home of Stanley Sinclair for half an hour because Auntie Lil insisted that an innocuous blue sedan parked in the driveway was really an unmarked police car. T.S. humored her and passed the time by relating Lilah Cheswick's indiscretion to Auntie Lil. For once, she had little to say and merely patted his hand in an understanding way, shaking her head at his disappointment. Finally, two men who were clearly detectives emerged from the modest house and drove away in the car.

"You were right," T.S. admitted before she rubbed it in.

"Not very big, is it?" Auntie Lil remarked, looking at the two-story house and neatly trimmed lawn. "Don't they pay him much?"

"You'd be surprised at how much that house costs," T.S.

pointed out. "All those years of rent control have spoiled you. You've lost track of real estate values."

"Yes, I imagine so." She got out of the car and he followed. They stood in front of the house on the sidewalk, looking at the front door.

"How shall we do this?" he asked.

"Leave it to me," she said, charging up the path.

Her idea was direct and to the point. The moment the door was opened by an almost attractive woman, younger than T.S. had expected, Auntie Lil grasped the woman's hands between her own and said quietly, "We've come to help."

The woman stared at Auntie Lil but did not draw away. She had been weeping and her eyes were puffy.

"My name is Lillian Hubbert," Auntie Lil said in the same quiet and earnest voice. "This is my nephew, Theodore Hubbert." She nodded toward T.S. "He's a friend of your husband's from Sterling & Sterling. Perhaps Stanley spoke of him."

"Stan never talked about work," the woman said quietly.

"We know he's in danger," Auntie Lil continued. "Terrible danger. And we know that he didn't steal a penny from Sterling & Sterling. He is simply too devoted to the firm." Auntie Lil spoke in near evangelical tones, emphasizing certain words in a cadence that enthralled the listening woman.

"Stan told you?" she asked.

"Some of it," said Auntie Lil. "May we come in ?" She looked behind her shoulder out at the street. "We waited until the police left. We want to keep this private."

The woman stood aside and they entered a drab but comfortable middle-class home. It was a narrowly built house and steps ascended steeply upstairs as soon as one stepped inside. Mrs. Sinclair led the way into a small living room, furnished in green and brown. T.S. suppressed a shudder and studied Sinclair's wife instead. She was thin and plain, but not homely. Her looks might easily have been redeemed by a beautiful smile or winning gesture, if only she had possessed one. Certainly she neither gestured nor smiled now, just sat woodenly on the sofa next to Auntie Lil, who had practically leapt to make herself comfortable and was patting the cushions beside her in a friendly fashion.

"Theodore," Auntie Lil commanded. "Perhaps Mrs. Sinclair would like a cup of tea?" Mrs. Sinclair nodded and started to rise.

"No, dear. You stay. You've been through a lot. Theodore will handle it. The kitchen must be that way." She pointed through a rear door and the woman nodded.

"What is your name, dear?" Auntie Lil asked, taking the woman's hand again.

"Muriel," she said.

"May I call you Muriel?"

T.S. left the room as she was nodding. He hurried to find the kitchen and tea. *Stan*? She had called her husband "Stan." It was odd to think of anyone calling Stanley Sinclair "Stan." It was odd, in fact, to think of him as having a wife and a home and a personal life. T.S. was suddenly ashamed of his animosity toward the treasurer and felt a vague sense of foreboding.

Auntie Lil sat in silence and watched Muriel Sinclair dissolve into a fresh round of tears. "Here, dear," Auntie Lil said, handing over a handkerchief.

The woman took it and sniffed something resembling a "thank you" through her sobs.

"The police were very hard on you, weren't they?" Auntie Lil asked sympathetically.

"Yes." More sobs followed and Auntie Lil patted the distraught woman's hair.

"They think your husband stole money from the bank and killed the partners?"

The sobbing figure nodded and Auntie Lil's voice grew strong with indignation.

"Rubbish!" she cried. "Such a dedicated man as your husband would never steal!"

Muriel Sinclair stopped crying and sat up straight, staring at Auntie Lil.

Auntie Lil continued passionately. "I know your husband

would never kill anyone. I know your husband would never steal a penny. I'm right, aren't I?''

"Yes," Muriel Sinclair whispered. "Stan would never kill anyone. And he is honest. He isn't very charming and doesn't have much of a sense of humor, but he is honest."

"He's in danger, isn't he?" Auntie Lil said this matter-of-factly, one eye on Muriel Sinclair.

"Yes. He said he was afraid for his life."

"And that no one must know where he is?"

"Yes," she nodded tearfully. "He says if he's found and brought back, that whoever killed Mr. Cheswick and Mr. Boswell will kill him, too."

"Did he tell you who he thought it was?"

"No, he said it was better that I not know." She bent over the handkerchief again as a fresh round of sniffles threatened to escalate into full sobs. "He said he would handle it. That Mr. Hale would know what to do."

"Hale? Did he speak to Edgar Hale?"

The tearful woman shook her head. "Stan tried to call him last night right after he got home from work but had to leave a message. Later that night, someone called him back. He seemed much relieved by the time he hung up. That's when he said that Mr. Hale would know what to do."

"Did you answer the phone when Mr. Hale called back? How did he sound?"

"No," the woman's tears grew louder. "It wasn't Mr. Hale that called back. It was some lady. But I think she knew what was going on. I couldn't really hear. Stan turned his back to me and whispered." She seemed to consider her husband's secretiveness as a personal affront and looked ready for a fresh round of tears.

"We have information that may help him," Auntie Lil said quickly, before she lost her audience to hysteria. "I must find him to talk to him. We can help him."

T.S. returned with a cup of tea. He looked around for a table and, finding none, sat it at Muriel Sinclair's feet.

Auntie Lil looked at him expectantly. "Where's my cup, Theodore?"

"I didn't know you wanted one."

"For heaven's sake." She was clearly annoyed.

"You can have mine," Muriel Sinclair said in a tiny voice as she nudged the saucer with a foot. "I don't want it."

"Nonsense," Auntie Lil said. "You need it and you'll drink it." She picked up the tea and held it out to the woman. Muriel Sinclair took it obediently and balanced the cup and saucer on her knees.

"Listen to me, Muriel." Auntie Lil looked the woman right in the eye and leaned toward her as she spoke. Her voice was gentle but firm. "Tell us where Stanley is hiding out. I know that he loves you very much and would tell you where he was going. I understand that you can not tell anyone else because his life is in danger. But we can help him if we can only talk to him."

"I can't tell you," she began hesitantly.

"Can you call him? And let me speak to him?" Auntie Lil asked.

T.S. tried to think of the reaction if he were to ring up Stanley Sinclair at that moment and announce, "Stanley, my man, it's Hubbert. Your archenemy from Sterling & Sterling. I understand someone's been trying to bump you off."

"There's no phone there," Muriel Sinclair answered. "There's no service except in the summer."

"He's gone to that lovely summer home of yours he spoke so much about?" Auntie Lil guessed. "Please, I wouldn't have told you to call him if we weren't sincere."

The woman hesitated and T.S. spoke up. "It's okay, Muriel, we really do want to help. I could find out the address easily, but we must move quickly. Please tell us."

Perhaps it was hearing the male authority of his voice. Perhaps she was just beaten down by hours of interrogation. Or perhaps it was Auntie Lil's gentle voice and demeanor that prompted her to tell them where Stanley Sinclair was hiding.

Auntie Lil wrote the address down in her notebook, then asked, "Can you give us directions?"

T.S. could hardly believe her nerve, but the tearful Mrs. Sinclair gave her quite thorough directions in a halting voice.

They were to return to the city and take the Lincoln Tunnel to Highway 3 West, then follow that to Interstate 80. Their home was in the Poconos, just past the Delaware Water Gap.

They rose to go and Auntie Lil seemed not to mind the fact that one of her best lace handkerchiefs from County Cork was still clutched tightly by Mrs. Sinclair.

"Do you have a sister?" Auntie Lil asked.

The woman nodded. "A sister-in-law."

"I think perhaps you should go stay with her immediately. You know that you may be in danger, too."

The woman looked up with startled eyes.

"Promise you'll call her?" Auntie Lil asked once more on her way out the door.

Muriel Sinclair nodded again and watched as they drove away. T.S. could see her reflected in the rearview mirror, a thin and vulnerable creature outlined in the doorway of an overpriced house in a not-quite-ritzy-enough section of a Long Island suburb. He sighed. As soon as he saw Stanley Sinclair again, he swore he'd be nicer to him.

6 "Can't you drive any faster, Theodore?" Auntie Lil looked anxiously at her elegant watch and sighed.

"No, I can't." They were zooming down Interstate 80 headed west at seventy miles per hour. "This road is swarming with state troopers. What are we supposed to tell them if we get stopped?"

She sighed again. "I know we're getting near, but I have this feeling we're always a step too late." He knew what she meant. He increased his speed, checking the rearview mirror.

It was a typical Poconos community resort home: a shingled A-frame house with a wrapping redwood deck that was situated on an acre plot around a man-made lake. Every house looked empty and, this early in March, only the evergreens provided any privacy among the bare trees. For the next few months, at least, houses would be clearly visible on either side of the Sinclair's. The overall effect of the community was that of giant Monopoly houses thrown down around the lake from above.

They saw no signs of occupancy as they pulled into the driveway. Indeed, T.S. was not sure it was even the correct house.

"Are you sure this is it?" he asked Auntie Lil. "These all look alike."

She consulted her notebook. "Yes. This is it."

"It looks very quiet." He automatically went around to her side and helped her from the car. They stood, his hand still on her arm, looking up at the silent house. Neither wanted to pull away from the other.

"He would hardly be lounging about in the open." But Auntie Lil spoke uncertainly.

"Where do you suppose his car is?"

"I'm sure he was smart enough to park it at another house. Or perhaps down by the lake." She shivered and T.S. began to take off his jacket. She waved it away. "No, I'm not cold. I just don't have a good feeling about this." She took a tentative step forward and stopped.

"What is it?"

"It is quiet, Theodore. No birds, no sound of water. No wind. Like the whole world is waiting." She shivered again. "We're being watched."

"Nonsense." He spoke loudly, hoping to find real courage in his false bravado. "Only by Stanley Sinclair."

They moved forward to the bottom of the stairs. "I'll go up first," T.S. told her, waving her behind him. She fell obediently into place.

"Stanley!" he called out. "It's T.S. Hubbert. The police are looking for you." There was no reply. "I know you didn't do anything. We can help you. I want to help."

They mounted the steps slowly, Auntie Lil lightly touching his waist from behind.

"The door's unlocked," T.S. announced to break the ominous silence. He swung open the door and peered inside, then abruptly turned around and faced Auntie Lil. "Go back to the car," he ordered.

"No." She stood her ground. "Something has happened, hasn't it?" He didn't answer. "It's no good, Theodore. I'm not in this for a lark.'' She tried to push past him again and he moved to block her way.

His voice was grim. ''No. Wait here. At least let me make sure it's safe.''

''It's safe for us,'' she called after him. ''I don't think it's you or me they're after.'' When she got no reply, she followed him in and found T.S. standing in the middle of an arched, rectangular living room. Stairs to the right led up to a sleeping loft. The downstairs room was dominated by a large stone fireplace. Stanley Sinclair lay on the hearth, part of his head removed by a gunshot. The fireplace stones nearby glistened with blood and a dark pool had collected around his skull.

T.S. and Auntie Lil stood shoulder to shoulder staring down at the body. T.S. was thinking about the thin figure of Muriel Sinclair, framed in the doorway of their house. Auntie Lil was thinking of how close they had been to preventing the third murder.

''There's the gun,'' Auntie Lil said softly. Her words seemed to reverberate loudly off the empty walls and T.S. jumped reflexively. She pointed to the right of Sinclair's crumpled body. A blue-gray handgun glinted in a beam of afternoon sunlight streaming in through the skylight above them. The gun seemed too small to have created such harm. The sunlight reflected the amber of the cedar shingles and a fine dust of gold swirled about them as they stared at the dead body.

''Do you think he did it to himself?'' T.S. asked, more out of hope than conviction.

''No, I don't,'' Auntie Lil responded immediately. She pointed and he followed her lead. Stanley Sinclair's fly had been unzipped. T.S. saw that he'd been wearing royal blue briefs and looked away. Auntie Lil stared down at the gun. ''I've never seen a real gun up close before.'' She bent to get a better look.

''Don't touch anything,'' he warned.

She stood up and glared at him. ''Of course not, Theodore. I'm not an imbecile.'' She moved closer to the body and T.S. followed unwillingly.

"He's quite dead,'' she said. "It doesn't seem like he could have any blood left in him. How long do you suppose he's been lying there?''

T.S. stared at the pool of blood. He had always expected it to be red, but it was dark purple in the reflected sunshine. He imagined he could see it almost pulsating. "I couldn't say.'' He bent down and touched the dead man's skin, pulling his hand away quickly as if burned. "He's not really warm anymore.''

"He may have been dead by the time we talked to his wife.'' She said this for the same reason T.S. had thought it. There had been nothing they could do to prevent it.

"We should call the police.'' T.S. said this doubtfully and her response was immediate and swift.

"Not yet, Theodore. I really don't think we can afford to waste an evening being questioned about why we were here. We haven't anything to tell them, yet, and we've got to buy some time to pull it all together.'' She stared down at Sinclair. "We'll call them anonymously after we leave.'' She straightened and looked around the room. "See if he gave us any help before he died. Here—use this.'' She rummaged in her pocketbook and produced another frilly handkerchief from her endless supply, tossing it to T.S. with a distressingly professional air. He combined it with his own handkerchief to create crude mitts and avoid leaving fingerprints. Auntie Lil kept her customary gloves on.

T.S. searched the house. It was sparsely furnished with mass-produced modern pine tables and chairs. A wood frame couch that folded out into a bed with a futon mattress added the only color to the room. On top of its flowered cushions lay a copy of that morning's *Post*.

"He saw the article about Boswell's death in the paper this morning.''

"Yes,'' Auntie Lil answered. "Perhaps he had intended to go in to work but something in that story made him change his mind. Something confirmed what he had suspected yesterday. You said he was puzzled. Perhaps his question was answered by something he read. Look around some more.''

They moved cautiously about the quiet room. Between their whispers, tiptoes and the soft afternoon light, T.S. began to feel he was in a church. He looked back at the dead man and did, indeed, wish for the comfort of a church.

Auntie Lil was carefully poking about a long counter that jutted out from one end of the room and marked off the kitchen area from the main living space. It seemed the only lived-in spot in the house. Several bar stools were pulled up to its tiled surface and papers and books were stacked at one end. She moved them cautiously with one finger. ''Brochures about tourist traps,'' she remarked with little interest. ''A notice about garbage pick-up and recycling instructions.'' She pulled a section of the *Post* off the top of a stack of books.

''Bingo.'' She nodded toward the pile. ''Another dead boutonniere. On top of a stack of library books. Listen to the titles—*Psychology of the Criminal Mind; Women and Violence; Deviant Behavior and Manifestations of Anger*.'' She looked up at T.S. ''Sounds like he had someone definite in mind.'' She moved down the counter. ''Here's a cup of coffee.'' She sniffed at it. ''Not old. He must have brought it here with him.''

T.S. opened the refrigerator. Inside was a loaf of bread, a large, unopened package of sliced bologna, a jar of mustard and a new bottle of Pepsi. He was reminded of lunches when he was a little boy. It saddened him deeply. ''I guess he was planning to stay for a while,'' he said.

''Food?''

''Yes. Bologna and bread.''

Auntie Lil sighed. ''He hadn't time to think of anything else. Hello, what's this?'' She was peering down at a memo pad. ''Looks like he stole his memo paper from Sterling & Sterling.''

T.S. peered over her shoulder. ''We all do. I even have a few pads at home myself.''

"Look what's written on it." She stepped aside and he bent over to see the note better.

"R.I.P." was written across the top of the page in Sinclair's fussy, spidery handwriting. The letters were heavily underlined.

"Rest in peace?" T.S. wondered aloud. He reread the pad. "That's certainly morbid. It's his handwriting, though." He sighed, then stopped and looked up at Auntie Lil.

"Ralph I. Peabody," they said together.

T.S. was elated. He was in the game, no longer one step behind.

"I think it's time to pay him a visit," Auntie Lil added quietly.

CHAPTER NINE

1 They searched the upstairs sleeping loft carefully but nothing more of interest was found. By the time they left the house, the sun was low in the afternoon sky and an evening chill enveloped them. Auntie Lil shivered in her cardigan sweater, reminding T.S. of her age. He helped her into the front seat of the car and ordered her to stay put while he checked to make sure they had left no signs of entry. This time she obeyed.

They drove quickly away from the lakeside resort community, passing no other cars on the road. They reached the main highway and T.S. pulled into the first rest stop they reached. Afraid to call the police directly for fear he would be taped, he dialed the operator and explained that he had passed a house while birdwatching, seen an open door and entered to find a man shot to death. He doubted anyone ever really birdwatched, but for a cover story it would have to do. He did not give his name or any other details, other than the address, and hung up before the operator could protest that it wasn't her job to report murders. Let them do whatever they wanted. Nothing would bring Stanley Sinclair back.

He drove slowly back to Manhattan, being careful to observe the speed limit. He did not want to be stopped for any reason. There must be nothing to connect them to the carnage they had left behind.

If he had any qualms about leaving the scene of a crime, they vanished quickly once Auntie Lil outlined what she saw as their next step.

"Do you agree that embezzling or insider trading is not

behind this, dear?'' she asked him after nearly a half hour of brooding silence.

''I think so. Stanley Sinclair monitored the firm and partners' accounts, but he didn't really have access to any of the in-house systems that could manipulate funds. He would have had to have accomplices in several areas and that's unlikely. Besides, I don't think he was very smart but, like his wife, I do believe he was honest.''

''That's it. Just your feeling?''

''Yes. And the fact that the three people killed so far have no real connection to each other, at least none that I know of. Cheswick was on the investment side at Sterling & Sterling. Boswell was on the banking side of things. And Sinclair was essentially administrative. They couldn't have been helping each other, they operated in far too different spheres. I can't figure out what the connection between them could be.''

''That's what bothers me, too,'' Auntie Lil admitted. She gazed out the windows at the mountains as they passed by. They loomed large and forbidding in the early evening darkness. ''Do you want to hear what I think?'' she asked.

''Do I have any choice?'' he wondered out loud, but smiled when he spoke. He felt a great need to smile and erase some of the sadness they had left behind them.

''Perhaps it is only because I'm an old woman,'' Auntie Lil began, ''but it seems to me that the truth lies in the past. It's the only time everyone's paths crossed. Besides, there's such passion in these deaths. Someone is hurting badly and not letting go.''

''And that's why you want to talk to Ralph Peabody?''

''We have to,'' she said simply. ''Who else is there?''

''Abromowitz would tell you that Sinclair killed the others and was referring to their deaths when he scrawled 'R.I.P.' ''

''Then killed himself with John Boswell's gun?''

''Yes.''

''First unzipping his pants so he could relieve himself more easily upon death?'' she asked brightly. T.S. longed to put her up against the lieutenant in a sarcasm contest.

"That does seem unlikely," he conceded. But he could recall no personnel incidents involving the three dead men. "Are you saying they had somebody fired or disciplined and now this person is out for revenge?"

"No, not that simple." She leaned her head back on the seat and sighed. "I'm afraid sex is involved somehow and sex is never simple."

"Why would you think that?" he asked. He hated it when Auntie Lil talked about sex. Far from being embarrassed, she actually talked *louder* about sex, he suspected, just to prove that the topic didn't faze her in the least.

"Think, Theodore," she said. "Every man with his zipper pulled down?" She crossed her arms and shook her head disapprovingly. "Now that's just nasty."

2   T.S. arrived at the office early the next morning, despite a restless night plagued by ominous dreams and images of Sinclair's dead body. In his dreams, a Spanish dancer named Magritte whirled about, offering tables of dead men large glasses of frosty margaritas, while Sinclair's wife, Muriel, cried in a corner and Auntie Lil hovered about taking photographs. When he finally awoke, T.S. felt exactly as if he had a horrible hangover. His head was pounding and his stomach fluttered ominously.

Even worse, no one in the department mentioned his absence or even seemed to have noticed that he had been missing the day before. He couldn't decide if he was grateful or if his feelings were hurt. He had not seen any mention of Stanley Sinclair in the newspapers and no messages from Edgar Hale awaited him. The word had obviously not yet filtered in from Pennsylvania.

He had hardly removed his hat when Sheila charged into his office, flopping into his visitor's chair unceremoniously without bothering to take off her coat. T.S. stared at her but she took no notice of his scrutiny. After prying frantically at the plastic top on her coffee cup, she sipped at the steaming liquid in a desperate manner before leaning back with a sigh.

She ran a hand through her tousled hair. "It was Xanax," she announced.

"I beg your pardon?"

"Xanax." Sheila repeated patiently. "John Boswell was drugged by Xanax before he drowned."

"What in the world is Xanax?"

She shrugged. "A couple of our employees could give you a more colorful description, but as I understand it, it's a relatively new anti-depressant commonly given to people in pill form. Induces a sense of euphoria."

"He jumped off his boat in a fit of happiness?" T.S. could be willfully obstinate in misunderstanding people when the mood struck.

"Of course not. It can also introduce artificial psychosis. But that's not the point." She spoke in a superior manner. Pharmaceutical knowledge was one of the few areas where she had it over T.S. "If it was given to him in combination with enough alcohol, it would do a very good job of knocking him out. Like shooting a horse, in fact. Boom!" She slapped her hands together and he jumped. "He'd go right over."

"And then someone could just toss him overboard?"

"That's what it looks like to me. Also to six million readers of the daily papers." She tossed a final edition of the *Post* on his desk.

John Boswell's murder still occupied the front page. "*Wall Street Whiz Drugged and Dumped*," ran the headline. "*Autopsy Reveals Shocker*." He pushed the paper back without comment.

"Why Xanax?" he wondered out loud. "Was he taking it for something?"

"No," she answered at once. "He had slightly high blood pressure and took medicine for that. But that was about it. I'm sure he wasn't taking Xanax. I looked through his file to make sure." She stared at T.S. expectantly.

"You were working with John Boswell on his medical coverage?"

"Well, of course," she said somewhat uneasily. "Partners are worse than clerks when it comes to trying to get every penny back from the insurance company." She shifted under his scrutiny and sipped at her coffee. "Why are you staring at me?" she asked in an accusatory tone. "I work with everyone here at one time or another."

He shook his head, hoping to clear his thoughts. He was surprised at her defensive reaction. "Nothing. I was just wondering about the Xanax. There must be a hundred more common drugs that could give the same effect."

The question didn't puzzle Sheila for long. She unfolded her long frame from the chair, struggling out of her coat on her way to the door. "Beats me. Maybe someone wanted to be on the cutting edge of innovative poisoning."

"Sheila," he called out before she could disappear. "Could you find out where Ralph Peabody is these days? Someone wants to know."

She paused before answering, "I'll check the files, but I think he's in a nursing home somewhere. He's not in too good shape. You need it soon?"

"As soon as you can get it," he replied.

"Doesn't everybody?" Her voice trailed off and she was gone, leaving the faint scent of lemons behind.

T.S. called Edgar Hale shortly after 9:00 but the Managing Partner had not yet arrived. Despising his deception, he asked Mrs. Quincy, "Did Stanley Sinclair show up yet?"

"No, he hasn't," she said quickly, happy to pass along information to any employee evidencing an interest. "But Mr. Hale says he and the accountants worked through the night. So far, the books are immaculate. The records are clean. It doesn't look like Mr. Sinclair took a cent."

"Curious," was all T.S. could manage to reply, and it was an effort at that.

"I just can't figure it out," Mrs. Quincy was saying. "Why would he just disappear like that? Where is he?"

He had no wish to enlighten anyone early. "Perhaps he's afraid a maniac is on the loose?" he suggested.

"That's nonsense," Mrs. Quincy said firmly. "Who would bother to kill Mr. Sinclair? He's not even a partner." She then pulled one of her abrupt and overly confident changes of subject. "I must speak to you about Anne Marie. She's supposed to be helping me out, not hindering things. She's most unreliable. If I didn't know better, I'd say she was enjoying playing the tragic figure. Coming in late, leaving early, making mistakes, carrying on in the bathroom. Being rude to her co-workers. I simply cannot tolerate such unprofessionalism."

T.S. sighed. So, the war between the two women was heating up. "She's lost the man she worked for most of her life," he tried to explain patiently. "You should try and be a bit more patient. It might help smooth things over."

The silence on the other end of the line was eloquent and he was finally compelled to defend himself. "Besides, I'm not the Personnel Manager any longer. If you really want to complain, speak to Miss Fullbright." Women. That was just what he needed. A memo war between Mrs. Quincy and Anne Marie. Miss Fullbright would probably have Anne Marie brought kicking and screaming up to the trauma team room for grief analysis or some such nonsense.

He sighed and rang off, then went to check the employee attendance reports. News was bad. Apparently, Anne Marie was not the only one finding it difficult to cope, and not everyone subscribed to Mrs. Quincy's theory that only partners were being bumped off. Absenteeism was nearly at the sixty-percent rate.

It would likely get worse. The news about Stanley Sinclair hit Sterling & Sterling around 11:00 A.M., just before Sheila came back into his office with a current address for Ralph Peabody.

"He's in a nursing home near Garden City, just off the expressway," she said quietly, handing him a piece of paper with the address written on it.

He looked up at her. "Thanks. What's wrong?"

She stared at a point over his head. "They found Mr. Sinclair last night. He either killed himself or was shot. I put a call through to . . . to Brian for details."

He was a bad liar and opted not to feign any surprise. She didn't seem to notice. "How did you find out?" he asked.

"On the radio. It was the weirdest thing." She shook her head. "I was up in the cafeteria getting coffee. You know how they play that music over the loudspeaker all the time?" He nodded. "Every once in a while some guy with an obnoxiously deep voice interrupts and gives you all the news in about thirty seconds."

"What did he say?"

"It was one of those moments when everyone in the cafeteria decided to take a deep breath at once and, for a couple of seconds, all conversation stopped. We all heard it at the same time. The news guy distinctly said that the state police in Pennsylvania had identified Stanley B. Sinclair as the male found slain the night before in a resort home. An anonymous tip led police to the scene."

"Did they mention Sterling & Sterling?"

"No, they hadn't made the connection yet."

"Do the New York police know yet?" T.S. asked.

"I'm sure they do by now. They're going to be pretty angry that they weren't told right away." She shrugged. "I guess the media will make the connection with us by this afternoon."

He was sure she was right. But he couldn't afford to wait any longer. He took his coat and the address she'd given him, made a quick call to Auntie Lil and ducked out the door without being noticed—although he did have to hide in the Xerox room for a few tense seconds when he heard Miss Fullbright approaching, chatting earnestly with a bearded man who evidently headed up the employee trauma team.

T.S. was in no mood for a discussion about trauma.

3 "Xanax," Auntie Lil said. Her voice wavered between wonder and scorn. "They think up a new drug every day. I can't say it's such a wonderful thing, Theodore." They were heading out of the city toward Long Island and traffic was light. She looked out the window at the gray day. It was drizzling again.

T.S. shrugged. "To some people, these drugs can change

their lives. It's supposed to be quite effective in combating depression.''

"The *modus operandi* seems a little confused," she said, relishing the official-sounding phrase. "An old knife, a new drug. And a stolen gun." She had obviously been reading her detective magazines again.

"We don't know that yet. It might not be Boswell's gun."

"Of course it's his gun. This murderer is not stupid. It's the perfect weapon. The police can trace it back to the second murder and no further."

"But why a gun? Why not a knife?" He was unwilling to give the killer credit.

"Simple," Auntie Lil said. "The killer knew Stanley Sinclair suspected he was being followed. The element of surprise was gone. I would think that a knife would be more difficult to use effectively, shall we say, when the victim is on his toes. Particularly if the murderer is physically inferior to the victim."

T.S. didn't know a whole lot of people physically inferior to Stanley Sinclair; an anorexic dwarf perhaps. Just about every other man had more meat on his bones. He realized the implication. "You still believe the killer is a woman?"

"Yes," she said confidently. "I do."

"How can you be so sure?"

"The zippers," she said.

"The zippers again? That could mean anything."

"Maybe to you it could. To me, it seems to mean one thing." She folded her arms and waited for his curiosity to get the best of him.

"What?" He swerved to avoid a bus that suddenly pulled in his path and almost collided with a delivery truck merging into the center lane. Auntie Lil didn't flinch.

"It means you should have kept your pants zipped up, Theodore," she told him briskly. "That's exactly what it means."

4   Nursing homes had changed since T.S. visited his grandfather in 1961. Based on this memory, T.S. thought of rest homes as long white clapboard buildings with spacious porches, rocking chairs and shade trees surrounding all. But the massive brick skyscraper looming over the Long Island Expressway did nothing for his utopian vision. It more closely resembled a prison or hospital than a home, and this impression was hard to shake. He and Auntie Lil entered through silent sliding doors to find an empty and sterile reception area. Groups of muted orange chairs clustered around glass coffee tables gave the room a distinct hospital waiting room air. The receptionist sat inside a Plexiglas cage and directed them to the fourteenth floor with little more than a shrug.

They waited in front of the elevators silently, T.S. intimidated by the hushed atmosphere and Auntie Lil rendered anxious by the warehousing of adults her age.

The elevator was as smooth and white as an egg. T.S. expected the theme from *2001* to begin at any minute, but not even elevator Muzak penetrated the silence.

"At least it's clean," he tried in an attempt at conversation.

Auntie Lil looked around her grimly. "This place is absolutely horrifying, Theodore. It reminds me of the inside of a crematorium."

"Now, now. Have you ever been in a crematorium?" he asked.

The doors opened on the fourteenth floor. "Yes, I have." She led the way to the nurses' station. He didn't have the energy to ask for details.

The nurse was expecting them. She was enormously fat and very businesslike. She had a large red whistle looped around her neck and T.S. found himself wondering why. Perhaps she whistled for help getting back on her feet whenever she slipped and fell.

"Are you a relative?" she asked, staring at Auntie Lil over large round glasses.

Auntie Lil summoned cheer into her voice. "No, just old friends, dear. *Very good* old friends."

The nurse gave her a careful once-over and Auntie Lil

straightened as if she were afraid they might seize her and keep her should she fail to pass physical muster.

"I'm an old colleague of his," T.S. explained, placing a reassuring hand on Auntie Lil's shoulder.

The nurse made a check mark on her clipboard. "Well, he didn't recognize either of your names, but that isn't surprising. He's having trouble recognizing his own." She began to waddle down a long white corridor and they fell in behind her, unable to keep from staring at her curious rolling gait.

"He doesn't recognize anyone these days," the nurse added. "I'm afraid he's grown a bit senile and never having visitors doesn't help. You two are the first people to ask for him in three months."

"What about his family?" Auntie Lil asked, appalled.

"There's a daughter that lives in the city," the nurse replied. "In Mr. Peabody's old home, if I'm not mistaken. But we don't see much of her." She gave a derisive snort and waved them into a large sunroom. It was curiously empty of furniture, deliberately so to make room for wheelchairs. A group of women were gathered in front of a blaring television set at one end of the room, their heads bobbing as they watched intently or spoke to each other. T.S. thought of a mental hospital immediately because they were all dressed so closely alike, nearly every woman wearing a navy blue cardigan wrapped tightly over a flowered dress.

A tiny figure sat hunched in a wheelchair at the other end of the room. T.S. hadn't realized how much hope he had piled on the shoulders of Mr. Ralph I. Peabody until it evaporated at the recognition that the lonely figure was his man. He remembered Ralph Peabody as a proud man with careful posture, his hair always impeccably groomed and his dress immaculate. But Ralph Peabody today was a gnarled, gaunt old man, huddled in a wheelchair, who stared out the window at nothing but fog.

"You have some visitors," the nurse shouted in the old man's ear. She turned abruptly, rubber soles squeaking on the linoleum floor, and walked briskly to the television to turn the volume down before sailing regally out the door.

T.S. and Auntie Lil stared at Ralph Peabody, uncertain of how to proceed. The old man appeared not to notice their presence. Behind them, the old ladies laughed uproariously at a commercial involving dancing dogs.

"Pull us up some chairs, Theodore," Auntie Lil commanded. She bent over the feeble figure and took one of his hands in her own.

"Hello, Mr. Peabody. I am Lillian Hubbert, Theodore Hubbert's aunt. Do you remember Theodore Hubbert?" She spoke in a normal but firm tone of voice. The old man appeared to be listening. Suspicious eyes peered out at her from a mass of wrinkles and scaly skin. His beard lay in stubble around the folds. It was clear he could not shave himself and that a careless aide had not tried very hard. His eyes had obviously once been blue, but now were milky and curtained.

"No," he said in a voice tinged with phlegm. He coughed fitfully and stared at her, pulling his hand away. "Are you a Jehovah's Witness?"

Auntie Lil sat in the chair provided by T.S. and drew closer to the man's wheelchair. "No, I am Theodore Hubbert's aunt. Do you remember Theodore?"

"He doesn't know me as Theodore," T.S. hissed with some satisfaction.

"Of course," Auntie Lil murmured. She said more loudly. "This is my nephew, T.S. Hubbert. He is the Personnel Manager at Sterling & Sterling."

Ralph Peabody leaned forward slightly and pulled his sweater more tightly around him. "Sterling & Sterling? I worked there once. They've forgotten all about me. Yes, they have."

"I'm sorry," T.S. shouted, following the lead of the nurse.

"You don't have to shout!" the old man yelled back. He lowered his voice to a grumpy growl. "I hear perfectly well." He stared at T.S. "Who the hell are you?"

"I'm T.S. Hubbert. I have your old job at Sterling & Sterling. I took over your job when you retired, remember?"

The old man peered at him. "Nonsense. Some overconfident young twerp took my place."

"That was me," T.S. replied, feeling foolish.

"Are you one of the Sterling boys?"

"Me?" The old man's confusion was contagious. "No. I just work there," T.S. said. "I worked there, I mean. I was Personnel Manager. I retired, too."

The old man appeared not to have heard. He stared back out the window. "Cockleshells," he said.

"Do you ever see any of your old friends from Sterling & Sterling?" Auntie Lil said, trying to draw his attention back to the room.

"That place." He snorted. "They've forgotten me. They forgot me the day I walked out the door." He shook an angry finger at T.S. "You retire and that's it. You may as well never have been there." He glared at Auntie Lil's hat. "Are you sure you're not a Jehovah's Witness?"

"I'm sure, Mr. Peabody." She leaned forward again. "There's been some trouble at Sterling & Sterling." He appeared not to hear. "They've stabbed Robert Cheswick."

"Who?" he asked loudly, swatting at the empty air.

"Someone has killed Robert Cheswick and John Boswell and Stanley Sinclair," she said more loudly.

The old man stared at his hands. "I don't remember them," he said. T.S. knew he was lying.

"Yes, you do," T.S. interrupted. "They were there when you were Personnel Manager."

"I don't know who you're talking about," he said firmly. He looked around him. "Is my daughter here?"

T.S. automatically followed his gaze. "No. No, she's not."

"Thought not. Do you suppose she's died?" The old man laughed. "That would be something. Maybe I'd get my house back." He leaned forward and looked at Auntie Lil. "Are you sure you're not her?"

"No. Of course I'm not." She looked at T.S. and he shrugged.

"Then, who are you?" the old man demanded. "I'm not interested in any Seventh Day Adventists, you know. I may need my blood transfusions."

Auntie Lil sat primly in her chair, hands folded carefully in her lap. She stared at Ralph Peabody very quietly for a moment, then she took a deep breath and looked him right in the eye. "Meet me for margaritas at Magritte's," she said.

Ralph Peabody sat straight up in his chair and a puzzled look passed over his face. "You?" he cried. He pulled his sweater close around him. T.S. thought he might have shivered. "It's you? Why I would never have guessed." He looked closer. "You look so old. Must be your conscience." He leaned back and glared at her. "You should never have done those things, you know."

"I'm sorry for them," Auntie Lil replied. T.S. looked on, mystified.

"It was nasty. Very nasty business. Caused those boys a lot of trouble." Ralph Peabody wagged a finger at Auntie Lil. "I never believed you were telling the truth. They might even have lost their jobs."

"But they didn't," Auntie Lil replied.

"No. They didn't. Thanks to me. I kept it quiet." He grew indignant. "I'm the one that had to cover up and read your filth." He leaned forward again. "That's a very sick mind you have there, missy."

"I know," Auntie Lil said apologetically. "I'm sorry now for what I've done."

"Don't you go thinking everyone will forget," the old man warned. "I've got the proof. I've got the proof. Words alone don't excuse it."

"What proof?" Auntie Lil widened her eyes and injected worry into her voice.

"What proof?" He turned to T.S. and snorted. "What proof, she asks?" He folded his arms and glared at Auntie Lil. "You never thought about that when you sent those letters, did you? All those filthy letters and postcards and such.

Those nasty photos.'' He shook his head. ''Trouble. A whole lot of trouble.''

''I was ill,'' Auntie Lil said to him. ''I didn't know what I was doing.''

He huffed. ''I should hope not. Very improper behavior. You should be ashamed.''

''I am. Deeply. I am deeply ashamed.'' Auntie Lil took his hand in hers again but he pulled it away indignantly.

''Do you know this woman?'' he asked T.S.

''Yes.'' T.S. was unsure of what else to reply. ''I've known her for . . .''

''She is dangerous,'' the old man interrupted. He tapped the side of his head. ''Not well. She may look fine, but she's not well.''

Auntie Lil stood and went to the window. She stared out at the fog, thinking. Then she turned back to the old man. ''I am well now. I want to destroy all traces of my old life. Please give me my letters back. Please give me the photos back.''

Ralph Peabody looked almost fierce in his anger. ''You won't get them back from me, missy. I've got the goods on you. I've kept every one of your filthy accusations and they're safe. Away from the eyes of others. Proof positive that you're as crazy as a bedbug and a hundred times more evil.'' He wheeled his chair around away from them, staring at the other end of the room.

T.S. and Auntie Lil exchanged a glance. T.S. shrugged. ''We didn't mean to tire you,'' he said to the old man. ''Let me take you back to your room.''

The old man made no reply and T.S. slowly wheeled him out of the room. Auntie Lil remained behind, staring out the window.

''Which way?'' T.S. asked. He steered down corridors so relentlessly alike that he could not even remember which direction he'd come from.

The old man waved to the right and T.S. slowly made his way past open doors. Inside nearly every small room, an old man or woman lay on the bed. Some slept under the sheets, obviously infirm. Others lay on top of the spread, staring out the door at nothing. A name tag marked each doorway and T.S. slowly wheeled Ralph Peabody along until they came to his room.

"I don't want to go back to bed," the old man declared suddenly.

"No, of course not. Where would you like to sit? By the window?"

Ralph Peabody did not reply and T.S. wheeled him over to a small curtained set of double windows. The old man stared down at the highway far below. Cars whizzed by silently. It was a hell of a view for a bedbound person.

He appeared not to notice as T.S. quietly searched the room. He opened a set of built-in shelves against one wall and bent down to check beneath the bed. He found nothing, not even dust. He checked a small end table with drawers that stood beside the bed, and even looked behind the curtains on the window sill. There were very few personal effects in the room and nothing resembling papers or a file. T.S. was peering into the closet when Ralph Peabody finally spoke up, his voice startling T.S. into bumping his head on the clothes bar.

"Are you sure that woman's not my daughter?" the old man asked.

"Yes. I'm sure." T.S. rubbed his head and moved to stand beside him. "Who do you think she is?"

"Don't play games with me, young man." Ralph Peabody glared up at him. "If she's who she says she is, you better watch out, buster." He shook a finger at T.S. "Just keep your pants on, sonny. Keep your pants zipped and you'll be okay."

T.S. nodded. He was getting used to the advice.

"Cockleshells!" the old man cried again. He turned back to his window view. There was nothing more T.S. could do.

"Take care of yourself," he called from the doorway.

"Margaritas, indeed," Ralph Peabody replied gruffly. "Tell them I'm sick and tired of these damn Jehovah's Witnesses!"

T.S. left the old man muttering by the window and went back to retrieve Auntie Lil. She was waiting quietly in her chair, watching the backs of the little old ladies clustered around the television set. He sat down and took her hand, patting it gently. It seemed very frail and dry.

"He doesn't have all his wits," T.S. said.

"Perhaps he doesn't want to. But like a lot of old people, he can remember events that happened long ago clearly. It's the recent past he has trouble with."

"He seemed to think he knew who you were."

"Yes, he did. It's beginning to make some sense. Did you find anything?"

"No. There wasn't much at all. He told me to keep my pants on, though."

"What exactly did he say?" Auntie Lil looked up suddenly.

"He told me if I didn't keep my pants zipped when I was around you, I'd be in trouble."

Auntie Lil stared at T.S.

"It was just a saying, Auntie Lil."

She shook her head. "No. I don't think so."

"But he said he couldn't even remember Cheswick, Boswell and Sinclair."

"Maybe not. Maybe he was protecting them. But he sure knew something later. He has the evidence, he said. Letters. Postcards. Photographs."

"Of what?"

"I don't know. That comes next."

"Where would he keep them?"

"There's only one other place," Auntie Lil said. Her chin was propped on her hand and she frowned as she thought. "The nurse said he has a daughter living in his old home. It has to be in that house."

"You want us to break into a house?" T.S. was incredulous, but not surprised.

"Nonsense, Theodore. I'm not a burglar. I am, however, an excellent liar." She rose and walked briskly to the door, ready to put the nursing home behind her.

The enormous nurse was ensconced behind her desk, a box of cookies open beside her. She was reading the latest issue of the *National Enquirer* and looked guilty at being caught.

"Belongs to one of the orderlies," she explained, pushing the paper away on her desk. "It's quite amusing."

"Young lady," Auntie Lil interrupted somewhat sharply. "I asked Mr. Peabody about a number of cherished items I gave him." She lowered her eyelids and added more softly, "We were once very good friends, you understand. I'm talking about souvenirs of some very special times. Why aren't they in his room?"

The nurse looked bewildered. "Whatever they bring, within reason, they can display," she said.

"He is most upset he does not have them."

"Perhaps he left them at his house. He was already a bit forgetful by the time he arrived." The nurse looked vaguely uncomfortable, as if expecting Auntie Lil to accuse the staff of stealing.

Auntie Lil's manner changed abruptly to one of extreme graciousness. The nurse's relief was obvious.

"But of course," Auntie Lil said. "He must have left them in his home. I'll go by and speak to his daughter. I'm sure she won't mind my bringing them to him."

"Suit yourself," the nurse replied as she reached for the box of cookies.

"Could you save me some time and trouble and give me her address?" Auntie Lil asked sweetly. T.S. stood to one side, staring studiously down the corridor. He found it difficult to look the nurse in the eye.

"I couldn't do that," the nurse explained, her mouth stained dark with chocolate cookies. "It's against our regulations."

"That's silly. I'm not going to burglarize the place. I'm only going to talk to his daughter." Auntie Lil paused and no one spoke in the silence. "I could go and ask him but he drifts in and out so. For a moment there, he thought I was his daughter. It would be so nice to have those souvenirs for him to look at and remember. During those precious few moments when he's lucid.'' She sounded positively enraptured at the thought of a contented and lucid Ralph Peabody. ''It wouldn't be hard to find out somewhere else, but it would save us so much time.''

The nurse shrugged her roly-poly shoulders and gave them a final close look. T.S. took the hint and handed her a ten-dollar bill. She palmed it quickly and stashed it in her enormous bosom. ''Look, only because you're the only ones to take an interest in him. Might do the poor man good.'' She pulled open a file drawer and rummaged around for a few seconds, emerging with a thin brown folder. She flipped this open expertly and copied down a name and address on a piece of paper.

''You didn't get it from me, of course,'' she said in reply to Auntie Lil's thanks.

''No, of course not.'' Auntie Lil tucked the paper away in her sweater pocket, then leaned and clasped the nurse's hammy paws in her own elegant hands. ''You're so very kind. I feel better just knowing that Ralphie is in good hands.''

T.S. mumbled his own thanks and gently dragged his aunt to the elevator. They rode alone down to the pristine lobby.

''Ralphie?'' T.S. asked. ''A bit thick, don't you think?''

''Of course not.'' Auntie Lil sailed through the empty entrance room. ''They think all old people are either sentimental or senile. Why not take advantage of their ignorance?''

He opened the car door for her and she slid in. ''Get me out of here, Theodore,'' she commanded. ''This place gives me the creeps.''

CHAPTER TEN

1 Ralph Peabody's former home was a narrow, white clapboard house on a quiet tree-lined street. The yard, while small, was lushly green and the lawn was carefully trimmed. Bushes grew in rigid rows and rimmed the property precisely, proclaiming to all that intruders were not welcome. The lawn was steep and T.S. had to help Auntie Lil up the meticulously bricked stairs. They rang the bell and heard chimes reverberating inside. They could hear someone running lightly down a staircase.

The heavy wooden door practically exploded open and a young boy appeared in front of them, standing warily behind the screen door. He was wearing a set of headphones and held a half-eaten banana in one hand. He stared at T.S. and Auntie Lil without comment.

"Hello, young man," Auntie Lil said. "Is your mother home?"

"She's shopping," he volunteered willingly, his mouth full of banana. "I'm supposed to be doing my homework."

"With your headphones on? Can you concentrate?" Auntie Lil had a tendency to be sidetracked by situations where she felt her interference was needed.

The child shrugged. "Who are you?" he asked abruptly.

"We're friends of your grandfather's," T.S. explained.

"He's not here anymore. He lives in a home." The child was blissfully unconcerned about his grandfather's whereabouts.

"Yes, we know. We've just come from visiting him."

Auntie Lil erased all traces of the sweet tone she usually adopted when speaking to children.

"You went to see Grandpa?" he asked.

"Yes, he seems in good health," Auntie Lil volunteered.

"He's confused," the young man said, settling the subject in his own mind.

"Yes, well, that's why we're here. Your grandfather said he had forgotten to bring some special items of his to the nursing home with him. He asked us to stop by and see if we could find them."

The boy stared curiously at Auntie Lil as she spoke. "Do you always wear hats like that?" he asked.

She touched the brim and pushed a drooping flower out of her face. "This is my visiting hat. Your grandfather liked it quite a lot."

"It looks like the hat the horse wore when Mom took me for a carriage ride last Christmas. We went around Central Park and everything."

Auntie Lil looked discomfited. T.S. decided to take charge. "Your grandfather seems very anxious about his things. Would it be all right if we just took a look in his room to see if they're there?"

The boy chewed the last of his banana thoughtfully. "Mom turned it into a sewing room."

"Are his things in the attic?" T.S. suggested.

"He doesn't have very many things. And we don't have no attic." He laughed heartily, as if this were a great joke.

"We don't have *an* attic. Could we take a look around? Under your supervision, of course," Auntie Lil offered.

"Under my supervision?" The child considered this. "I guess I could do that." He opened the door and they walked into an overstuffed home filled with rugs, too much furniture and a profusion of framed oil paintings of the kind sold in a suite at the Holiday Inn twice a year. T.S. noticed that the couches and chairs were covered in plastic. Ralph Peabody's style had not been inherited by his daughter.

"It's upstairs," the young boy said, and they followed him obediently up the narrow stairway. T.S. tagged along behind

Auntie Lil, ready to give a push if needed. But she stepped lightly forward, craning her head from side to side as she absorbed the house about her.

The boy led them to a small room next to the bathroom. Only one tiny window admitted light. If Ralph Peabody had been banished here, he probably was better off at the nursing home. A sewing machine and table took up most of the space, though a twin bed was pushed against one wall and a low set of shelves held some paperback books. "Not much to look at," the child said. "Unless you like patterns and junk like that." He kicked a cardboard box full of carefully preserved sewing patterns with his foot and pushed a heap of material to one side of the table. "Mom is teaching Mary Beth how to sew. I think it's dumb, myself."

Auntie Lil picked up a pattern, looked at it critically, and tossed it back in the box. "I quite agree, young man," she said cheerfully. She began lifting up fabric and peering beneath it. T.S. moved to the closet and opened the door, sending a faint smell of mothballs wafting through the room.

"Grandpa will probably die soon," the child said suddenly.

"Why do you say that?" Auntie Lil opened the top drawer of a small wooden dresser and rummaged around inside.

"Mom says so," he replied confidently.

"That's too bad, dear." She started in on the second drawer and found nothing more than fabric scraps.

"This house is really his. It won't belong to us until he dies."

"That's nice," Auntie Lil said absently. T.S. had found nothing but a collection of old boots and shoes and some moth-eaten winter coats in the closet. He knelt on the floor and peeked under the bed.

The young man grew weary of his supervisory role. "Could I go finish putting the wheels on my truck?" he asked. "I've nearly finished and if Mom comes home, she'll be mad I'm not doing my homework."

"By all means," T.S. agreed heartily. The thought of the boy's mother coming home gave his stomach a slight jump.

Ralph Peabody had been grouchy enough. Suppose his daughter had inherited his temperament?

"This is easier than I expected," T.S. said, once they were alone.

"I know," Auntie Lil interrupted. "That's the advantage of being so old. Everyone trusts you. But just the same I'd like to get the hell out of here before his mother comes home, wouldn't you?"

"Exactly." There was plenty of dust and a pair of old socks beneath the bed. He was idly looking behind a framed portrait of Jesus when Auntie Lil uttered a triumphant hoot. He turned to find her kneeling in front of the low bookshelves. A stack of paperback books surrounded her, but she held a heavy cardboard box file in her hands.

"I've found it," she said. "This has to be it."

"Where was it?"

"He'd pushed it flat against the wall, behind the books." She flicked dust off the cover fastidiously. "Do you suppose anyone in this house reads books?"

"I doubt it." He knelt beside her. "Are you sure that's it?"

"Of course not." She pried the rusty clasp open with her thumb and lifted the lid up. It was attached to the box by a heavily taped spine that had been torn away at the top. "This is pretty old."

He looked carefully at it. "It looks familiar," he admitted. "I think Archives has some old file boxes like that."

She ran her finger down the first paper. "Who is Francine Claremont?"

"I have no idea. Why?"

"She stole $200 from the United Way fund box in 1956."

He grabbed the file from her. "What is this?" He paged quickly through the papers and blinked.

"What do you think, Theodore?"

"I think the old buzzard went through the personnel files before he left and pulled out every embarrassing or incriminating memo he could find. Why, most of these people aren't

even partners! They're clerks or messengers. Why would he
do that?''

"An attack of conscience," Auntie Lil suggested. "Perhaps he was tired of being Big Brother."

"Perhaps." He snapped the lid shut. "This is it. Let's get
out of here."

She reached and tried to tug it back. "Let me just take a
quick peek right now."

"Absolutely not." He held it out of her reach. "Let's get
out of here immediately."

They quickly straightened the books back on the shelves
and tried to leave the room exactly as they had found it. With
the goods in hand, both of them had been seized by an impulse to flee as quickly as they could move. They scurried
down the stairs and over the porch, hopping quickly down
the brick steps. T.S. forgot to open the car door for Auntie
Lil and simply slipped behind the wheel in a mild panic. He
stuffed the dusty file under the front seat. Auntie Lil climbed
in slowly and gave him the evil eye.

"In a hurry?" she asked.

"To get out of here," T.S. muttered back. He pulled out
of the driveway with a screech and took several unnecessary
turns simply to be away from the house. Then he made his
way back to the main street.

"You're making me nervous, Theodore," Auntie Lil com-
plained.

"I'm making *you* nervous?" He turned to look at her and
narrowly missed colliding with a bus. "You want to know
what makes me nervous? The way you can lie so easily and
be absolutely convincing. Now *that* makes me nervous."

2   "I've found it," he said simply, holding a batch of papers of various sizes and colors in his hand. He sat on the
floor in the middle of Auntie Lil's living room, while she sat
on a small footstool nearby. They were surrounded by loose
papers and memos, stacked in piles on the sofa and on nearby
chairs and tables.

"What is it?" Auntie Lil produced the hated pair of eyeglasses and put them briskly on without a thought to her vanity. She reached out a hand. "Let me see."

"Not so fast." He held up a hand and smiled. "I'm the one who found it. I'll read you *selected* portions."

"For heaven's sakes, Theodore." She blew a strong gust of breath out of her mouth and clutched her hands together. "You can really be quite annoying."

"That's all right. You were right about Ralph Peabody, so I get to be annoying."

He looked at the cover sheet and read aloud: *"Memo to the Partners. From Ralph I. Peabody, Personnel Manager. Date: February 27, 1959. Re: Patricia Ann Kelly. Gentlemen: After a thorough investigation and discussion with all parties involved, I have come to the conclusion that there is no basis for Miss Kelly's continued allegations. In fact, I believe that her actions and the recent flurry of disturbed letters and correspondence clearly indicate that the young lady in question is suffering from a severe case of mental illness. I would suggest that we extend her health coverage for an indefinite period of time in an attempt to aid in the treatment of her troubles, but I do not recommend that action be taken against any of the other parties involved. There is no proof of poor judgment or misbehavior on anyone's part, other than Miss Kelly's word, and that word clearly is cast in doubt by the strange and irrational manner she has adopted.—R.I.P."*

"What are all those papers attached?" Auntie Lil demanded.

"It's fascinating," T.S. said, thumbing through them. "It's just as Mr. Peabody said. He has the proof carefully saved."

Auntie Lil slapped her hand down on the surface of a small side table. "Damn it, Theodore. Stop teasing me. Let me see those papers."

"We'll look at them together." He removed the chaotic piles of papers from the coffee table and sat on the couch. Auntie Lil joined him and they unclipped the many documents and envelopes from Patricia Kelly's file and spread all of the items out in front of them.

It was a varied mixture of letters, postcards and photographs addressed to different partners. The earliest were dated 1958, but some of the newer letters and cards were dated as late as 1972.

"My god," Auntie Lil breathed. "This is so sad."

T.S. could do nothing but agree. The collection represented years of physical and mental deterioration. The earliest letters were addressed to Robert Cheswick. Several months later, John Boswell, Edgar Hale and Stanley Sinclair were added to the mailing list. Still later, she had included Ralph I. Peabody, Frederick Dorfen and three or four other partners as well. All of the letters held a common theme, expressed in various sentiments but quite clear in their thrust.

"Listen to this," Auntie Lil said sadly. She held up a small blue notecard. The handwriting was neat, precise and flowery. The kind T.S. instantly recognized as Catholic school script.

"Dear Robert," Auntie Lil read. *"There is room in my bed here at the hospital for at least nine more. Even the sheets are hot. Won't you come meet me for a margarita at Magritte's? I long to see my tiger again. You could always bring your friends. They seem like so much fun. I looked around the other day and found that I was gone. What do you think of that? Love always from your sensuous Patty."*

They looked at each other in silence. The words were bad enough on paper, but read aloud they were sad and pathetic.

"Bingo on the margaritas and Magritte's," Auntie Lil said.

"That's pretty tame stuff compared to this." T.S. stared down at a piece of notebook paper. The woman's careful script had deteriorated into an angry scrawl. The letter was peppered with various sexual suggestions, and a crude drawing of a woman being attended to by a sexually aroused man dominated the page.

"Who is that addressed to?" Auntie Lil demanded. "How very ghastly."

T.S. peered at the envelope attached and sighed. "This one seems to have been sent to Edgar Hale. But look." He held up a batch of similar pages stapled together. "She's gone and sent carbons to at least five others."

"Look at this." Auntie Lil held out a reproduction of an early French pornographic postcard. A dark and bored-looking woman with a drooping body and heavy face lay on a couch, dressed only in a pair of beaded panties. She was pinching the nipple of each breast artfully between her fingers and smiling at the camera. The postcard was addressed to John Boswell and the sender had written in a flowery hand: *"Come and get it. Soup's on. Hot and Spicy. Sweet and Sour. Come and get it like you like it, hour after hour. Meet me for a margarita at Magritte's?"* This time there was no signature. Auntie Lil paged through the pile and pulled out several similar postcards.

"Oh my," T.S. said. "Look at this." He held out a photograph nearly identical in pose to the French postcard. It showed a slightly heavyset woman lounging on a modern sofa, dressed only in what looked like the bottom of a leopard-skin bikini. She was garishly made-up in heavy mascara and lipstick, and her hair had been teased high in the fashion of the early 1960's. She wore a pair of high heels and her legs were thrown uncaringly over one arm of the couch. She, too, was pinching her nipples in the stylized fashion of the earlier photograph. She smiled gaily at the camera but her eyes reflected a vacant, almost unseeing stare. The picture was framed oddly, as if someone had set the shutter on automatic timer without bothering to check the frame.

Auntie Lil placed both hands over her lips and made a clicking sound with her tongue against her teeth. "Oh, Theodore. The poor woman."

T.S. tossed the photograph back on the pile. "The poor woman? She may be going around killing people." He held up a carbon of a neatly typed list. "Oh. My. God." He pronounced each word slowly and distinctly. "Under any other circumstances, I might have enjoyed this list." He stared down at the paper.

"A list? With names? They may be in danger."

He showed her the list and they scanned it together. Ten names appeared. The first three were Robert Cheswick, John Boswell and Stanley Sinclair. They were followed by Edgar

Hale, Frederick Dorfen, Ralph Peabody and four more names.

"Are all of these men partners?" Auntie Lil asked.

"No. Just Cheswick, Boswell, Hale and Dorfen." He looked the list over carefully. "Sinclair and Peabody you know about. Two others retired early. Very early." He stared at Auntie Lil. "The other two left Sterling to work for other companies."

"What's the date on that list?" She peered at the smudged paper.

"It doesn't say."

"What *does* it say?" She leaned over to read the hand-written notes that appeared next to each neatly typed name. "Oh, my." She sat back and looked the other way.

T.S. looked down at it again. "Performance Evaluations" was typed neatly at the top. This was followed by the list of names. Each name, in turn, led to a line or two of hand-written comments. He read the first few entries:

> *"1. Robert Cheswick—Average. They say the first is al-
>   ways the best—unless the first doesn't know what to
>   do with it. Better at bonds than bed, Bobby?*
>
>   *2. John Boswell—Needs Improvement. If only he were as
>   good as he thought he was. With all that practice,
>   you'd think he would have learned.*
>
>   *3. Stanley Sinclair—Needs Improvement. You really
>   wanted mama, didn't you, little boy? But I guess if
>   you weren't so little, you wouldn't be such a boy.*
>
>   *4. Edgar Hale—Satisfactory. And you thought you were
>   the only one? You weren't even the best, just the one
>   who wanted it the most.*
>
>   *5. Frederick Dorfen—Superior. They say an older man
>   knows just what he's doing. I say that practice must
>   make perfect. How about it? Ready, Freddy?"*

"I don't think I can read any further," T.S. said.

"To your great credit. But what's it say about Ralph Peabody?"

T.S. scanned the list and steeled himself to read the next entry:

> *"6. Ralph I. Peabody—The Best. Because when you think about it, he screwed me to the wall without even coming near me."*

Auntie Lil stared at the wall without comment. T.S. dropped the list back onto the table.

Auntie Lil coughed politely and he raised his head to look at her. "Two things come to mind, Theodore," she said briskly.

"What two things?"

"Number one—I'm glad to see you're not on that list. Number two, that's a carbon. Where is the original?"

They searched the pile but found no other copies of the list.

"I guess this is it," he said, holding it carefully between two fingers as if it might bite or, at best, smell bad.

"That's it, all right," Auntie Lil replied grimly. "Right down the line. And if she was still using carbon, it was probably written no later than the early seventies, wouldn't you say?"

He stared at the collection of obscene correspondence. "That's right. It would have been before 1973 or surely I would have seen these before. I don't know how Peabody kept them from me." He touched the pile of correspondence with his hand. "This is so pathetic. It makes me ashamed. Of what, I'm not sure."

"Yes, poor woman." Auntie Lil sighed again. "And yet, Theodore, I can't help wondering . . ."

Her voice trailed off and he was forced to prompt her. "Wondering what?" he asked.

She placed a hand on the pile of letters and patted them gently. "How much of what she says is true."

CHAPTER ELEVEN

1 Patricia Kelly's file left no doubt in even Auntie Lil's mind that it was time to turn the matter over to Lieutenant Abromowitz. After much discussion, they decided that T.S. should reveal the killer to him and Edgar Hale at the same time, thus improving his own reputation in one fell swoop. It seemed more practical than Auntie Lil's idea to demand an audience with the chief of police.

T.S. felt it was a lucky coincidence that, as soon as he arrived at work on Thursday morning, Sheila informed him both men were waiting for him in the same conference room where Cheswick's murder weapon had been originally displayed. He gave Sheila instructions to locate Patricia Kelly's old medical file and, if possible, her present whereabouts. Sheila stared after him with a disturbed look on her face as he hurried to meet the men.

Edgar Hale had shriveled up even more since T.S. had last seen him. With Stanley Sinclair dead, he was left without a scapegoat and this seemed to have taken the wind out of his sails. He sat quietly, a remarkable event, with his hands clasped and his mouth drawn in a tight, unsmiling line. His tie did not even remotely match his suit and his wrinkled shirt was further evidence of his despair.

"I heard you wanted to see me," T.S. said without preamble. No sense wasting polite chitchat on these two. Abromowitz stood in a far corner of the room, as if banished there due to his own shameful actions.

"We're ruined," Hale said. "It wasn't Sinclair. The police say he could not have killed himself. The angle and distance are all wrong. He was murdered by Preston Freeman."

"I beg your pardon?" T.S. was shocked. Preston Freeman? He wouldn't leave his work long enough to murder somebody.

The old man sighed. "Sterling & Sterling is ruined. The police have Preston Freeman in custody. They say he's the one."

"That's absurd," T.S. said, blinking at the idea of the junior partner committing violence of any sort. "All he ever thinks about is mergers. Murder would be the last thing on his mind." T.S. thought back to the meeting when John Boswell's death had been announced so spectacularly by Mrs. Quincy. It was true Freeman had remained calm at the news—but was he ever ruffled about anything?

"The gun that killed Sinclair was definitely John Boswell's. So it has to be someone close to both of them," Edgar Hale interrupted. "And they have concrete evidence that it was Preston Freeman."

"Not exactly," Abromowitz corrected in a rather smug tone. "But we're close. I can't divulge the details, but suffice to say that my original hunch was right."

"Forget hunches," T.S. said, receiving a glare in return. "What's the evidence? I'm talking about fingerprints, hair samples, witnesses. Not hunches. You can't arrest people without evidence."

"We've pieced together an airtight theory." The lieutenant folded his arms in front of his large stomach and smiled at T.S:

"A theory? Theories aren't airtight. Let me guess—it's the IRS."

The lieutenant stared at him. "For your information, we've uncovered letters in John Boswell's files from clients complaining that Cheswick had been mishandling accounts. We believe he hoped to cover his mistakes by generating enough money through inside trading to replace the lost funds before anyone noticed. Cheswick enlisted Preston Freeman's aid in obtaining illegal takeover and merger information, but came to regret his actions. He planned to confess all, but Preston Freeman, worried about his own career, tried to stop him. Cheswick refused and was killed. Cheswick's personal files are missing. We believe Freeman stole them at the time of the murder because they might have contained evidence of his and Cheswick's wrongdoing. But Cheswick had already confessed to Boswell, and Freeman killed him to silence him as well. I'm confident we'll discover evidence during our searches of Freeman's homes."

"Oh, come on," T.S. said. "There's evidence Cheswick was preoccupied and making some mistakes, but that's about it. It's not like he was embezzling."

"Give us time," the lieutenant said confidently. "The evidence will turn up. Preston Freeman is a proud and arrogant bastard. He'd kill to save his own reputation."

Translation: Freeman had not been cooperative with Abromowitz and he was getting his chops busted as a result. "Then why is Stanley Sinclair dead?" T.S. asked.

Edgar Hale sighed and spoke. "We think he discovered what was going on when he checked the partners' personal financial records. That he tried to blackmail Freeman and, when he heard about Boswell, panicked and ran. He was hiding out from Freeman, but bungled it, as usual. Everyone knew he had that summer house, including Freeman."

T.S. stared at the lieutenant's nose, which appeared to be suffering from an exotic skin rash, then glanced at Edgar Hale. The old man looked more tired than anything else. The anger fueling him was now squelched in hopelessness.

"Why would Cheswick go to Preston Freeman for help in the first place?" T.S. demanded. "Freeman is the last person I'd ask to break the law."

"Cheswick was blackmailing Freeman into giving him insider information," Abromowitz answered stiffly.

"Blackmailing him based on what? Oh, wait—don't tell me. Preston Freeman had murdered before!" T.S.'s imitation of a sarcastic Lieutenant Abromowitz was wasted.

Edgar Hale raised his head. "Preston was arrested for manslaughter when he was in college. There was a large fight among a number of drunken students and someone fell and hit his head on concrete and died. He was charged and got probation because no one was really sure which one of three students had actually delivered the fatal punch."

T.S. could not imagine Preston Freeman noticing other human beings, much less doing them harm. "How do you know this?"

Lieutenant Abromowitz took over. "We discovered his record during a check of all partners and executives."

"I would have gotten that information before he was hired," T.S. protested. "During a routine background check."

"Well, you didn't," the lieutenant pointed out happily. "Apparently, it's obvious that John Boswell intercepted the police report before it got to the Personnel Department and kept it in his confidential files. If you had checked your records better, you would have noticed that Boswell had recommended Preston Freeman be hired. Freeman's the son of a good friend of his. No doubt someone in the mailroom or, more probably, your department preferred to be loyal to Boswell, not you." He gave T.S. a sympathetic smile. "Boswell got the file on Freeman first and kept it from you as a favor to his friend. We suspect Cheswick somehow found the report, perhaps going through Boswell's drawers for information on his wife, and used it to force Freeman to cooperate."

"Information on his wife?" T.S. asked faintly.

"Rumor has it that Lilah Cheswick and Boswell were involved," Abromowitz explained. "If I heard it, Cheswick probably did."

"How do you know Boswell ever received the police report on Freeman in the first place?" T.S. countered, hoping to change the subject.

The lieutenant smiled sweetly. "Because I received Freeman's original police report record anonymously in the mail yesterday and it was still in an inter-office envelope, cracked with age, addressed to John Boswell. Face it: someone in your department passed it on to him before you could get ahold of it. Too bad you didn't know what was going on in your own department.''

"I may not have been here at the time," T.S. replied, trying very hard not to sink to the lieutenant's level. "Aren't you curious as to who so conveniently discovered this missing police report and incriminating inter-office envelope?''

"Perhaps Boswell's wife discovered the report among his papers at home and, not wanting to be involved, merely mailed it to me. You know how those high society ladies are about staining their reputation with police involvement.''

"Did you ask her?" T.S. inquired calmly. "I wasn't aware that the world at large knew you were heading up the investigation and possessed your name and address.''

"Of course I didn't ask her." Abromowitz waved a chubby hand impatiently. "What good would that do? The report was sent anonymously. Obviously, the source plans to remain unknown. Who's going to confess? As to my heading up the investigation . . ." His voice trailed off and he inspected his fingernails for cleanliness. "I'd say that it wouldn't be unusual for word to get around that they've brought in a top gun to head up things. I've got quite a reputation, you know.''

Yes, T.S. did know. Sheila had told him. But it probably wasn't the reputation Abromowitz imagined. T.S. shrugged. "I suppose you think Boswell was engaged in insider trading, too?''

The policeman shook his head. "No. We think he started poking around after Cheswick started acting strangely, and discovered what was going on. He may even have been the one to eventually persuade Cheswick to turn himself in. Several witnesses saw them arguing before their deaths.''

"You've got it all figured out," T.S. admitted, "although I confess that the idea of Stanley Sinclair blackmailing Freeman is rather startling. It goes against his character to even disagree with a partner, much less double-cross one. I myself never would have been able to make the great logical leap from bungling accounts to insider trading, hidden police reports, wife-stealing, teen-age murderers and cowardly blackmailers.''

Abromowitz missed the edge of sarcasm in T.S.'s voice and preened importantly by the window.

Edgar Hale finally spoke up. ''My best man. Preston Freeman was my best man. He brought millions into the firm. We paid him millions.'' He shook his head sadly. ''I wouldn't care if he strangled his own grandmother on the banking floor.''

T.S. patted the old man on the back. ''He's wrong, Edgar. I'm convinced the lieutenant is wrong. All they really have is information that Cheswick was botching his accounts. Worried. Upset about something. Perhaps he was simply under tremendous strain for some other reason. A reason that has to do with his murder. Have they found any evidence of wrongdoing in Cheswick's trading accounts to back this theory up?''

''No, but they will. It fits too well with what I saw with my own eyes. I can no longer deny it. Cheswick had been under some great strain. Boswell was angry at him about something.'' Edgar Hale looked up at T.S. with as grateful an expression as he was capable of—one bordering more on distaste than thanks. ''You've really tried, T.S., I know that. I appreciate it. But I think it's time to give it up.''

''Listen to me. Abromowitz is wrong.'' T.S. ignored the lieutenant's incredulous laugh and pulled out the chair next to Hale. He placed the musty file box on the table in front of them. ''Do you remember Patricia Kelly?''

Edgar Hale looked up at him in horror. ''This is hardly the time or place to bring that mess up again. It's long over. We have enough trouble as it is.''

''It's not over,'' T.S. spoke so emphatically that even the lieutenant moved over unwillingly and placed a finger on the file.

''What's this all about?'' he demanded.

''I went to see Ralph Peabody,'' T.S. explained to Abromowitz. ''He was Personnel Manager many years ago.''

''Don't go into this,'' Edgar Hale commanded, his im-

perious manner returning. But his hands trembled and he
placed them against the tabletop to stop the shaking.

"No, Edgar. It's vital. I'm convinced there is a connection." T.S. removed the old letters, postcards and photos
from the file and spread them out across the table. He opened
the individual personnel folder on Patricia Kelly that he'd
found hidden with the other papers and spread it in front of
the men. A faded black-and-white photograph of a hopeful-
looking young woman stared up at them. "Look at this. This
is a woman who was a secretary here more than thirty years
ago. She seems to have had affairs with quite a few men here
at the firm. Men who later became very important. Partners.
Heads of other firms. Then she went off the deep end, starting writing obscene letters. Ralph Peabody has stripped all
mention of her from the files, as if she never existed."

"We were all very young then," Edgar Hale interrupted.
"She was unstable. Imagined it all. Poor woman. Let it be.
It's in the past."

"No, it's not in the past," T.S. said once more. "Look
at these." He handed the lieutenant various letters. "Read
them. These are clearly the work of someone who is mentally
unstable. Look at this list." He held up the list containing
names and sexual ratings. "The first three names. Cheswick.
Boswell. Sinclair." His voice faded and trailed off as he
suddenly realized he was approaching Edgar Hale's name.
Best not to bring everything up at once. He deftly slipped
the list back into the pile.

The lieutenant grabbed a particularly pornographic postcard and studied it. "Where did you get this stuff?"

"From Ralph Peabody. He had hidden them. When he
retired, he apparently culled the files of nearly every embarrassing memo he had ever put in a file."

"What?" Edgar Hale was outraged. "Why, I paid him
to . . ."

"He had an attack of conscience. I think he was ashamed
of himself. To be perfectly honest, I know how he felt,"
T.S. said. "You paid me well, Edgar, but not well enough

to be Big Brother and still sleep soundly at night. At least not every night.'' He cast a reproachful look at the old man.

''You're saying that this woman is killing off the men she slept with years before?'' the lieutenant asked incredulously as he paged through the notes and letters. ''She'd be, what? Fifty, sixty years old by now? And a nut case to boot?''

''She didn't sleep with anyone,'' Hale sputtered angrily. ''It was wishful thinking.''

''Look what was found on Boswell's boat,'' T.S. told the lieutenant, ignoring the partner's distress. ''A pitcher of margaritas.''

''Big deal,'' the lieutenant mumbled, although he was rapidly scanning the file with a panicked look on his face.

''But Cheswick and Boswell were arguing about meeting someone at Magritte's for a margarita the week before they both died,'' T.S. said.

''Where'd you hear that?'' Abromowitz demanded, staring at T.S. suspiciously.

''I have inside sources,'' T.S. interrupted. ''Just let me finish. Look how she signs all of her letters and postcards. 'Meet me for a margarita at Magritte's.' ''

''Magritte's?'' the lieutenant echoed, stumbling over the unfamiliar name.

''Who knew what she meant?'' Edgar Hale shouted angrily. ''She was deranged. Don't you understand?'' He shook his head. ''God, what trouble this woman caused.''

T.S. resisted the urge to point out that, technically, it was unlikely she had caused the trouble on her own. Someone had no doubt taken his pants off. ''You've got to admit that there are some strange coincidences here,'' T.S. pointed out.

The lieutenant was scratching his head. ''I'm taking this with me,'' he finally announced, pulling the file box over to his side. T.S. pinned the woman's official personnel folder firmly to the table—he wasn't letting go so easy.

''Not so fast,'' T.S. told the lieutenant indignantly. ''I figured it out. I think you should at least give me the courtesy of participating in . . .''

''You stumbled onto this by blind luck. You should have

known earlier and given it to the police right away," the lieutenant decreed. "I haven't got time to mess around with amateurs who think that—"

A firm knock at the door interrupted his warning speech.

"Go away," Hale shouted, his anger returning.

"It's me," Sheila called out. "I have something for Mr. Hubbert. He said it was urgent."

"I sent her to pull out the old medical files on this woman," T.S. explained. "We may be able to figure out where she is now. One of those memos indicates that Sterling agreed to pay for her treatment, at least for a while. We know she was eventually committed to a mental hospital. Sheila's been calling around trying to find out when she was discharged."

"Come in, then," Hale barked in reply. "I'll have your badge for breakfast if you've leaked anything about Preston Freeman to the press prematurely," he warned Abromowitz.

"I've explained the situation," T.S. told Sheila. She was holding a slim file in her hand and gazing apprehensively at Edgar Hale. "What did you find out?"

"She's dead," Sheila said, tossing a manila folder on top of the table. "She died last month." She stared down at the official file beneath T.S.'s hands and leaned forward for a better look, peering at the old photograph. Her eyes blinked.

"What?" T.S. looked at her. "Are you positive?"

Sheila was still staring at the photograph. She blinked again, as if to banish its vision, then swallowed and finally turned to T.S. She spoke more slowly than before. "Am I sure? Absolutely. The poor woman never even got out of Creedmoor the last three years of her life. She died there, a ward of the state. No family. I called a friend in administration. I deal with her all the time, since some of our employees use their outpatient services. She double-checked for me. Patricia Kelly is dead. There's no question about it."

T.S. was too stunned to reply. He surveyed the letters and postcards spread across the table with mounting horror. What had he done, dragging up this mess without more proof? He looked up. Hale and Abromowitz were exchanging a glance that clearly indicated T.S. was now part of the problem, rather than the solution.

"It's a good thing you go on evidence," the lieutenant told him with a smile. "Rather than mere theory."

T.S. stared apologetically at Edgar Hale. "I was so sure. It made so much sense."

Hale pushed the file away with a quick, angry shove. "Get this trash out of here," he thundered. "And don't ever remind me of it again." He glared at T.S. "Maybe it was time for you to retire. Of all the things to bring up."

"I was only trying to help," T.S. said helplessly.

"Give him some credit," the lieutenant said soothingly. T.S. stared at him with sudden suspicion. Abromowitz had picked a sheet of paper out of the mess and was reading it with great appreciation. "T.S. was only trying to score points with the boss."

"See here," T.S. began, but was quickly interrupted by Abromowitz.

"After all, Edgar," the policeman said, sliding the sexual performance rating memo across the desk, "with Sinclair gone, look who's next on the list."

Edgar Hale glanced at it briefly and threw it back across the table. "So what. My name and a lot of other people's. Don't be impertinent."

"He could have saved your life," the lieutenant pointed out obnoxiously. "Let's see what she has to say about you—ah, here it is. You were satisfactory. Not bad, I suppose. And you wanted it the most. Now, is that a compliment or an insult?"

Edgar Hale's mouth tightened so firmly it all but disappeared. He stood and walked to the door. "Meeting's adjourned. Do what you have to do, Lieutenant. And T.S., for god's sake, try to make up for this lousy idea by doing a thorough job on damage control with this Preston Freeman thing. Don't leave it to that silly replacement of yours. Not that it will do any good. Sterling & Sterling is ruined."

He left a speechless Sheila staring at T.S., while Abromowitz whistled happily. T.S. gathered the rejected files into his arms and walked silently out with Sheila.

"I'm sorry, Mr. Hubbert," she said apologetically.

"You're absolutely positive?" he asked her.

"Yes. I checked crazy Miss Turnbull's obituary file. It's in there, too. Here, you take it." She handed T.S. another file. She punched the elevator buttons angrily. "I saw the letters on top. I know what they said. You don't have to pretend. Why would that poor woman even start something like that unless there was some basis in fact? It takes two to tango." The elevator doors opened and they stepped inside. She began to pace across the small square of carpet. "That's just like a bunch of men to blame the woman," she declared bitterly. T.S. coughed discreetly and Sheila finally noticed the presence of several stupefied employees standing against the back elevator wall and watching with great interest. Her mouth closed and she stood quietly by T.S. He could almost feel Sheila's anger. It was palpable in the air and he wondered at its intensity.

2   "No, Theodore," Auntie Lil protested over the phone. "That can't be. There must be a mistake about her death. It fits too well."

"It can be," he corrected her. "And it is. She died all alone at a mental hospital without a dime or a friend in the world. I'm looking at the obituary now."

"I want to see it for myself," she demanded. "Bring the files with you to dinner."

"All right. But I've had enough of this sleuthing. I made an ass of myself today."

"No one ever died from looking like an ass," Auntie Lil reminded him.

"That's scant comfort."

"I still believe we're right."

He sighed. "See you tonight."

"Good. In the meantime, I'm going to the mental hospital."

"It hasn't been *that* exasperating."

"Don't be absurd, Theodore. I'm going out to where Patricia Kelly died. I want to hear it for myself. We'll swap notes at dinner."

"You don't trust anyone, do you?" he told her.

"Not quite. I still trust you."

T.S. hung up and rubbed his temples. Was that a compliment? Oh, what he wouldn't give to see Lieutenant Abromowitz properly humbled. Maybe even humiliated. He amused himself by imagining scenarios in which Abromowitz was properly punished for his insufferable cockiness. In one particularly vivid daydream, Abromowitz was being forced to march around the employee cafeteria in his undershorts.

A ringing phone in the distance permeated his satisfying fantasy. Sheila's line shrilled persistently, then jumped to his own phone. He waited for the receptionist to answer it and when no relief came, reluctantly picked it up himself. No doubt one of the blue rinse set looking for juicy details. Or Miss Turnbull reporting a new death.

"Personnel," he said crisply. "Sheila O'Reilly's line. T.S. Hubbert speaking."

"T.S.?" a male voice asked. "Is that you? It's Brian O'Reilly. Sheila's husband."

"Hello, Brian. I'm afraid Sheila must be away from her desk."

"That's okay. Just tell her I'm back in town. I'll see her at home tonight."

"Back in town? I thought you were working on the murder case."

"What murder case?" Brian O'Reilly was clearly confused.

"The Sterling murders," T.S. said.

"Sterling murders? Hey, what have I missed? What's been going on? I've been upstate, fishing Lake Ontario for a week with some buddies. Who got killed?"

T.S. stared at the phone. "I thought you participated in the investigation of Boswell's boat," T.S. finally said.

"*John* Boswell's boat? The partner with all that white,

snowy hair? He was killed? Holy shit.'' There was a whistle
on the other end.

"You've been gone a week?'' T.S. asked him.

"Sure. Caught a twenty-nine-pounder. But looks like I
missed the really big one. Tell Sheila to bring home all details.''

"I will.'' T.S. hung up the phone and stared at the wall.
How had Sheila gotten the details on Boswell's death? His
coffee soured in his stomach and he reached for the phone.
Perhaps Auntie Lil could reassure him.

She had already left her apartment. T.S. listened to the
dull ring of her phone fifteen times before he placed the receiver back in the cradle and stared at the clock on the wall.

Let it be anyone else but Sheila, he thought. Anyone else
at all.

CHAPTER TWELVE

1 It had been months since her last attempt at driving and Auntie Lil was the first person to admit that her motoring skills were rusty. The second was the driver of the Dodge van that she forced onto the sidewalk when turning right against a red light after forgetting that the maneuver was illegal in New York City. He shook an angry fist after her as she glided slowly past, careful to keep her speed down. She forgot what the official limit was within the city, but figured twenty miles an hour was safe enough. The other drivers on the road were less law-abiding. They zoomed angrily by, the more polite honking maniacally. The less polite were much more imaginative. Auntie Lil saw hand gestures she had never seen before in her life, not even during a recent tour of the Balkan countries and Turkey.

Only one other motorist seemed content to follow her good example. She peered into the rearview mirror. Naturally, he was not at first glance an impatient American. She could not see his face well, but he appeared to be an older Asian man in a blue Buick. He was quite willing to follow carefully behind her, despite the angry shouts of other more careless and obviously reckless drivers. She approached another intersection and felt instinctively that the traffic light was getting ready to turn yellow at any moment. She would not risk an accident, given the importance of her mission. Unfortunately, her hunch proved incorrect and an angry line of drivers honked impatiently behind her. Well, let them wait. She was sure it would turn yellow eventually and after about ten seconds or so, it did. She waited patiently for the yellow to

turn to red. No sense taking any chances. If she had an accident, Theodore would never let her forget it. He had been
after her for years to get rid of her car but she wasn't about
to let go. Lose your car and lose your independence, she
believed. Besides, she didn't see him giving up his car. All
that nonsense about her being a terrible driver was just jealousy on his part. She knew for a fact that he had once received a speeding ticket and had tried to hide it from her. If
she hadn't accidentally found it in an unmarked file in a
drawer in his personal desk one day—while he was out fetch-
ing her a certain kind of Danish she craved—she might never
have known about it at all. Of course, it would have been
indiscreet to have mentioned her discovery, not to mention
embarrassing to explain her methodology, so she kept the
information to herself. Even if it had been fifteen years ago,
it was still proof positive that she was the better driver.

Besides, without a car, she would not be on her way to
Creedmoor, the mental hospital where Patricia Kelly had
lived out the last few years of her life. She was certain that
the woman would lead them to an important clue and she
debated just what that clue might be. Lost in her thoughts,
she crawled slowly toward the hospital, no longer aware of
the blue Buick behind her. It inched forward as determinedly
as her own car, turning right when she turned right and dropping back at times, as if the driver had thought better of being
too obvious.

The parking lot at the hospital was nearly full and by the
time she'd discovered and claimed a space for herself, the
Buick had elected to pull up by the curbed entrance instead
of searching for parking itself. The driver watched as Auntie
Lil climbed out of her Plymouth and headed for the main
entrance. He slouched back against the seat and slid halfway
beneath the wheel, keeping a watchful eye on her progress.

It was just as Auntie Lil imagined it. No cleaner, but no
dirtier either. Patients moved about the carelessly kept
grounds sluggishly, in slow motion, peering about at the grass
and shrubs as if seeing them for the very first time. Several
huddled on concrete benches with relatives. Everyone looked

sullen and angry, as if the rate of progess toward normalcy was never fast enough for anyone concerned.

She found what looked like a reception desk but it was several more minutes before she could find a person. After assuring the pouting girl that she was here solely to speak to some of the staff who had known her dear niece during her last days on this earth, Auntie Lil was unceremoniously allowed to wander among the winding sidewalks, searching for the proper brick building.

No doctors could be seen and nurses were few and far between on both the grounds and the floors of the buildings she peeked in. Even nursing aides were scarce. The facility was obviously having difficulty with either paying for or finding a proper staff or both. She was so intent on her thoughts that she crashed into a hulking man and careened off his barrel chest to bump into a building doorway. He continued on without a word and she wisely let him go. He hardly seemed aware of his own existence, much less her brief presence in his world.

It was Auntie Lil's opinion that there was no such thing as an insane person. Rather, the mentally ill were *too* sane. They could not keep up the everyday delusions that so-called normal people used to sustain their desire for life. The mentally troubled saw life too clearly, in all of its naked and unsatisfying truth, and reacted, appropriately enough, with overwhelming despair.

"Can I help you?" The question was asked by a plump black woman. She sat in a chair by the building entrance, sunning herself and flipping through a magazine devoted to the lives of the famous. "I don't recognize you. Are you new? Don't you look pretty today?" Her accent was low and melodious, tinged with Caribbean. She spoke to Auntie Lil as you would address a child.

Auntie Lil stared at her for a moment, digesting this question. When she fathomed its meaning, she hastened to answer. "Good heavens, no." She managed a laugh. "I'm not a patient, I'm afraid." Why in the earth did she feel the need to apologize? "I'm here to speak to some of the people who

took care of my niece before she died. Her name was Patricia
Kelly. Have I got the right building?"

The plump black woman stared at her impassively. "Patricia was here, all right. She died last month. What do you
want to know? You planning to sue or something?"

"Heavens, no." Auntie Lil placed a hand to her throat as
if the very idea shocked her. "I just want to know what her
last years were like."

"That's good. Because she died in her sleep. Not restrained or anything, you understand. Just asleep. She shuffled off this mortal coil without any help from me or anyone
else." The woman stared at Auntie Lil placidly.

My goodness. A nursing aide who quoted Shakespeare.
Auntie Lil felt immediately better about the future of mankind.

"You're from the islands?" she asked the woman. "Haiti,
perhaps?"

"That's right." For the first time an emotion crept into
the woman's voice. Unfortunately, it was suspicion. "How
did you know that?"

Auntie Lil flashed her broadest smile. "I had a seamstress
from Haiti who worked for me once and who had an accent
just as beautiful as yours. She was quite good at her job, you
know. Quite good. As I suspect you must be as well."

The woman nodded. She was either unimpressed, immune to flattery or had been nipping at the patients' medication. "What was it about Patricia you wanted to know?"

Auntie Lil looked around her. "Is there a private place
where we could talk? A bench somewhere perhaps?"

"Can't. I'm on duty. Someone in there might need me."
The woman gestured with her thumb toward the building
door. Auntie Lil did not point out that, if she were so concerned about patient care, she could probably keep a better
eye on them if she were inside the building and actually with
them.

"This building's got what we call ambulatories living in
it," the woman explained, as if she could read Auntie Lil's
thoughts. "Most are out and about for a walk this time of

day. Had one wander over to the grocery store across the boulevard last night," she offered. "Manager called up about 9:00 P.M. Knew she had to be from here. I had been wondering where she'd gotten to. But she was fine. It was jus¹ that she'd tried to steal a twenty-pound frozen turkey and got caught. Can't imagine why. She'd tied it around her middle and put a sweater around her, like a big old baby was in there. When they caught her, she started screaming and going into labor pains before she'd let that sucker drop. Wanted to hold it when she was through. Why the manager thought that was so unusual for New York is beyond me."

"Is there a chair I could pull up?" Auntie Lil asked faintly. Best to ignore the woman's line of narration. It could open the floodgates to all sorts of stories.

"Help yourself." She pointed inside and Auntie Lil crept quietly through the doors. The building smelled of ammonia. She shivered and dragged a plastic chair outside, placing it on the sidewalk next to the aide's.

"What's your name?" she asked the woman. As usual, she checked the chair carefully for unidentified wet stains before sitting.

"Evelyn." The woman sighed and folded up the magazine, tucking it beneath her chair. "Patricia was your niece, huh?" She shook her head slowly and eyed Auntie Lil. "Sure had a lot of relatives who never bothered to come see her when she was alive but rushed right over after she died." She stared at Auntie Lil.

"I've been living abroad, I'm afraid," she lied. "I've been unable to get by until now. I feel a bit guilty about it, you know. That's why it's so important for me to know how her last days were spent."

Evelyn stared intently at Auntie Lil. "What side of the family are you on?" she asked abruptly. "The rich one?"

"What do you mean?" Auntie Lil demanded, alert for information.

"Rich old man came out last Friday asking questions about Patricia, too. Said he was her uncle, wanted to see if she needed any money. He looked rich, all right. Custom suit. Leather shoes. *Acted* rich, too, if you know what I mean.''

Auntie Lil nodded in agreement. "That would perhaps have been Cousin John or, perhaps, dear Cousin Stanley?" she asked.

The woman shrugged. "Wouldn't know his name. For someone so concerned about his niece, he seemed pretty calm about hearing she had died. Satisfied in fact, if you were to ask me. Hmmph . . .'' She crossed her arms and stretched her sturdy legs out into the sun. "Damn fool Walter told him everything he could. Had the notion the guy would give him money or something for taking such good care of her. Of course, Walter's the same idiot who spends half of his paycheck on lottery tickets. That man didn't fool me. He could have waved his wallet under my nose and it wouldn't have done him a bit of good. I know damn well there's no such thing as a rich *and* generous man. You don't get rich by being generous. Not in this world, anyway.''

"Walter?" Auntie Lil asked sweetly.

"That's the other day aide," Evelyn explained. "He's at lunch. Probably for the next three hours, knowing Walter. But he didn't know Patricia as well as I did. I took care of her on and off for ten years, you know. Came over with her from another building just about the same time. She used to be worse, was parked in one of the locked wards. Got better, they kept saying. Better than what, I wanted to know. But I wasn't about to spill my guts to Mr. High and Mighty, so I let Walter do the talking. I could tell he wasn't going to part with a dime, no matter how fast Walter shuffled. No sir. Your Mr. Cousin was not the type to be either generous or grateful.''

"He had white hair. Like snow? A fine figure?" Auntie Lil asked.

Evelyn shrugged. "Maybe. Who knows? All of you white people look alike to me. I just take care of you folks. I don't bother to remember you.''

Auntie Lil let the comment pass. "Did my niece die peacefully?" she asked.

"I'll say. As many drugs as she was taking. Couldn't get more peaceful and still be breathing. Thought at first she'd taken her own life." The woman's voice softened. "Wouldn't have blamed her if she had. Poor thing didn't have much left."

"You thought it was suicide at first?" Auntie Lil's brain raced as she spoke, connecting and discarding theories.

"Sure. On account of a lot of pills and such had been stolen from the medication room a couple of days before. So they did one of those autopsy operations. She had plenty of drugs in her blood, mind you. But none that weren't supposed to be there." She snorted in contempt and lapsed into silence.

"Was she lonely while she lived here?" Auntie Lil asked. "Did she have visitors?"

"Everyone is lonely who lives here," Evelyn replied. "Everyone who works here is lonely, too. This is a lonely place."

"So no one ever visited her?"

"No, I didn't say that. She did have one friend. Came to see her maybe once a month, but Patricia would refuse to see her most of the time. But she did see her just a day or so before she died. Didn't seem to make much difference to Patricia whether this friend came or not, sad to say. Never saw her smile. Not even one time."

"What did this friend look like?"

Evelyn stared at Auntie Lil suspiciously. "Why would you ask me that? Same thing the rich man asked me. I'll tell you the same answer. I don't remember. Like I told you, all of you white people look pretty much the same to me."

"Now, I don't really believe you mean that," Auntie Lil said gently. "And I won't insult you by trying to bribe you. You're angry because she was neglected by her family and friends and you're a caring person. So I'm going to tell you the truth."

The woman looked back up at Auntie Lil, her calm eyes lighting with a curious gleam that hovered between interest and respect. "Well, I believe it is about time someone told the truth. Cousin Whoever certainly didn't."

"I think that something terrible happened to Patricia many years before and that it is coming back around again to hurt people."

"What goes around comes around," the aide pointed out.

"It does indeed. But innocent people may be getting hurt. Even killed. Can't you tell me what this friend looked like?"

Evelyn shrugged. "Just a regular lady. Dressed nice. Wore a scarf around her head and big sunglasses. Even on cloudy days. Couldn't even tell you her age. Ashamed to be seen here, I expect."

Auntie Lil sighed. "Did anyone else ever visit her?"

Evelyn thought carefully. "A priest now and then. An old nun, could barely walk, would come by every couple of months. These are the forgotten people, you know. Relatives put them here to forget." She sighed deeply, her tough facade finally punctured by a breath of sympathy. Auntie Lil thought she wasn't so bad after all.

"Yes. They are forgotten. But I don't plan to forget." Auntie Lil sat quietly with her hands in her lap, staring at a nearby hedge. It needed trimming badly.

"It's a funny thing about people," Evelyn finally murmured. "You think you know them, but you never really do."

"What do you mean?"

"Here is this woman, Patricia. She lives and nobody cares. Then she dies and the whole world comes snooping around. And then there's the flowers."

"Flowers?"

"She got flowers every week for years. Never a card, never a note. Just flowers. Who would be sending flowers to a dried up old woman, confused in the head, trying her hardest to die?" Evelyn shook her head.

"Flowers every week?" Auntie Lil inquired.

"Every week. Nice ones, too. Smelled so good. Smelled expensive." The aide breathed deeply of the air. "Good for her, I say. Good for her for having a secret."

"How badly ill was she?" Auntie Lil asked.

Evelyn shrugged. "Worse than some. Not so bad as others. But unpredictable. One minute she'd be climbing all over the men patients and even poor Walter. The next she'd be lying on her bed staring at the ceiling for days. Refusing to eat or talk."

"What drugs were stolen? You said drugs were missing just before she died."

Evelyn shrugged. "When drugs get stolen around here, you don't ask questions. Best not to know. People start thinking you've got ideas of your own. Drugs are drugs and I've never met one I like. Probably just some patient or another aide looking to make some money." She sighed again. "Always someone willing to pay for drugs."

Auntie Lil thought this over. "Isn't there anything else you could tell me?" she asked the woman.

Evelyn looked her right in the eye, her placid exterior restored. "Whatever happened in that lady's life, it didn't happen here. People come here to avoid life. They don't come here to live it."

Auntie Lil rose and smiled her thanks. "Thank you. You've been most helpful. You didn't have to help me at all and I know it."

"No, I didn't have to help you," Evelyn agreed. "Time to get going. I better start rounding everyone up. There's a lady comes in once a week and tries to get them to make clay pots. You should see the ashtrays we got in there." She jerked her head toward the building and rolled her eyes. "I asked her why she couldn't come up with something but clay pots once in a while. Why can't they paint for a change? She just tells me that it's good for them to get their hands into the clay and squeeze hard." Evelyn stopped and shook her head in disbelief. "I told her not to tell the patients that. Don't be talking about getting their hands around anything and squeezing, I said. Wouldn't want to give them any ideas." She opened the door and disappeared inside, a cloud of her jasmine scent and building disinfectant lingering behind.

* * *

2 "Why would Sheila kill them?" Auntie Lil asked, spearing a shrimp and popping it briskly into her mouth. Her appetite was obviously better than his own. He had been unable to touch a thing on his plate until he blurted out his suspicions about Sheila.

"I didn't say she did. I just think it's curious she knew so much about Boswell's death. And lied about Brian being on the case."

"Well, I doubt she would dig her own grave by giving you such details if she was the murderer," Auntie Lil pointed out. "Give her a chance to explain."

"No, I guess not." He clung to that hope. "I couldn't find her this afternoon."

"Let's see Patricia Kelly's other files," Auntie Lil commanded. She pushed her nearly empty plate aside, having polished off a full order of scampi, new potatoes and asparagus in less than five minutes, much to the amusement of a gentleman dining alone at the table next to theirs. She had even quickly filled T.S. in about her hospital trip at the same time, doing a credible Haitian accent with a mouthful of shrimp. Both had agreed that John Boswell was the mysterious Cousin Whoever. But neither could come up with an identity for Patricia Kelly's female friend.

"All I've got is her old personnel file. You saw most of that. And the old medical files Sheila was able to dig up," T.S. admitted.

"What's this?" Auntie Lil held up a newspaper clipping.

"It's the Kelly woman's obituary. Courtesy of the Bride of Death."

Auntie Lil looked at him curiously.

"We have a crazy retiree named Miss Turnbull. She sends Sheila all the obituaries of retirees who die. Keeps a regular death count of Sterling & Sterling kick-offs. She never married, so we call her the Bride of Death. It's from an old *Shadow* episode . . ."

"I know where it's from," Auntie Lil said crisply, scanning the clipping. "And it seems a bit beneath you, Theodore. She must be a very busy woman lately."

T.S. stared at his liver and onions, having been conned into ordering it yet again. "Why don't you ever order this yourself if you like it so much?" he demanded.

She stared at his plate with distaste. "Who says I like liver and onions? I think it's disgusting."

She returned to her clipping with great concentration. "This is very curious, Theodore."

"What's curious? She died. She made the papers."

"A woman that obscure would never make the papers in this area. You said she died penniless, without a friend in the world. But this is a paid obituary."

"So?" He chewed a liver chunk dispiritedly.

"Well, who paid for it? You said she died all alone. No family."

T.S. considered the question. "A friend?" he suggested. "The mysterious female friend? Or the nun or the priest."

"Perhaps. Who else? Not much opportunity to make friends in the mental hospital, I should think. At least not the kind who compose tributes and have the wherewithal to have them published in the paper. And what a curious memorial poem."

"Why? What's it say?" He knew he should have reviewed it prior to handing it over to Auntie Lil. She was no doubt about to solve the entire mystery, having snatched it from under his nose.

"It's not really a death poem," she said, moving her lips silently as she read and re-read the lines. "And yet, it seems very familiar.

"Listen to this—" Auntie Lil held the yellowed clipping up to eye level and began carefully to enunciate the words, drawing more interested glances from the gentleman dining nearby:

> "Patricia Kelly—1938 to 1991.
> Nothing Old, Nothing New.
> Nothing Borrowed, Nothing Blue.
> Perhaps in death, you can regain
> The dignity they took from you."

She finished with a flourish and stared at T.S. He gulped down his liver and thought it over carefully. "It's a curious epitaph," he finally acknowledged.

"Curious?" She sniffed. "I think bizarre might be a better word. Does it sound familiar to you?" she demanded.

He thought it over. "A little. That part about nothing old and nothing new. Isn't that an old folk saying?"

"I think so," her voice trailed off. "But there's something wrong . . . *Something*. That's it, Theodore!" The waiter screeched to a halt by their table, but Auntie Lil waved him away and bent toward T.S. in great excitement. "That's it. It's *something*, not nothing!"

"I beg your pardon?"

"It's 'something old, something new, something borrowed, something blue.' It's a wedding saying. What the bride wears at her wedding."

"Yes?" he asked, mystified.

"And if you don't have a wedding, you wear nothing, right?"

"I beg your pardon?"

"If the man won't marry you, you wear nothing old and nothing new. Don't you see?"

"No, I don't see." He thought perhaps the last Bloody Mary had pushed her over the edge. He had warned her to take it easy.

"Stop being patronizing," she snapped at him. "She's supposed to have died alone, but this announcement was paid for by someone. There is a distinct reference to no wedding. To having been robbed of her dignity." She stared at T.S. expectantly and he looked nervously around. "What was the worst thing that could happen to a nice Irish Catholic girl thirty years ago?" she finally demanded.

"Getting pregnant," he said immediately and automatically.

"Exactly. Getting pregnant and not getting married." She stood up and pushed her chair firmly back into place. "Get the bill, Theodore. This is it."

"It is?" He gestured to the waiter, who was watching Auntie Lil nervously.

"Yes, it is. Patricia Kelly may be dead, but I'll bet anything she has an illegitimate daughter who is very much alive. Alive and angry. And we have to find her. Think of the wilted boutonnieres found at each murder scene. When does a man wear a boutonniere? At a wedding, of course. This changes everything. How old would you say the daughter would be by now?"

"Twenty-five. Twenty-six. Late twenties. Something like that."

"Well, then. We have a handful of suspects, at least."

"Why are you so sure it's a woman?" T.S. asked. "Maybe it's a son."

"The zippers and John Boswell's floating bedroom of a sailboat."

"How can you be so sure it's someone we already know?"

She shook her head. "Too much access to the building and the victims without leaving hardly a clue. Specific files missing, as if the killer knew where they were. Those men knew her. She was able to get close. Would a complete stranger have been able to pull that off?" She left her questions unanswered. "We'll have to consider any employee in that age range, especially anyone attractive. Even Sheila, I'm afraid."

"But we know her mother," T.S. protested. "For god sakes, you had brunch with her. Sheila can't be Patricia Kelly's daughter."

"She could be adopted," Auntie Lil pointed out. "Anne Marie herself admits she was gone from the job for a year and a half."

"Who wants to march around in front of everyone pregnant?" he asked.

"Or not pregnant." She let this sink in and continued. "Of course, this theory lets Lilah Cheswick out." She looked at him over her glasses. "Lucky for you."

He pressed his lips firmly together to squelch his retort. Best not to open that Pandora's box again.

"I think this new angle also makes it worthwhile to look more carefully into the background of every woman involved with the dead men in any way. Can you get their files?"

"Of course." He was silent and waited for instructions.

"First thing tomorrow, you can start checking their files," she ordered. "Especially against what we have on Patricia Kelly. Look for inconsistencies. Items that don't make sense."

"I did that before I approved them for filing in the first place," he pointed out.

"Yes, but now you know that something is there," Auntie Lil said, tapping her fingers briskly against the table top. "I will pursue other angles while you do that."

"What other angles?" When was he going to catch on to this detecting business?

"Well," she mused thoughtfully, "they say the dead can't talk. I'm not so sure."

He stared at her. "You're not going to bring in psychic nonsense, are you?" he asked. Anything beyond the rational did not belong in the Hubbert way of thinking.

"Don't be foolish, Theodore. I'm going to take a look at Patricia Kelly's grave," she decided. "I want to know if it's being kept up. Or if the groundskeeper remembers any visitors. That would be proof the daughter is alive and in the area. Besides, maybe it will inspire me. Perhaps the epitaph has another clue." Her mouth curled in a smile and he could tell she was still pleased over her earlier triumph.

Before he could reply, she stood up and marched right by the dessert cart without a glance, heading for the door.

Their neighbor gazed after her in admiration. "That's some lady," he said to T.S. approvingly. "Got a lot of spunk. Good appetite. I like that in a woman."

T.S. stared at him. The man was dapperly dressed in an expensive suit and was obviously a retired man of some means. With excellent hearing, apparently. "Get your own. She's taken," T.S. growled as he threw money on the table and hurried after his aunt. He caught up with her near the front door. "That man practically asked me for your phone number."

"Did he?" She stood on tiptoe and peered back into the dining area. "He looks quite interesting. Did you give it to him?"

"No," he protested loudly. Several people waiting in line turned to stare at them curiously. "You better be careful," he warned her in a calmer voice.

"Of what? Old mashers?"

"No, tomorrow at the graveyard."

"Worried about the living dead?" She smiled at him and shrugged on her coat.

"Yes, as a matter of fact, I am. Where are you going now?"

"Home, of course. It's so much nearer all the graveyards. It will make my search much easier to wake up in my own bed ready and raring to go." As if she ever woke up ready to do anything but go.

"I'll help you get a cab," he offered.

"No need. No need." She waved him away and headed for the door. "I can manage by myself."

Of course she could, he reflected. She could manage better than he.

Auntie Lil did, in fact, snag a cab immediately. Little old ladies were excellent passengers late at night, as they didn't tend to pull out pistols and demand money. Cabbies always screeched to a halt for her.

As she slid happily into the backseat and chirped out her address, neither she nor T.S. noticed the shadowy figure of an older Asian man leaning against the wooden wall of a nearby construction site. He pulled his coat tightly around his body. Shadows shielded his face as he watched Auntie Lil's exit. A blue Buick was parked nearby.

CHAPTER THIRTEEN

1 T.S. once again spent the night fighting off dreams of murder. This time, he and Auntie Lil were locked in a linen closet at the rest home. He was peering out the small porthole window while Auntie Lil poked him from behind with her umbrella. Ralph Peabody rolled jauntily by in an enormous wheelchair with Sheila on his lap. She snuggled against him happily and ruffled his hair as they took turns inhaling from a small oxygen tank and giggling together. As they passed the window, Sheila's face began to age, skin cracking and wrinkles swelling around her eyes and mouth. Her hair bleached gray and faded to white. She looked over her shoulder at T.S. and he saw that she had turned into Lilah Cheswick—without her teeth. Suddenly, Robert Cheswick appeared at the end of the long hallway, crawling slowly along the corridor and leaving a trail of purplish blood behind him. T.S. watched in horror as Cheswick was crushed beneath the huge wheels of the chair, neither Lilah nor Peabody even noticing. Cheswick began to scream and Auntie Lil joined in, the sound filling the tiny closet.

No wonder he woke screaming himself, to find that he had once again overslept yet was still exhausted. How long had the alarm been buzzing? Brenda and Eddie meowed at him in reprimand as he dressed hurriedly and dashed out the door.

To be rising at 9:00 A.M., he thought in the subway on his way in, to be waltzing into Sterling & Sterling just after 10:00 and in disgrace yet—his discipline was going to seed much more quickly than he'd ever dreamed possible.

"Sheila in yet?" he asked Margaret as he flew by, hat in

hand. He was determined to jump into business immediately and quickly clear up this nonsense about Sheila being the missing daughter.

"No," the receptionist answered tersely, ringing phones surrounding her. "She called in and she's taking a personal day. She won't be in until after the weekend." She turned her back to him and spoke hastily into two phones at once.

Was it his imagination or had she treated him with less respect than usual? Perhaps word was already out—he'd made a fool of himself yesterday in front of Edgar Hale and was now in disgrace. An exemplary thirty-year career ruined by one foolish mistake. He hoped fervently that Auntie Lil was right about Patricia Kelly's daughter, despite the fact that he knew nearly every suspect personally. He could think of nothing else that might salvage his reputation or that of the firm.

Miss Fullbright rushed past, looking extremely harried, and ignored T.S. when he called after her. Effie must be doing a good job of referring media requests to her line. Or perhaps the absentee rate had continued to climb. The lobby and elevator had been deserted. There was no doubt that the firm was in chaos. Soon the only employees reporting to Sterling & Sterling would be Miss Fullbright's trauma team. They'd have to sit around in an empty building and analyze each other.

Not even that thought cheered him. It seemed to him that he had been removed from the inner circle, that the many and varied tasks he had dispatched so well were now in the all too capable hands of Miss Fullbright. He sighed and settled in at his desk. What was he doing here anyway? His time had passed.

How dare Miss Fullbright not even return his greeting? What in the world could be so important that he would be ignored?

In revenge, he would examine her file folder first. The thought of Miss Fullbright being led away in handcuffs, a sea of Sterling & Sterling employees parting for her exit, lifted his spirits.

His satisfaction evaporated after a close examination of her file. There was nothing to indicate she was not who she was and he was suddenly ashamed of his animosity. She was just a hardworking single woman, brought up by her mother, who had paid her own way through City College and aspired to greater things. If she had attained those heights, even at expense to his pride, who was he to question her worthiness? He felt very small and mean, peering through her file. Her father had died when she was young, according to her application. It could not have been easy for either her or her mother.

He pushed the folder away and mused. Might the dying father be an excuse for no father at all? Surely not. But where had she been the last few days? He had not really seen her alone since she had interrupted his discussion with Herbert Wong and made fun of the old messenger. She had kidded him about Bruce Lee movies and then pointed out to T.S. that Wong was on the list of people who had checked out late the night Cheswick was murdered.

The list? T.S. sat up straight and stared at her file. How had Miss Fullbright known which employees were on the list and facing investigation by the police? He had not heard of any of them being questioned yet. The guards would know to keep the names to themselves. Even if Abromowitz had questioned Miss Fullbright, he wouldn't have revealed the names to her. She was a stranger to him, and the investigation had been compromised enough. Yet she'd spoken so confidently, T.S. decided, as if she were privy to information denied him.

Once he began to suspect her, other questions emerged. Why had she been so sunburned the Monday after Boswell's death? What better place to get sunburned than out on a boat on an unexpectedly sunny afternoon? Why had she attempted to pump him for information on what he'd found out? Where had she rushed off to just now? Was this what Auntie Lil had meant by pieces that didn't fit?

Perhaps an unconscious desire to regain his position of esteem at Sterling & Sterling fueled this immediate suspicion against Miss Fullbright. Perhaps he was simply afraid. Whatever the reason, his anxiousness caused him to blurt out his unanswered questions to Miss Fullbright herself, when she appeared unexpectedly in his doorway.

"Sorry, T.S.," she said. "I didn't get a chance earlier to say good morn—"

So now she was trying to butter him up, deflect his suspicion. "Why did you stay late the night Cheswick was stabbed?" he cried, not falling for her little trick. She stared at him in astonishment. "You left the building more than an hour after leaving my party," he remembered angrily. "Where were you during that time?"

"I was moving my things into my new office. Why are you asking me this now?" Her voice grew in pitch as she realized his implications.

"Then where did you get your sunburn last weekend?" he demanded loudly, even his ears shocked by his fury. "How did you know Herbert Wong was on the list of people who checked out late?" He rose from his chair and took a step toward her. "Where were you the Sunday that Boswell died?" Much to his own embarrassment, he found himself pointing the classic accusatory finger at her.

For a moment Miss Fullbright simply stared at him, mouth open and face gone white. Then she darted forward and he realized the foolishness of what he had done. If she had a weapon, he would be next. But all she did was slap him solidly across the face with amazing strength. Rubbing her hand, she marched to the door in visible disgust, stopped with one hand on the doorknob and fixed him with a withering glare. "It's none of your damn business what I do on my time off!" she shouted. "It's no one's business but my own!" She slammed the door in his face.

T.S. stared at the door's smooth surface in surprise, his heart pounding. What had gotten over him? Was the panic sweeping the employee population affecting him as well? He took a deep breath. There were disturbing questions about Miss Fullbright, that was true, but it didn't prove she was the murderer. He had acted foolishly. Had allowed his per-

sonal feelings to interfere with his job. It had never happened
to him before.

In that moment, he realized the precarious hold he had on
his own composure and how deeply he mourned the loss of
the Sterling & Sterling he had known and loved. He felt a
much closer kinship to Edgar Hale than he ever had before.
He vowed not to give up on the investigation until the truth
was uncovered, no matter who was to blame. Not even if it
was Auntie Lil herself.

He would look like an ass, he might turn out to be a fool,
but he would do no less than his best in finding out who was
responsible for this destruction of years of caring and pride.
And he would begin by looking through the remaining files.

He had not even opened the first of them when the phone
interrupted his thoughts. Perhaps Auntie Lil was calling in
with a progress report. He did not like being out of touch
with her.

"Mr. Hubbert, thank god you're there!" Effie's unmistakable operator voice carried sharply over the phone line, her
crisp military tone throbbing with the emergency announcement she was about to impart. "We have a real crisis, sir,"
she said. "Mr. Hale won't see anyone. He's just sitting alone
in his office and refusing to let anyone in or even any calls
through. Which, of course, means that Quincy is in a tizzy
and taking it out on all of us. I thought she was going to slap
Anne Marie this morning for coming in late. I tell you, sir,
the situation is escalating."

"If you have a problem with any callers or visitors, send
them to me," he said reluctantly. He had better calm her
before she ran through the Main Floor of the bank shouting,
"Mayday! Mayday!" and spreading panic like wildfire.

"Roger, sir. I knew you'd be able to help." He listened
to her abrupt click and felt some small satisfaction. At least
she still had faith in his abilities.

Edgar Hale had gone into shock. Sterling & Sterling would
grind to a halt. Who was there to take charge? He was unable
to ponder the problem long. He had been unconsciously
aware of Sheila's phone ringing in the next room and it chose

that moment to jump to his line, startling him from his reverie.

"Personnel," he barked, unwilling to go into an entire introduction.

"That you again, T.S.?" He heard Brian O'Reilly's voice with some distaste. "What did they do? Demote you to receptionist?" He laughed heartily at his joke.

T.S. really could not understand how Sheila could have married such a buffoon.

"Hey, is my wife there?" he asked. It occurred to T.S. that perhaps the man had been drinking. His hale and hearty Irish manner was a shade too hale and hearty.

"No, she took a personal day," T.S. said curtly. "I assumed to spend with you." Not that he could imagine anyone wanting to spend a day with Brian O'Reilly in such a disgraceful condition.

"A personal day? What the hell for?" the Irish cop barked through the phone. "Certainly not to get personal with me!" He laughed loudly at this joke and, for the first time, T.S. detected a slight roar in the background. A murmur of voices and clinkings. He looked at his watch. Good heavens, it was barely noon and the man was whooping it up in a bar. No wonder Sheila wasn't home.

The question remained—where was she?

"Do me a favor, would you, T.S.?" Brian O'Reilly's voice was infected with a growing hostility that T.S. was not at all sure he liked. "When you see my lovely wife, would you ask her where the hell she was last night on my first night home?"

T.S. heard the angry bang of the phone being slammed down, followed by a sudden and complete silence. He stared into the dead receiver and thought, "It's time to talk to Anne Marie again."

2 Anne Marie looked pale and thin as T.S. ushered her into his office. "I hope this doesn't take long," she said almost apologetically. "With so many people out, I've had to take on quite a lot of extra work and I can only stay so late tonight. That Quincy is really taking advantage of the situation. Ordering me around right and left.'' Anne Marie looked as well turned out as ever, but tiny wisps of hair fluttered uncharacteristically about her face and she wrung her hands tightly as she spoke. Her voice hardened when she mentioned Mrs. Quincy.

"No, of course, I won't keep you long," he agreed absently before deciding on a roundabout tack. "Do you know where Sheila is today?"

She looked in the direction of her daughter's empty office. "She's taking a personal day, I believe. She called me early this morning and said not to wait for her at the subway stop." She spoke lightly, but her eyes narrowed and she watched him with some suspicion.

He considered her answer in silence. Why would Sheila need a personal day so suddenly?

"Why do you ask?" Anne Marie inquired faintly, fidgeting in her chair. "Personal days are allowed, aren't they? She rarely takes hers."

"Yes, yes, of course they are. It's on page 19 of the personnel manual." He thought hard. "Did she call you from home?"

"Of course she did," the woman replied a bit too quickly.

"Are you sure?" he asked.

She stared quietly at the rug. "I assumed she did." Was it his imagination or was she evading his eyes? Perhaps more direct action was called for.

"Anne Marie—if you know where she is today, you must tell me."

The woman looked up at T.S., and he saw that she was clearly upset. "What is so important about where Sheila is?" she asked him. "I thought personal days were personal." Her voice swelled indignantly.

"They are," he assured her. "But to be perfectly frank, there are some troubling inconsistencies and coincidences in Sheila's absences and appearances lately. With the murders and all, everyone is under suspicion." He noted the instant alarm on her face and hurried on. "Not that Sheila is *really* under suspicion. Not for a moment. But I've been asked to verify her whereabouts during certain times, and it appears she did not tell me the entire truth.''

They were both silent and when no answers were forthcoming, T.S. continued. "You can see the importance of the truth under the circumstances, can't you?''

"It's so distressing," Anne Marie said. Her mouth trembled and she removed a handkerchief from her pocketbook. T.S. hoped she would not break down in tears. He didn't know if he could deal with yet another woman in tears.

"I assure you I will keep whatever you tell me in complete confidence," he said.

She hesitated and dabbed at her eyes. "Sheila and Brian are . . . having marital problems. She's been unhappy for some time." She gave a sigh that caused her shoulders to heave. "I can sympathize. It's not easy being married to a policeman and when he drinks as much as Brian does, well . . .'' She let her words trail off, but her eyes flashed with a sudden anger and she glared unexpectedly at T.S. "No doubt he suffers from the same problems as my husband," she said bitterly.

"Problems?" he inquired, his voice an octave too high.

"Not for him, of course. The inability of a husband to remain faithful is really only a problem for the wife, wouldn't you say?" She stared at T.S. and he flushed, looking away for comfort. He remembered the lieutenant's failure to locate Tommy Shaunessy the day Anne Marie was being questioned and how Abromowitz had kidded about her husband's obvious infidelity. Well, it was now apparent that Anne Marie knew everything and was clearly not as amused as the lieutenant.

"I've always found it strange how policemen find it impossible to keep either their guns or . . . or their private parts where they belong, haven't you?" She stared at T.S. sweetly but an angry fire smoldered in her gaze.

"I hadn't noticed," T.S. assured her hastily. Oh god, the things he had to learn about people. Was no one as honorable as they seemed? "Where has Sheila been?" he prompted her gently. "Brian called and said she never came home last night."

The woman looked up at him with genuine surprise. "I assure you, I don't know the answer to that." She clamped her lips together and stared thoughtfully out the window. "I thought you meant *today*. Today she's going to see a lawyer. To see about a separation and, I suppose, a divorce." This final admission pushed her over the brink and she began to quietly cry.

"Now, now, Anne Marie," T.S. said, nearly as distressed as she was at her unhappiness. "People get divorced every day. It's not a crime."

She looked up at him with tear-stained cheeks. "Try telling that to Father O'Donnell. She'll likely be excommunicated from the Church."

"Surely they don't bother with"—he groped for the right word—"*official* excommunication these days."

"Oh, you'd be surprised," she sobbed in reply. "But a divorce is the best thing for her. I know that." She stared at the wall and paused dramatically, tears dripping down her cheeks. "Better to suffer excommunication than be put through the kind of humiliation I've had to endure." She glared again at T.S. "Men are all alike."

He was quite offended and spread his hands wide in protest. He was not like that at all. He had always thought he was rather unique. But at least she had told him some, though not all, of what he needed to know. If Sheila's home problems were that severe, perhaps she had simply been staying at a girlfriend's. He watched Anne Marie sob into her handkerchief for a moment longer before deciding that, so long as she was crying anyway, he might as well take the plunge.

"Anne Marie—is Sheila adopted?" he asked.

The effect was startling. She stopped her crying immediately, handkerchief raised halfway to her nose, and stared at him in astonishment. An emotion he could not fathom—anger, suspicion, panic or fury—ripped across her face and was gone.

"Is Sheila adopted?" he asked again.

"Who told you that?" she hissed, tears forgotten.

"I . . . well, no one. I'm just guessing."

"You don't guess about things like that." Anne Marie leaned forward, anger replacing her distress. "What do you know about that?" She leaned forward and repeated her question even more loudly. "What do you know about that?"

"Nothing," he replied, astonished. "Honestly. I'm just guessing."

"They swore to me that it would always be kept a secret," she declared bitterly.

"Who is they?" he asked, ignoring her reproachful glare.

"The nuns at the agency."

"You adopted her through the Church?"

"Of course I did." She sat up straight in her chair and blew her nose daintily. "I suppose now you'll want to know why we couldn't have children of our own," she said somewhat nastily.

"No, no, no." He was appalled at this swipe at his good manners. "Not at all. I can't explain it to you right now, but it's important that I know whether or not Sheila is adopted."

"I'll tell you anyway," Anne Marie declared. "It's because the great Tommy Shaunessy is sterile. That's right! The big tough guy can't father a child." Her voice dripped with scorn. "But does he let that bother him? No, not at all. No thought to the anguish he has caused his wife. Oh, no." She glared at T.S. with a malevolence that frightened him. "Instead, he's used it as an excuse to play around for years. My husband has been unfaithful to me for decades, all because he can't father a child!"

"Please, Anne Marie. Please." He was practically begging her now. He wanted to hear no more about unfaithful husbands and sex. How quickly the genteel turned tawdry when you looked beneath the surface. "Just tell me about Sheila. It's for your daughter's own good," he pleaded with her. "Please, Anne Marie. You've known me for years, surely you can trust me. We could find out other ways, you know."

"You wouldn't find out much," she said nastily. "Those records are sealed."

"We could get a court order," he countered, returning her angry tones. He was tired of her nonsense. "And I will if I have to."

Her manner changed abruptly. "Not even Sheila knows," she told him. "Just her father and I. And . . . one or two other people." She twisted her handkerchief. "When we couldn't have children of our own, it was terrible. Everyone kept asking when we were going to start a family. They whispered that it was me, of course. No one would dream that one of the Shaunessy boys could be shooting blanks." She laughed bitterly and T.S. sighed. He didn't want her to get started again on *that*.

"You can imagine, back then, what it was like," she said sadly. "Living in a Catholic neighborhood filled with young girls and boys and having none of your own. We were the only family on our block without children." She was staring again at the wall, lost in her own thoughts, many miles and many years away from where they sat. "Finally, we contacted a monsignor at another church on . . . on Long Island, I believe. It was my mother's idea, rest her soul. She was actually the one who arranged it. She felt it would be easier on Sheila, although we didn't know it would be Sheila at that point, if no one suspected that she was adopted. And easier on Tommy, no doubt."

She blew her nose daintily again and continued. "To make a long story short, we didn't have to wait long." She looked up at T.S. with indignation. "There were no alternatives, you understand, for pregnant women in those days." He nodded. "Nowadays, of course, it's . . . different." She stopped as if aware she was in danger of wandering off the track once more. "At any rate, we were put in touch with an agency and heard about a young girl who was expecting to deliver in six months or so. I went to stay at my aunt's house in Maine and the story went around that I had been ordered to bed for the whole pregnancy. When Sheila was born and turned out to be Sheila, Tommy and I simply collected her at the hospital and brought her home and no one ever knew. Since I hadn't been physically pregnant, I was emotionally unprepared for the enormity of how much I would love her.'' She broke down again and began to sob.

"I don't want her to know anything," she begged T.S. through tears. "She'll hate me for not telling her first. I don't want her to know." Her sobs grew louder.

"I won't say anything unless I have to," T.S. quickly assured her. Why in the world hadn't she told Sheila when she was younger? What was the big deal? God, everyone was so on edge. He couldn't take the tension much longer.

"I couldn't bear to leave her and go back to work so soon after getting her," Anne Marie whispered. "Mr. Cheswick kept my job open an extra year for me. He was the only one who knew the truth." She paused in her story, tears on hold, and looked at T.S. closely. "How did you know?" she asked him again.

He shrugged. "She doesn't look a bit like you or her father," he pointed out, feeling a need to defend himself. "Look at her blonde hair. Look at yours. It's blue-black."

"Oh, who really does look like their parents?" She stared at him a moment longer but saw she would get nothing out of him. "Anyway, Sheila mustn't know."

"Are you sure she doesn't know already? Children have a way of sensing the very things we try to hide from them."

"Of course I'm sure. She's never even considered the possibility or brought it up," Anne Marie said quickly. "And I don't see why we have to now."

He stared thoughtfully at his desk. Auntie Lil had been right about Sheila being adopted, but that did not prove in any way that she was the murderer or that Patricia Kelly was her real mother. Not in any way at all. His thoughts were interrupted by the ringing of his telephone, a shrill intrusion that caused Anne Marie to jump.

He picked it up hesitantly, not having heard a thing but bad news by phone thus far in the day. "Hello?"

"Why the hell are you harassing Felicia Fullbright?"

Lieutenant Abromowitz's angry and obnoxious voice was unmistakable.

"What do you mean?" T.S. asked faintly, one eye on a squirming Anne Marie. She twisted a handkerchief in her hands and stared at him curiously.

"You know damn well what I mean. Accusing her of murder. Asking where she got sunburned. If she killed John Boswell. Implying she stabbed Cheswick."

"That's not what I said, I only asked her—"

"I don't care what you said. *Lay off her.* She was with me that Sunday afternoon when she got her sunburn, okay? Not that it's *any* of your business. I want the harassment of her stopped or I'll have you in for interfering with a murder investigation. Better yet, I want *all* activity on your part stopped. Playtime's over."

T.S. was speechless. Miss Fullbright and Lieutenant Abromowitz? My god, what if they married and reproduced? The receiver went dead in his hand and T.S. stared at it.

"Who was that?" Anne Marie asked. She leaned forward anxiously.

He looked up at her. "You say Sheila went to see a lawyer today?"

"Yes. Then she's meeting me here later. We're going to see the Ice Capades tonight at the Garden. Who was that on the phone? What were you talking about?"

T.S. rubbed his temples wearily. "No one, Anne Marie. Please don't ask. Just go back to work and forget it." He felt as if he had not slept a wink last night. He sighed deeply. "I must see Sheila when she arrives," T.S. told Anne Marie. "Immediately. I have some very important questions to ask."

Anne Marie stared at T.S., searching his face for clues. A dark and troubled cloud settled over her features. Their eyes locked but he would not give in and she finally rose, straightening her skirt automatically. "Well, of course. I'll bring her up. Can't you tell me why?" She looked at him anxiously and he sighed.

"I know she's done nothing wrong," he assured her quietly. "I have more faith in your daughter than anyone else at

Sterling & Sterling, but there are several questions I must ask her myself.''

If only T.S. felt as confident as he sounded. He rose and walked to the window, prying apart slats in the blinds to stare down at the street below. Strangers passed by and he wondered what secrets they concealed. Lost in thought for several long seconds, he did not even turn around when Anne Marie finally spoke again.

''Are you going to tell her she's adopted?'' she asked in a tiny voice from the doorway.

He thought it over. ''Only if I find it necessary. Although I don't see why you don't tell her sooner or later.'' He let the blinds fall back in place and sighed.

She whirled around and slammed the door behind her with a violent crack. T.S. stared after her, astonished.

CHAPTER FOURTEEN

1 T.S. sat behind a pile of employee files and looked at his watch impatiently. It was nearly 2:00 and he had not yet heard from Auntie Lil. He had been through most of the remaining files thoroughly and could find no discrepancies in the backgrounds of the women. He had pulled the files of all female employees in the right age range with any reason whatsoever to come in contact with the dead men, even including three dining room employees. There were more than three dozen possibilities in all and every one of them seemed to be from good homes and good schools. No one had any strange or suspicious gaps in their employment—they'd never have been hired in the first place if they had—and all had references from reputable people covering virtually every period of their lives: teachers, pastors, scout leaders, community figures.

Again, he found it reassuring to remind himself, proof that Sheila was adopted was not proof that she was the killer.

His search was made all the more maddening by Auntie Lil's insistence that something had to be there. He sighed. Edgar Hale refused to return his calls, Sheila would not be in until later and he didn't know where Auntie Lil was. What was there for him to do?

The phone rang as he was contemplating the necessity of going through the files once again.

"I've found her," Auntie Lil cried immediately, in great excitement.

"The daughter? Be careful, she could be . . ."

"No. No. The dead woman. She's buried in Brooklyn. It

took me all morning to track her down. I had assumed she'd be buried in Queens since she was Catholic." Auntie Lil seemed to find this amusing and T.S. listened to her merry laugh with distinct relief. She was safe. "I checked grave records for hours and finally found her. I'm on my way there now. I just wanted you to know I was fine."

"I was getting a bit worried," he admitted. "You're not driving, are you?"

"No. I'm not a fool. Where would I park? Did you find anything?" She hurried to brush aside any hint that she might not be able to take care of herself.

He told her about Sheila's adoption.

"Don't fret about Sheila," she told him. "You're an excellent judge of character. This marital business explains some things. You'll feel better when you've talked to her yourself. What about the files on the other women?"

"Nothing. Everyone looks clean. I don't know what I'm looking for."

"Anything that could tie her into Patricia Kelly. Maybe she's named for Patricia's mother. Or grew up in the same borough. Went to the same school. An address that matches. Have you memorized the Kelly information?"

"Well, no," he admitted. "You just said to go through the other files."

"For heaven's sakes, Theodore. Use some initiative. Compare them to the Kelly file. Look for a Magritte. Anyone have a relative named Magritte?"

"No. Now that's something I would remember."

"It's odd and very puzzling." She was still a moment. "I know that 'Magritte' is important and I don't know where to start. Are you sure the files are clean?"

"They seem to be. I'll compare them to Patricia Kelly's one more time but after that I don't know what else to do."

"Then why don't you try to talk to Mr. Dorfen again? We've got to find out who Magritte is."

"Heavens. On a Friday? Who knows if he'll even be able to walk."

"Perhaps he'll surprise you, Theodore. After all, three of

his colleagues have been murdered. That's enough to sober anyone up.''

''I'll give it a try,'' he promised.

''Good. I'll check in later,'' she said. T.S. could hear the sounds of traffic whizzing by in the background. It made Auntie Lil seem very, very far away and he was seized by a sudden fear. Of what, he did not know.

''Call me back soon,'' he asked. ''I'm trying to reach Sheila. Maybe I'll have good news.'' He would offer her a carrot to make sure she kept in touch. Besides, he *was* trying to reach Sheila. He could think of no easy explanation for her knowledge about Boswell's death, but she deserved the chance to explain.

''I'll call you after I've seen the grave,'' Auntie Lil promised. ''Now you go through those files and speak to Mr. Dorfen again. Remember—think inconsistencies.''

''Right.'' He hung up the phone and stared at the files in front of him. Think inconsistencies.

The first inconsistency turned out to be a whopper. When he reached for the Patricia Kelly file, he found that it was missing.

2   The March day was glum—clouds and smog hid what sun there was—and the air had cooled perceptibly by the time Auntie Lil reached the cemetery in Brooklyn. My god, but she had seen more graves in one day than she had ever thought the earth had room for. She supposed they were already burying them in layers. The thought of being confined, even in death, by another coffin below or above her, was not a pleasant one. She made a mental note to remember to change her will and demand burial upstate alongside her beloved brother.

The trek to the far side of the cemetery was long. It seemed to stretch endlessly, bounded on all sides by wide thoroughfares and highways where drivers raced and honked with abandon—respect for the dead ignored in favor of life in the fast lane.

Shadows formed at the edges of the grave sites when the

afternoon sun finally broke through. Auntie Lil wrapped her coat collar more tightly around her neck and shivered in the breeze. The cemetery operators had resisted being entirely greedy and a few large shade trees remained along the outskirts, bordering a low stone wall that separated the graveyard from the sidewalk. In the cold March afternoon, the bony tree branches stretched out over the wall's barren stones with a distasteful grasping look. Auntie Lil hurried by them quickly. The sun slowly inched its way toward the west, casting unpleasant shadows on the path in front of her.

Behind her, concealed in the darkness beneath a large tree, stood the Asian man. He waited calmly in the dark haven, motionless, his hands in his coat pockets. Only his eyes moved slightly as he followed Auntie Lil's progress. When he saw a third figure approach in the distance, he stepped back further into the shadows and, unobserved, continued his careful watch.

Oblivious to anything else, Auntie Lil gave a small cry of triumph when she spotted the grave she was seeking. She knelt in front of it and caught her breath. The gravestone was as simple as the epitaph:

Patricia Kelly, 1938–1991
Beloved Friend & Mother

But it was not the stone that captured Auntie Lil's greatest interest. She brushed her gloves off daintily and lifted up a huge rotting bouquet of flowers stuffed into a cheap gold-painted plastic vase. It was not at all appropriate for the dead. It was, in fact, she was quite sure, a browned and withered bridal bouquet. The ribbons were a dirty and tattered white satin, bound around what had been a large bunch of white roses and lilies of the valley. Dried baby's breath and selected ferns completed the arrangement. Lifting the flowers into the air had revealed a combination of items carefully placed about the grave site. A cheap oval wooden box was propped against the headstone. The top was garishly painted in bright colors—the kind of inexpensive trinket made in Mexico that you could buy at any import store. She opened the lid slowly and found nestled inside a diamond necklace of such brilliance that it sent out tongues of fire in the waning afternoon light. Its quality confirmed John Boswell's excellent taste in jewelry.

She placed the necklace next to the withered bouquet and began to brush dirt off a buried square, quickly unearthing a slim book bound in a heavy plastic library cover. She scraped mud off of the front and *Women and Madness* emerged as the title, splashed across a lurid red-and-black illustration of a woman screaming. Auntie Lil flipped to the inside back cover and discovered ''Property of Little Neck Public Library'' stamped on a small manila pocket. Little Neck? That was Stanley Sinclair's hometown.

Another object was lodged in a mound of dirt piled against the grave—a large sterling paperweight shaped like a spoon. She read the inscription slowly, noting the decades-old date and expected words:

> *"To Robert, with warmest congratulations.*
> *You're on your way to the top.*
> *R.I.P."*

She placed the objects in her lap and stared out at the distant traffic. An item to connect each of the murders. Carefully chosen items, she was sure. Auntie Lil held up the paperweight and murmured, ''Something old.''

She tilted the necklace and it sparkled in the light. ''Something new,'' she whispered.

''Something borrowed,'' she thought, staring at the book. ''Followed one day soon by something blue.''

She was so absorbed that she did not notice a tall young woman with unruly blonde hair step lightly around a corner and pick her way carefully over the soggy ground in high-heeled shoes. Her head was down, lost in thought, and she looked up only when she stumbled over an errant tree root. Her green eyes focused on Auntie Lil, her face registering both alarm and surprise. She stopped short several rows from

Patricia Kelly's grave and stood still, staring at Auntie Lil's kneeling figure. The blonde woman trembled out of fear, excitement or both.

Under the tree, the Asian man took his turn staring, his eyes darting from one woman to the other. He knew the younger one. What was she doing here?

Auntie Lil caressed the objects with a delicately gloved finger. The crux of the entire mystery had been brought home to her very simply and infinitely sadly with what she had found. Something old, something new, something borrowed, something blue. Objects for a woman who had never had the opportunity to fulfill the wedding tradition when alive. Auntie Lil sighed. It seemed to her that Patricia Kelly had not yet found any peace or dignity, even in death. That her unfilled hopes and abused dreams still roamed the earth, restless and mourning. She touched the withered bridal bouquet.

The younger woman continued to stare intently as Auntie Lil carefully replaced the objects and leaned the bouquet back in place against the grave. Auntie Lil reached a hand out and gripped the gravestone, trembling with exertion as she eased herself to her feet.

Auntie Lil was too absorbed in her sadness to notice when the blonde finally moved from her spot. In an almost complete reversal of Auntie Lil's own actions, the woman dropped quickly to her knees at the nearest grave and wrapped a scarf, which had been at her neck, tightly around her face. She inched the bouquet she'd been holding onto the grave and bent her head as if absorbed in prayer. When Auntie Lil passed by with an absently murmured kind word, the young woman appeared too lost in sorrow to reply.

Auntie Lil carried herself tensely, as if she were in a terrible hurry. She eyed her original path and it seemed a long way out in the afternoon shadows. She turned and surveyed the low stone wall that marked the cemetery's far boundary, only a few yards from where she stood. She walked carefully over the spongy ground and stared down at the sidewalk. A three-foot drop. Could she pull it off?

The kneeling woman's eyes slid slowly to one side, then she turned slightly and gazed at Auntie Lil poised at the top of the wall. She put a hand down to the earth and started to rise, but when the Asian man stepped quietly out of the shadows, only his silhouette visible against the fading sun, she relaxed and turned back to her praying. The man moved silently toward the wall and stood a few yards behind Auntie Lil.

"Oh, dear." Auntie Lil clenched her hands into fists and banged her thighs in frustration. She leaned over the wall and eyed the nearby corner. A phone booth, miraculously empty, stood waiting. Gritting her teeth, she first sat on the top of the wall and then gave a quick hop. Although the distance wasn't great, it was far enough to hurt when she hit the sidewalk with a painful jar. The Asian man stepped away from the edge and back into the shadows, watching as Auntie Lil rubbed her ankle and hobbled toward the corner phone. He looked behind him at the praying woman and at the sidewalk crowded with people hurrying home. Having reached a decision, he leapt lightly over the wall and, blending in with the bustling crowd, hurried toward the corner and Auntie Lil.

She was too busy searching for quarters to notice Herbert Wong walk quickly past, hat pulled low over his face. He turned the corner and disappeared in the crowd.

3   Where could the blessed file have gone? T.S. searched every drawer in his makeshift office, knowing he would not find it. It had been taken deliberately. But by whom? By Miss Fullbright to give to Lieutenant Abromowitz? Was he having second thoughts about his own theory? After several fruitless minutes of search, T.S. sat back in his chair. It was useless. The file was gone. Taken by someone here at Sterling & Sterling.

He sighed. There was no use comparing files now. There was only one thing left to do until he could find Sheila. He would talk to Frederick Dorfen again.

For once, the old man was clearly sober. He answered his

phone immediately, almost jauntily, in fact. "Frederick Dorfen here," he said cheerfully. "At your service."

"Frederick? It's T.S. Have you got a minute?"

"I don't really know," the old man replied happily. "I'm terribly busy these days. Filling in for poor Cheswick and Boswell, you know. Business must go on and it appears that I'm about the only one who completely understands their areas and has the time. Would you believe it? The clients still remember me!"

"That's wonderful, Frederick. I'm not surprised at all. But it is important. Shall I come down?"

"No, no. I'll pop up now," Frederick Dorfen declared. "Plenty of energy in these old legs yet. Won't take but a minute, you say?"

"Just a minute," T.S. promised.

"That's good," he said cheerfully. "Because I've really got to get back to work."

Frederick Dorfen was a changed man when he entered T.S.'s office. He walked tall and proud, his shoulders thrown back. A clean handkerchief poked elegantly from his breast pocket and his hair was carefully brushed. He sat with great dignity in the visitor's chair, carefully straightening the crisp crease of each pants leg.

"What can I do for you?" he asked T.S. graciously.

He had to quiz the old man on Patricia Kelly. But he did not want to scare him off or elicit a horrified reaction like Edgar Hale's.

"Do you remember the last time I talked to you?" he asked the older partner.

"Certainly I do," Dorfen replied with calm dignity. "It was right after Boswell's death, I believe. Day before yesterday, was it?"

"On Monday," T.S. corrected him. "You made a remark. A curious remark."

"Did I?" He waited quietly for T.S. to continue, composed but watchful.

"About meeting you for margaritas at Magritte's." In the

silence that followed, T.S. stared at him carefully. It seemed like the old man's shoulders stiffened.

"Maybe I did," the partner admitted slowly. "So I did. It was careless of me."

"You said you could not remember where that saying had come from," T.S. prompted gently. "Have you thought about it since?"

"No need to," the old man replied very quietly. "I'm quite well aware of where that saying came from now. Being sober has its advantages."

"It's of life-or-death importance that you tell me."

"I know. Sinclair's death has proved it." The old man sighed with such sorrow and intensity that his backbone seemed to float out of him with the sound. He leaned back against the soft leather of the chair and rubbed his eyes. His shoulders slumped and he shook his head. "The world has changed, T.S.," he said. "It will never be as it once was. I remember when I was a young man just starting out. What responsibility and dignity there was attached to a job here at Sterling. How each one of us felt keenly aware of our role to protect and advise clients."

His voice grew heavy with memory and regret. "Now money is the name of the game. Forget honor and integrity." His shoulders straightened slightly and he stared at T.S. "It changed very quickly. By the time I was a partner, nothing was the same. The men you see now, heading up this firm, are as different from me as night and day. And the young men beneath them even more different. Each year is worse."

"About Magritte?" T.S. prompted gently.

Frederick Dorfen shook his head. "I don't really know what happened there that night. I guess I never wanted to know. Their fathers were friends of mine. She was just a young secretary from Queens, I think it was, or maybe Brooklyn. Her word against theirs. And Ralph Peabody assured me . . . Later, when she wrote those things about me, I *knew* she was lying. So I became even more convinced she'd been lying back then." His voice trailed off into silence.

"It's Patricia Kelly you're thinking of, isn't it, Frederick?" T.S. kept his voice soft and low. The old man's sorrow was nearly contagious.

"Yes." He sighed again. "Patricia Kelly. That poor child. She hadn't a chance. She wasn't very strong. Mentally, I mean. But lovely. Very lovely."

He coughed and his voice took on new strength. He sat up straighter and looked evenly at T.S. "Magritte isn't a person. *Magritte's* was the name of a private club that used to be just around the corner. The building's still there, but it's been called something different for years. Now it's *The Bull Pen* or some kind of nonsense like that. Something happened there one night to Patricia Kelly. In a private room upstairs. I don't know what. It was long ago. I was only told because I was Managing Partner at the time. It was my first inkling that the world was changing and that I wouldn't be able to keep up. Ralph Peabody handled the situation. He said he investigated thoroughly. That her charges were unfounded, not true. The product of a sick imagination."

"What were her charges?" T.S. asked firmly. "What were the charges?"

"Rape," Frederick Dorfen answered simply. "I believe she accused the men of rape. Sexual assault they called it, in those days. It was all we could do to persuade her not to go to the police."

"Who were the men she accused, Frederick? It is most important that I know."

He looked up at T.S. in surprise. "Why, it's obvious. Robert Cheswick. John Boswell. Stanley Sinclair. And Edgar Hale."

"Edgar Hale?" T.S. repeated automatically. "No one else?"

"No one else but Edgar," Dorfen confirmed. "He has always been their leader."

4   As soon as Auntie Lil left the graveyard, the young woman with blonde hair rose from her position and moved to where Auntie Lil had knelt. She approached the site slowly, feeling her way forward over the ground as if she'd been struck suddenly blind. She leaned forward and moved her long fingers over the name chiseled into the stone. In an imitation of Auntie Lil's earlier gesture, she knelt before the simple epitaph and raised the withered bouquet in the air. Objects tumbled to the ground before her and she picked up each one in turn. Her head bowed low as she examined the collection and remained bowed for many minutes. When she raised her head again, tears ran slowly down her cheeks and glittered in the waning afternoon sun. She ran a trembling hand through her closely cropped hair, pushing the scarf off her head and back around her shoulders. Lost in thought, she searched the sky for an answer, absently picked up each sad object again in turn. Her lower lip had started to bleed, she was biting it so tightly, and tears glistened on her cheeks as brightly as the diamond necklace.

Ignoring the book, she tucked the necklace and its box into her purse. She weighed the heavy silver spoon paperweight thoughtfully in her palm, then placed that in her purse as well. Rising from the grave, she headed for the low wall. She stopped at the edge and stared down the sidewalk. Spotting Auntie Lil at the corner phone, she melted back into the shadows beneath the trees, much as Herbert Wong had done only moments before.

Auntie Lil was in great pain—her ankle throbbed from the jump. She wrapped her coat more tightly against the growing cold and waited anxiously for T.S. to answer. To her intense relief, he picked up after the third ring.

"Theodore," she cried breathlessly into the phone. "I've hurt my ankle, but we've really found it this time."

"Found what?" His voice came tinnily over the wire and she strained to hear.

"The connections. The proof. It *is* the daughter. I'm absolutely sure. I can't talk about it now." Auntie Lil stopped and looked around suspiciously. "I may be watched for all I know."

"Don't get carried away," T.S. said wearily. His mind was preoccupied with what Frederick Dorfen had told him.

The world was turning nasty all round him and he didn't like it one bit. "What exactly did you find out?" he asked.

"The paperweight and the necklace and one of Sinclair's library books," she explained. "Arranged across the grave as a kind of offering. It was terribly sad."

"Get out of there immediately," he ordered her, his voice growing sharp. "And leave things just as you found them. We can't let her know she's been discovered, whoever she may be."

"Of course," she promised, rather affronted at having her story broken into so rudely. "I'm on my way now. We must warn the men on that awful list from Patricia Kelly's file."

T.S. sighed. "You better be absolutely sure, you know."

"I am. I saw the objects. What did you find out from re-checking the files?"

"Nothing. Someone took Patricia Kelly's file off my desk this morning."

There was a brief silence on the other end. "This morning?"

"This morning." His voice was dull. "I'm sure. It was here earlier this morning and now it's gone."

"Well, that's good news," she said hesitantly.

"It is?"

"Yes. That means the killer is probably at Sterling & Sterling."

"How reassuring," he told her drily.

"Better there than right behind me," she explained indignantly.

"Yes, yes. You are quite right." He was relieved by her reasoning. "At least I have people around me."

"What did you find out from Frederick Dorfen?"

"You were right about there being fire where there's smoke. He says that *Magritte's* was a private club near the bank. Around the corner. Something happened there one night to Patricia Kelly. There were allegations of rape involving her, Cheswick, Boswell and Sinclair. Plus one more."

"One more what?"

"One more man."

"Who?"

"Edgar Hale."

There was a silence on the other end, then her voice came through sharp and clear. "This is not a game, Theodore," she said. "I found objects on the grave belonging to the dead men. Edgar Hale is next. You must warn him."

"He'll never believe me," T.S. said simply. "I made a fool of myself last time."

"Then I'm coming in to tell him myself."

He stared helplessly at the clock. "He'll be gone by the time you get here," he pleaded. "Let's call the lieutenant. Tell him what we have."

"You call the lieutenant. Then call Edgar Hale and tell him to wait. We have to talk to him today."

She hung up before he had a chance to protest, her abrupt action prompted more by the shock of sudden and unexpected recognition than hurry. She had been staring across the street at a tiny church while she talked, her mind unconsciously noting every detail of its small but charming facade. It was a skinny stone church squeezed between two enormous apartment buildings, and its spires, not more than several stories tall, were dwarfed by the high-rise neighbors.

But it was not the architecture that caught her eye. It was the name. An unusual name for a church. One she had heard before. It was etched deeply in stone. Not even centuries of smog would be likely to ever erode the letters: "*Our Lady of Perpetual Help.*"

"That's what *we* need," Auntie Lil thought. "Perpetual help." But where had she heard that name before? She let her mind roam over the days since Robert Cheswick had been found stabbed. Someone, somewhere had mentioned that name. It was maddening to be so near. She pulled her notebook out of her pocketbook and began to flip through it quickly, then stopped just as suddenly.

It had been the very act of pulling out her notebook as efficiently as an experienced stenographer that had jogged her memory. Anne Marie. Anne Marie had gone to school at Our Lady of Perpetual Help. T.S. had thought it so appropriate for a secretary.

But would there be any connection? Could there be any connection?

As if in answer to her thoughts or, perhaps, her unspoken prayers, an elderly nun turned the corner near the church and inched toward the building's stone steps. She moved slowly with the air of one plagued by arthritis. An old-fashioned marketing basket was slung over one arm and she was dressed in a traditional black-and-white Roman Catholic habit.

An old nun. A very old nun. One who had trouble walking. What had the aide at the mental hospital said? That Patricia Kelly had very few visitors. A mysterious lady. A priest now and then. And an old nun who could barely walk. And where else would Patricia Kelly be buried than across from the only place where she was still remembered?

Auntie Lil checked the coin return automatically for quarters, scanned for traffic and crossed the street. She would reach the front door at the same time as the nun.

Behind her, Herbert Wong moved out slowly from his hiding spot around the corner. He had not gone far. He watched Auntie Lil cross the street and greet the elderly nun. His face was puzzled and anxious. Only when he saw Auntie Lil enter the massive oak doors of the church did he relax. He leaned against the stone wall and waited.

Behind him, in the shadows of a nearby oak tree, Sheila crossed her arms and waited, too.

5   T.S. dialed Abromowitz to tell him of Auntie Lil's finds. Things had gotten nasty. It was time to turn the whole thing over to professionals, like it or not.

"Who is this?" the Lieutenant barked rudely. His version of "hello."

"T.S. Hubbert. I've got some new information you may find . . ."

"I'm not interested. Butt out." He hung up without comment, the bang of the receiver ringing in T.S.'s ears.

Damn them all. They could kill each other off for all he

cared. But Auntie Lil's words reverberated in his mind: "This is not a game, Theodore."

T.S. dialed Edgar Hale's number with resignation, prepared to be hung up on yet again.

"Hale," the familiar disagreeable voice boomed into the receiver.

"It's T.S., Edgar." He was met by an underwhelming silence.

"What do you want?" the old man finally barked. "Clever of you to wait until Mrs. Quincy is away from her desk to call me."

T.S. spoke quickly, anxious to get it all in before the old man could hang up. "Edgar, I know you think I'm crazy but Auntie Lil is absolutely convinced she's uncovered evidence that's a matter of life and death."

"What rot," Edgar Hale said.

"Life and death for you," T.S. cried in desperation. The anguish in his voice convinced Edgar Hale to listen.

"I'm waiting," the Managing Partner finally said, "but it better be good. I suffered through an extremely humiliating lunch with Frederick Dorfen today, who talked of nothing but the Patricia Kelly affair. It took us decades to bury that mess and you go and dig it up."

"I apologize again, Edgar. I don't know exactly what Auntie Lil has, but she's on her way in now and feels that you may be in danger. Can you wait until she gets here?" He'd let *her* have a try at convincing him that Patricia Kelly still lived, at least in spirit. Not that Edgar Hale deserved a warning. He had known all along what *Magritte's* meant and had chosen to conceal it.

The old man snorted. "I can wait all night. Haven't you heard? I'm the only one doing any work around here! Preston Freeman is sitting in his lawyer's office not saying a word, and it's taking days to go through his two apartments and three houses in four different states. How many homes does one man need? Meanwhile, I've just discovered that before Cheswick died, he didn't just neglect accounts, he practically destroyed them." The old man sighed and in the sudden silence that followed T.S. heard the distinct echo of a distant crash.

"What the hell?" he heard Edgar Hale shout. "What is it now?" The phone was dropped with a thud and T.S. heard screaming and cries in the background.

"Stop that!" Edgar Hale's voice boomed out from a distance. "Stop that. What's going on in here? Get out! Get out, I tell you! Frederick—get some help!"

T.S. didn't wait to hear more. He was already halfway out the door.

CHAPTER FIFTEEN

1 It was natural enough for Auntie Lil to offer to help. The elderly nun was huffing and puffing too much to protest when Auntie Lil took the market basket from her, gripped her elbow and guided her inside the church.

The observers watched the scene with interest. As Auntie Lil disappeared inside the church, Sheila looked at her watch and bit her lip, then turned resolutely away and walked briskly through the far exit of the cemetery. Herbert Wong continued to lean against the low brick wall, staring at the church doors.

While the nun fussed over her packages, Auntie Lil stood in the darkness of the entrance room and wondered where the old sister could possibly reside. The building looked the same inside as it did outside—as if the brick apartments on either side were squeezing the life from its stones. A narrow aisle ran between short rows of pews but the altar made up in depth what it lacked in width. The floor was green marble inlaid with stars of white, but the pews were nicked and scarred. The windows were high and skinny, their beauty vanquished by the apartment buildings that blocked the light that used to stream through the stained glass. It was a pity. The expressive faces of saints now lurked in darkness, any hope they might have symbolized lost.

The old nun appeared not to notice or care that the life was being squeezed from her home. She smiled her thanks at Auntie Lil and headed briskly for a wooden door hidden in the shadows of the altar, leaving Auntie Lil to her prayers.

Accordingly, Auntie Lil uttered a short one and answered it herself. "Sister," she called out. "May I speak to you?"

The nun stopped, one foot on the altar step, and turned to stare at the stranger. Auntie Lil looked harmless enough—elderly and clean. Nicely dressed with perhaps a too-jaunty hat, but at least her head was covered. So few women bothered these days. A step up, in fact, from the usual crowd. All the same, it was best to be careful. Sister Bridget Mary had learned that over the years. God resided everywhere, but was sometimes elbowed aside in New York City.

"If something is bothering you," she told Auntie Lil gently, "perhaps I should call Father Davies. He's much better at this kind of thing than I am."

"No, it's not that." Auntie Lil moved carefully closer, inching her way down the darkened aisle. "It's you I want to speak to. About someone you may have known."

The nun stared at Auntie Lil without moving, then placed her bundle down on the step and moved slowly forward. Her former briskness gone, she put a hand out and grabbed the top of each pew as she passed, moving her way back up the aisle toward Auntie Lil. Her face settled into a grim mask, as if she knew what Auntie Lil was going to ask and dreaded opening up the subject.

"About who?" she asked softly, slipping into a pew by Auntie Lil. She slid along its polished surface and waited patiently for Auntie Lil to speak.

Auntie Lil could not bring herself to tempt fate so brazenly as to lie to a nun. Nor could she face the woman's trusting features with anything less than the truth.

"It's about Patricia Kelly," she said quietly. The empty air within the church stirred with her words and soft echoes fluttered up the aisle. "She was a member of this church, wasn't she?"

"She once was," the old nun admitted sadly, her sign of the cross discreet and automatic. "She's in the hands of God now."

"Yes. I know. I've just been to her grave. It's a very sad story, isn't it?"

"It depends on how much of the story you know." The nun had moved almost imperceptibly away from Auntie Lil and her voice had grown more wary.

"I am not going to lie to you, Sister," Auntie Lil whispered urgently. "The truth is, I did not know her. I was not even certain that she was a member of this church, but when I saw the name it reminded me of someone else. Someone who I suspect must have a connection to Patricia Kelly. I have come here to find out if that is so."

"Who is this person?" The nun glanced toward the altar and Auntie Lil wondered where the priest might be.

"Her name is Anne Marie Shaunessy," Auntie Lil said. "I know that she went to school here."

"We have no school here," the nun said emphatically.

"Not now. That's obvious. But perhaps, many years ago, you did."

"Perhaps." The nun folded her hands as if in prayer and stared down at the marble floor. "There was no Anne Marie Shaunessy at the school," she said quietly.

"That is her married name. She would have been known by another name back then." Auntie Lil stared at the bowed head. She would break down the woman's defenses slowly, she was not the type to keep up a lie for long. Sister Bridget Mary was used to a kinder world than the one in which Auntie Lil moved. It was a pity to intrude upon the sanctuary she had sought in the Church, but Auntie Lil had no other recourse. "I think you know who I'm talking about," she told the nun.

Her answering sigh was as faint as the rustling of silk. "What do you want to know? Even if you are not a Catholic, surely you believe in letting the dead rest in peace?"

"I do believe in that. Most definitely. But I don't think that Patricia Kelly is resting in peace. In fact, that is the very reason I am here. To bring her peace."

"How did you know to speak to me?"

Auntie Lil shifted uncomfortably on the hard wood. "I visited the hospital where she died. They told me that one of her very few visitors had been a nun."

"An old nun, no doubt." The woman managed a smile, which she hid with her hands as if God might somehow be offended.

"Perhaps. I'm not one to throw stones," Auntie Lil

pointed out. "She also had another visitor at times. A woman. They could not give me a description."

"That would have been Anne Marie," the nun answered quietly. "She loved Patricia very much. She was, I think, the only one who could understand how much she had suffered. What she had given up."

"How had she suffered?" Auntie Lil asked. "I have no wish to disturb the dead or bring up sad memories that are better left alone. But I am concerned with the living and many people are being hurt. What you have to tell me may be important."

"She has been back here quite often in recent days." The old nun sighed again.

"Who?"

"Anne Marie. I think, perhaps, sad memories are coming back on their own."

"How had Patricia Kelly suffered?" Auntie Lil prompted gently.

The nun sat back against the pew, her habit rustling. She tucked her hands beneath the bib and stared up at a huge stained glass rendering of Jesus that dominated the wall behind the altar. This window alone was lit from behind and golden light poured through the halo that encircled his head. His face drooped with a permanent sadness as hands helped him down from the cross.

For the first time in many years, Auntie Lil felt close to God and the small infusion of strength gave her the courage to press on. "I don't know what else to tell you except that I need to know," she said.

"I knew that nothing good could come of it," the old nun said sadly. "We see a lot of sadness here, you know. People bring it to our door every day. Lay it out. Ask us to make it better." She sighed again, deeply. "A long time ago, I thought we had the power. Now . . ." Her voice trailed off and she shrugged, then her shoulders straightened and her voice grew more confident. A decision had been made.

"To tell the story of Patricia Kelly and Anne Marie Gallagher, you'd have to go back many years. Many, many years.

It was before we sold the lot next door. When the school still stood there and we had rooms for the sisters. There were more than a dozen of us then. I'm the only one left, you know. I take care of Father Davies. I don't think any one else in the Church really remembers we exist. We had to sell the land because we had no money and the people of our parish have greater needs these days than learning how to type.'' She grimaced and shook her head.

"Patricia and Anne Marie entered the school together. They held hands their first day, I remember. We knew their families well. Both lived only a few blocks over, within doors of each other. It was a nicer neighborhood back then. Neither Patricia or Anne Marie had any sisters. Both came from huge families filled with boys.'' She looked at Auntie Lil keenly. "I confess I have often thought that it would have been better if we had all been born men in this world.'' Auntie Lil nodded in understanding.

"Naturally, they gravitated toward one another. Anne Marie was the tomboy back then. She was always as brown as a little Indian. She could ride bicycles and sail and fish better than any of her brothers. The Bay was still clean then. She practically lived on the water. Used to bring us fish for our Friday meals. Patricia was different. She was the shy one, followed Anne Marie in all she did, but without Anne Marie's enthusiasm. Patricia's mother had been very old when she was born. Old for those days, at any rate. Anne Marie took the place of Patricia's mother in many ways, I always thought.

"But their positions changed once they came here for training. There had been no question about what they would do. Nice young girls in those days came here for secretarial training. Period. We doubled as a high school. I was the typing and shorthand teacher.'' She held out her chubby palms and stared at them. "Can you believe I was once quite good at it? I don't think they even teach shorthand anymore. Why bother? Tape recorders. Video cameras. Who needs it?

"They were both good students. Top of the class. Anne Marie was first, of course, but Patricia was close behind. They grew into beautiful young ladies. Patricia especially,

she was so tall and striking, a Nordic princess, perhaps.''
She laughed, briefly, covering her mouth again as if the sound
were inappropriate.

"They had gone through a year or two of wanting to be
nuns, but it was clear from the looks of both of them that it
wasn't going to last. Boys were already lingering around the
corner before either was even fifteen. I don't know their private lives, but there was soon no more talk of being nuns.

"By the time Anne Marie graduated, she was a proper
young lady. No more being a tomboy for her. Always dressed
up, gloves even. Hair carefully groomed. What little makeup her mother would allow. Patricia had changed as well.
She wasn't so docile, so willing to follow Anne Marie. She
was the tomboy by then, loud and laughing and boisterous.
Caused commotion after commotion in class. But to tell you
the truth"—she stopped and looked at Auntie Lil—"it was
Patricia I preferred. She was loud, but so honest and so much
fun. As if she had just discovered life and it was too mar-
velous to believe. I used to look at her and feel that, because
of her, I wasn't missing out on so much myself. Anne Marie
was ladylike, it was true. But controlled. Too controlled.
Still, I knew she would do well in life.

"They both took a job at some Wall Street firm, earning a
top salary for those days. I wasn't surprised they went to work
together, they were still inseparable. After that, I lost track of
them for several years. Most of our girls go through that period.
They haven't time for church. They're building a life, starting
families, thinking of other things. Or else they've married and
moved away. Switched over to their husband's diocese. I believe I never really expected to see either one again.''

The small door behind the altar opened. An old man exited,
dressed in street clothes. Only the stiff white collar gave him
away. He stepped briskly across the worn floor, glanced briefly
at Auntie Lil, then raised a hand and continued on outside.
Sister Bridget Mary waited a few seconds before she continued.

"Patricia came to see Father Williams a few years later. He's
gone now. Dead, like so many of us. Sometimes I envy them,
you know. They want me to retire, but I haven't any money,

and what would I do? Who would take care of things here?''
She stared again at her hands. ''Patricia's problem was not
surprising. We got quite a few problems like that in those
days and I am only sorry that the alternative is so readily
available these days. But I *was* surprised at it being Patricia.
She was going to have a baby and she wasn't married. She
was afraid it would kill her parents if they knew. Knowing
her parents as I did, I must say that I almost agreed. She had
a plan. If we would help her find a place to stay and have the
child, she had a friend who would raise it. A friend who had
been married several years but could not have children and
was desperate for one of her own. It was Anne Marie, of
course. She had married that awful Tommy Shaunessy, God
alone knows why. Although I can guess why He saw fit to
deny him a natural son.'' She shivered in distaste, but did
not elaborate. Auntie Lil did not want to know.

''I argued against it. It was, perhaps, the only time I ever
disagreed publicly with the Father. But I did not think it was
a good idea to place the child with someone Patricia knew.
It would always be there, so close, you know, to remind her
what might have been. She had already changed, you see. I
could see it in her eyes. A lost, almost wild look. I was
worried for her even then. I felt that having the child nearby
would hamper her ability to get on with a new life and, despite what people say about the Catholic Church, we do care
very much for the living.

''I was overruled and Patricia was sent away. The adoption
was arranged. I thought, for the second time, that the story
had reached an end.'' The nun produced a tissue from beneath her bib and held it up near her bulbous nose. Her voice
quivered but she continued on, her face well averted from
Auntie Lil's sympathetic gaze.

''Many years later, I received a phone call from Anne Marie. She was in tears, genuinely so distraught that I could hardly
make out the words. Patricia had been committed to a mental
hospital, it seems. After behavior so . . . so shocking and
troubling that her family had disowned her. There was no one
to care, no one to see her through. I believe it was too much

for Anne Marie to bear. Would I go and see her? she begged me. What could I say?'' Sister Bridget Mary shrugged and her face sagged with the sadness of remembering.

"That began the first of many, many years of visits to Patricia in those kinds of hospitals. I did not think she should be forgotten. Sometimes, they would let her out to move among us, but I don't believe that she was ever really herself again. Not even for a moment. She walked in some different world she found necessary to build. I never prayed for her to die, that would have been wrong, but I sometimes asked God why he couldn't see fit to somehow ease her suffering.''

The old nun dropped to her knees on a low padded bench that pulled back from the pew in front of them. She stared intently at the stained glass window. "I've seldom seen or spoken to Anne Marie in decades. Not even in the last few weeks when she has been here praying. But I continued to visit Patricia every month or so until she died. I just wanted her to know that someone remembered who she had been and that someone still cared. Someone besides God.''

With that, the nun laid her cheek on the back of the forward pew and began to cry softly. It was a sad and raspy sound that filled the emptiness of the church. The deserted corners seemed almost to welcome the noise, embracing the sobs as if the stone walls fed upon the loneliness. Auntie Lil looked around her at the shadows and darkness, then back to the stained glass window. She knelt beside Sister Bridget Mary and gently patted the woman's heaving shoulders. "I'm so sorry,'' she whispered to the nun. "So sorry to make you remember.''

Despite her forthrightness, in many ways Auntie Lil believed deeply in the privacy of the human soul. She left the old nun weeping in her sorrow and moved slowly out of the church into the last of the March afternoon. The fresh air cleared her head, sweeping away the painful passing of years that had been laid so barely at her feet. But it did not remove the agony nudging at her own heart. Sheila was Patricia Kelly's daughter. Who better to avenge her mother's death? Auntie Lil had not planned on breaking her own nephew's heart. T.S. would never be the same.

She stood on the stone steps, then turned and slipped back inside the church. It was empty. Sister Bridget Mary had escaped to the familiar comfort of her own room. The votive candles flickered forlornly to one side of the altar. Only five had been lit. The poor box was battered and dented and the lighting sticks scattered in disarray. Auntie Lil knelt before the bank of candles and slipped a twenty-dollar bill into the metal box. She carefully lit three of the misshapen mounds of wax. One for Patricia Kelly, one for Sheila and one for her dear Theodore.

2   A dozen different scenarios raced through his imagination as T.S. dashed down the fire stairs. Edgar Hale being throttled to death by the murderer came immediately to mind. Maybe by someone he knew. Perhaps even Sheila. Where was she today? In his confusion, he even imagined Lieutenant Abromowitz straddling Edgar Hale, Sterling's antique fire poker raised high above his head.

He flew down the Main Floor with the abandon of a wild man. Had he the time to notice, he would have been surprised to see how few people looked up to watch him race past. The fact was, most were already crowded into the Partners' Room. A wave of sound buzzed and lingered around the edges of the crowd as T.S. shouldered his way through a thick pack of Sterling & Sterling employees. The excited hum of their voices formed an indistinct backdrop for his own confused thoughts. He could hear shouted phrases, but could not make out the words. He was vaguely aware of employees hooting and shouting as if they were at a football game. "Cheering on a murderer?" he vaguely thought. The world had gone mad.

Madder than even he imagined. He burst through the crowd and found himself in a roughly defined circle beneath the portrait of Samuel Sterling and his sons. The fireplace tools and screen had tumbled across the rug. Edgar Hale stood to one side, his mouth open in silent rage and his face pulsating an alarming shade of purple. Frederick Dorfen stood on a chair, his old legs shaking beneath him. He had his arms spread wide and was attempting to shout above the crowd, calling for order that never came.

In the center of the circle stood Anne Marie and Mrs. Quincy. They faced each other like angry gladiators, arms outstretched and fingers tensed for battle. A long scratch marred the side of Anne Marie's face and blood oozed from a cut on Mrs. Quincy's nose. Anne Marie's hair flew about her face in angry wisps and her dress had been ripped—the sleeve hung limply like a broken wing. One of her shoes came off as she lunged at Mrs. Quincy before retreating to her corner of the makeshift ring with what looked to be a deflated raccoon dangling in her clenched fist.

Mrs. Quincy gave an angry, high-pitched shriek and T.S. looked up, startled, at the old secretary's contorted face. Her hair had disappeared, to be replaced by a mottled and strangely colored patch of stubble that dotted her egg-shaped skull like underfed and dying grass.

Anne Marie waved the wig above her head like a trophy, shouting at her foe. "You've got your nerve," she screamed. "Saying I dye my hair. This isn't even yours!" She waved the wig again and T.S. realized with horror that several people in the crowd were shouting encouragement.

"Let her have it, Anne Marie!" a heretofore dignified executive cried. T.S. shot him a look that inspired the man to fall silent immediately.

"Stop! Someone stop this nonsense!" Frederick Dorfen shouted.

Mrs. Quincy seized the opportunity to dart forward and kick Anne Marie in the shins, shouting a phrase that T.S. had never imagined she knew.

Anne Marie was less surprised. She flung what was left of Mrs. Quincy's wig to the ground and spat on it. "I'm not afraid of you!" Anne Marie screeched, her formerly modulated voice now replaced by the shrill nasal tones of an angry young girl from Brooklyn. "I'll take you on. Come on! Come on!" She actually put up her fists as if to box and T.S. decided that things had gone far enough.

He dashed between the two women and was rewarded with

an astonishingly powerful right hook to his jaw. His anger was so great, however, that it didn't stop him for long. He grabbed Anne Marie by both hands and twisted her roughly to one side, pinning her arms behind her. "Get Quincy. Move!" he ordered Edgar Hale. The partner obeyed, grabbing his secretary's frail arms with little enthusiasm. All the fight went out of Mrs. Quincy at her boss's touch. In fact, she looked suddenly frightened. She stared at the crowd with horror, any hope of maintaining her dignity shredded. Tears welled in her eyes as Frederick Dorfen proved he truly was a gentleman by taking control of the crowd.

"That's it!" he shouted from his perch on the chair. "Enough is quite enough. Leave this room immediately. Without hesitation. I mean that. Leave this room *now*." He stood above the crowd like a policeman directing traffic from a stadium, pointing to slow moving employees with a warning glare. Eventually, employees began to group together, shaking their heads, muttering in disbelief and grumbling that their fun had been interrupted.

"Everyone may go home early!" Dorfen finally called out in desperation and the pace toward the doors quickened. "The firm is closed for the week. Go home now!" He had discovered the magic formula. Within minutes, the room was emptied of everyone but Edgar Hale, T.S., the two women and Dorfen.

The oldest partner climbed slowly down from his chair. He eyed both women, then shook his head sadly and put a gentle arm around the now sobbing Mrs. Quincy. "Now, now, Mrs. Quincy," he told her gently. "We all lose control sometimes. We've been under great strain. Everyone will soon forget all about this." He led her down the hall toward the private conference rooms.

T.S. had less luck calming Anne Marie. She muttered angry threats beneath her breath and T.S. caught snatches of her long-buried Brooklyn accent.

"Anne Marie, please," he pleaded. "Take a deep breath. Calm down. We've all gotten overexcited." He repeated his command until she began to relax. Edgar Hale took a step toward her but she tensed up again and T.S. had to ask him to leave the room, a task the partner undertook with enthusiasm. In fact, he nearly mowed Sheila down on his way out the door. She burst into the room, gasping for breath, and her eyes flew to T.S. and then to her mother. She lunged forward, shouting, and Anne Marie twisted away to run into her daughter's arms. She fell against Sheila and broke into sobs like an overgrown child. Sheila stroked her mother's hair back into place and glared at T.S.

"What happened?" she asked angrily. "What's going on?"

"I haven't the faintest idea," he protested. "Where have you been?"

Sheila ignored him and attempted to calm her mother. T.S. pulled up the chair Frederick Dorfen had used for a stage and sat in it with a dull thud. "What in the world were they fighting about?" he asked wearily.

Anne Marie whispered frantically to her daughter and Sheila looked up at T.S. with pleading eyes. "Please, Mr. Hubbert," she asked, "it's something Mrs. Quincy said. Mom's been so on edge. You can't imagine. Please let me handle it. The doctor gave her some tranquilizers earlier this week. I'll make her take one. It'll be okay, I promise. I'll take care of it. Just leave us alone."

"Where have you been?" he insisted. "I've been trying to find you all day. I must talk to you immediately." Was she avoiding him?

Her face took on a new desperation. "I know you do. I have to talk to you, too. *Alone.* Please. Can't you wait for me in your office? I'll be up as soon as I can."

He saw no other option. He had no idea what could be going on. "All right," he told her as sternly as he could manage in his worry. "I'll wait for you upstairs."

Sheila was already guiding her mother gently toward the nearest ladies' room. T.S. had not even gotten halfway up the aisle of the Main Floor when Effie Abacrombie appeared at his elbow. She had left her operator post at the reception desk in such haste that a pair of headphones still dangled about her neck, the disconnected wires crossing her ample chest like a gun belt.

"Have you ever seen anything like it, sir? What a battle that was. A regular sortie. I'd have to call it a draw. Both sides fought with courage. They were worthy opponents. But it's a very good thing that no clients were present this late in the day."

"A very good thing," T.S. agreed. He felt about a hundred years old. His orderly life had dissolved into insanity. He would not have been surprised to hear Effie yell, "Once more into the breach!" before leaping into the potted palms.

"I really must go upstairs now, Effie," he told her. "I haven't got the energy to talk."

"I thought you'd like to know, sir," she whispered urgently. He could sense departing employees around them, slowing in their movements, leaning forward to hear. He grasped her elbow firmly and guided her down the hall toward the elevators and into a private alcove.

"Let me know what, Effie? Just give it to me straight. What is it I should hear?"

"What it was that started the skirmish, sir. I heard the whole thing. I was just leaving the ladies' room."

Whatever it was, he doubted he wanted to know. But what choice did he have anymore? There was nothing left in this entire mystery that would make him happy now. "What was said?" he asked the head operator.

"Quincy called her crazy," Effie informed him importantly. "She was leaving right behind Anne Marie, and Anne Marie stopped to straighten her pantyhose. Quincy bumped into her and didn't even say excuse me. She just said, 'Wake up, why don't you, Anne Marie? You're right in the middle of the doorway. You're just as crazy as she was.' "

"Just as crazy as she was?" T.S. repeated. "Who's 'she'?"

"I don't know," Effie admitted with a shrug. "I just overheard that one part. But believe me, that was enough. Anne Marie flew at her like a cat in heat and started scratching at her face. The next thing you know Quincy is scratching and punching back. Just like those lady mud wrestlers on television. The two of them rolled and kicked each other down the hall and tumbled into the Partners' Room with half the firm hot on their trail. I only followed to help prevent injuries.''

''Yes, I know,'' T.S. murmured weakly. ''I saw that much.''

''Could you believe it when she ripped Quincy's hair right off of her head? Thirty-two years I've known her and never suspected it was a wig.''

''You never know,'' he agreed wearily.

''If you ask me, Quincy's half right, you know,'' the receptionist offered.

''How's that?'' He forced himself to turn and punch the elevator button. He'd get the next car and escape to the peace and quiet of his office.

''This entire place has gone crazy. Just completely crazy.''

3   Auntie Lil realized how stupid they had been halfway through the subway ride toward Sterling & Sterling. They should have guessed the truth. Cheswick's missing personal correspondence files, plucked so easily from their spot. Someone had known where to look. Boswell's weakness for blondes and his readiness to go for a sail with someone he knew and trusted. Someone knowing right where to look to find a hiding Stanley Sinclair. Anne Marie insisting that Robert Cheswick had been the same before his death, when others had argued he was under pressure. Her silly lie about Cheswick sending the flowers to his wife, when all along they had been going to Patricia Kelly. Anne Marie had been protecting someone near and dear to her and the strain had been showing. Protecting someone near and dear to them all. It would break Theodore's heart to find out it was Sheila.

Auntie Lil had called T.S. immediately after leaving the church, but no one had answered the phone, not even the department receptionist. It worried her. Sheila had been missing for the entire day. There was no telling where she had been or what she was up to.

* * *

4   T.S. hovered anxiously near his desk, filled with foreboding. Effie Abacrombie was absolutely right. The world
was going mad around them.

Calm down, he told himself. Face the truth squarely. What
was the worst that could happen? The worst was that Sheila
was Patricia Kelly's daughter and the murderer, he supposed.
But if it was Sheila, then she would soon be in his office and
could not be putting Auntie Lil's or Edgar Hale's life in danger. Only his own. It was hardly a reassuring thought. Perhaps it was unwise to be alone with anyone until he knew
which end was up.

He need not have worried. Sheila arrived with her mother
in tow. Anne Marie's eyes were red from weeping but she
appeared much calmer than before. He wondered how many
tranquilizers she'd been munching. He ushered them inside
solemnly, unable to meet Sheila's eyes.

Both sat almost primly in their chairs, facing T.S. with
grim expressions. Even if their physical appearances were
worlds apart, their mannerisms were not. Sheila looked more
guilty than her mother, perhaps, but both of them fidgeted
nervously with their hands carefully folded in their laps, as
if waiting to be asked to dance.

"What is this all about, Mr. Hubbert?" Sheila asked anxiously. "My mother has insisted she be present. I'm not
being fired, am I?"

"Fired?" He laughed perhaps too loudly. "Fired? Of
course not." What put these ideas in people's heads? Then
he remembered. He did.

"It's very embarrassing," T.S. began.

"Then perhaps you had better just spit it out," Sheila
piped up. Her voice was unnaturally loud and she cast anxious glances at her mother, as if Anne Marie might jump up
and flee from the room. But Anne Marie sat in a near trance,
her eyes fixed on some unknown point.

At least Sheila had not lost her spunk, he thought. This
gave him courage. "I must ask you some questions," he
started slowly. "I know it's most disturbing and you'll think
I don't trust you, but . . ." He stared down at his hands,

then looked her in the eye. "It appears you may have lied to me and I need to know why."

Her reaction was immediate. She flushed a deep scarlet and looked away.

"You must tell me the absolute truth now," he warned her.

"Fire away," she mumbled. "I'll certainly try."

"Is there anyone who can vouch for your whereabouts the night that Robert Cheswick died? Or the Sunday afternoon John Boswell drowned? What about the day that Stanley Sinclair was shot? An alibi for just one of those times would help. I know that Brian was out of town, I've talked to him on the phone. Was anyone with you?"

"Yes," Sheila said after a short pause, her face flushed a deep scarlet.

"Who?"

"Sergeant William Perry. Of the Third Precinct." She recited his name flatly, as if name, rank and serial number were all he'd drag out of her.

"Oh, sweet Joseph," her mother murmured, turning to stare at her daughter. "That's your father's precinct. Oh, my god." Her eyes opened wide.

"Please, Anne Marie," T.S. pleaded. "Let me handle this. Better she be unfaithful than accused of murder." Anne Marie looked unconvinced, but she shut her mouth at the mention of murder.

"Murder?" Sheila turned to stare at him. "You think *I* did this?" She waved her hands around as if the bodies were lying about the room. "I thought that you trusted me," she pleaded. "You know I would never . . ."

"I'm only asking you the questions the police will ask you." Tears welled in her eyes, but he steeled himself to go on. "You were *friends* with this Sergeant Perry?" he asked delicately.

"I *am* friends with this Sergeant Perry."

"Another cop? What good is that going to do?" her mother suddenly shouted. Anne Marie stood, ripped sleeve still dangling, her calm abruptly vanishing. "You know what they're like! You've seen it your entire life. How *could* you?"

"He's not like Dad or Brian," Sheila shouted back. She started to rise, then stopped and stared defiantly at her mother. Sheila's voice softened and she reached a hand out and tugged at Anne Marie's torn-away sleeve. The last threads ripped and the sleeve came off in Sheila's hand. The three of them stared at it for a second until Anne Marie snatched it angrily away from her daughter. "I'm sorry, Mom," Sheila pleaded. "I'll help you fix it. Just sit down and calm down. You're right, okay? You're absolutely right."

Sheila leaned forward in her chair and appealed to T.S. in quiet tones. "Do I have to go on with this in front of her? It might be better if she could leave."

"I'm not leaving," Anne Marie announced. "Just try to move me."

T.S. eyed her and spoke firmly. "Sheila is right, Anne Marie. I think it's best that you give us a few moments alone. Why don't you wait outside in the reception area? I'm sure it will only take a moment or two."

Anne Marie stood sullenly and moved to the door, stumbling slightly where the two rugs joined. Sheila watched her go anxiously, her eyes narrowed in concern.

T.S. sighed as the older woman disappeared from view. "Very well. Let's go on. How did you find out the information I requested on Boswell's death when Brian was out of town?"

"My friend," she said simply. "You sounded like you needed it and Bill was happy to do something for me." She shot the empty doorway a worried glance. "*Please*, Mr. Hubbert. I need to ask you some things." She picked up her pocketbook and began to twist the leather handles together.

"Me first," he insisted gently. "And then it will be your turn. So last night, you stayed with this Sergeant Perry?"

"Yes. And we slept in this morning." She stopped and had the good grace to blush. Her color, in fact, had been excellent all week and now T.S. knew the reason why. Ah, love, he reflected. Or, perhaps, love. He prayed with all his might that it was love that had produced such a flush.

"I didn't lie about my personal day," she added anxiously. "I went to see a lawyer this morning. She says that because Brian hit me, I'll have no problem getting a quick divorce."

"He hit you?" T.S. repeated blankly. Why, that son-of-a-bitch. If ever he ran into Brian O'Reilly again, T.S. would waste no time on pleasantries.

5 Herbert Wong was the first to arrive at Sterling & Sterling, having found tailing Auntie Lil an easy task. She moved so slowly with her bad ankle that he'd had to continually hang back to avoid being spotted. And the crowded subway made it a snap to blend in. Besides, it didn't take a genius to figure out where they were going. He nodded at Albert, who was guarding the lobby, signed his name in the log and disappeared up the narrow stairway that curved into the marble wall of the lobby and led up and around to the Main Floor. He had gotten little more than halfway up the stairs, however, when he suddenly stopped and crept slowly back down until he hovered on a step that barely turned the corner and gave him limited visibility of the lobby.

"Okay, Albert," Frank was saying to the elevator man on duty. "Off you go. Have a good evening."

"I'll go as fast as I can," Albert replied jovially. "I don't mind saying that this place is starting to make me nervous." He retrieved his coat from beneath the sign-in podium and cheerfully donned it. "Are you sure Timothy will be here soon?"

"Sure," Frank said. "He called in. Just a few minutes late. No bother—you go on." Albert headed for the outside door, passing Auntie Lil on the way in. He tipped his hat and melted into the sparse sidewalk crowd.

Frank's attention was caught by the elderly woman now hobbling in the front door. "Why, Miss Hubbert," he cried solicitously. "Let me help you. Here." He quickly brought a chair forward and helped Auntie Lil sit. "Have you hurt yourself?"

"It's nothing, Frank," she said, massaging her ankle. "Just a bit sore from walking on it." She had to get to T.S. and Edgar Hale quickly.

"Meeting Mr. Hubbert tonight, ma'am?" he asked.

"Oh, yes." The ankle was swelling slightly but she'd endured worse.

"I wonder if he might be able to spare me a moment before you leave," the guard asked her politely. "That lieutenant is giving me a hard time again."

"I'm sure he'd be delighted to. Why don't you come up with me now?"

"I'm waiting for the regular night guard. He should be here any second. I'll be up in a minute." He moved to the sign-in book. "Here, let me sign you in. It is Hubbert, isn't it? I was right about that?"

Auntie Lil stood and tried her ankle. "Oh, yes indeed. I'm a Hubbert, all right. Well, that's a little better. Onward and upward." She hobbled toward the elevators, Frank hovering at her elbow.

"Shall I call Mr. Hubbert and tell him you're on the way up?" the guard offered.

"Oh, no," she reassured him. "He's expecting me."

"Best take it easy on that leg," Frank warned her. He pressed the fourth floor button for her and the elevator doors glided shut.

Inside, Auntie Lil stared at the button panel, deep in thought. Frank would be up to see T.S. in a moment and, since T.S. had been unable to find Sheila all day, he was safe for the time being. But who was protecting Edgar Hale? He needed to be warned before anyone else. As was her habit, she did not hesitate.

Had Frank not been distracted by the entrance of the night guard, he might have noticed that Auntie Lil's elevator car, instead of continuing up to Personnel, stopped at the Main Floor first. This fact did not, however, escape the attention of Herbert Wong. He watched the floor indicator with a frown on his face, then hurried up the steps.

If he moved quickly, he could get there first.

CHAPTER SIXTEEN

1   The Main Floor was dark. It seemed that everyone had taken up Frederick Dorfen's suggestion to leave early. It was now approaching 6:00 P.M., and no one had cared to linger behind, working alone.

To search for a light switch in the cavernous room was hopeless. Auntie Lil did not even know where to begin. Desks and chairs stood eerily in the shadows like silent ghosts. She limped carefully down the hall, her injured leg making a peculiar scraping sound against the marble floor. She heard a rustle in the darkness and froze, peering back toward the elevators. Had it come from that clump of potted palms? She shook her head briskly, banishing fear. It was only plants rustling in front of the heating vent.

Ahead of her, light flowed from beneath the swinging doors of the Partners' Room. She moved toward this beacon gratefully.

Herbert Wong moved behind her, invisible in the internal night. His natural grace served him well as he darted from desk to desk, lost in the darkness. He had a duty to perform and he would not fail.

2   It was most disagreeable and unfair to Anne Marie, but T.S. simply had to ask Sheila to clear the air completely. It was crucial to learn the truth.

"Sheila," he asked as gently as possible. "Are you aware that you're adopted?"

She sat up warily and a new look crossed her face. It was suspicion mixed in with confusion, gradually giving way to

something very near fear. "Yes. Dad told me ages ago . . ."
Her voice trailed off and she stared out the empty doorway,
running her tongue nervously over dry lips.

"Your father told you?" He had been certain that Anne
Marie did not know.

"Yes." Sheila looked back at him absently, her mind elsewhere. "We didn't tell Mom because we knew she'd get
upset. It was no big deal. I found the papers once when I
was going through the desk in the study. Dad says they got
me through the Church." She sat up straight and stared at
him intently. "Are you telling me that this has something to
do with what's going on?" Her face betrayed such genuine
fear that T.S. could not decide whether to be relieved or
frustrated.

3 Edgar Hale sat hunched over his huge desk, shuffling
through papers almost blindly. The truth was, he could not
seem to get a single thing done. Was there any way the firm
could be saved now? He just did not know what to do.

Auntie Lil's discreet knock interrupted his anguish. "I'm
so sorry to intrude, Mr. Hale," she said.

He stood immediately. "Come in. Come in, Lil. I remember you well." He remembered her as a charming party guest
who could drink him under the table if he wasn't careful.
"Please, call me Edgar." He wondered how such a remarkable woman could have a nephew like T.S. Hubbert. Perhaps
she was unaware of her nephew's extracurricular snooping
activities. But wait, hadn't T.S. said that she was involved?
Oh, dear. He sighed. It was best to get it over with now.

Auntie Lil stood tentatively in the doorway. "I know this
sounds ridiculous," she began. "But I understand that T.S.
told you the unfortunate story about Patricia Kelly yesterday."

"He didn't have to tell me," the old man said sharply. "I
remember it well. It was nonsense. All nonsense."

"Yes, yes. Of course it was." Auntie Lil moved further
into the room, her progress slowed by her injured ankle. "I

know what's done is done. That it's in the past. But I'm afraid the story is not over yet.''

Edgar Hale looked up at her and in the curious light cast by his old-fashioned brass lamp he looked like an animal trapped in the headlights of a speeding car. ''What do you mean by that?'' He smoothed the front of his wrinkled shirt nervously, as if afraid Auntie Lil was going to accuse him.

''You needn't look quite so alarmed,'' she assured him. ''We've found out in time and now we can prevent any more killings. I have evidence.''

Edgar Hale opened his mouth and shut it abruptly. His eyes widened. If Auntie Lil had been worried he would not take her seriously, she worried no more.

''I'm afraid she has a daughter who appears mentally unbalanced and—''

''Don't do it!'' Edgar Hale suddenly cried, almost leaping across his desk.

He was too late. Auntie Lil's words were cut off in midbreath by a length of blue silk twisted tightly around her neck, choking off all air.

''Sit down,'' a strident female voice commanded, the echoes of a Brooklyn accent rising with each word. Edgar Hale immediately sat. ''If you make one move,'' the voice continued, ''I'll kill her and then I'll kill you.''

Anne Marie Shaunessy held a gun in one hand and pointed it calmly at Edgar Hale. The sleeve ripped from her dress was now wound tightly around Auntie Lil's throat. Her bare, pale arm almost shone in the dimly lit room, in vivid contrast to her flushed cheeks. Never had her Irish coloring been more striking. She was a strong woman made stronger by anger.

''It's you,'' Edgar Hale said faintly. ''You've known all along. T.S. was right. It's this Patricia Kelly thing.''

''No, I didn't know all along,'' Anne Marie replied angrily. ''If I had known all along, you would have been dead years ago. She kept it from me. Even from me.'' She smiled suddenly, her aim held steady as any policeman's wife would have been taught to do. ''This *thing* as you call it, this minor

incident in your life, destroyed the person I loved more tha
anyone in the world.''

A gust of wind blew through the room and the curtain
rustled in front of a slightly open window. A shadow move
among the shadows behind Anne Marie. Unaware, the sec
retary tensed, tightening her grip on the blue silk sleeve
Auntie Lil kept perfectly still and tried to keep from choking
She watched Anne Marie and Edgar Hale out of pained bi
still determined eyes. Auntie Lil had no intention of givin
up just yet.

"She never told me," Anne Marie repeated. The sickl
smile had faded from her face. "She was too ashamed. Sh
never told anyone. Not after Ralph Peabody. That taught he
a valuable lesson. She trusted him like a father, he'd bee
the one to give her a job. But when she went to him with he
story, what did he do? He turned it against her. Destroye
her with it.''

She looked up at the painting of Samuel Sterling and hi
sons, then quickly leveled her gun back at Edgar Hale. "Yo
men. Playing in your houses of money. Thinking you ca
buy the world. I told her to stay away from men like Rober
Cheswick. Men like you. I warned her you were only inte
ested in using her before you married someone more sui
able. That's why she wouldn't tell me. Because I turned o
to be right." Anne Marie's grim self-control only made he
more frightening.

"She kept it inside her all those years," she said quietl
"Lied to me about Sheila's father. I don't know why. Mayb
she wasn't sure. Maybe she still wanted to protect Rober
But where was he when she needed protecting? Who wa
there to protect her? Who?" She screamed her last questio
and raised the gun higher.

"For god's sake," Hale said. "The old woman's don
nothing. Let her go.''

"No," Anne Marie answered, dragging Auntie Lil for
ward. "I really don't think so. She's the one person wh
seems to have figured this whole thing out.''

"It won't do you any good. T.S. knows everything." Hale stuttered in his fear.

"Then I'll kill him, too," she told him calmly. "Do you know what it did to her to keep that inside? Did you ever visit her when she was locked away for years, staring at walls, hardly blinking her eyes? Never laughing. Never talking. Not even *looking* at the one person closer to her than any other person in the world? Not even looking at *me*."

Edgar Hale put a hand out and gripped the edge of his desk tightly.

"And all that time it was killing her, I was right here working for you. Smiling good morning. Answering your phones. Asking you about your families." She took a step forward, dragging Auntie Lil beside her. The sleeve slackened momentarily and Auntie Lil gulped in a quick burst of fresh air, then kept as still as she could.

"You thought I knew, didn't you?" Anne Marie wagged the gun at him. "That's why you always gave me so much money. That's why I earned so much more than anyone else. Not because I was good but because you thought you were buying my silence. You thought I could be bought just like everyone else." Anne Marie shook her head lightly and let out her breath in a slow, deliberate stream as she steadied her aim. "I can't, you know," she told him quietly. "I can't be bought and it makes me angry to have people think I can. But before you die, I think there's something that you should know."

4 Frank was whistling as he stepped into the near darkness of the Personnel Department. He knew that Mr. Hubbert would take care of things for him. Make sure that awful lieutenant didn't put a note in his file like he'd threatened. Why, he *was* telling the truth about the sign-in log. Was it his fault the lieutenant didn't believe him? When he noticed the light on in T.S.'s office, Frank thought nothing of simply pushing open the door. "Mr. Hubbert, I wonder if you'd speak to—" He stopped and looked at Sheila in surprise. "I'm sorry," he mumbled, backing out the door. "I didn't

know you were busy. I thought it would just be you and you
Aunt Lil.''

"Auntie Lil?'' T.S. turned to Frank. "My Aunt Lil's ar
rived?''

Frank touched his hat briefly. "She said she was on he
way up to see you, sir. About five minutes ago.''

Sheila was staring at T.S. wide-eyed, unmindful of th
guard. "I've answered your questions. Now you have to an
swer mine. I need to know some things. I need you to tel
me what—''

"Sheila, please, as my friend,'' T.S. pleaded, "I just hav
a few more questions. Understand that I'm only—''

"You're the only one I can turn to, I need your help—''

"I want to help, but I can't unless—''

"Listen to me. You have to let me talk.'' Sheila's voic
grew louder. She fumbled in her pocketbook urgently
searching.

"No. First, you must answer all of my questions. Yo
can't avoid them any longer.'' T.S. raised his own voice an
leaned forward toward her.

Frank had listened quietly to the exchange but now h
interrupted. "Mr. Hubbert, sir,'' he pointed out, twistin
his hat nervously in his hand. "I think she's trying to tell yo
something. Why won't you let her?''

"I am. I am trying to tell you something,'' Sheila cried
bursting into tears as she pulled a small oval box from he
purse. The lid tumbled to the floor and a rope of light sli
into her palm. She held it up in the room. It dazzled as i
swung slowly back and forth between them.

T.S. sat, stunned, behind the desk, staring at the bracele
He had not been listening because he was afraid of what h
would hear. Because he did not want a confession to com
tumbling from her mouth. Because he wanted someone els
to be Patricia Kelly's daughter. And now the evidence wa
literally dangling before his eyes. The bracelet that John Bos
well had bought. What a lousy detective he was. Here was
murderer trying to confess, and he couldn't bear to hear it.

"Mr. Hubbert, please,'' Sheila pleaded through her tears

"You have to tell me. What does Patricia Kelly have to do with the murders? Why did Auntie Lil go out to her grave today? I know who Patricia Kelly is, I've seen her before. When I saw her photo on her personnel file that day in the conference room with Mr. Hale and the lieutenant, I remembered her from when I was little. I used to call her Aunt Patricia. She would come and bring me toys. But now my mother is lying to me about her. She says she never knew her, but I know that's not true. I *remember* her." She stared at T.S., wide eyes pleading for an explanation. "I called my friend at Creedmoor yesterday. She told me where Aunt Patricia was buried. I went to her grave. I brought flowers. I thought, maybe . . ." Her voice trailed off, then regained strength. "I thought maybe if I prayed there, everything would be all right. I would understand what this all had to do with my mother lying. But when I went out there this afternoon, Auntie Lil was already there. And this was on Aunt Patricia's grave."

Sheila offered T.S. the bracelet and he took it slowly, turning it over in his hands and rubbing its links nervously. It was cold and hard.

"I know that bracelet," she told him in a voice dulled by fear. "Mr. Boswell used it to try and get me to go out on his boat with him last Sunday afternoon. He tried to buy me with it. How did it get on Aunt Patricia's grave?"

T.S. stared at her, astonished. Sheila knew she was adopted, but didn't know who her natural mother was. But if the killer wasn't Patricia Kelly's daughter, who was it?

"You have to tell me," Sheila pleaded. "Please, Mr. Hubbert. How did that necklace get on her grave? Mr. Boswell had it with him that day at the marina. He made me meet him there and I agreed, but only to beg him to leave me alone. Sergeant Perry can back me up, he was waiting in the car." She leaned so close to him, he could smell the shampoo in her hair. She fumbled in her purse and produced the silver spoon paperweight. It hit his desk with a dull thud. He knew immediately what it was and where it had come from.

"This was on the grave, too," she explained. "You have to tell me what this has to do with my mother lying to me."

"Anne Marie lying?" He said it tentatively, but even as he uttered the words, the truth became apparent. He had been blind. Where was Anne Marie now?

"I'm afraid," Sheila admitted, wiping her nose unconsciously on her sleeve like a young child. "She's not the same anymore. I told her I recognized the photo of that woman and Mom said I was crazy. But it's her. That's my Aunt Patricia."

T.S. stood up abruptly and stared out the doorway. Frank stirred uneasily, and looked nervously over his own shoulder.

"What is it, Mr. Hubbert, sir?" he asked T.S.

"Anne Marie!" T.S. called out loudly, toward the door. "Anne Marie? Are you out there?"

"There's no one there, sir. The department is empty. Kind of spooky, in fact." Frank stared from T.S. to Sheila.

"We've been so stupid," T.S. shouted on his way out the door. Frank was pushed aside roughly and caromed off the door frame, crashing into a racing Sheila. She was already following T.S. The guard straightened his hat on his head and lost no time sprinting after them.

T.S. raced toward the elevators but saw that the doors were closed. He ran through the darkness, pursued by the others. He reached the fire stairs, burst through the heavy door, kicked the doorstop out of the way and scrambled down out of sight. The door clicked shut behind him, locking. Sheila and Frank pounded on the other side screaming, but T.S. heard not one sound.

Auntie Lil. Where was Auntie Lil? And where was Anne Marie? He would check her desk. He would warn Edgar Hale. He would find Auntie Lil in time.

It was his second race down the steps against time that day, but this time the prize was beyond value.

5   "How do you know it was one of us?" Edgar Hale pleaded in a desperate voice.

"Because, contrary to what you tried to make her out to be," Anne Marie replied in acid tones, "Patricia never slept with anyone else before you and your friends. And no one for a long time after. Not until she changed. Not until she began to believe all the things you said about her. She loved Robert. And he used that love to get her to *Magritte's* that night. He broke her heart first and then her mind. You helped. She told me everything before she died. It was your idea, wasn't it? *Your* idea. You didn't think think she was good enough to be a future partner's wife. You wanted to prove to Robert that she was trash and when he wouldn't believe you, you made her trash." She inched closer to Hale's desk, dragging Auntie Lil along.

If she kept her body very, very still, Auntie Lil could draw in small puffs of breath through her nose without being noticed. Concentrate on something else, she thought. Forget the cruel cloth twisting off your breath. Concentrate on the throbbing in your ankle. She began to count each stab of pain, unable to relieve the pressure.

"You said it yourself," Hale pointed out quickly. "She slept with us. She knew what was going to happen when she agreed to meet us. She went along with it. She liked it. Look what she did with all those men afterward. That's proof she liked it."

Oh, dear god, Auntie Lil thought to herself. Does the fool have a death wish? If only she could speak.

"*Liked it? Went along?* Is that why she hid herself from me for a week? Told me she had fallen down her basement steps when I asked her about the bruises? Is that your idea of going along?" Anne Marie extended the gun closer toward Edgar Hale and the senior partner began to shake. "You destroyed her. What she did with all those men in the years afterward was your fault. She thought that was all she was worth because you taught her that. You. And you destroyed Robert, too, long before I did. Destroyed the love he had for her, leaving only guilt. Guilt that he thought flowers could satisfy. At first, I thought his guilt would be enough. I sent him letters pretending to be Patricia, tortured him that way and enjoyed his pain. But then I realized that it wasn't enough. He'd have to die. All of you would die.''

"Think of Sheila," Hale cried, holding his hands up in front of his face. "She's still your daughter. You love her.''

"I am thinking of her. Believe me. I followed Sheila to the marina last Sunday. John Boswell lured her out there. My daughter. It wasn't enough that he helped destroy my best friend. He had to go after my daughter, too. I'd seen him sniffing around her. I knew it was going to happen again. That's when I understood that I'd have to stop all of you. You all thought it was your *right* to play with other people's lives. If I hadn't taught Sheila not to trust men like you, she might have gone out on the boat with John. When she refused, I knew he'd keep trying. I knew. I *had* to stop him, I realized. For good." She laughed, an ugly barking laugh that went on too long and too loud. "After she left, it was so easy to get him to take me out on that boat. It was still so easy.''

"But if what you say is true, you could be murdering Sheila's father if you kill me." Edgar Hale trembled uncontrollably, his chair quivering on its hinges.

"Gee," Anne Marie replied in a sympathetic voice. "I really hope so." She shook her head in mock sadness. "I'm only sorry Patricia isn't here to enjoy this with me. I let her help, you know. I used the drugs she gave me at the hospital to poison John. I thought it was only fair. She would have liked that, helping me kill him. She never could bring herself to hate Robert but she never stopped hating the rest of you.'' She steadied her pistol and squinted one eye in aim. "And you helped, too. I called Sinclair and said you wanted to meet him somewhere private. Somewhere like his summer home. It was so easy to do. But don't worry. I'll make it quick. One shot. That's all it took for Stanley Sinclair. My husband was good for one thing, you see. He taught me how to shoot like a regular Annie Oakley.''

At exactly that moment—just as T.S. flew breathlessly through the swinging doors—Herbert Wong exploded out from behind the curtains, one leg reaching in a savage kick that slashed at Anne Marie's wrist and knocked the gun aside.

The retired messenger dropped to the ground and scrambled away as the pistol exploded with a booming shot. The sharp crack swelled in the room and reverberated in waves of sound that rolled across the Main Floor.

Edgar Hale shouted and dove beneath his desk. Auntie Lil twisted, grabbing at the sleeve and digging her good foot into Anne Marie's instep. T.S. leapt from the doorway onto Anne Marie's back, knocking her to the floor and dragging Auntie Lil down with them into a whirling blur of legs kicking and hands grasping. T.S. rolled on top of Anne Marie and her fingernails raked at his face. Blood blinded him and he had to relinguish his grip. He could feel her pulling free. She stood and reached for the gun.

A panting Herbert Wong rose and took a running dive, tackling and knocking Anne Marie to the carpet again as he shrieked in Chinese. He straddled her, his forearm locked across her neck, and pinned her firmly to the floor. She tried to raise her head only once before giving up and staring soundlessly at the ceiling, tears trickling down her cheeks.

The near silence that followed the fight was eerie. Auntie Lil and T.S. sprawled on the rug together, both breathing heavily. Slowly Edgar Hale peeped his head above his desk and stared at the scene before him. "Who are you?" he barked at Herbert Wong, and T.S. would not have been surprised if he'd cried out "Friend or foe?" instead.

Herbert looked down at Anne Marie, as if to warn her not to move, and eyed the senior partner angrily. "I work for you for fifteen years, that's who I am. This whole damn thing your fault."

"Herbert's a retired messenger," T.S. hastily explained. He, too, stared at Wong. "What *are* you doing here?" he asked him, not ungratefully.

"You tell me I can be of no help, but I know better," the messenger explained simply. "I follow her to make sure she's okay." He nodded at Auntie Lil and she nodded back. Anne Marie flopped beneath him and he gripped her arms tighter.

"Don't move!" a loud voice shouted. Edgar Hale dove beneath his desk again.

Frank, the security guard, stood in the doorway in a classic pose, his knees bent and his gun extended in both hands.

"Don't shoot! Don't shoot!" T.S. cried. "For god's sake, Frank. Don't shoot."

"He won't shoot." Sheila's voice wavered as she stared at her mother. She entered behind Frank and put an arm on his shoulder. T.S. turned just as she reached for Frank's gun.

She touched the barrel lightly with a finger. "Keep your gun on her," Sheila ordered sadly, walking over to the fireplace and staring down at her mother's discharged pistol. She picked it up curiously by the edges, turned it over in her hands, then slowly raised it to her face and examined it more closely before turning it toward T.S. Tears welled in her eyes and she did not notice that he flinched. "Dad's gun," she said softly, handing him the still-warm piece. "Oh, Momma.

"It's okay," she told her mother sadly, kneeling beside her on the floor. Sheila smoothed the hair from Anne Marie's forehead, but her mother's eyes remained unfocused, tears trickling from the outer corner of her eyes into the soft curves of her ears. "We've got her covered. Mr. Wong, I think it's safe to let her go."

Herbert Wong moved slowly off of Anne Marie and the sobbing woman shut her eyes. "I did it for you, too," she told her daughter in the silence. Her voice was blank, devoid of emotion. "I didn't want the same thing to happen to you."

Sheila lifted her mother's head and placed it gently in her lap. She continued to smooth the hair from her mother's forehead. She looked up at the others, who waited silently and respectfully in a semi-circle around them. "Mr. Hale, call the cops," Sheila reminded him quietly. Her voice wavered and she sighed, looking back down at her mother. "Momma, I'm sorry. I'm so sorry that it was you. I love you very, very much."

Anne Marie opened her eyes again and stared blankly at her daughter. Sheila raised her face and gazed at T.S., silently pleading for his guidance. She was hurting but she was also ready to do what was right. The glint of steel in her intense, smoky green eyes was unmistakable.

T.S. knew one other person with eyes like that. He turned to Edgar Hale and his suspicions were confirmed—the resemblance was exact.

As if she knew what he was thinking, Sheila slowly turned away from her mother and stared at Edgar Hale. Their eyes met and they blinked at one another in slow, unwanted recognition.

"She's crazy," Edgar Hale sputtered, emerging from behind his desk. He pointed to Anne Marie. "Patricia Kelly was confused and ill. This whole mess has been because of nothing."

"Has it?" Sheila's eyes half-closed in anger as she scrutinized Edgar Hale. He froze and stared back into a face whose resemblance to his own, once suspected, was clearly apparent. "My mother did what she did because she loved me and she loved her friend too much," Sheila said evenly. "What's your excuse?"

Edgar Hale's mouth opened but no words came out. Everyone in the room stared at him in silence. He ran his tongue around dry lips and swallowed. They still stared.

"I don't know why we did what we did," he finally whispered in an old man's croak. "I don't know why we did it."

"Then shut up and sit down," Auntie Lil said firmly.

Edgar Hale did just that.

CHAPTER SEVENTEEN

1 They held the victory dinner at Harvey's Chelsea Restaurant, although T.S. considered it a Pyrrhic victory at best. But when Auntie Lil pointed out that at least they had undisputably triumphed over Lieutenant Abromowitz, T.S. agreed that a celebration of some sorts would not be too unseemly.

Auntie Lil invited Lilah Cheswick without telling T.S. first. He retaliated by insisting Herbert Wong be there.

"Of course," Auntie Lil had agreed enthusiastically, promptly puncturing his revenge. "I'd love to have him join us. He should be the guest of honor!"

T.S. wore his dragon tie and was highly annoyed when Herbert Wong did not even notice. In fact, he hardly paid T.S. any attention at all. Perhaps it was Auntie Lil's hat. She had truly outdone herself this time. T.S. was afraid to ask if she had concocted it on her own. If there were others in existence, it was best he not know.

The hat was as big and round as a manhole, made of bright green straw and centered by a flat crown piled high with enough fake fruits, vegetables and flowers to constitute an entire bicentennial exhibit of Midwest agricultural products. T.S. was tempted to ask that the hat be seated at its own table, perhaps upstairs, where it had a chance of being mistaken for the buffet and somehow spirited away.

The hat was not going anywhere. Nor, it seemed, was Auntie Lil's coat. There was the usual tussle at the coat check area, with Auntie Lil finally consenting to relinquish the coat only after Herbert Wong promised to keep a faithful eye on it during their meal.

"And you know what good eyes I have," the retired messenger pointed out, ogling her monstrous hat as if to prove it.

Frederick himself came over for their bar order, calmly parting the various dangling and sprouting flora of Auntie Lil's hat with his hands as if he *always* served drinks in the jungle. "The usual?" he asked T.S.

Before T.S. could reply, Herbert Wong broke in. "Little Solly Fishbean!" he cried out in delight. "How is your father?"

T.S. looked at him in irritation. "This is *Frederick*, the bartender."

"No, it's not." Herbert Wong playfully tweaked the big bartender's handlebar mustache. "This is my friend Hiram's youngest son. We play mah jongg together on Tuesday. I beat your father big time last week." Herbert Wong wagged a finger at Frederick and smiled.

"I'm sorry, Mr. Hubbert," Frederick apologized quickly with a nervous glance at T.S. "Solly just doesn't seem like the right kind of name for a bartender here."

"Oh, never mind," T.S. commented grumpily. The impertinent young pup. Was no one who they purported to be these days?

"Not the usual," Auntie Lil decided. "We'll start with margaritas all around."

"*Margaritas?*" T.S. repeated thickly. "Isn't that a bit macabre?"

"Not at all," Lilah chimed in. "I'd love a margarita."

He was outflanked and acquiesced graciously. Besides, when the drinks came, Lilah turned to him with a radiant smile. "Here's to you, Theodore," she told him gaily, raising her glass in toast. "And to your brilliant Aunt Lil."

"Indeed," Auntie Lil agreed. "It was a brilliant sleuthing job."

T.S. made a mental note to move modesty down a couple of notches on Auntie Lil's list of attributes, but he toasted nonetheless.

"I did make *some* mistakes," Auntie Lil added in a brief stab at self-effacement.

"A mistake? You?" T.S. looked incredulous but Auntie Lil breezed right past his sarcasm with her usual aplomb.

"Perhaps one or two . . ." she admitted graciously. "Tiny ones, of course."

"One or two *significant* ones," T.S. corrected. "But all's well that ends well."

"It was human nature," Auntie Lil explained. "I included human nature when I examined each suspect, but I forgot to include my own."

"What do you mean, Lillian?" Herbert Wong asked in hopeless admiration. He had been fluttering at her elbow all night, pulling out her chair, opening doors for her, and springing to his feet when she visited the ladies' room. In fact, he'd been popping up and down all night like a human jack-in-the-box. But it was his sudden refusal to address her as "Auntie Lil" like the rest of the world that made T.S. most suspicious of all.

"I've never had children you know, Herbert." She patted the messenger's hand fondly and he beamed. "I have a very romantic idea of what it would be like. Once I learned that Sheila was Patricia Kelly's daughter, I just misread Anne Marie's lies entirely. I thought of her as a fierce mother tiger protecting her cub. I should have listened to T.S. He never believed it could have been Sheila."

"I've had years of experience reading people," T.S. pointed out. "After all, it was my job."

"Yes, but I was guilty of something even worse than misreading people," Auntie Lil confessed. "I assumed that because John Boswell had gone out willingly on the sailboat with the killer, that she had to be young and blonde and beautiful. That he wouldn't bother with anything less. That an older woman would never be attractive to him."

Lilah choked lightly on a bread stick and averted her gaze.

"Are you all right?" T.S. asked anxiously. He pounded her lightly on the back in what he hoped was a chivalrous manner.

"Yes, yes," Lilah murmured, her voice a bit faint. She reached for his hand and held it briefly. Her touch burned T.S. like a momentary flame.

"I find older women most beautiful," Herbert Wong declared with enthusiasm. "The older, the better. Beauty begins with character." He gazed rapturously at Auntie Lil. She primped, pleased with the compliment, while T.S. exchanged an amused glance with Lilah.

How far he had come, T.S. thought happily, from being tongue-tied with Lilah to sharing secrets with her. Perhaps something good would come of all this sorrow, after all. They had solved three murders, he reminded himself. After such a feat, anything was possible.

"Tell me the truth," Lilah Cheswick inquired in her smoky voice, "was I ever a suspect?" She leaned over and smiled at T.S., the candlelight sending flickers of orange dancing across her nearly white hair.

"I refuse to answer on the grounds that it may incriminate me," he answered firmly. Herbert Wong laughed loudly and T.S. decided that the retired messenger was a wonderful fellow after all, even if he did encourage Auntie Lil to show off.

"You were never a suspect in Theodore's eyes," Auntie Lil assured Lilah. "I was the one who suspected you, briefly. But not Theodore. Not for an instant. He was completely bowled over by your many charms."

"Really?" Lilah leaned closer to T.S. "And what are those charms?"

The room grew much warmer. T.S. was conscious that everyone around the table was staring at him, waiting for him to speak.

"Ironic, don't you think?" he said brightly, praying an abrupt change of subject would rescue him. "That Edgar Hale loses three friends and gains a daughter?"

"And early retirement," added Lilah. "Though we don't know for sure that Sheila's his daughter."

"No," Auntie Lil admitted. "A blood test will prove it.

But I saw those eyes, just as T.S. did. I'd say there's a very good chance.''

"Mr. Hale must believe so himself," Herbert Wong added politely. "I heard he is offering to give Sheila money to pay for Anne Marie's defense."

They considered this quietly. "How very unlike him," Auntie Lil finally said. "I thought he was immune to guilt."

"He's lucky he's immune to prosecution," T.S. pointed out angrily. "There's no one left to tell what really happened at *Magritte's*. All we really know for sure is that Robert arranged to meet Patricia there late one night, after the men returned from a cotillion ball uptown."

Lilah paused, glass half raised to her lips. "I was probably at that ball," she said meekly. "I was one of the proper young women Anne Marie hated so."

"I'm sorry, Lilah," Auntie Lil said kindly. "But it does appear that Patricia was in love with your husband all these years."

"You needn't be sorry," Lilah answered quietly. "I'm convinced Robert was in love with her, too. I understand now what broke his spirit so many years ago. I don't mind. It's nice to know he was capable of such feelings."

What a remarkable woman, Auntie Lil thought to herself. Why, she reminds me of myself.

"Poor Robert," Lilah murmured. "He must have been so ashamed."

"Yes, I believe your husband was. He came to realize that he had loved her all along and still did. That he had destroyed what he adored." Auntie Lil shook her head. "Perhaps if the times had been different. It is a tragic story all around."

"What will happen to Sterling & Sterling now?" Herbert Wong asked sadly.

"Preston Freeman will probably happen to Sterling & Sterling," T.S. told them. "Out with the old, in with the new. Frederick Dorfen won't be able to keep up the pace. He had his last moment of glory, though, and I salute him."

"But will Sterling & Sterling survive the new?" Lilah wondered.

"They'll survive," T.S. said confidently. "Believe it or not, the murders appear to have given the firm some sort of panache it lacked. It's ghastly, but true. The *nouveau riche* have discovered Sterling & Sterling now. It's a whole new market for the firm. And this is before the inevitable story in *New York* magazine."

"Let us discuss Miss Fullbright and Lieutenant Abromowitz," Herbert Wong suggested eagerly. "It appears that love is in the air." He hummed a happy tune.

"I did enjoy the look on his face when he walked into Edgar Hale's office," T.S. reminisced. "I like to think he'll end up writing parking tickets in Canarsie."

"He won't," Lilah told them. "I've already asked. Don't forget—the case *was* solved. He'll get the credit publicly. But, privately, I heard from a friend of Robert's and . . ." She held up her glass in toast. "The lovely lieutenant has been assigned to the new White Collar Crime Task Force forming downtown. He'll be poring through security transactions for the rest of his life."

It was, perhaps, the single most enthusiastic toast of the night.

Unexpectedly, T.S. sighed so sadly that it cut their merriment short. "I wish Sheila could be here," he admitted. He had not seen her in a week, not since that terrible day. And she had only called him once since then, to say that she was surviving and would not be coming back to work at Sterling & Sterling.

"We cannot blame her for failing to find celebration in the situation," Herbert Wong pointed out.

"No, we cannot," Auntie Lil agreed.

They all stared quietly at their drinks.

"Will she be okay?" Herbert Wong asked solemnly.

"I hope so," T.S. said. "She's going through with the divorce from her husband. Let's hope the new man is a good man." He was surprised to find that repeating this news triggered a spark of jealousy in his heart.

"Let us hope he is," Auntie Lil echoed. "She deserves some happiness."

There was a mournful silence, finally broken by Lilah. "If it is any consolation, Edgar Hale has no other children. Sheila is likely to be a wealthy woman one day."

"Money is not much solace when you lose two mothers at once," Herbert Wong declared wisely.

"It's too true," Auntie Lil agreed. "Though she is standing by Anne Marie and visits her every day. But let's not talk any more about Anne Marie," she decided. "Or we'll forget that we are celebrating."

The group stirred and murmured, nodding their heads.

"Then here's to Patricia Kelly," T.S. said softly, raising his glass. "May she rest in peace." He thought of the initials, R.I.P., and smiled. Their first big clue.

"Rest in peace," the group repeated, clinking their drinks together.

"It was a somewhat disillusioning experience," T.S. admitted, shaking his head.

"Poor Theodore." Auntie Lil was instantly sympathetic. "Despite all your background checks and experience, you still expect people to be good at heart."

He looked up, feeling foolish. "I would settle for *decent* at heart."

"No, you wouldn't," Auntie Lil teased him, her good spirits returning. "Theodore wants the world to be perfect," she explained to Lilah and Herbert. "Theodore wants people to be perfect." She dropped her voice to a most dramatic level. "But Theodore, perfect people are so boring."

Auntie Lil raised her glass in yet another toast. "So here's to the world's imperfect people. They're much more interesting." The collection of imperfect people surrounding the table joined in the toast enthusiastically.

"Hey," announced Herbert Wong happily. "I know a good place to go dancing after dinner. Who wants to go? Lillian?" He turned to Auntie Lil.

"Pour me another margarita and count me in," she said immediately. "Another one of these and my sore ankle will be history." She held out her glass and they busied themselves fussing with the pitcher.

"What do you say, Theodore?" Lilah asked T.S., leaning closer and taking advantage of their momentary privacy. She radiated a warm gardenia smell. "Now that you're retired, you need a hobby," she coaxed him softly. "Dancing's not golf, but it's a start. Don't you agree?"

T.S. nodded as if in a daze, acutely aware of her closeness. There it was again, that same old feeling. Something big was about to happen.

"Sure, I'll go dancing," he agreed, to his own surprise. He'd never gone dancing in his entire life. Well, his mouth was moving of its own accord. Perhaps his feet could do the same.

He blamed it on the gardenias. T.S. loved their smell. It reminded him of years long gone, of peering through fragrant hedges at the exotic woman who lived next door, of dreaming of the mysteries of men and women and wondering when his turn would finally come. Oh lord, it was definitely the gardenias.

"You know what I like about you, Theodore?" Lilah purred into his ear. She slipped a slender arm through his and whispered, "You just keep getting younger every day."